There ... Marylyle Rogers ... of

She brings to life
exquisite tales of love set amid
the blaze of medieval pageantry.
Now, she parts the swirling mists of the
past to bring us a breathtaking romance
of timeless dreams and desires.

"What I feel for you cannot be halted simply because you order it so."

Linnet was heedless to either the consequences or the pride-crushing secret her words revealed.

The sparks in the Eagle's eyes exploded into a fire threatening to consume its tender prey. This was dangerous. This was wrong. And, God forgive him, this openly offered love was also what he hopelessly wanted beyond all reason.

Although shaking his head against the errant deed he could not stop, in one fluid motion Rhys rose and stepped over the bench to sweep the trembling songbird into his arms.

With every sense atuned Linnet felt the approach of his kiss and yearned upward. She tightened her arms around his neck, crushing herself against him, wanting to be closer still.

The damsel's action brought Rhys potent memories. "I could forfeit everything to claim all that you are—anything, save my honor. And my honor is the price I would be required to forfeit for taking you as my own. . . ."

Books by Marylyle Rogers

Dark Whispers
The Dragon's Fire
Chanting the Dawn
The Eagle's Song
Hidden Hearts
Proud Hearts
Wary Hearts

Published by POCKET BOOKS

THE EAGLE'S SONG

MARYLYLE ROGERS

POCKET STAR BOOKS

New York   London   Toronto   Sydney   Tokyo   Singapore

This book is a work of fiction. Names, characters, places and incidents are either products of the author's imagination or are used fictitiously. Any resemblance to actual events or locales or persons, living or dead, is entirely coincidental.

An *Original* Publication of POCKET BOOKS

A Pocket Star Book published by
POCKET BOOKS, a division of Simon & Schuster Inc.
1230 Avenue of the Americas, New York, NY 10020

Copyright © 1992 by Marylyle Rogers

ISBN: 0-671-74561-1

First Pocket Books printing December 1992

10 9 8 7 6 5 4 3 2 1

POCKET STAR BOOKS and colophon are registered trademarks of Simon & Schuster Inc.

Cover art by Steven Assel

Printed in the U.S.A.

Author's Note

When William the Conqueror died in 1087, he left his most proudly held possession, the duchy of Normandy, to his oldest son, Robert, and the kingdom of England to the next elder, William. This second William was known as Rufus *not* for red hair, as he was as fair as his mother, Matilda of Flanders, but rather for his ruddy complexion. A third son, Henry, was left with little, but in the end claimed and held it all.

For King William Rufus, like most men of his era and class, war was his business. Yet, once the crown was his, he both demanded absolute obedience to royal laws and ruled with unusual violence. Amidst even this violent age he was denounced by the clergy for his brutality . . . and his infringement on church rights. He spent most of the year 1092 in battles on the Scottish border. In 1099 while hunting in the New Forest with friends he was killed by a stray arrow, believed to have been shot (accidentally?) by a companion, Walter Tirel.

When the Conqueror took England, several Welsh princes and Scottish lords swore fealty to the Norman king. A practice repeated by their heirs just as the heirs of those who'd been given lands and made vassals by the first William were constrained, in order to continue holding those lands, to pledge their oaths to future monarchs.

Two facts need to be pointed out.

First, several languages were spoken on the Welsh/English border. The conquering Normans spoke French, while the conquered spoke English. Among these two peoples it was imperative that those in daily contact learned enough of the other's language to communicate. However, across the border into Wales, the people, of course, spoke Welsh. It could and did on occasion create communication problems which added to the constant conflict brewed by greed for more lands and all to be resolved with spear and sword.

Second, the church forbade marriages between peoples related within seven degrees—even those related by marital bonds rather than blood.

PROLOGUE

November 1066

LIGHT FROM A SINGLE CANDLE GAVE THE APPEARANCE OF A halo to the white hair of an aging and bedridden man. Long in years and physically infirm as he might be, Siward's eyes were clear. Piercing in their intelligence, they measured the proud, vital young man squarely facing him.

"To avert certain bloodshed I will peaceably surrender," Siward said, "providing you swear to grant me the few paltry sops to my honor which we've discussed."

Half-lowered lashes shielded Godfrey's sour thoughts from the Saxon lord's penetrating gaze while he lifted his chin in defense against the old man's reminder of his youth. What matter his age when Duke William had found his support during the battle at Hastings worthy of so fine a reward? Though Godfrey had been born of an important Norman family, it was for his loyalty and valor that the duke had bestowed upon him more than a small parcel of land. Godfrey had been entrusted with a great stretch of the western border and with a charge to defend it against Celtic marauders from across the boundary line with Wales.

"We are agreed." Godfrey had near to grit his teeth to speak the unwelcome words. He would have preferred to wield the much greater force at his command and lay low all who stood in his path. Only the oath given his duke restrained him. Following the carnage at Hastings and aware of the ravages which the Norwegians had a short time earlier wrought upon the Saxons, Duke William had cautioned prudence to those supporters whom he'd granted lands. Their commander had warned them of the need for plentiful and healthy serfs to till fields and serve their lords' interests. Further battles would of a certainty cost the Normans dearly in terms of adequate hands to toil.

A faint sad smile barely moved Siward's cheeks, already heavily creased by the years. "Then do you pledge an oath upon the Holy Cross to honor and hold inviolate the strip of land on the western border, which upon her marriage my daughter, Emma, took as dowry to the Welsh prince, Griffith of Cymer?" Siward paused, his unswerving gaze seeming to demand that the oath be given.

"Aye." Godfrey curtly nodded, refusing to glance toward where the Saxon's three golden-haired children stood in the stark and poorly lit chamber's shadows, solemn witnesses to words deeply resented by them all. Godfrey silently berated himself for the imprudent initial decision that had permitted a subtle shift in negotiating strength during this confrontation between master and mastered. Despite his position as leader of a conquering force, Godfrey had begun with a major concession. Instead of forcing the vanquished Saxon to appear before him, crawling if need be, he had come to the man's bedchamber, a bedchamber now rightfully Godfrey's own. Here he stood alone before a reclining foe, as if their positions were reversed. Godfrey fairly steamed while his face went ruddy with bad temper.

"And upon the Holy Cross you pledge your oath to

gift my only surviving son with a small wedge of the northern border?" Siward's attention shifted to a short, sturdy boy of four and ten. Siward's elder son, fighting at Harold Godwinson's side, had fallen 'neath a Norwegian sword. He hoped that his humiliating submission to this young and arrogant Norman would leastways save Osric's life and that his desperate negotiations would provide security for his son's future.

Godfrey's attention also turned to the adolescent bitterly watching, listening for the promise that would name to him a mere morsel from the cake composed of vast lands he'd expected to inherit. An endless emnity glowed in the boy's gray and glacial stare. Long tense moments passed while the unyielding gazes of boy and foreign conqueror did battle.

This was the part of the pact Godfrey most wanted to reject. Only the sharp wits that had gotten the unimportant younger son of a Norman noble this far and that recognized the truth in William's warning prevented the denial in his heart from reaching his lips. With little harm to his battle-hardened warriors, Godfrey could order an assuredly victorious attack upon the already dying Siward, his immature son, and their untrained and ill-equipped serfs—but few would remain to work the land. Moreover, those who survived likely would choose an honorable death over toiling for the monster who'd needlessly, brutally taken the lives of a pair doomed to fail, one by age and one by youth.

"Aye. By this oath I grant Osric the subfief of Northland." Godfrey saw hatred flare in the gray eyes, as deadly as a honed blade. "But the grant is given by Norman feudal law. Afore Osric assumes Northland's reins, he must swear fealty to me as his lord, and with it vows of loyalty owed and duties accepted."

"It will be done as you demand." Siward solemnly nodded. Osric was clearly disappointed, but he was the younger son and never meant to rule the land. Leastways this pact would see the boy with some portion of lands for himself, and he ought be appreciative to his father for arranging things thusly.

His father's promise merely intensified the hostility in the hard gaze with which Osric steadily assaulted his Norman foe.

Beneath the pale glare, Godfrey shifted uneasily. But with the ready assurance of a man who had seldom failed and was confident of his abilities mentally, he shrugged aside the silent threat of this mere boy, a member of the defeated race.

"Lastly, upon the Holy Cross do you pledge your oath to wed my daughter Morwena?" Siward's dislike of Normans strengthened his determination to see his younger daughter wed to this victorious Norman. Their marriage would ensure that in the fullness of time Siward's own bloodline would continue to rule Radwell—a goal important to him.

"Aye." As Godfrey gave the oath he glanced sideways to the younger Saxon damsel. Of ten and six years she was golden-haired, voluptuous, and plainly welcomed her pairing with an important man, conqueror though he might be.

"And, too, by accepting Morwena's dowry—a narrow strip of land upon Radwell's southern border—do you confirm it as dower for her and her heirs?" Siward was no fool and had no reason to trust any man of Norman blood. Had not the Norman duke lied in staking his claim upon England and then used force to take what was not lawfully given?

"Aye," Godfrey repeated. "You've my oath that I will take your daughter Morwena and keep her dowry inviolate to her and her heirs." Godfrey chose his words with great care. Over time, he comforted himself, these secret oaths would become meaningless. It was plain that Siward had not long to live. Once the elderly man was gone, only the boy and his

4

two sisters would remain as witnesses. In years to come, who of import would believe the word of three Saxons over that of a Norman lord?

Siward heard the treacherous change in wording but, knowing the danger in trusting a Norman, he had arranged for more than spoken words to guard the upholding of crucial oaths.

"You've my earnest gratitude for allowing me these small morsels to lessen the pain and humiliation of surrender. Moreover, I am certain that as a man of honor"—Siward sent Godfrey a bland look—"you'll not hesitate to sign the document wherein these oaths have been written by our village priest."

Siward turned away from the Norman's abruptly white face and nodded toward his son. Osric moved to open the door. A cowled figure who waited just beyond stepped inside carrying a rolled sheet of vellum, a small container of precious ink, and a sharpened quill.

A neatly trapped and coldly furious Godfrey put his name to the carefully written page.

"Once Father Bertrand has signed as witness," Siward continued while taking the quill into his own hand, "by my command Osric will take this parchment and place it in a well-hidden niche"—Siward paused and, as Bertrand added his name to the sheet, gave the Norman lord an angelic smile—"for safe-keeping."

When the ink was dry and the vellum again curled into a neat roll, Osric hastened from the chamber to execute his assigned task while his two sisters departed at a more leisurely pace.

Siward kept Godfrey with him to discuss lesser matters remaining to be settled. His first concern involved arrangements for Osric's public oath of fealty. Siward urged that the ceremony be done with haste in order for his son to quickly assume control of Northland and thus enable the family to move from

Castle Radwell to the subfief. Also they debated which personal belongings the family would be allowed to keep and which would remain. These and other matters kept an impatient Godfrey occupied and confined to the dim chamber for more hours than he'd ever thought to give.

1

Late Spring 1092

CAPRICIOUS CLOUDS DRIFTED RESTLESSLY ACROSS THE PALE face of a moon turned half to the dark. Thus the cool orb shed an ever-changing pattern of light and shadow over Castle Radwell's soaring tower as if conspiring to disguise the extraordinary sight of a figure steadily scaling the fortress's sheer stone walls.

With tenacious care Rhys sought firm holds in crevices between thick blocks, sporadically dislodging pebbles. He was impervious to dangers of which he was forewarned by the pebbles falling for a distance in silence before skittering down a steep, rocky hill to end with a faint splash in the deep waters of the moat at its base. His objective's importance blocked thoughts of the deadly consequences of failure in this initial feat. Permitting his concentration to be diverted would have been to threaten the whole, for attaining the ultimate goal depended upon first securing the prize of this night's hazardous but carefully planned action.

At last he reached the summit. Cautious to make no sound, Rhys swung over the ledge and dropped to the far side's parapet walkway. He crouched in sheltering gloom for a long moment, waiting until easy breathing was restored and full strength revived. Then, an unseen shadow, he rose and moved toward the lone night guard standing squarely in a firebrand's ring of light.

Atop an invulnerable tower and gazing out over the motionless countryside at its front, the guard had no earthly reason to be wary of approaching danger and even less to fear the immediate presence of a foe. A single blow from behind proved the folly of his complacent assumptions.

Tapers clustered atop a silver platter cast flickering lights across Linnet's bath as she finished wringing water from a wealth of hair and shifted to lean back against one side of the wooden tub resembling an overlarge barrel's bottom half. All day she'd dutifully met expectations placed upon the sole lady of Castle Radwell, the daughter of its lord. She was anxious to be done with the task at hand and for a brief time released to enjoy the comforts of heated water, the peace of private moments . . . free to delight in impossible dreams.

While steaming water lapped at the creamy skin below her shoulders, Linnet allowed the weight of her freshly washed hair to tumble over the tub's edge to the floor. She then lifted the bone-backed brush waiting beside a rapidly drying ball of sweet-scented soap on the stool drawn near. After first bringing order to tangled locks, she continued stroking them with slow and soothing regularity. Her tresses, though neither the glorious gold of the Saxons native to these lands nor the raven black of the Welsh who bordered them, leastways were thick, and as they began to dry, their soft umber hue gleamed with warm highlights.

Abundant hair, however, was small comfort when secretly she wished for the peacock beauty that could never belong to a humble linnet bird. Her name, she'd always known, was singularly, depressingly appropriate. A linnet she was—plain and drab-colored, worthy only of an indulgent father's admiration. Oh, 'struth, one day a husband might deem her a prize. But she had no illusion but that 'twould be for the assets of her sizable dowry and the valuable alliance with a powerful family that such a match would ensure.

A faint shudder passed over Linnet. Unbidden, her mind filled with the features of the most recent supplicant for her hand. One of the few Saxon lords who still held lands in Norman England, Lord Osric was a gruff man notorious for his impatience and his violent temper. Why her father had sent his all-important young heir to Lord Osric for fostering Linnet had never understood. Yet by the fact that he had, she'd known her most heartfelt pleas would fail to persuade even her indulgent sire to refuse the Saxon lord's suit. Her silent relief that negotiations for their union had apparently come to a halt was so great that it dulled the pain of a blow to her already humble self-image. That talks ended shortly after Lord Osric first met her had convinced her that the disgusting man found her appearance wanting. Linnet had deflected his unspoken insult with the shield of a certainty that she found him infinitely less appealing —not that a woman's opinion of a prospective spouse would be sought or considered of any worth.

Linnet determinedly averted her thoughts from the unpleasant subject of arranged marriages and far more unpleasant lords. With her back turned toward the chamber door and with the tangles smoothed from hair that was almost dry, she was free to slide down and rest her head atop the tub's nearly shoulder-high rim. Her pale brown eyes gazed through the thin opening of an arrow slit on the facing wall and dreamily searched for brief glimpses of the mysterious half-moon alternately peeking flirtatiously around and then hiding behind the dark silhouettes of aimlessly drifting clouds. Soon Meara would return from the hall below with a towel heated by the fire in its central hearth. But until then . . .

Linnet relaxed and welcomed the anticipated delights of warm waters and equally warm fantasies. Predictably the latter were drawn from the oft repeated and well-known mythical deeds recounted of an evening in her father's great hall. But quite to the reverse of those tales, the hero of Linnet's exciting adventures was a mysterious, devastatingly handsome stranger of whom, with the exception of one recent humiliating experience, Linnet had caught only rare glimpses.

He looked like a man born to lead, standing out amid many others, if not by height alone, then by virtue of the hair falling below impressively broad shoulders and so bright it seemed to glow with inner lights. And his eyes! His eyes were as dark as the midnight sky, piercing but perversely lit with humor as if he were laughing at the world and everything in it.

Linnet was a well-born maiden and naturally reserved, but on the few occasions when he'd unexpectedly appeared, she had found herself helplessly staring at him while the sharp mind on which she prided herself went as soft and about as clear as mud. She'd sought, albeit surreptitiously, to learn the elusive man's name—and more. Her quest had met with no success. Either she was too reticent in her attempts or honestly nothing was known of him. Likely both possibilities were true. Yet the fact that his identity remained hidden only made the golden-haired, dark-eyed stranger the more enthralling.

Linnet would never have had courage enough to boldly approach the man. Her cheeks burned even a fortnight later under vivid memories of the day when she'd glanced over her shoulder to find *him* a mere two paces behind her. Although, to compensate for her plain appearance she ever strove to maintain a modicum of grace, at his sudden nearness she'd gone clumsy. Tripping on her own gown, she'd fallen into an inelegant heap at his feet.

Sir Basil, the guard captain, had clearly been aghast at the prospect of ill befalling the earl's cherished daughter in his presence. Fearing the blame would be laid upon him, the knight had instantly lifted her from the ground—but not before she'd caught a glimpse of the stranger's lips curling with faint disdain. Rather than come to her aid, her hero had quickly stepped back and disappeared into the concerned crowd gathering about their lady—an action of questionable gallantry.

Despite this apparent fault, which she bleakly accepted as a justifiable response to her disgusting awkwardness, he had remained at the center of her daydreams and had invaded her night dreams as well. More shocking still, she could no longer confine her fantasy hero's actions to brave deeds done. No. Now, fresh from victory over evil, the golden warrior inevitably returned to his lady love—a linnet magically transformed into a beautiful peacock by the amazing power only shining dreams could provide. 'Twas a shameful secret. But, Linnet consoled herself, no one need ever know. Thus she excused adding his ardent vows of endless devotion to the growing list of embellishments for the second portion of her every fantasy, that scene rapidly becoming the most important.

Willingly Linnet drifted into the mists of her whimsical imagination while before a background of fickle moonlight her champion did honorable battle against a wicked foe. Time advanced unnoticed by the one lazing in mystical realms wherein a golden hero, in the guise of Saint George, valiantly met a ravenous dragon.

Under an unaccountable but growing uneasiness, the vision began to fade. Although no sound bestirred the chamber's silence, a prickling sensation assaulted the back of Linnet's neck. She shifted nervously, and water that of a sudden seemed to have gone cold sloshed in gentle waves against the tub's thick, tightbound planks.

"Meara?" Frightened and lacking the courage to glance behind her, Linnet could do precious little more than whisper. No answer.

She was alone in the solar, Linnet realized, sharply rebuking herself for her illogical fears. Of a certainty she was. Nonetheless an erratic thumping shook her heart. The drawbridge was upraised, leaving no way across the wide, deep moat. Moreover, the iron portcullis at the castle entrance was lowered. 'Twould be impossible for any foe to gain access to the fortress of Radwell. That sane, rational reassurance lent a comfort remarkable for its small and feeble proportions.

Enough of this nonsense! Linnet scolded a pigeonhearted nature long admitted but distressing all the same. You've spent too much time in witless dreams of daring deeds. You've lost reality somewhere in midst of exciting events which, given substance, would melt you into a pool of craven terror. Turn about and see how witless are your fancies. Knowing a moment's hesitation would smother every last glimmer of courage, she suited action to her silent command.

Linnet's lips opened, but under the collision of shock and fear, sound perished unborn in her throat. It seemed certain that either she had truly lost her right wits or a fearsome otherworldly force had given life to her dreams. Before her disbelieving eyes her breath-stealing fantasy hero stood in the flesh, so tall, so devastating in his masculine beauty, and with so potent an aura of power that the image seemed too perfect to be real. Linnet shook her head in a vain attempt to disperse this apparition, which proved the truth behind priestly warnings that such dreams as hers were a sinful wrong that good women must disallow. Overwhelmed by belated guilt, Linnet inwardly confessed her fall to a tempting lure she should have resisted.

Still—despite negatively shaken head, thick lashes repeatedly blinked, and fervent silent prayers beseech-

ing forgiveness—the image would not fade. Linnet
was left to absorb the staggering fact that his presence
was no illusion bred of a too fertile imagination but
real, very real. Far worse than that, his broad shoulders rested against the closed door of the room where
she sat covered by clear liquid alone!

"Milady . . ." Apparently at his ease, the intruder
grinned with wicked sensuality while mocking eyes
visually caressed the creamy shoulders half turned
toward him and exposed above the tub's rim. During
the decade Rhys had spent as an unwilling guest at the
Conqueror's court in Normandy he'd become accustomed to women, well born and commoner alike,
figuratively throwing themselves at him. But only this
coy, pampered daughter of Radwell's earl had gone so
far as to actually fall at his feet in a ploy to gain
attention. Now that she had won his interest's full
force, Rhys wondered how sincerely she would rue his
giving of the gift besought. The wry thought widened a
white smile, which lost none of its potent charm for
the cynicism in its depths.

Barely able to breathe and despite thoughts in total
disarray, Linnet knew the impossibility of producing
more than an embarrassingly inadequate squeak of
protest. She abruptly turned about and sank down
until her chin was below the waterline. Through the
narrow opening on the far wall she glared at the
betraying moon, irrationally blaming it for her predic-
ament while a blush bloomed with such heat that by
rights her bathwater should have boiled. She wished it
would. A froth of bubbles could provide a flimsy cover
of sorts between her nude form and a pair of night-
dark and far too penetrating eyes. Failing that, she
wrapped her arms about her uplifted knees and
pressed tightly back against the wooden wall between
the intruder and a forbidden view.

"Who are you?" The question Linnet had long
sought answer for popped into being without forein-
tent. She could have bitten her tongue. Leastwise,

Linnet comforted herself, she'd recovered her voice, although its usual calm tone had turned husky and came out little better than a whisper. "How did you get in?" This hastily added question was more to the point.

The uninvited visitor ignored her first query to cryptically address the last. "Eagles fly."

"Eagle?" No-o-o. This man, this hero of her dreams, couldn't be he. Linnet's heart pounded so hard it threatened to suffocate her while the implications of such a possibility curled like poisonous vines around her sweet fantasies. Only hours past, her father had taken the castle's entire garrison, save Edolf, the one guardsman atop the tower, to rush forth and meet his arch foe in battle. Her golden champion could not, simply could not possibly be the man her father hated more than the devil himself. Asides . . .

"The Eagle is Welsh." Water invaded Linnet's mouth, turning the last word into a sputter as in desperation she seized upon this frail argument to wield against an awful truth. By the circumstances of his arrival, this man had proven himself an enemy, but her mind fought against accepting a fact that would make her dreams the acts of a traitor.

"Aye, that I am." Rhys grinned. He could nearly see the damsel's confusion, although her face was turned away from him and, by the sound of it, buried so deep she was in danger of drowning. He had not envisioned coming upon the earl's spoiled daughter at her bath as a part of the plan, but he saw no reason to regret the fact. During the few advance forays he'd made into his enemy's home, this tender creature had sent him an abundance of smoldering looks. Surely any female bold enough to repeatedly issue such melting gazes knew full well the precise nature of her dangerous invitations.

Throughout the goodly number of years he'd spent

in the company of Norman damsels who were more than anxious to know him better, similar enticements had been turned upon him too oft for him to have any question as to the reward expected. He had proven himself loath to disappoint them. Nor would he have been averse to indulging in similar meaningless but pleasurable games with this small linnet who was clearly willing to become the eagle's prey.

Linnet's hair, near the same golden brown as her eyes, pooled on the floor as she tilted her chin upward to safely draw deep breaths in an urgent attempt to tame a thundering pulse and regain some semblance of normality. How could what he claimed be true? The Welsh were a dark-haired race. This man's mane was as bright as sun-ripened wheat and as fair as any Saxon's. More importantly, *much* more importantly, how could any of this be happening to her—quiet, sensible, dutiful Linnet?

That Lady Linnet had yet to scream for help, as surely any timid virgin caught unclothed by a man would do, reinforced Rhys's belief that her reticence was an act calculated to draw him nearer. So be it. He moved forward with the soundless stealth of a hunter.

"Lady Linnet is Norman, as is her sire. Thus, rightly she should be as dark as he. But you are not. Now you are eight and ten, you must have learned that all things are not as might be expected." He learned that same lesson anew by discovering, despite tightly wrapped arms that did more to emphasize than to hide her lush curves, she had physical attractions more than sufficient to compensate for a misleading initial impression of pale charms. And not slender limbs of alabaster and generous curves alone. Standing near for the first time, Rhys saw what he'd failed to look close enough to acknowledge before—a complexion of pure cream and thick sable lashes certain to emphasize the gold of her eyes. Candlelight caressed his fair mane as he shook his head in mild irritation with his own limited perceptions. Pursued too oft, he'd stopped bothering to return enticing examinations in detail.

Linnet gasped. The rough velvet voice came from directly above. What should she do? What could she do? She dared not scream. Whatever else was unclear, his reason for coming was obvious—to take her captive—and to cry out would be to summon the one whose presence must remain hidden. Mentally flailing about for an alternative answer, she stumbled over the meaning of words barely heard above the ever more frantic pounding of her heart.

How did he know she'd recently passed that mark of age? How? Linnet grimaced with self-disgust. With her own eyes she'd seen him come and go in Castle Radwell at will. Plainly he was far more successful in learning what he sought than she'd been in learning more of him. It was irritating, frustrating, to know that the Eagle had discovered so much about her while she knew so little of him. Even now she knew only that she'd spent far too many hours in treacherous, wicked fantasies about a man proven to be the deadly enemy who had led his people in repeated raids across Radwell's border.

"I am not Lady Linnet." Linnet recognized the ridiculousness of the lie the moment it was spoken. Nonetheless, she resented the mocking laughter with which he greeted it.

"Oh, but you are." Rhys's deep voice went lower to purr a scant distance from her ear. "We both know I've visited here often enough to be aware of you— your soulful stares and well-timed tumble guaranteed that I would."

A new wave of embarrassment swept Linnet from the tips of her toes to the top of her head, and she buried a rosy-hued face in cupped hands resting atop knees just breaching chill bathwater. He knew how she'd watched him! Linnet wished she could simply dissolve into the transparent liquid that left no place to hide. She could hardly justify her action by confessing an inability to prevent her gaze from following him as if it were some inferior metal and he the lodestone. More appalling still was his taunt that she'd purposely fallen at his feet in a wordless demand for his attention. His accusation forced her into greater depths of humiliation.

Rhys frowned. Her reaction was unexpected. After those many sidelong, come-hither looks her retreat from his answer to their call was annoying. Cynicism lent a cold glitter to his eyes. Lady Linnet's response, it would seem, proved her to be a too oft indulged female who teased but never fulfilled. Mentally shrugging, he acknowledged that despite his initial thoughts an impenetrable wall had already been placed betwixt them—first by their respective positions in life and second by the constraints of the task under way. Still . . . He meant to warn the pampered maiden just how dangerous it was for tender prey to bait an eagle.

One long forefinger slid across Linnet's collar bone, leaving a wake of tingling fire on its journey to the dip at the base of her throat. Stroking out to the tip of her chin, with gentle insistence Rhys urged her heart-shaped face up until the back of her head again rested atop the tub's rim. Robbed of sanity by eyes burning with the hypnotic power of a predator for its quarry, Linnet parted her softly bowed lips on a silent gasp. Dark flames flared beneath half-lowered lashes as the hard curve of a very real mouth descended. Rhys took possession in a succession of exciting, tormenting kisses that demonstrated to Linnet just how feeble had been her inexperienced dreams. The heavy pounding of her heart seemed to fill her throat until a faint, strange sound whispered out.

Knocked off-balance by a sweetness he could almost swear tasted of innocence, Rhys was irritated by this weakening to a woman's surely practiced lures. To punish her he deepened the kiss with blatant expertise, building it to a fever of hungry passion he believed no inexperienced maiden could match. Another helpless sound welled up from Linnet's depths, in part a cry of fear for the unknown but more a supplication for him to ease needs whose existence she'd never suspected. The oddly vulnerable sound broke Rhys free of a rapidly escalating desire sending blood coursing through his veins with the speed of windswept flames. He forced himself to break their bond.

As the invading mouth abruptly lifted, to Linnet's shame, hers followed in silent plea for its return. Feeling bereft, lost in the unfamiliar mists of passion, Linnet opened her eyes to the daunting view of a mocking smile curving masculine lips. It brought from her a whimper of distress, and yet she could not look away.

Gone still as stone, Rhys frowned. His open hand absently caressed the cream silk of Linnet's throat while he studied the wild blush on her dazed face and the hurt in eyes gone to molten honey. Wordlessly he reminded himself that it mattered not at all whether she was experienced, a manipulating tease, or truly a virginal woman. She could never be his! It was a fact that made the suspicion sweeping over him all the more disturbing, the suspicion that he was going to regret permitting himself even this small taste of a sweetness he'd never forget. He angrily rejected the mere notion that any single female, let alone the coddled daughter of a despised enemy, could so deeply affect him.

The sound of a door latch lifting sliced between them as cleanly as any sharp-honed blade. With incredible speed, Rhys swept Linnet's discarded gown from the floor where it had been allowed to fall as she stepped into the tub. Cloth caught in the strong arm wrapped just below her shoulders, he pulled the maid to her feet. The same arm holding an improvised cloth shield across the damsel's front, permitting her a modicum of modesty, urged her back to lean full against his broad and overwhelmingly powerful form. A dagger simultaneously appeared in his free hand and moved to hover a tiny fraction above the graceful arch of her exposed throat. Together they faced a slowly opening door.

Stunned by the Eagle's rapid reactions, Linnet was barely aware that she still stood in the tub. Her haphazardly draped gown's bottom edge floated atop wild waves breaking against her knees and sloshing over the rim to flood the floor about her captor's feet. She knew who and what to expect. Yet for all that Linnet would have forestalled the inevitable, had it been possible, she watched helplessly as a sturdy woman of considerable girth rolled into the chamber with a neatly folded cloth square in her arms.

The instant the newcomer's attention fell upon the threatening sight she loosed a bloodcurdling scream.

"Meara, stop!" The implacable command shocked Linnet at least as much as it shocked the onetime nursemaid and lifelong companion who had never bowed to the will of any save Earl Godfrey. Nonetheless, it was effective. Meara's scream came to an abrupt end. Likely too late.

Whatever the Eagle intended for her, Linnet had hoped to rob him of an even more powerful weapon, hoped somehow to save her twelve-year-old brother from his hold. Truth be told, she'd have savored, if only silently, the knowledge that she had outwitted a man who thought he knew so much of her and of events in the Norman stronghold of Radwell.

"Meara? Linnet? What evil imp has frightened you?" A boyish version of Linnet thrust his way past the human barrier near blocking the doorway. Certain some feminine and unjustified panic lay behind the piercing cry—a fearsome spider, mayhap—Alan charged forward, a teasing grin brightening his face. Then, one step beyond Meara, he came to a sudden halt.

"So . . ." High above Linnet's disarranged curls

amused satisfaction glittered in dark eyes. "Radwell's young heir is in residence. A boon unexpected but most welcome."

The boy's hands curled into fists. He'd have sworn it was impossible, but here stood an intruder with his dagger at Linnet's throat! "Release my sister or I'll . . . I'll . . ."

"Hmmm?" Brows arched while a mocking yet surprisingly gentle smile curled Rhys's mouth.

Alan's thin chest heaved with frustration set to boiling by the impossibility of a successful fight against this foe of such size and undoubted strength.

"By your quick defense, I see the honest affection you harbor for your sister." The golden man's deep voice wielded more force for its quiet tone. "And man to man, I offer you a bargain."

Alan's pale brown eyes narrowed to a fierce glare glowing with animosity. "Don't hurt my sister."

"As you wish to see Lady Linnet protected, best we come to terms by which I'll ensure she comes to no harm."

Certain that unpleasant conditions would follow, the youngster met this unexpected promise with mute suspicion.

Rhys acknowledged the lad's right thinking with a broad smile even as he continued. "I will ensure her good health so long as you do as I command."

Refusing to verbally agree, yet deeply aware of the gleaming blade so near Linnet's throat, Alan nodded once. The action trapped light in the soft umber curls covering his head.

Rhys respected the boy's blatant reluctance but lost no moment in stating his requirements. "Fetch first a gown from your sister's chamber. Her cloak as well. To that add your own cloak. Then, without word to any other, return directly here. To do elsewise will place at risk the one you would see safe."

Linnet watched as the boy, painfully conscious of the futility in refusing, turned to do as he was bidden.

During the unequal confrontation she had all but forgotten the sharp weapon so near, but once Alan disappeared through the door, awareness of its dangerous threat returned.

The boy's departure had a similar effect upon Meara, who suddenly found her voice again—and a booming voice it was. "Best you not harm my wee linnet bird or my lord earl will see you dead. Be assured of that fact. One bruise, one hair disturbed . . ."

Rhys's dark and formidable scowl put an end to the flow of accusing words. "Your earl has long desired to see me dead, has long done his all to achieve that end. But as you see"—abandoning the responsibility for keeping Linnet's lone covering in place to the damsel's own desperate hold, with his freed hand he motioned toward himself—"your lord has yet to win his goal." He slowly shook his head in feigned sympathy, and candlelight seemed to burn more brilliantly for being reflected by blond hair. "And I warn you, 'tis a goal he is unlikely to secure—even should harm befall either your lady or the all-important heir."

Although irony cast a momentary shadow across dark eyes, the sight of this shrewish guardian's frustrated temper building to an explosion revived Rhys's mocking humor. Wryly amused, he yielded to the laughing imp of temptation and set out to tweak the dragon's tail and bait her to a greater fury. Rhys moved a slight distance back and brushed his sword-callused hand over the maiden's lush mane from the crown of her head, through the center of her back, and down to where tresses ended on the smooth curve of her derriere.

Under the unfamiliar sensation of a man's hand intimately touching her, Linnet went rigid. No man had the right to treat her thus. Certainly never this man, this foe. Yet, even through the thickness of her hair, his touch sparked the excitement of a danger greater even than that of the gleaming blade still held menacingly close to her throat. Though Linnet had made the silent confession, she laid the blame for this wicked wrong squarely at the Eagle's door. Lent a momentary bravado by the sense of injustice roused by his action, she pushed aside the threatening dagger and half turned to send him a burning glare that decried his touch. Yet all the while, inside her treacherously melting soul, a mocking voice gleefully pointed out that 'twould be more effective were she able to honestly claim she found his caresses an unwelcome affront.

When the intruder's strong arm snapped out to pull the defiant damsel back against his powerful form, Meara immediately protested. Unfortunately Meara's wail, blocked by a deep fury, was no louder than Linnet's had been upon first discovering her fantasy hero leaning against a closed door.

A rueful grimace passed over Rhys's handsome face. He regretted having allowed his sense of the absurd to urge him into shocking this overweight protector of virtue with an action that had assuredly embarrassed the damsel in his hold. An unintended result.

"Waste no more breath in threats as useless as the young heir's." Rhys resumed his warning, every hint of amusement stripped from his voice, while he resheathed his dagger. "Rather, come. Take your wee linnet bird and see her readied to don the garb, which I hope will soon arrive."

The powerful arm wrapped about Linnet shifted from shoulders to waist. In one sweeping motion he lifted her from the tub and lowered her feet to the chill of a bare plank floor. At near the same instant Meara rushed forward to envelop her charge in the huge cloth square she'd warmed by the fire below. The towel had lost its heat, but Linnet welcomed both its enshrouding folds and the block Meara's wide body had inserted between herself and the dangerously attractive man.

After thrusting Linnet safely behind her considerable bulk, Meara turned to again boldly face the unwelcome visitor.

"You say Earl Godfrey has long sought to see you dead." Her voice was flat and hard. "Then you are . . ."

"Prince Rhys ap Griffith, though doubtless you know me best as the Eagle—and privately name me much worse." Amused by the questionable need for this second introduction, he made a slight bow without taking his gaze from the woman who repeatedly sought to confront him.

Meara had suspected as much from near the moment she'd entered the chamber. "I warn you"—her glare held the fierceness of a mother bear protecting her cub—"that I mean to tell Earl Godfrey every detail of the dreadful wrongs you've committed here."

"I give you my gratitude for becoming my messenger." The faint smile on Rhys's lips failed to thaw eyes gone to black ice. "And if you wish to see the earl's children safely home, with the news of their taking I pray you will tell him, too, the price for their return." He paused to emphasize the import of his next words. "I demand that what is mine be restored."

Meara frowned, not so much in anger as in confusion, an expression mirrored on Linnet's face. The endless skirmishing between Norman and Welsh meant the constant shifting of borderlands. Though a warrior renowned for his fierceness in battle and for his uncanny successes, surely this Welsh prince was not so witless as to expect the forfeiture of every small piece of land he might think to claim?

Rhys's humorless smile deepened, but still it did nothing to lighten his bleak expression. "Earl Godfrey will know precisely what I seek."

Before Meara could press further, Alan hustled into the chamber overburdened with garments, which dragged on the floor and threatened to trip him. As Rhys moved toward the boy, whose cheeks he as-

sumed had been stained a ruddy hue by haste, Alan
abruptly dropped the clothing to the floor. Thus lay
revealed the glitter of a sword, small but doubtless
honed to a biting edge.

"I won't let you take Linnet—or me!" With that
wild claim, Alan hurled himself and his weapon
toward the threat too near.

Impressed by the youngster's courageous attempt to
defend both himself and his sister, still Rhys easily
sidestepped his less than half-sized attacker. Speed
and direction fixed at the outset, the boy bypassed his
target while Rhys reached out with the invisible
swiftness of a striking adder. He grasped the child's
wrist so tightly in his far more powerful hand that
brief moments later the sword fell from fingers gone
numb.

His tender pride bruised, Alan determinedly refused to shed tears of frustrated rage, though his eyes
sparkled with moisture even as his successful opponent retrieved the short blade.

Holding the confiscated weapon overhead, Rhys
drove its sharp point deep into a wooden beam high
above, placing the weapon beyond the reach not only
of the boy but of the two women as well. The
unavoidable humiliation his action heaped upon the
young heir was regrettable, though generous when he
could as easily have used his dagger to defend himself.
Such an action had never truly been an option, for to
have done so would have had deadly results and have
defeated his purpose in coming. His reason for endan-
gering himself by taking the night's perilous actions
permitted neither killing nor maiming. Rather he had
come to capture the woman—and now the boy as
well. Any harm to them would lessen their value
when, for their safe release, Rhys firmly believed he
would win the ransom he sought—if not in the first
round of his joust of cunning with the earl, then in the
second.

Clutching the towel tight to her chin, Linnet shared

Alan's ignominy in having his brave attempt at defense so easily thwarted. But simultaneously, at the sight of the living hero of her fantasies demonstrating the prowess with which her imagination had endowed him, a secret thrill renewed the rosy heat of her cheeks. Here was proof the stunningly handsome man was all she had dreamed him to be.

Remorse drove its barbed tip into her tender conscience. Aye, the Eagle was skilled at combat. It had to be so for him to have been so successful in fighting her father. 'Twas shameful to be thrilled by the dangerous abilities that threatened every member of Radwell's own—not least of all Alan and her!

Linnet nibbled her lower lip to renewed berry brightness, scolding herself for allowing an errant imagination to make her susceptible to wrongful admiration of this most fearsome of foes. Thick lashes descended over guilt-filled eyes. She had an alarming suspicion that such worthy admonitions would do little to strengthen her ineffectual attempts to resist his unintended but potent lures. This probability was made the more hazardous by her forbidden hero's unknown intentions.

Meara, ignoring the two males of widely divergent ages, scooped up the garments Alan had so carelessly let fall. Separating bright linen from the dark wool and warm fur of two cloaks, she frowned. For Linnet to wear, Alan had brought only this lightweight scarlet gown, no camise or headcloth or . . . Meara shook a head barely covered by thinning gray hair. What needs be must be. Leastways raglan sleeves, wide at shoulder, grew so close at wrist that excess cloth would ruche half down to Linnet's fingers. Turning toward the younger woman with the determined air of a warrior who would not be waylaid, Meara lifted the scarlet linen gown above the cloud of her charge's softly glowing locks.

Only when the bright-hued garment dropped over Linnet's shoulders did she loosen her grip on the towel. White folds fell as the gown replaced them in providing a modest covering. She faced Meara, whose girth blocked the view of either male and who quickly drew the front laces together and tied them primly at her throat.

Once Meara's task was done, she gave Linnet what she believed to be a reassuring smile along with a pair of dainty kid leather slippers. Linnet's fine brows creased with concern for the meaning of her mentor's grimace while she bent to don the slippers, but as she straightened again, the startling weight of a dark brown cloak descending from behind drove that question from her mind.

Rhys had gallantly waited until the damsel was modestly garbed, but when Meara took a step back from her charge, he moved quickly to smooth his hands across Linnet's slender shoulders to settle the cloaks' generous fur-lined folds more comfortably. Looking down upon the mass of flowing curls still loose, he felt a near unmanageable urge to again savor their silky texture. To end this weakening to foolish temptation, which had struck him at the worst possible moment, he turned a penetrating look upon the bristling Meara and with it issued a curt order.

"Tell your sorry lord that I swear by the Holy Cross to safely return to him those who shall be his once he recalls his mercenaries from lands that are mine—and once I have received his written oath to forever hold their boundaries inviolate." Rhys paused, and the moments of silence that followed were as tightly strained as once-soaked leather cords bared to the summer's midday sun. "Warn him that there are limits to my patience. For a fortnight I will guard his offspring against harm. After those fourteen days . . ." His slight shrug did more to frighten Meara than any spoken words ever could have done.

While her captor addressed Meara, Linnet gazed up at the granite profile, and faint puzzlement furrowed her delicate brows. Why was she, a pigeon-heart, not overwhelmed with fear by his unspoken threat?

Fire flared in Meara's eyes and earned a sardonic smile from Rhys. "Now so long as your earl follows my directions, you both need only pray that I hold my honor and the sanctity of oaths made upon sacred relics more dear than he."

Linnet was stunned by this insult to her father. All her life she'd heard him lecturing foster sons, knights, and guardsmen on the all-important principle of unsullied honor as the standard every well-born man must hold most dear. And with that duty, he'd repeated again and again, must come a willingness to sacrifice even one's life to preserve its purity. By the fervor of those speeches she was certain that no person could possibly be justified in impugning the honor of Earl Godfrey of Radwell.

Ignoring Linnet's wide eyes and Meara's horrified gasp, Rhys next looked toward the boy. Now would begin the final step in the night's mission.

"Alan, don your cloak and lead the way while I escort your sister to the bottom of the stairs, her safety ensured both by my sharp blade and by your unfaltering compliance with my commands."

Alan glared at the enemy he dared not defy. Comforting himself that his father would surely see the man dead for these actions, he obeyed.

HELD CROSSWAYS ATOP A MIGHTY STEED BY ITS MASTER, and for the moment hers, Linnet nonetheless sat upright, determined to maintain a small distance between herself and the Eagle's broad chest. Now that no dagger was held to her throat she should fight her abductor. She should, but the sensible side of her nature argued that to struggle against a man easily tenfold stronger than she would merely make her look the more foolish . . . not that his opinion of her could have gotten much poorer. Reduced to showing her resistance by holding her back stiff and herself rigidly separate from him, Linnet tilted her chin up toward the moon. Her gaze became a reproachful glare for this symbol of the betrayal in her fantasies.

Three horses, their riders, and the two captives had rapidly left the cultivated fields of Radwell behind and melded with the black silhouette of the dense forests at their border. Close-grown trees and thick undergrowth trapped ground mists, which transformed the dark outlines of common objects into strange and deceptive shapes. Never having traveled at night, and never into the forest, Linnet stared apprehensively at eerie shadows that would have seemed infinitely more ominous had the worst not already befallen her.

As once-gentle hills became ascents much steeper, Linnet's unyielding posture was more difficult to maintain. But that challenge was not as troublesome as the discovery that her refusal to look into the Eagle's face did nothing to dispel the deeply regretted but continuing fascination he effortlessly exerted over her.

Although she sensed rather than saw the cynical smile lifting one corner of his lips, it grated over her already ragged nerves. More than ever before in her life she rued her lack of courage. Surely, had she possessed the bravery required to resist and distract her captor, she and her brother would have had a chance to win their freedom. But instead, Alan had led the Eagle and his female hostage into the castle's great hall. There the Welsh prince had stood with an elsewise exposed back against a stone wall and a blade to Linnet's throat while, by his command, the drawbridge had been lowered and the gates opened, allowing his two cohorts to enter and guard their exit.

Though believing herself to be as lacking in courage as in beauty, Linnet prided herself on possessing quick wits and good sense. Exercising the latter, she excused her inaction with the sensible argument that any such rash measures would likely have gotten the servants, Alan, or herself killed. Hah, her guilty conscious immediately ridiculed, her good sense was otherwise known as cowardice. Discouragement robbed her posture of defiance although still she held herself separate.

"Were you to relax, you would find the journey far less trying." A low voice stroked its near irresistible temptation to yield over a proud profile held determinedly aloof. "What danger is there in accepting the small measure of comfort I offer when, with my men and your brother behind and able to see every action we take, you are hardly in danger of being ravished."

Ravished? Despite all the dangers this golden man did in truth represent for Linnet—from the pain of a sharp dagger to her humiliatingly clear fascination with him—this possibility had never occurred to her. Why should it have when even the kiss he'd taken as she lay vulnerable in her bath, while devastating to her, had seemed no more to him than mildly amusing, a jest at her expense. Moreover, his taunting comments about her supposed pursuit had made it painfully obvious that he saw in her none of the allure she found in him.

Linnet nibbled her lip when a strong arm curled about her shoulders, pulling her to lie close against him. Shamed as she was by words reaffirming his lack of interest in her, still his aura of masculine warmth and power overwhelmed her. Even her most exciting fantasies had left her ill prepared to fight such potent enticements. Whether or not she wished it so, Linnet found herself melting.

While the small damsel lay within the circle of his arms, the subject of ravishment, mockingly raised and honestly declared impossible, haunted Rhys as well. Vivid memories of Linnet at her bath, a delicious sight, flooded back with unwelcome force. It had been a mistake to steal that glimpse of creamy skin and lush curves. He could only be relieved that neither she nor their companions would see the self-contempt in his eyes as he inaudibly cursed the return of an unruly physical response.

Rhys sent a blind glare toward the well-hidden path ahead, a path only those familiar with it could find, even in daylight. Once again he acknowledged the many layers of the impenetrable wall between them. He couldn't claim Lady Linnet. Neither here and now nor at any later time. Rhys prided himself on being a man of honor—unlike her father. And though but the outer layer of the barrier between them, he had given an oath to see the damsel returned to her own unharmed—for a price. That vow was a wall of steel that couldn't be broken. Still, his acceptance of an honorable oath did nothing to cool the heat of his blood.

As their silent journey continued, Linnet clenched her eyes shut, too conscious of the breadth and strength of the chest beneath her cheek. Unfortunately the action merely left her more sensitive to muscles rippling as the Eagle controlled the steed's direction. The dark forest's quiet ached with such a depth of awareness that she was relieved when his low-spoken words sundered its too warm embrace—until their meaning came clear.

"Do I take it that the fact I am Welsh has soured the sweetness of your success in winning from me the attention you sought?"

Having come to the conclusion that this plain linnet was all the more dangerous for her subtle attractions, Rhys had produced the sharp blade of taunting words to slice through the tentative bonds of her hold.

"Never did I seek your attention!" Linnet immediately pulled herself free of his treacherously welcome arms to sit upright and unyielding. "Never!" The words spurted out on the small explosions of a fierce temper Linnet had never suspected herself capable of feeling, much less putting into an audible snarl.

"Of course not." His words were thick with disbelief. "After a glance in my direction you merely fell at my feet."

"I tripped." Linnet's words were a hiss while under the shaming confession the heat of her scarlet blush burned.

"You make a habit of tripping?" Sarcasm fair dripped from the question.

"Nay, I do not." Fearing the heat of her own newborn temper, Linnet sought to smother its flames with logic. "Surely you must see that, had I intended to seek your attention, I'd have chosen some method that wouldn't require me to show myself lacking not only in beauty but in grace as well."

Rather than lessening, Linnet's fury grew ... but only with herself, for making this humbling admission of her own limitations. She tightly compressed her lips, refusing to let pass a single word more.

His head tilted to one side, and across it slid stray beams from a moon nearing the end of its journey and hovering on the western horizon. Defying that orb's color-stealing properties, his hair glowed gold while he pondered the fuming female determinedly holding herself separate from him—an assuredly difficult task, given the steepness of their climb. Had her fall truly been an accident? His suspicion that her statement had been true was the least of the doubts raised by her quick and likely inadvertently revealing defense. Linnet's bright embarrassment and the surprising lack of self-esteem revealed by words ringing with honesty caused Rhys, who rarely had reason to change his opinion, to uncomfortably question his initial assessment of her as the vain and too pampered daughter of the Norman earl.

As they continued to ascend the sharp incline, barely visible in darkness intensified by a cloud drifting across the face of the moon, Linnet's mild discomfort grew to an honest pain increased by each jarring stride of their steed. She would far rather have walked the whole way from Castle Radwell to ... to wherever they were going. Even as the thought formed, Rhys brought their horse to a halt. Peering over the beast's twitching ears, Linnet could just make out the dim shape of an odd structure near buried in a copse of trees. As she watched, a small, bent figure hustled out and immediately came to take the Eagle's reins.

"Ya did it, lad, ya did it!" A dry cackle that passed for a laugh rattled from the man, who was old enough to regard the infamous Eagle as a lad.

"Aye, Milo, I did what I set out to do." Without looking her way, but with care, as Rhys spoke he lowered his feminine burden to ground rendered spongy by a thick layer of dead leaves trapped in tangled grasses. "Did you doubt it?"

"Be a fool I would to think you likely to fail at whatever you set out to do, even be it that a bleedin' miracle was required—and this un near did." Eyes bright and curious as a magpie's examined the damsel standing diffidently to one side.

"Not quite." Rhys grinned as he swung down.

The Eagle's fondness for this wizened fellow was clear as he gave to Milo the first honest smile Linnet had seen on the man's lips. It was stunning, and when unexpectedly turned toward her, its potency robbed her of breath.

While Milo took the reins of all three horses, the Eagle's two cohorts moved forward to join their prince. Their action gave Linnet her first opportunity to closely view the pair. The husky one carrying an innocently dozing Alan was near the same age and height as the Eagle, with an untamed black mane but well-trimmed curls covering his cheeks and chin. In short, a bearded bear of a man. The Eagle's second supporter, also dark but reed slender and standing respectfully behind the other two men, Linnet suspected was little older than she.

After exchanging with the pair a few brief words, so softly spoken Linnet couldn't hear what was said, Rhys took her hand and turned to lead the way into the shadows of another secret path. With twists and turns that would be impossible to retrace, he directed their course up and then down one steep hill after another.

By the time they'd climbed the first of these many hills, Linnet's feet, encased in naught but thin kid leather slippers, were violently protesting such ill treatment. Her error in thinking she'd have preferred to walk rather than ride a horse became clear—painfully clear. Never before had she been compelled to hike such a distance or under such adverse conditions. Still she refused to complain and give her abductor further excuse to jeer at her supposedly coddled way of life. Though stinging tears of pain glittered at the ends of a thick sweep of lashes, she kept her gaze on ground mists trapped by dense-grown trees and held low by abundant foliage. The view was obscured, but the ground clearly was littered with unseen rocks that jabbed through her flimsy shoes and into her tender flesh while branches whipped at her legs and ankles and dew-moistened undergrowth made the climb treacherously slippery.

At long last the Eagle paused at the brow of a particularly grueling ascent. Linnet, grimly concentrating on the path that was no path in a desperate attempt to suppress the agony of her tortured feet, walked straight into the broad impediment. Stepping back, she slid on a pile of the previous autumn's decomposing leaves and landed hard on her derriere. Weary frustration brought on a fresh bout of tears. Dashing them away with a dirt-streaked hand, she scrambled to rise, only to fall again. This time she collapsed flat atop a sharp rock.

"God's teeth!" Linnet's growled oath was as much a shock to her as to the three men who'd quickly gathered about her. Never had she used unfeminine language, let alone sworn with such fierce abandon.

"Linnet, Father would punish you for saying that!" Wide awake, Alan stared down at his sister, aghast even as he struggled to be lowered to his own feet.

The subject of this rebuke had risen on her elbows but, recognizing the futility of her struggle, dropped back. This was it, the end. Her swollen feet hurt, her posterior ached, she was certain to have been bruised all over by the second fall . . . and, worse still, her lone gown was a filthy mess. The last, illogically, seemed the most monstrous insult of all, as she would be forced, for the next however many days in her hero's company, to wear the same torn and dirty gown. Silent tears continued to flow with an abandon she was certain to regret but could not halt.

To ensure that she was all in one piece Rhys crouched down beside the fallen damsel and lightly ran his hands over her form from shaking shoulders to . . . Unequal to the harsh wear they'd been asked to endure in recent hours, her slippers had fallen to shreds, and the soles of her feet were in little better condition.

"Bloody little fool. Why didn't you tell me?" He was irritated with her for not speaking and more with himself for having apparently alarmed her so badly she preferred suffering to the unknown risks involved in telling him.

Linnet met his glare with one equally as fierce. "And be accused, *again*, of seeking your attention?"

The expletive he used was even harsher than her relatively mild curse of moments past, but when he lifted her into his arms, his hold was gentle. No further words were spoken while, through the eerie, colorless light of predawn, Rhys set a steady pace down the path toward a group of buildings in the deep ravine below.

"He said what?"

Close-cropped in the Norman style, abundant gray hair near standing on end seemed as physical a demonstration of Earl Godfrey's ire as his tightly curled fist smashed against an unyielding stone wall, though the earl was too lost in temper to feel the pain.

"The Eagle, hah! More like some carrion-eating raven!" For all the great hall's size, it reverberated with the furious words. He whirled to glare at the bearer of terrible news as if meaning to wreak his vengeance upon her. "I rode out to do battle with him, but did he meet his foe face to face like an honorable warrior? Nay, he waited until the strong were distracted and then like a cowardly crow he preyed upon the weak!"

Near steaming under the heat of his anger, Godfrey marched directly toward the hefty woman who had met him at the door and welcomed his return from an unsuccessful sortie with this wretched news.

Exercising incredible speed for one of her size, Meara moved aside as her lord approached and refrained from pointing out that leastways no blood had so far been spilled. The thought of bloodshed so soon after the end of her confrontation with the Welsh prince sent a cold shiver snaking down her spine.

"Surely, no matter the Eagle's method of attack, you'll surrender what he demands to win the return of your children?" Meara said. Fear of the earl's rage was a weak match for her instinct to protect the two youngsters, her precious charges for so long. To secure their freedom she would gladly have faced any danger.

Godfrey's eyes flashed with the sulfurous light of two burning coals. "How dare he threaten me with outrageous talk of honoring oaths! How dare he!"

Meara knew that here lay the core of his anger's fire. Oh, aye, Earl Godfrey hated the Eagle and doubtless hated him the more for the wicked taking of heir and beloved daughter. But worst of all, with his reference to oaths honored or forsworn the Welsh prince had dared to challenge the earl on a painful subject, had dared to pick at an injury unhealed in lo these many years by demanding the earl's written oath that he would return the disputed lands and hold them inviolate.

She alone among Radwell's people knew facts injudiciously revealed long ago by another woman's temper. She alone, and never would she have been foolish enough to so much as allude to a wrongful deed best forgotten, let alone peel back the scab and probe the festering wound beneath. Only for the children's well-being would she force Earl Godfrey to face the issue, only to guard their safety and see them home once more. Her determination was strengthened by confidence that a loving father must care as much and be as willing as she to pay any price for their well-being. He would rant against the Eagle, fight to again hide the ugly sore, but surely for the sake of his children . . .

Linnet was aware of her captor's irritation, despite the gentleness of his arms cradling her like a recalcitrant child against his broad chest. She had kept her head lowered and her eyes closed all the way down the long descent. Yet without the distraction of passing sights, she became even more aware of his awesome strength, his ability to carry her so far with so little apparent discomfort. Beneath her chin Linnet curled her fingers into childish fists to prevent them from spreading across the tempting expanse of steely muscles beneath her cheek.

Not even the creak of an opening door, which proved they'd arrived at their destination, offered incentive enough for her to lift the heavy lashes hiding her amber eyes. Only after being lowered into a large chair, lent comfort by a single cushion, did Linnet peek up and catch a glimpse of the bearded bear leading Alan up a steep wooden stairway in one corner of a large hall.

"Give me your feet, one at a time."

Startled, Linnet glanced toward the speaker and found him settling atop a three-legged stool nearby, a resting place surely unequal to bearing a man of his impressive size.

"I'll bandage them before carrying you to join your brother in a bedchamber above." With a faint half-smile for the shocked expression on the winsome face near lost amid clouds of honey brown hair, Rhys absently nodded toward the figures disappearing into the dark beyond the highest step.

When the Eagle placed a small earthen jar on the floor to one side, Linnet realized that already he had rinsed his hands and dampened one of the several cloths laid across his lap. A brief visual search revealed the ewer from which he had poured water into the basin beside it. The two vessels sat upon a bare plank table at the near end of this sizable but sparsely furnished room. With cool efficiency her host had prepared for the task while her concerned attention followed Alan and his guard.

From his inadequate perch, placed on angle with Linnet's chair, Rhys reached out, lifted an abused foot, and set it crossways atop his thigh before she could think to question his intent.

"I can do it." Realizing of a sudden what this powerful man meant to do, Linnet instantly sought to pull her foot free. No warrior, and even less a prince, ought tend a woman's minor injuries. It was a shame to her that the Eagle thought her so incapable when in truth she, as a woman trained to be mistress of a castle, knew the ways of treating even the serious wounds of battle. Though painful indeed, the battered soles of her feet were nowise that gravely harmed.

Rhys held her limb secure and sent her a chilling glare that would have turned her to ice but for the warmth of his intoxicating nearness, a dangerous proximity that with every step they'd taken during the full length of their journey had ever increased the heat of her awareness.

With deft fingers Rhys searched the cuts. Then to cleanse dirt and crushed foliage from bruised and broken skin he employed the cloth earlier dipped into spring water. It had in no way been a part of his plan to see the Norman damsel harmed, and he blamed himself for these injuries. Having seen the flimsiness of the shoes fetched by Alan, who'd had no notion of the need for others more substantial, he should have sent the boy back for a better choice. The attack made with a child's sword had distracted him from that wiser course, but that was no worthy excuse for having allowed this to happen.

Linnet couldn't prevent her gaze from sliding over the hard planes of this intimidating and unbearably attractive man's face. Although she deemed it a wicked, treacherous wrong, still this man, this foe, was inextricably bound in her mind to the champion of her fantasies, and the touch of his fingers was a painful delight.

As Rhys, in silence, gently spread a soothing salve over flesh carefully dried, he felt the sweet caress of soft brown eyes to the depths of his soul. With equal care he lightly bandaged the treated foot while a muscle flexed in his cheek over a jaw tightly clenched against the growing awareness stretching between them.

The Eagle returned her one foot to the floor and lifted the other, but in his gentle hold Linnet found an ominous threat. By Radwell's endless gossip vines ripe with hushed whispers of terrifying deeds done and forbidding specters of more to follow, she knew that he had earned his fearsome reputation by standing undefeated in battle and unyielding in confrontations. Aye, a warrior he was . . . and a menacing predator. Yet 'twas this unexpectedly tender treatment which, rather than calming the few fears she'd felt, stoked them. Capture by her father's worst enemy had failed to alarm her. His tenderness was terrifying! The Eagle's careful touch represented a graver danger than had his dagger's sharp blade. It robbed her of the will to fight a far greater peril—his potent allure. Never before this night had she spent so much as a single moment alone in the company of a man not of her kin. Thus she possessed no experience in the methods to defend herself against his wordless, likely unintended assault on her senses.

The damsel's intense scrutiny disturbed Rhys in an

unexpected way. 'Twas as if she wielded some strange feminine magic to sunder the thick chains across the gates to his citadel of cynicism. He inwardly lowered additional bars to keep her from strolling with ease straight to his core—the heart no woman had ever been allowed to approach.

While seeking to block the entry of this deceptively helpless damsel, he erred in meeting an amber gaze. Although her eyes were wide with fear, in their depths lurked a heat he sensed would turn them to molten honey were he to give what from the first she'd sought—though whether innocently or knowingly he couldn't of a certainty say.

So scant a distance separated them that Linnet clearly saw the hot glitter in his black eyes. Too, she saw thick dark lashes lower as his gaze suddenly dropped with fierce intent to her parted lips. She shivered. Nothing in her fantasies had prepared her for the shock passing like a lightning bolt from him to her.

Rhys knew all too well the danger in this visual exchange. With considerably less care than earlier demonstrated, he finished fastening the last bandage and lowered her foot to the floor. Best he, if not she, remember they were enemies by heritage. 'Struth, he must, or they would both lose far more than either dared risk. Brows of dark gold scowled as he abruptly rose.

Gazing up at the coldly angry man of a sudden looming over her, Linnet felt his wordless rejection like a dagger blow landed sharp to point in her heart. The Eagle's fierce expression made it all the more unexpected when he bent and swept her up into his arms. Permitting himself no downward glance, he carried her up the wooden steps and into a window-less chamber poorly lit by a single tallow candle. It was there that an anxious Alan huddled beneath the watchful gaze of the bearded bear.

Linnet steadily watched the two silent men until a heavy oaken door closed off the sight, leaving brother and sister alone. Only then did she turn to Alan and see the anxiety in brown eyes at odds with the determined set of his young jaw. Plainly he'd spent the time awaiting her arrival concocting desperate plans.

3

Linnet paused and glanced over her shoulder at the pale glimmer struggling through a crack between shutters closed over the window at corridor's end. That narrow strip of daylight stretched the full length of the hallway to where she stood just above the outset of the stairway's descent to the great hall.

The night past she had been unable, under the Eagle's distracting nearness, to take rational stock of her surroundings. But now, while hovering in the shadows of a position offering a fine vantage point, she remedied that failure. What she found surprised her. Surely the prince of Cymer's lodgings should be more impressive than this timber structure. True, it was large and the single sizable room at ground level contained a very fine central hearth of mortared stone, but judging by the number of doors leading off from the corridor, there were but three chambers on the upper level. Where did his servants reside? Of more immediate import, where lived his warriors?

Ignoring the discomfort of feet first bandaged by the Eagle, then more recently wrapped and rewrapped in the multitude of cloth strips she had torn from a bedcover in the chamber where their captors had deposited them, she crept down the first step. Linnet motioned a fuming Alan to remain safely behind while she continued descending with stealth and caution. Though the hall below seemed empty, she hardly dared believe it true.

Once their captor and his burly cohort had left them alone in the small, dark, and windowless chamber, Alan had urged her to escape with him as soon as the building settled into silence. The night was all but past, and with the faint glimmer of a promised dawn already touching the sky Linnet had argued against that too impetuous and poorly thought out plan. Besides, they were too weary to flee with any haste.

Alan had reluctantly admitted the right of her reasoning and fallen asleep with the ease of childhood while Linnet sat staring into the shadows of a chamber lit only by a single flickering candle. She had reviewed the events that had so recently turned her life upside down and tangled the cords of her safe and well-ordered daily routine. That each day, for her, was a constant repetition of the one past she admitted while refusing to acknowledge an additional, equally accurate but less positive fact: her days were also boringly predictable.

Along with the realization that her steady path had been thrown off kilter came an unfortunate and utterly wicked thrill of excitement. Guilt brought a more vivid awareness of another terrible truth, half admitted while the Eagle treated her abused feet. It lay in the confusion between her dream hero and her abductor. That confusion had kept her fear restrained, even while her captor held a dagger to her throat. Struck with shame by this confession, which placed her in the greatest danger of all—the danger of losing the will to fight wrongfully imposed restraints—she became determined to seek release no matter its price.

Reaching the bottom step unchallenged, Linnet let out a deep breath. Her gentle face warmed with a small grin while she waved her brother down to join

her. Apparently their arrival late the previous night—
or rather early this morn—had led the Eagle to
oversleep. Linnet's amber eyes narrowed. In so doing
he had foolishly underestimated his hostages' resolve
to defeat him and win their freedom. Irritated on the
one side by his poor opinion of her and her brother
while on the other encouraged by their minor success
in getting even this far undetected, Linnet led the way
to the outer door as boldly as possible with pillows to
walk on.

Linnet had known that before they could attempt to
flee their captor her feet required a further covering of
one sort or another. So, while Alan slept, she had
quietly shredded their second coverlet. In these long
strips of cloth Linnet had wrapped her sore feet until
they looked like overstuffed cushions—awkward but
surely adequate to see her free of the enemy she'd
been traitor enough to admire.

Once done, she'd stifled memories of the Eagle's
gentleness in caring for her injuries and cudgeled her
mind for some plan to see herself and her brother
miraculously liberated. But by the time Alan stirred,
she'd become resigned to making this desperate and
likely ill-fated flight against great odds.

Facing the outer door and filled with bravado,
Linnet smiled, albeit grimly. She had inwardly sworn
to take any risk to free herself from the Eagle's
physical hold and hoped by that victory also to win
release from the bonds of fascination he'd unknowingly wound around her thoughts and dreams. A faint
flicker of hope glowed, though no brighter than the
cloudy day.

"We've made it thus far with no interference from
the Eagle." As Linnet reached for the latch, she
glanced down into her young brother's solemn eyes.
"Pray God we can as easily make it into the shielding
shadows of the forest."

"The Eagle is nowhere about and not a threat to

your flight but . . ." From the depths of a dark corner came the quiet words.

Not French words such as those Linnet had spoken to Alan but words from the Saxons' English tongue—which, as 'twas the language of Radwell's natives, both she and her brother understood. Just as plainly, the speaker understood but chose not to speak French.

Linnet realized this difference in one instant but in the next, heedless of her sore feet and the cumbersome bandages, whirled to see a young, slender, and raven-haired woman step forward into the central fire pit's circle of light. A woman alone in the Eagle's home so early in the morn? His wife? That too likely possibility hit Linnet with the force of an unexpected blow and robbed her of both breath and quick response. Why had it never occurred to her that a handsome man aged somewhere near a score and ten, particularly a man as important as a Welsh prince, must be wed?

"Even assuming you know in which direction to travel," the woman continued in a tone so flat it fair screamed of restrained contempt, "these mountains teem with many who may not share Rhys's goal in keeping you safe—or alive." While the words utterly lacked emotion, the woman's dark eyes glittered in a way that left Linnet little doubt but that the speaker found the latter prospect pleasing. When the danger-ous gaze shifted to Alan, Linnet instinctively moved several steps from the door and placed the barrier of her body between the woman and her brother.

"What reason have they to kill us?" Intending to divert their foe's attention, Linnet asked the question without honest desire for answer.

"What reason had your sire to kill their kinfolk?" The answer, snapped back without hesitation, crack-led with bitterness.

"Our father would not kill without reason, would not kill but to protect his own." Alan boldly stepped out from behind his sister's skirts, irritated in the first instance that Linnet had again relegated him to the position of helpless child. He was half done with his training to knighthood and well able to stand strong for himself.

Flame light gleamed over a dark head shaken while the woman's lips tilted into a crooked smile filled with cynicism near a replica of the Eagle's own and containing as small a measure of real humor.

"The young accompanied by the naive—how sweet." The woman made the belittling comment as she slowly circled Linnet, subjecting her to a minute examination from head to toe.

Linnet watched as the woman completed her circuit and saw the expression of disdain no longer hidden.

When the woman looked up, her gaze met Linnet's questioning eyes. She shrugged and gave an explanation, uncaring of the further insult it contained. "I had wondered if the Eagle's determination to claim you for hostage sprang from some deeper purpose than the one he's given. Clearly not. You are hardly the sort a man—Rhys least of all—would risk his life to possess."

The barb struck dead to point in Linnet's tender self-esteem. Nonetheless, had her childhood training taught her naught else, she had learned the importance of standing proud against all adversity, and her only response was an uptilted chin. She would not wilt before this female plainly venting the anguish of an earlier jealousy. Although the woman's suspicion of unfaithfulness had now been soothed, such fears seemed likely to have proven justified in the past. Linnet had only to consider the Eagle's earlier actions —the kiss in Radwell's tower and his tender treatment of her injuries—to believe it true. She felt sympathy for the woman and disgust for her own ungovernable response to the golden man's lures.

The pity glowing in Linnet's pale brown eyes both startled and irritated the woman. She immediately lashed out. "No matter the Eagle's discriminating tastes, you would be in great danger were you to attempt to pass through lands where men might covet a taste of pedigreed meat."

"They'd best not try to harm my sister!" Alan had had enough of women ignoring his presence and disregarding his abilities. "I will protect Linnet with my life."

Dark eyes softened with a gentle amusement resented by its recipient. "I fear you'd be forced to surrender that final defense, and it would be inadequate to secure your goal. On Radwell—or other Norman lands—your wishes might be respected because of who you are and what your future holds. But here in Cymer men, battle-hardened by conflict with your father over his unceasing greed for what is theirs, would brush you aside like a pesky fly to reach the prize they seek."

Alan straightened to his full height. The top of his head still failed to reach his opponent's shoulder. He was young yet mature enough to recognize when nothing of further use remained to be said and thus confined his response to a glare brimming with animosity.

Linnet restrained an urge to reach out and comfort her brother for the verbal blow to his pride. Alan would assuredly deem any such gesture from her a further affront. His response Linnet understood, but the woman's gentle tone and apparent regret for the insult in what she must view a necessary warning was more difficult to comprehend. Linnet wondered why the other's heart, hardened against the feminine hostage, softened for the boy.

"Nay." Again a dark head shook in rueful denial. "Truly it is best that you remain here under the Eagle's protection until what he seeks is returned."

In these words, too, Linnet found reason for curiosity. It was odd that this woman continually refer to her husband as the Eagle. Did she purposely distance herself from him by refusing to call him by his given name? Had his infidelities hurt her so deeply that she felt a need for barriers this flimsy? Even before Linnet could ponder this matter, the door behind silently opened.

"Aye, best you stay safe within this eagle's aerie until my lands are restored."

Startled by the unmistakable voice of rough velvet coming from so close to her back, again Linnet whirled about. Her swirling skirts traitorously caught at one awkwardly bundled foot and knocked her off balance. Entangled, she'd have fallen had he not instantly wrapped his arms around her and pulled her near. He had saved her from a bruising fall but not from either humiliation in this further demonstration of a clumsiness apparent only when he appeared or guilt for the thrill she felt in his unexpected embrace.

Cradling the damsel in the safe haven of his arms, Rhys gazed intently down into wide honey-hued eyes emphasized by thick lashes. Although an amused smile tilted one corner of his mouth with a gentle, unspoken gibe for near falling at his feet once more, he calmly stated a fact the pair had failed to consider.

"No matter your strategy, the guard posted outside would've permitted you to journey no farther afield than the bottom of the outer stairs."

Anxious not to appear the utter fool she felt, Linnet scrambled to gather her scattered wits and restore them to some semblance of order. How was it that she must ever appear before him like a fool? And a doltish jester she must look with pillows for feet, bedraggled gown torn across one knee, and a wild tangle of hair flowing free as no well-born woman should permit. While seeking words to respond, she twisted her fingers in a skirt already greatly abused. Before she succeeded in her quest, the other woman intervened.

"Until *your* land is returned?" The dark woman's sneered words addressed his initial statement. "Further proof you lived too many years as a Norman. You've forgotten, Rhys, that Welsh princes, unlike

Norman kings and their barons, do not own their people's lands."

"Nay, Grannia," Rhys flared back. "I have forgotten nothing—neither during the ten years of my absence nor in the five since I came home."

No hint of humor remained on a face gone cold and hard. Never since his return had Rhys's sister given him so much as a quiet word, even less one warmed with a sister's affection. True, she'd been naught but a toddling when he, given as an honorable and well-treated hostage, had departed. But her tender age was no explanation for why she blamed him still for events not of his choosing—and that she did was an inexplicable yet undeniable fact.

"'Tis you who refuse to remember I was dispatched to Normandy for the sake of securing the peace and safety of Cymer's people." Rhys's tone was so firmly controlled it turned harsh. "The same people I now rule by more than right of birth. I rule by both their will and right of combat."

Held in the unintentionally tightening iron bands of his arms, Linnet gazed up and saw his eyes harden to black ice, glittering with rebuke. She couldn't look away while he continued his rebuttal of this Grannia's statements, particularly not when what she'd suspected—that the two were wed, though apparently not happily so—seemed to be confirmed by the Eagle's next words.

"Moreover, by virtue of our bond, the lands in question *are* mine."

"Whatever off-tune note of discord roused this subject, Grannia"—a new voice sliced through the growing tension—"you should be thankful to Rhys for his efforts to force the avaricious earl to acknowledge the falseness of his claim and see that Abergele Farm is restored to its rightful owners."

Linnet saw Grannia's face go white as she looked to the man standing in the open door, the bearded man who had aided his prince in taking hostages the past night. Yet, when the slurs heaped upon her father sank through her still muddled thoughts, Linnet went rigid in mute rage.

Rhys felt indignation burning within the slender body he held and forestalled the defense trembling on rose lips before it found voice.

"Owain speaks only the truth. The lands that I demand the earl return were Grannia's dowry and her mother's dowry before—lands which many years ago the Earl of Radwell swore to hold inviolate."

From amber eyes flashing with an amazing fire, Rhys looked toward Owain and gifted him with a slight smile. "And I am pleased that, without the need for me to decree it be so, Owain saw the right in speaking only in a language you will understand. 'Tis best you know what is said, even be it not to your liking. To do elsewise would be to plant deep suspicions which, like mushrooms, grow in darkness."

Heavy black brows creased as Owain grimaced a wordless admission that he had not actually paused long enough to make any such decision. Rather, he had merely interrupted without forethought in the same language as that spoken in the original dispute.

Linnet recognized and appreciated the rationale behind the choice to speak in a common language but the topic was of far less interest than the claims the Eagle had made about dowries and oaths.

Amber eyes glanced sidelong to the dark-haired woman's face. Its cold, hard lines were a silent testament to the truth in the Eagle's statement. Linnet frowned. There was some mistake. She didn't know how or what, but still she was certain the father so proud of his honor and whom she admired could not possibly be guilty of a forsworn oath. 'Twas a firmly grounded belief unshaken by even the Eagle's further condemnation.

"Aye, Earl Godfrey swore to recognize and respect the boundaries of this border freehold." Rhys saw the disbelief on Linnet's dainty face and was irrationally vexed by her misplaced trust. "That he has now seized Abergele, ruthlessly murdering an aging man in order to do so, proves how willing he is to forsake an oath and forswear his honor."

While Linnet urgently sought chilled words capable of shattering with freezing cold this strange and surely untrue claim, Alan exploded with fervent heat.

"How dare you speak such wicked lies of our father!" In a fury over the degrading words Linnet had failed to immediately refute, Alan launched himself at the culprit's back and attacked with flailing fists and kicking feet.

With one hand Rhys reached back to grasp the neck of the boy's tunic, lift him from the floor, and hold him at arm's length. "Owain, take this fiery lordling away."

"I pray you will learn better manners, including the appropriate response to a fellow noble's hospitality." Seeing Alan's face turning purple with pent-up anger threatening to erupt, Rhys shook his head in warning. "Had I wished it so, I could have treated you as the prisoner you are, could have chained you and your sister inside a gloomy hovel with only pigs for company."

"We'd have preferred an honest farm animal's company to that of a buzzard." Alan unhesitatingly spoke for both himself and his sister. "That's what eagles are—just buzzards preying on the weak."

"So . . . I am the buzzard and your father my prey—my weak prey, hmmm?" Rhys couldn't restrain a grin. "I gravely doubt your sire would appreciate a defense wherein his son and heir termed him weak."

Despite his precarious position dangling some distance above the floor, Alan saw a glance of mocking amusement pass between the two men. His sense of injustice boiled the more fiercely, but he could do nothing to prevent the burly Owain from scooping him into a gentle yet inflexible hold.

Rhys shook his head and spoke to Owain. "Let us hope your brother's company will provide an entertaining diversion for this confused—nay, deluded—child."

The burly man taming Alan's wild struggles with ease gave a grunt of disgust that was half laugh and half growl.

"Aye, it'll be a challenge for David." With that Owain carried Alan from the house where the lad's sister remained under the Eagle's control.

Feeling as if her last hope of freedom were being inexorably severed, Linnet peered around her captor's broad shoulder to watch the bearded bear and his struggling burden move through the open door. She saw, too, where a young man, the third of those who'd entered Castle Radwell, stood guard with broadsword at the ready and dagger prominently tucked into a wide belt. Yet, even if no guard had been posted, Linnet would never have left without Alan. Likely the Eagle knew it was true and had chosen to separate her and her brother as a further impediment to their escape.

"He refused my suit outright!" Osric snarled the words. A hefty man, he irritably marched from one side to the other of the tiny cottage where some daft inspiration drove his sister to reside. His once-blond hair, thinning and streaked with both gray and brown, brushed his meaty shoulders as he shook his head with fury. "Dared me to proclaim him dishonorable to the whole of Christendom, saying too much time had passed, and now that Father Bertrand is dead, no one would lend credence to my words!"

Morwena sat at a rickety table that looked as near to ruin as did she with her long gray hair uncombed and in wild disorder. Yet for all that she was bent near in two, and her hands were unsteady, the sharpness of her mind had dulled not one whit. Rather the bitterness of years had honed it to a more piercing edge . . . but with an odd curve and single purpose.

"Moreover," Osric said, continuing his seething litany of acrid complaints, "he has taken his heir from my fosterage. Means to send the sniveling brat to Normandy."

"Aye, you've grievances, but of what interest are they to me?" Morwena turned her gaze upon the speaker, who had never been comfortable beneath a steady look from eyes whose irises were so pale a gray as to be almost indistinguishable from the white surrounding them. "Did you come to *my* aid when I had need of you?"

"Ah, but, sister, of what use could I have been when 'twas an accomplished deed already done?" Osric turned, bent to lean forward with palms flat atop the unsteady table while he directly met her penetrating gaze. "I could do nothing then, but now we can both see he pays for the many wrongs he has done us."

Like a bird searching for a tasty worm, Morwena tilted her head to one side, chin jutting out. "Vengeance would be sweet, but 'tis justice I demand as the price for my aid in any scheme you devise."

"What to you would be justice is to me a higher form of retribution, and we will both wrest from him what we seek." He pulled a chair out and lowered himself onto it, taking care to test its strength before trusting it with the whole of his considerable weight. Its rickety condition increased his disgust for her choice of abode. Lower in the valley lay a sizable wooden structure more appropriate for the holder of the land and people of this valley, but she lived there only when her son came to visit, which Mark rarely did.

She stared down into the dregs of ale in a simple earthen tankard while her unblinking gaze gleamed with a hatred growing colder with every word her brother spoke.

"Even as I made plans to come to you and see our blended voices raised against our foe, news arrived. News of an event that we can use to our advantage . . . " Osric rubbed his hands together as if in anticipation of a fine feast.

"News? What news?" Morwena looked up and leaned nearer, the war between suspicion and curiosity plain in every tense line of her gaunt form.

"I had feared our nephew would get in the way." Osric put on a mock frown of regret. "But it seems we could have asked for no better cohort—an unknowing accomplice. Rhys has abducted not only Godfrey's daughter but his heir as well!"

Morwena's strange light eyes blinked for the first time since the conversation had begun.

"So send for your son, call him home." Osric clapped his hands with glee. "The hour of revenge and justice draws nigh."

And, Osric silently resolved, while Morwena wrote her message he would write another to be sent deep into western Wales.

4

"PRAY LET ME HELP YOU." WITH THE QUIET PLEA LINNET
rose from the same big chair she'd been lowered into
upon her arrival near a sennight gone by. It and its
cushion had been placed close to the circular hearth,
leaving her to feel as useless as a newborn babe—but
far, far less welcome. For one who, though lady of a
castle, had rarely sat idle while others toiled, it was an
uncomfortable experience. Fingers tangled nervously
into a rough homespun gown, she quietly approached
Grannia. The woman whose back was turned to
Linnet while laboring over a bare plank table continued dicing parboiled meat for stew as if deaf to the
words spoken.

Where once Linnet had rued days too duty filled,
after enduring several greatly lengthened for having
nothing to employ hands unaccustomed to idleness,
she now longed to help her erstwhile hostess. Grannia
had been left to perform these household chores by
the departure of a stout and apple-cheeked woman of
middle years named Ynid.

Although the words exchanged between the two
Welshwomen were spoken in a language incompre-
hensible to Linnet, still she'd been given to under-

stand that these chores were normally this Ynid's responsibility. Seeing Linnet's questioning gaze, Grannia had grudgingly provided the terse explanation. The woman, seen by Linnet only the one time, had been summoned to treat a child who was seriously ill. Seemed she was the area's most capable healer. Moreover, though Ynid's husband and the oldest of her many children labored to work their prince's lands while she cared for his home, her first duty lay in responding to and treating the ailments of every native of Cymer.

Standing at the elbow of the unresponsive Grannia, Linnet acknowledged once again that despite the fact that, for the most part, only in her bedchamber was she without the Welshwoman's presence, she had never before experienced such isolation. The other woman rarely spoke to her and gave naught but the curtest of answers to any question asked.

Were it not for Pywell, Linnet would have been doomed to a near wordless existence. Fortunately, whenever tasks required Grannia to be gone from the Eagle's home for any length of time, she apparently preferred not to risk the remote possibility of a hostage's escape. As guard against that danger, she would summon to watch over Linnet the young man ever standing just beyond the outer door.

Thus the Eagle's slender cohort in her abduction from Castle Radwell had on several occasions spent some little time in Linnet's company. He was remarkably fluent in English and, once free of the awe-inspiring presence of his leader, had proven a cheery, talkative sort. Indeed, once his flow of words had begun, Linnet would have been hard pressed to dam them even had she wished to do so—and she hadn't. Pywell's honest smile was welcome. Moreover, he'd told her far more about the Eagle than she could ever elsewise have hoped to learn.

In their initial visit Linnet had learned Pywell was the son of Ynid and had been taught the Saxon tongue by his mentor, Milo, the keeper of the Eagle's steeds. And, not least of all, she'd learned just how whole-heartedly and openly he idolized his prince—as, he'd assured her, did each of Cymer's own. In later talks, Pywell had regaled her with tales of the Eagle's heroic deeds, his compassionate actions on behalf of those left in need by illness or battle, and his justice in dealing with the rebellious men he'd had to defeat in order to win back the right to his position as prince over them all. Only on the details of the latter struggle was Pywell loath to talk. His reticence merely served to increase Linnet's curious interest in this matter to which the Eagle had made an oblique reference during his argument with Grannia that first morn.

Yet, as much as she'd appreciated the openhearted Pywell's visits, the few truly bright spots in recent days were lent by infrequent glimpses of the golden Eagle himself. Despite her best intents and constant self-castigations, she could no more prevent her gaze from following the too intriguing man whenever he appeared than she'd been able to keep from watching him during his visits to Castle Radwell.

Believing it a sin to lie, even to herself, Linnet had days since confessed herself incapable of resisting such temptations. And it *was* a temptation, one so powerful that neither feelings of disloyalty to her father nor guilt for her helpless attraction to the husband of another could suppress it. Nor could she sunder the cords of his lure or halt insidious fantasies ever creeping unbidden into her mind. Indeed, with the experience of his embrace, his kiss, those fantasies had merely grown the more vivid.

Linnet compressed her lips with determination. She could, she *must* fight this fault in her nature. Her first step toward securing that goal was surely the diverting of wrongful thoughts and the blocking of endless daydreams with tasks able to keep mind as well as hands busy.

"Please . . ." Linnet candidly restated her case

while at the same time attempting to keep hidden its underlying thread of desperation. "Allow me some useful distraction from troubles that plague me." She could only pray Grannia would understand and despite her dislike yield this small concession.

"Hah." The scoffing sound was barely audible and quickly overshadowed by the disgust in words Grannia immediately added. "What useful chore could any well-born Norman lady perform?"

"Meara taught me from childhood how to manage a castle." Seeing that the image roused by the notion of a noblewoman's castle-management only deepened Grannia's contempt, Linnet rushed to reinforce her plea. "Meara believes it important for a lady to be proficient at any task she may require another woman to perform. This experience, Meara has counseled me, enables one to know of a certainty how much time should be allotted each task and how to recognize whether or not it has been done aright."

Dark eyes narrowed suspiciously but instead of questioning the logic in Meara's training, Grannia had a far different query. "You call your mother by her given name?"

Linnet's first thought was to ask why the other woman failed to call her husband by the same, but, prudent by nature and well aware that she was seeking a boon from the other, she explained.

"Meara is not my mother. My mother died bearing Alan. Rather, Meara is the woman charged with raising me. As mother's distant relation, after the marriage Meara accompanied her across the sea to Radwell. I was born within a year, but during the six years following, my mother lost four babes despite much time spent abed in an attempt to keep them.

"As mother's attention was thus drawn away from the castle's daily routine, both my care and Radwell's management fell to Meara." Pale brown eyes glowed with an affection that had been absent when she spoke of the mother she had barely known. "Meara kept me ever with her, teaching me how to take charge of a castle and how to do that which you doubt me capable of performing."

"Did you never play with other children?" This description of the Norman damsel's life was the very opposite of what Grannia had believed must be true. After all, everyone who'd any reason to know described Lady Linnet as the earl's beloved and indulged daughter.

"Other children?" Linnet blinked. Again Grannia's question pointed in an utterly unexpected direction. It caught her by surprise. She'd never before been asked such a thing, nor had anyone ever suggested her lack of playmates was a worthy concern.

A direct and truthful answer Linnet could have given easily enough. No need to confess how her healthy imagination had filled her childhood's lonely hours. And certainly no reason to admit that the same flights of fancy, strengthened by years of experience and a dawning maturity, had in the past few months spun thrilling dreams about a golden warrior who had proven to be a foe. Forcing an expression gone tight to relax, she spoke.

"The only other children in the castle were boys, older than I, who came to be fostered under my father's tutelage. Then Alan was born." A bright smile chased clouds from honey-brown eyes. "I was allowed to help care for him when he was a baby. Later we played games and shared other entertainments . . . until four years past when he was sent from Radwell to be fostered elsewhere." Caught in the desolate memory, Linnet was deaf to the aching loneliness in the tone of her last words.

Assailed by a twinge of guilt, Grannia drew her fine dark brows together in a slight frown. She had taken pleasure in seeing this surely spoiled female dressed in the overlong, drab homespun gown she'd lent her to replace the torn and begrimed rose wool. Had she been unjust? Nay! This fine lady was still the child of the man who'd destroyed the even tenor of Grannia's life. In irritation she pounded the cleaver more fiercely into the meat.

"Why was Alan sent away to be fostered when your father kept other boys with him for the same purpose?" Grannia's brows now arched with unhidden disgust for this strange habit of the Normans.

Linnet's lips tilted upward in a soft curve. Plainly Grannia had no appreciation for a tradition revered among the upper levels in a feudal hierarchy. "Every noble-born boy is sent away from home to be fostered, most usually with his father's overlord." She hoped her explanation would give Grannia an understanding of those who were, after all, her neighbors. "By first acting as pages the boys learn the manners of their class. Next in their quest for knighthood, acting as squires they are trained in martial skills and attend experienced warriors."

"And this knighthood is their ultimate goal? A sign of your kind of honor and loyalty?" Grannia already knew what the hostage had explained, and the faint sneer in her voice left little doubt as to her opinion on the subject.

"'Struth." Firelight from behind glowed about Linnet's dainty head. "The start of training for knighthood is a boy's first step toward manhood."

"Rhys was made a knight in Normandy." Grannia's unseeing gaze dropped to the meat, now hopelessly mutilated by hands that unthinkingly continued chopping while her mind was elsewise occupied.

"Rhys was . . ." Linnet's response trailed away under the sound of booted feet approaching, and she turned to face the subject of her words. The Eagle now stood a mere handbreadth away, and never had she been more conscious of the sheer size of him.

Golden brown brows furrowed as Rhys moved farther into his hall. He'd entered while the two women stood with backs to the door and in time to hear what was said between his sister's belittling of a clearly earnest plea for some task to fill empty hours and Linnet's repetition of his name. His glance passed from the startled captive, whose admission of a lonely past had unknowingly provided an insight into her character, to the blushing Grannia. Had the latter said or done something before his arrival to cause such a look of guilt? His sister wanted the Norman damsel gone as hastily as possible. Everyone knew that to be true, but to what lengths would she go to achieve her goal?

Rhys shrugged aside vexing but ultimately unanswerable questions and shifted his full attention to rest upon a "plain linnet" who was not truly plain at all. Flame light burnished to a bronze sheen the soft brown braids framing her face's piquant contours—high cheekbones tapering to a small, pointed chin while a short, straight nose led the eye to sweet lips, top gently bowed, bottom full and innocently promising. Here was a beauty the more potent for its subtlety—a fact able to alarm even the fierce warrior he was.

Beneath the intensity of a black gaze suddenly flaring with golden sparks, Linnet's creamy skin took on a faint crimson glow and her gaze dropped to the rush-strewn floor. Had she done something to cause the anger proclaimed by his scowl? Wildly she searched through words exchanged with Grannia for a possible wrong. Was he angry that his wife had told her even this little about him? If so, pray God he would never know the extent of Pywell's voluble discourses, though they were full of praise.

Rhys saw his hostage's confusion in a gently nibbled lip and fingers twisted into folds of too abundant cloth. Certain her distress was born of a misinterpretation of his irritation with Grannia, he gave Linnet a rueful smile while he explained his purpose in coming.

"I've returned to take you to see your brother." His return was a deed more easily stated than performed.

Earl Godfrey had dispatched his men to harry their foes all along the border in the hope of securing not only a route into Cymer but news of where his children were held. Rhys held a vital advantage, for while everyone knew the location of Castle Radwell, no Norman knew where perched the Eagle's aerie.

Amber eyes lit up with anticipation. Though she'd tried very hard to prevent herself from pondering what ills Alan might have suffered under the bearded bear's hold, she would be much relieved to see him still whole and healthy.

"Owain tells me that Alan fears the worst has befallen you in my charge. Thus have I arranged this visit to lend proof that his reasoning is faulty and, with a reaffirmation of my honorable intents, to allay future apprehensions."

Linnet nodded although she was certain her brother was no more likely than she to forget that a time limit had been placed as a condition upon the Eagle's promise of gentle handling. Rhys waved her toward the outer door, and what choice had she but to comply with the wordless command? Still she hesitated, casting Grannia a quick glance of regret for being called away before she'd the opportunity to lessen the other's burden.

Grannia allowed no flicker of response to cross the face she lowered to gaze at the table. As if already alone, she methodically continued her task, scooping the mutilated meat into a bowl. Then, never glancing toward the two who were lingering nearby, she carried this most important ingredient to the hearth and slowly dropped the chunks into a pot of liquid gently bubbling above low-burning flames.

Rhys saw small white teeth biting a soft lower lip, a sign of the pain aroused in Linnet by this further rebuff from Grannia. He wished for sufficient influence with his sister to ensure she would listen, and mayhap comply, were he to encourage gentleness in her dealings with the Norman damsel. Linnet had done Grannia no wrong. And Linnet, though she was Godfrey's daughter, didn't deserve to bear the brunt of Grannia's hatred for the man and his crimes.

A cynical smile came unbidden to Rhys's mouth as he put his large hand in the center of Linnet's back, urging her to turn with him and depart. The likelihood of his success in securing Grannia's consent to treat Linnet with even a modicum of consideration was as improbable as his winning of a rational explanation for her unfathomable resentment of himself.

Discouragement laid its heavy weight upon Linnet's shoulders as she allowed her captor to direct her toward a door apparently gone unclosed since his arrival. Grannia already resented her, and the Welshwoman's hostility would surely not be lessened by seeing her husband lead his female hostage into the woods on a solitary journey.

"Are you wearing the sturdy shoes I directed be made for you?" Rhys asked the question as he paused at pegs driven into the wall beside the open portal to lift Linnet's brown, fur-lined cloak and drape it about her slender form.

While fastening the garment beneath her chin with its enameled ring and pin brooch, Linnet looked up in time to see Rhys readjust his own black cloak over impressive shoulders. He was too close. Breath caught in her throat, and not daring to trust her voice, she nodded.

The arrival of the cobbler had surprised her, but the wiry man had marked and measured her nearly healed feet for the rugged shoes she wore now. Formed from multiple layers of hardened leather, they were far from pretty but most practical. On the trail between Radwell and the Eagle's aerie Linnet had learned the foolishness of putting beauty before usefulness—not that in that instance she'd had a choice. She only wished it were possible, in turn, to admonish this man on the value of the plain and practical as opposed to the ornamental but useless.

But neither he nor any other man would ever view a drab linnet as competition for a beautiful peacock. Besides, although decidedly a dark beauty, never could it be said that Grannia was useless.

Linnet gazed with distaste at the overabundant folds of her coarse homespun gown and found that, for all the good sense in arguments lauding the practical over the beautiful, she couldn't suppress an errant wish for fine garb. And, oh, how she wished to leastwise be seen at her poor best while in the Eagle's company. Her lips firmed into a resigned line. Such trappings of beauty were not to be hers, nor, considering the fact that he was a man wedded, ought she be sinful enough to wish to impress him.

"Let's be off." Rhys proffered his forearm to the slender damsel who was plainly nervous of him. Her attitude annoyed him. He'd done nothing to justify such a response.

In the next instant Rhys fought back a mocking laugh for the foolish thought, permitting only a wry smile to reach his lips. Done nothing? Merely had he held a knife at the damsel's throat and stolen her away from her home. Moreover, he'd repeatedly baited Linnet for her every response to him. In actual fact, the more appropriate question was how else but that she be nervous of him?

Light falling through the open door gleamed on golden hair as he gave his head a slight shake of self-disdain. For a man of considerable experience he'd been remarkably inept in his dealings with this dainty creature. In recent days he'd watched Linnet when she was unaware of his presence and had observed her to possess an innate grace. Yet, whenever she knew him to be near, she turned awkward. Because he was her foe? That could not be. She'd fallen at his feet before she had any idea who he was. A glittering amusement warmed his eyes while he waited for her to accept his offer.

While he no longer deemed her an experienced

woman using a blatant ploy to secure his attention, it was clear she was helplessly attracted to him. The danger lay in the fact that, rather than reinforcing the armor of cold cynicism encasing his heart, the prospect of her innocent surrender pierced it with a bolt of heat stronger than mere physical desire.

Linnet gingerly laid her fingertips atop a forest green sleeve and accompanied the Eagle into the daylight. Spring had given them the blessing of a shining sun and a cloudless sky. Almost could she push back the gloom born of Grannia's disheartening attitude and awareness of her own inadequacies. Indeed, she could have but for the lingering cloud of guilt hovering over her inability to quash a wrongful anticipation for this time alone with the husband of another.

"I heard Grannia tell you that I am a knight." Wanting to break a tension causing his companion to stumble as they walked, Rhys revived the subject his appearance had put to a quick death. It had seemed to catch her interest then, and he deemed it now the most promising avenue down which to turn her thoughts.

So much for the thought that his anger had been roused by Grannia's disclosure. Linnet cast a sidelong glance toward the devastating man too near to permit easy conversation and simply repeated what he'd doubtless heard said. "She told me you are a knight."

"'Struth." As if to steady her first walk of any real length on feet not fully mended, Rhys laid his free hand reassuringly atop the dainty fingers resting on his upraised arm. "I am a knight in Normandy, a prince in Wales, but only a foe in Radwell." He smiled down into amber eyes with a mockery plainly directed inward.

Linnet shook her head even as she fell prey to the dark welcome in his eyes. "Nay, you are both prince and knight whether here, in Normandy . . . or on Radwell lands."

Halting beside a small saddled donkey, Rhys shrugged, but despite his best defenses her quiet conviction warmed the outer layer of his cold armor of cynicism and allowed a rare true smile.

Breath catching at the potent response and hardly noticing the mount she'd been thoughtfully provided to save further wear on tender feet, Linnet rushed into words ill considered—words broaching matters rued in the next instant for doubtless containing as many stumble holes as the forest path that lay ahead.

"I don't understand why were you in Normandy in the first instance," she said. "Moreover, once there, why were you trained to knighthood?"

Having thought only to confirm that he was in truth a knight, annoyance narrowed his dark eyes. Yet Rhys realized that he himself was surely the source of this information, which he hadn't intended to be mentioned.

"On the day you attempted an escape, 'twas I who spoke of my decade in Normandy." The flat statement was soft but clearly laid as restraint over a disgusted growl.

Linnet bit at her lips and nodded. This she could admit without having to confess Pywell's many further revelations. Fearing what secrets might be read in her gaze, she lowered it from the uncomfortable sight of a frowning man to the rough coat of her "steed."

"I was sent there as security for the peace negotiated between my father and England's Norman conqueror." Even as the clipped words passed his lips, Rhys silently cursed himself for having made the initial comment leading to this opening of a subject he never discussed with anyone. Still, though he'd gone this far, he need not and would not speak of the last heated words that had passed between him and his father. That they'd argued fiercely while he fought against the unwelcome decision to send him away was a bitter memory. In the end he had obeyed, but he had gone in a coldness that disallowed so much as a single glance cast toward the father plainly hurt by his deed. This, too, was a painful memory, and he'd repressed thoughts of that confrontation for years—until now when a tender linnet had all unknowingly made a small breach in the iron barrier of an eagle's will.

To block out the image of an anguished father watching a stubborn son's departure, Rhys reached out to find a tiny waist near lost in voluminous folds and effortlessly lift his startled companion. She was as light as a dream. And, already angry with himself, he grew even more irritated for finding himself instantly too aware of the lush curves near fully in his hold. This was too dangerous a distraction. One fat shining braid brushed his cheek, and though silky-soft, it had as well been the lash of a whip reminding him of his oath to her father, reminding him of the importance of proving his word more honorably held than the earl's.

When without warning and with dizzying strength two strong hands lifted Linnet off her feet, she gasped and reached out to clasp broad shoulders as the only firm anchor in a suddenly tilting world. When she felt iron-hard muscle rippling beneath her touch, her breath caught somewhere between lungs and tight throat. The moment he settled her atop the placid beast's saddle she jerked her hands away from a contact that burned.

Rhys's mood was not improved by the hasty withdrawal of her hands. Fear or attraction? Mayhap both? While his attention rested heavily upon a path so oft traveled it was unneedful, an uncomfortable silence reigned as Rhys guided Linnet and her mount into the woodland's shielding dimness. In the end he felt driven by that silence to finish the unfortunate explanation he had earlier begun.

"In Normandy I was held hostage in a nobleman's hands. Unfortunately, from Count Marchand's viewpoint, the duke had forbidden him to keep me in irons or even in a secure dungeon cell. Thus the poor man was left with few options agreeable to him. Finding that my education in warfare was far different from his, he added a seventeen-year-old me to the ranks of his foster sons. And there, over the next few years, I served first as page and later as squire."

While black eyes glared at ruts and small stones below, Linnet was free to study the one whose harsh tone revealed what words had not. Having watched many boys pass through their training at Radwell, she knew what contempt he must have faced from much younger boys able to do what he had not earlier been taught. And worse, the open derision of grown men observing the whole.

"But you did become a knight." Linnet spoke with the assurance of having been told it was so.

"Aye." Rhys's tone was coldly triumphant. "My pride insisted I not merely learn but become the best at whatever challenge they threw into my path." That same pride glowed in the depths of dark eyes of a sudden glancing up into a pale brown gaze. "Time marched onward, and by the strength of my sword arm and my talent for creating tactics that won victory I earned a reputation as the fiercest of warriors—an Eagle."

Linnet's eyes warmed to molten honey; she was as impressed by the Eagle's fine accomplishments as ever Pywell had been.

For the purpose of warding off the subtle tendrils of attraction, which he was coming to realize this tender foe could easily weave about him, Rhys allowed his expression to become chilled as he added another fact certain to distract her. "But first I, along with my foster father's own son, was made knight by Duke William himself."

His impassive face revealed nothing of the cynical thoughts beneath. No need to tell Linnet how, during each passing day throughout the ten years he'd spent in their hold, he had been aware of the anticipation with which his foster father, and near every other Norman he'd met, had gleefully waited to greet his first misstep, his first failure. Never had he permitted them any reason for joy.

Linnet gasped. 'Twas a high honor to be knighted by the king and incredible that such a distinction had been bestowed upon a foreigner. Nothing sufficiently admiring came quickly to mind. Instead she made a lame and quickly regretted comment. "My father was one of King William's most ardent supporters."

Rhys's expression lightened not one whit, and Linnet was uncertain if what he said next was a response to her unfortunate words or merely a continuation of the last he'd spoken.

"I, like my father before me, swore fealty to the English king. Then together we spoke of Earl Godfrey . . . and of matters here."

Memory of that conversation concerning oaths made, which they'd agreed must be kept, lent a grim edge to Rhys's cool smile. And yet 'twas the most pleasant of the many memories he'd long repressed of a time past.

Linnet feared that, whatever the reason for his statement, the mention of her father was responsible for his increasing coldness. The branches of trees on either side near met overhead to lend a leafy canopy to the narrow path they traveled, and she nervously gazed down at ground dappled by sunlight and shadow while seeking to shift the focus of their talk onto a more pleasant topic.

"But then your return to Cymer must have been a joyous event." As the hasty words left her lips she wanted desperately to call them back.

"Oh, aye." Her lamented attempt at diversion drew humorless laughter. "So joyous that I was met with drawn blades bared and the news that another had claimed my right to rule."

"But how could that be?" Though obliquely warned

by Pywell's unusual reticence on the event, Linnet was distressed by this revelation of a reception far more hostile than any she'd imagined. "Surely your father—"

Before she could finish the question, Rhys flatly interrupted. "My father was dead . . . had been dead for nearly a year. Lloyd, a man almost his age, had taken my sister for wife, and in her name he claimed *my* patrimony."

"But you won it back." Again Linnet firmly stated an obvious fact, but the clear note of admiration in the depths of her lovely voice broke Rhys's bleak mood. An unusual response from the daughter of his greatest foe, and more than welcome.

Rhys sent the damsel a devastating look in which golden fires burned with such heat as threatened to see her melt into his arms.

"Pywell told me you had." Striving to keep from once more acting the fool and falling at his feet, she spoke the first words that came to a traitorous mouth. They were immediately followed by liquid fire brushing her cheeks with crimson. How was it that after a lifetime of being circumspect in every action she constantly allowed herself to become so flustered by this man that blundered words tripped from her lips as gracelessly as she had fallen at his feet?

"I fear one day Pywell's tongue will get him into more trouble than he can talk himself out of." A stray beam of sunlight caressed bright hair as Rhys tilted his head and grimaced with mock ferocity.

The comment struck a blow of greater guilt. Linnet flinched while worry creased her brow and small white teeth bit at a lower lip too oft abused thusly.

"Nay, you've no just reason for concern." Rhys instantly repented his jest. Repressing an insane wish to soothe tender lips with a kiss, he contented himself with laying his hand atop the two she'd so thoroughly tangled into drab homespun that the cloth seemed certain to be creased for all time. "I am fond of the lad and no more likely to punish him for speaking of the matter with you than I am to harm you."

This from a man who on the night of her taking had promised to see her safely held only the length of a fortnight ought not have been all that reassuring. Yet, with the ease of the sun, his words scattered the clouds of Linnet's anxiety to such an extent that a teasing smile accompanied her gentle scoffing of his wording.

"Lad? Alan *is* a lad and even he would resent the term. Surely Pywell has aged beyond that description."

Rhys laughed lightly, but his gaze grew more intense. True, she and Pywell were near of an age. Though the possibility was in direct contrast to what he'd come to believe her to be, he illogically wondered if her interest in him was naught but an infatuation so capricious that it could on a moment's whim shift to the "lad." Compared to himself, Pywell was that. An utterly unexpected, never before experienced stab of jealousy struck Rhys dead to point.

Thick lashes dropped to hide amber eyes Linnet feared would reveal how thoroughly and with what appalling haste she had fallen under the powerful thrall of his midnight gaze. But the darkness foolishly sought left her desperately struggling to fend off a growing awareness. Caught up in their battle, neither the donkey's abrupt halt nor Rhys's tying of it to a low-hanging branch won her interest. Her gaze remained fixed on the golden man.

Seated atop the small donkey, Linnet was near on a level with him. Stepping nearer, Rhys told himself he meant only to discover if her attraction to him was as ephemeral as that of the many fine Norman ladies for whom a man half Welsh and half Saxon had been merely a unique experience, a trophy worth bragging of to friends. Willingly he'd played their games and moved from one to another with little care as to who had sampled the same pleasures either before or after him. But the prospect of sharing

Linnet's honey sweetness with Pywell—or any other—burned.

Rhys silently ridiculed that feeling. Linnet was not and never could be his to claim. This acknowledgment did nothing to cool his heat or waylay his intent. Her nearness, eyes closed and breath revealingly unsteady, strengthened his need to prove to her that Pywell was, in truth, little more than a child and nowise equal to the sweet, hidden fires tasted once before and longed for every moment since. Submitting to the worst kind of folly, he lied to himself. Moving closer to the source of the addictive honeyed wine, he justified his action as merely intended to satisfy an idle curiosity, told himself it meant no deeper hunger.

Linnet sensed his approach, and the breath froze in her throat. Thought of resisting this wrong melted into nothing. Then a mouth, hard and warm, brushed lightly across her lips. She could prevent neither her soft whimper of immediate surrender nor the motion of her arms curling around his neck. Slender fingers wound into strands of gold that had been a temptation since her first sight of him towering amid the many lesser men in Castle Radwell.

Her headlong response caught Rhys completely off-guard and drove from his mind the duty to tame a forbidden hunger for this dainty creature forever beyond his reach. Mouth suddenly crushing down over hers, he took possession while his arms slid around her slight form to near pull her from the donkey and hold generous curves tight against the power of his own body.

He was very strong and the embrace was bruising. But for Linnet, weakened by the fever he had lit in the blood coursing through her like a river of fire, rational thought had ceased. She arched helplessly nearer. He was warm, so warm, and she wanted only to be closer. Glorying in the feel of his masculinity, his size, his strength, she was lost to reality.

The donkey, irritated by the shifting load, sidled farther to the side. Only the steely arms wrapped about Linnet saved her from the humiliating tumble to the ground at his feet she'd earlier feared.

"God's blood!" Rhys's rumbled oath was vehement. His heart was pounding a wild rhythm, but he held the damsel safe while reasserting his control over the errant donkey. As he glanced down into dazed honey eyes, Rhys's jaw went rigid under the will required to prevent his mouth from returning to drink deeper of the wine on red, crushed lips still trembling from his heated possession.

Exercising every trace of control he possessed, Rhys efficiently and impersonally placed Linnet securely in the saddle again before unfastening the reins. He turned without a word to continue leading the way toward their destination. During the long silence that followed, he told himself that leastwise now he knew just how dangerous was this too intoxicating damsel. And by the knowing he would stand better guarded against further invasions into the walled citadel of his emotions. Considering that surely only a few days remained of her time on his lands, it should be an easy goal to meet. That thought wielded an unexpected, completely unwelcome stab of regret and lifted one corner of his mouth in a cold smile of self-derision.

Linnet gazed forlornly at the point where tip ends of bright hair brushed the middle of a wide black-cloaked back. The Eagle no longer walked at her side but rather strode ahead, tugging the animal along at a faster pace than was its wont. Purposefully shifting her attention from the source of a confused tangle of responses ranging from merriment and pleasure to frustration and unhappiness, Linnet peered into the deep green of forest shadows on one side.

The quiet lengthened between them until it seemed almost to speak its own words of condemnation for her fall to a sinful fascination born of wrongful fantasies yet to be quelled. Linnet could not sincerely regret their embrace, despite a burning guilt for both the delights she'd found with another woman's husband and the treachery to her father she feared it meant. However, Linnet did regret the end their moment of passion had brought to her first real conversation with the man Pywell's words had led her to admire for more than his stunningly handsome appearance.

Of a sudden Linnet realized that the embrace had cost more than the opportunity to learn the details of an event even Pywell refused to discuss. While indeed she might never know the method by which Rhys had secured his right to the princedom of Cymer, it was even more disheartening to think the end to their talk meant the end to another matter even more earnestly rued. If left at the point where a passionate kiss had halted their exchange, the Eagle would assuredly believe Pywell the only source for her knowledge of his fight to rule. 'Twould be unjust.

Linnet had been raised to accept even unpleasant duties without hesitation or complaint. Thus she couldn't allow a new friend to carry the sole blame for an action proven abhorrent to the Eagle by Pywell's reluctance to state more than the one simple fact that a battle of one sort or another had occurred.

"It wasn't only Pywell," Linnet calmly stated, lifting her attention from the lower edges of a black cloak swirling about muscular calves to instead gaze hopefully toward a blond mane flowing over broad shoulders.

Although the claim made perfect sense to Linnet, Rhys's thoughts had gone far beyond their last verbal exchange and it held little meaning for him. Over his shoulder he cast a glance of black ice, shocking to Linnet, who was still wrapped in the fragile but lingering warmth of his embrace.

"I mean . . ." Linnet faltered only for a moment

before going determinedly onward. "It was from you I first heard of the need to retake your princedom." Before the man whose pace had slowed dramatically could speak and possibly question her statement, she reminded him of the scene wherein he'd spoken of the matter.

"'Twas the first morn, when you came upon Alan and me, frustrated in our attempt to flee. You reminded Grannia that you rule by more than birthright, that you rule both by right of combat and by the people's will."

The last two options were unfamiliar to Linnet. Oh, aye, men fought for control of lands. William had secured the crown of England by such means, but that was precisely why he'd taken such pains to be certain none of his barons would be able to easily do the same. He'd made it a well-enforced law that the property of any of his Norman nobles—those to whom he'd given English lands—who dared to make war upon others would be immediately forfeit to the Crown. The inflexibility of this law had been demonstrated many a time until only the most witless would dare defy royal power by such an action.

Despite a refusal to admit it was so, even to himself, Rhys felt shamed by the abrupt chill he'd turned upon the very one he'd so recently attempted to melt—with success all too sweet. Knowing as well as did she the rules under which the Norman feudal hierarchy existed, he realized what difficulties she would face in attempting to understand why he'd been forced to literally fight to regain his inheritance. It would be even more difficult for her to comprehend the role of Cymer's people in such a conflict.

Both to atone for his unjust treatment of one undeserving and to shift his thoughts from the bleak prospect of inevitably restoring Linnet to her own, he dropped back to walk at her side and finish the tale of his return to Wales.

"When I came home to be met with resistance from what then seemed the whole of Cymer, I had only one recourse. I challenged Lloyd to single combat. He agreed on the condition that, in consideration of his age, I allow him to choose another man to fight in his place." Rhys's jaw hardened against the memory. "I agreed, and he sent my childhood friend, Owain."

"Owain?" Linnet was startled. How could it be that the man who appeared to be the Eagle's most trusted supporter, the man now holding her brother captive, had once met him in earnest combat wherein the future of the princedom had swung in the balance?

The flash of a cynical smile accompanied Rhys's nod. "We were well matched. But the years I'd spent fighting in regional wars at my foster father's side stood me in good stead. The fierce reputation I had earned among Normans—including your father—had not spread so far as to reach Lloyd. He thought the 'boy' who'd spent too many years as hostage would be easily defeated."

"But you won," she softly stated with a touch of the pride he must have felt.

"As you say, I won . . . and spared Owain's life, although it was mine to take." Even the half-smile on Rhys's face seemed to freeze in place. "Then, in vengeance, Lloyd put a torch to my father's hall."

Linnet inaudibly gasped. Whatever pride he'd taken in winning the battle must surely have been smothered by pain and anger set alight by the thwarted foe's retaliation. As if to confirm her assumption, Rhys's next words smoldered with bitterness.

"He preferred to watch it fall to cold ashes rather than see me reclaim all that I had won or allow my return to the warm home of my youth."

"Then your residence was not your father's before you." Linnet's quiet musing sought no response. Merely did she ponder this answer, satisfying her curiosity of the first morn. It explained why, though large, his abode was so different from what she'd expected a prince's would be, and why it was so sparsely furnished.

Sunlight falling more strongly through trees less dense near the top of a steep climb gleamed over wheaten hair as Rhys nodded his head in silent affirmation. Moving beyond bleak memories, he spoke of his intention to correct a lack he saw as clearly as she must.

"One day, after I've won a peace of such duration as to allow me to see it so"—golden sparks took fire in dark eyes as he talked of future plans—"my hall will be restored to the rich glory I knew as a boy dwelling in the prince of Cymer's residence. From Normandy I brought back many trunks filled with booty, rewards for my sword arm's honorable labors. I had thought they would only be additions to my father's already illustrious hall." Rhys's expression again went bleak with regret until another shake of bright hair rid him of the useless emotion. "Now I'll furnish my own."

"I hope that time soon arrives." Linnet sensed the need in him and earnest words instinctively flowed from her heart to fill it in some small measure. "I will pray that peace soon lends you the opportunity to do what you plan."

A wry smile fleetingly crossed Rhys's face as he looked up into doe-soft eyes. Plainly she had not paused long enough to realize that such a peace would first require her father's defeat. Loath to say anything hinting at rejection of the gentle damsel's sincere good wishes, he chose to sidestep the issue and continue his tale down a different path.

"After winning the right to rule Cymer by virtue of successful combat, still I had to win my people's support—elsewise 'twould have been a hollow victory." Glancing sidelong, Rhys saw Linnet's bowed head and, in her concentrated effort to understand, the nibbling of a lip that was still passion swollen.

"They knew as well as I the terms of the pact under which I'd been sent away. They knew that I was to be returned should any ill befall my father. The people were told I'd been notified of my father's death. But when weeks, then months, passed and I failed to return, they easily believed the lie that I had chosen a Norman life over my Welsh heritage and its heavy responsibilities."

"The message was not sent?" Linnet lifted her eyes, and their flash of fiery defense earned from Rhys a small but potent smile, which in turn increased the rate of her heartbeat.

As he wearily shook his head, his bright hair caught another errant gleam of sunlight.

"I will try to explain why, here in Wales, 'tis so important for a prince to secure the people's support and hold it dear. Welshmen are not serfs. My people are free and so proud of their freedom that to guard it they'll gladly fight until the last drop of their lifeblood has been shed."

Rhys steadily met the damsel's serious gaze and, watching as she assimilated this philosophy foreign to her, saw proof of a sharp mind.

"Though I lead in this quest, I've no standing army. The men who answer my call to arms live throughout these rugged hills and valleys and are not dependent upon me for their daily bread. Nay, my soldiers, rather than lending aid in exchange for board, room, and wages, like the mercenaries your father employs, answer my summons knowing I will issue it solely for the sake of protecting our land, and thus their families and homes, from men who would steal it from us."

Even as Linnet parted her lips to challenge his oblique criticism of her father, Rhys lifted a hand and forestalled the words. Instead of permitting a useless debate on Earl Godfrey's qualities—whether fine or dishonorable—he returned her attention to the point in his tale where he'd left off to give an explanation of Welsh ways.

"While in Normandy I received no missive informing me of my father's demise, but the people of Cymer believed that I'd been told and had chosen not to return to them. After toiling for the past five years to win their trust, I can claim with assurance that they believe I would never willingly abandon them." Dark eyes narrowed on a sweeping curve ahead. "Only Grannia still refuses to accept my sworn oath on the matter for the truth it is."

A frowning Linnet glared at the innocent spring blossoms lending cheery colors to the woodland bordering their well-trodden path—yellow primroses and purple violets nestled amid green leaves and grasses while pale blooms on trees promised summer fruit. Considering that her host had been in Cymer for only five years and absent for the ten preceding, he must have wed Grannia since his return. Why had he taken for wife the one person who refused to believe him innocent of abandoning Cymer's people?

As Rhys impatiently urged the donkey to hasten its plodding pace around the last bend, his attention was so wholly given to an opening in the forest's green wall that he failed to see Linnet's perplexed expression. His black cloak rippled in a slight breeze as he lifted his arm to motion toward a peaceful view.

"Behold Newydd Farm . . . and our welcoming party."

Brown eyes widened to study a small meadow and the modest thatched cottage in its midst. The whitewashed structure was surrounded by the neat rows of a sizable garden, and several smaller buildings were clustered at its back. Linnet leaned forward to more clearly see where, on packed earth close to the cottage door, two boys almost the same size fenced with swords crudely formed of wood.

As they moved nearer, it was plain that Alan was being bested by an opponent whose head boasted a riot of black curls. Alan's weapon was knocked from his hand beneath an onslaught against which he was unable to defend himself. He tripped, fell back, arms outstretched and chest bared to what in actual battle would have been a killing blow. Though the width of the tilled field lay between them, Linnet heard Alan laughingly accept defeat with a grace echoed by the young foe who modestly waved his victory aside and extended his hand to aid Alan in rising. Then, as Alan brushed the smudges of dirt from the back of his chausses, he caught sight of the two approaching and his cheeks instantly went a glowing scarlet.

Knowing her brother as well as she assuredly did, Linnet recognized the source of his embarrassment. There was no doubt that Alan felt ashamed at having again lost his sword and failed before the Eagle. 'Twas bad enough that everyone, from Radwell guardsmen to his foster father, Osric, had scornfully teased him for having so much difficulty mastering the art of wielding a sword. But to have his lack repeatedly revealed to one who was a foe in earnest was assuredly as painful as salt added to an open wound.

"Not to worry, Alan." Linnet quietly comforted her brother once she was within speaking distance. "In time and with practice you'll become as skilled at swordplay as ever any man has."

Alan diffidently shrugged, implying the matter was of little import to him. "I only thought 'twould be a fine pursuit to while time away. Thus I and David"—on the name he paused to wave toward a husky boy standing motionless in the background—"searched until we found branches of just the right weight. Then David cajoled his brother into trimming them to the proper length to serve as our mock swords." Alan bent and retrieved his fallen weapon with a great show of nonchalance. "They were finished only this morn; and now, while David teaches me the tricks he knows, I'll show him what I've learned thus far in my fostering."

Linnet suspected the details of how harmless wooden blades had been formed were intended to divert attention from the clear truth that although the Welsh boy had never been taught, he'd easily defeated his years-in-training Norman opponent.

"Alan." Rhys's deep voice was calm and somehow soothing. "I was accustomed to a short sword until my seventeenth year. Then, when first given a broadsword, I found its great length and cumbersome heft difficult to master. But I learned."

Alan gazed at the speaker, pale brown eyes narrowed with suspicion of this famous warrior-foe's purpose in speaking to him of such facts.

"Having watched you at practice," Rhys encouraged, "I know you already possess the ability to wield a blade well. But many have died who in calm demonstrations were able to display such proficiency. Talent in swinging a sword wins no battle alone. Of equal or even greater import is the ability to remain calm and, when possible, to coolly evaluate an opponent's weaknesses—and advantages. Those who become flustered under attack will inevitably lose."

Too aware that he had recently demonstrated a complete lack of control under pressure to perform, Alan compressed his mouth and tilted his chin against what he saw as a direct insult.

"Nay, lad. I mean not to criticize but to offer counsel with a suggestion that may improve your chances in future competitions." Rhys first smiled into the boy's lingering suspicion and then turned toward David.

"Lady Linnet would, I feel certain, enjoy seeing more closely the young lambs in the meadow beyond." Standing still as stone, Rhys waited for the pair to retreat.

Frowning, David obediently turned to lead the way down a ribbon of use-smoothed dirt between the recently sown rows of an oat field. His shoulders were stiff with discomfort at being given responsibility for the entertainment of a Norman lady. It had been difficult enough during the first day or two he'd spent with her brother. The comparison calmed him. Since

David and Alan had no personal quarrel, the mutual hostility between them had eased once they became accustomed to communicating in a language not native to either of them. In truth, he enjoyed having the company of another near his own age—an experience seldom his. Casting a quick glance over his shoulder, David decided that likely this lady, in appearance much the same as Alan, was no more a vicious enemy than her brother had proven to be.

Linnet had a fair idea what purpose lay behind the Eagle's choice to send them off on an elsewise needless visit. Appreciating his willingness to lend Alan the benefit of his experience, she happily accompanied the Welsh boy to a low stone wall marking the field's far boundary and beyond which lambs tentatively ventured from their mothers' side. Knowing her guide was ill at ease, she sought to lessen his tension by asking simple questions about the farm and its animals. Each query was accompanied by a warm smile, and soon they were comfortably sharing soft laughter over the charming unsteadiness of fluffy creatures gamboling through thick grasses.

Once the two he'd dispatched moved beyond hearing range, Rhys crouched down, bringing his face to a level with an apprehensive Alan's.

"Instead of launching a wild attack the instant an armed opponent appears, I suggest you wait for a moment until he reveals his intent. Such a pause will enable you to recognize where his weakness lies."

Rhys's half-smile deepened as his young and unwilling student gave him a dubious look. "To pause, boldly facing a foe, is not the sign of weakness you apparently believe it to be. Rather it demonstrates a strength and control equal to any assault another may advance—and often hands you the advantage of intimidating him into more ineptness than is his wont.

"Thus waiting may lend your attack a far greater

likelihood of success." Rising to his full height, Rhys laid a hand on the boy's shoulder, winning an upward glance from steady brown eyes. "Are you willing, during another meeting between you and David, to test my suggestion?"

Warm daylight picked out the sun streaks in Alan's hair as he nodded, mouth again compressed but this time with a new determination.

Rhys called to the two leaning against the low rock wall preventing the small flock of sheep from wandering where they shouldn't go.

As David rushed back, anxious to continue a new and enjoyable game, he impulsively spoke before either Rhys or Alan could. "Are we to have another battle?"

Linnet saw the resolute expression on her brother's face and gave him an encouraging nod fortified with a smile of confidence.

A slyly grinning Alan wordlessly handed David his wooden sword. He then stepped back, holding his own at the ready. After a long pause, David leapt forward. Exercising both speed and grace, Alan stepped aside while in the same smooth motion tapping the left side of David's chest. The competition, begun and ended in the briefest of moments, awarded Alan the confidence previous years of trying had failed to extend.

"You're dead." Alan's happy laughter was a contradiction to the grim words.

As she heard the paradox, a shadow crossed Linnet's face but she immediately reminded herself that children had been playing games of war for centuries. 'Twas a pastime unlikely to soon end. Not wishing to dampen the boy's rising spirits, she bent and gave him a quick congratulatory hug.

Rhys saw Linnet's moment of sadness while smiling his own congratulations for the excited Norman lordling. He thought he understood, for beneath the warmth he felt for Alan's success lay a cold fear that these boys would one day play the game in deadly earnest.

"Who's dead?" The question was a rumble of mock alarm.

"I'm dead." A giggling David rushed to Owain's side. "But I killed him first."

"Oh, well." Owain shrugged his massive shoulders. "Be you fighting with a man what's already dead, it cannot count . . . unless he's a ghost . . . ooooh." With the exaggerated moaning of the last eerie sound, he bent and swept a boy up beneath each arm.

"Come. Though it required a deal of looking, I've found sufficient bowls to see us all fed." Still holding the wiggling children, Owain led the other two adults into the small but well-kept cottage, made cheery by the flickering flames of a roaring fire in the central hearth.

The two guests and both boys settled on benches running down opposite sides of a table whose planks were bare but for a chunk of dark rye bread and a mug of sweet well water at each place. The host picked up an earthenware bowl, which looked to be in distinct danger of being swallowed inside his massive hands, and approached an iron caldron suspended over the fire. Linnet's eyes widened. The caldron seemed perilously close to the flames below, and she watched in faint horror as Owain wielded a ladle to fill the bowl with a measure of the caldron's contents. As he filled one bowl after another with amazing dexterity, she watched, fascinated by the incongruous sight of the huge bearded bear undertaking domestic chores.

"Stew?" Rhys's single word was a wailed lament.

Taking his place across the table from the Eagle, Owain grinned while his thick black brows peaked in pretended amazement. "You've a misliking for stew, have you?"

Rhys grimaced. "Only when 'tis served day after day after day after . . ."

Apparently 'twas a private jest, for the two men broke into hearty laughter, which left Linnet perplexed.

Restraining a grin Rhys said, "Let me say only that I'll be greatly relieved when Ynid returns—and with her a diet of more variety."

Linnet frowned, watching the two men grin at each other, eyes gleaming. So stew was not a Welshman's steady diet, as she'd assumed it must be since 'twas all she'd been served since arriving in Cymer. But if Ynid knew other recipes, why had . . .

She calmly suggested what she could hardly believe this renowned warrior who'd so recently taught her brother the importance of strategy had failed to do. "Mayhap, in preparation for the next time Ynid is called away, you ought ask her to teach your wife to prepare other dishes."

"Wife?" The word was startled from Rhys. He looked toward Linnet for a long moment and then back to Owain with a slight shrug. "For the sake of a savory meal almost could I wish I had one."

"But . . . Grannia . . ." Linnet's voice trailed away beneath a penetrating dark gaze.

"Is my sister!" Shock lowered Rhys's golden brows. How could this damsel, his hostage for near a week, not know this fact? Had he been a wedded man, 'twould have been contemptible for him to embrace her as so recently he had. In the next moment he acknowledged it mattered little when, wed or not, 'twas equally wrongful of him to have embraced this virginal, noble-born daughter of a foe. Worse still, he'd fallen to the innocent lures of a hostage whom he had sworn to hold safe. The thought further reinforced the unpleasant truth that Linnet unknowingly possessed the power to see his control so far frayed as to threaten his honor. Once, but not again! His knuckles turned white with the strength of his grip on the mug, which miraculously failed to shatter.

While they consumed the disdained stew and rye

bread, a throbbing silence settled its uncomfortable mantle over the room. Rhys's frown deepened, but though Linnet knew she was responsible for his irritation, she couldn't repress either the bubble of happiness rising inside at the knowledge that he was not bound to another or relief that she was guiltless of enjoying the delights of another woman's husband. Only the undeniable truth that his being unwed made no difference at all to the fact that her admiration of—and growing feelings for—the Eagle made her a traitor to her father's every goal. She ate but could not later have said what ingredients the stew contained.

By the time the last spoon clattered into an empty bowl, Owain, feeling the weight of his role as host, forced words out to break the oppressive silence's hold.

"Aye, well, friend. You can see there's danger in getting us all to speak a language not our own. It's certain sure things we think we say may not be what we said at all."

"Owain, I'm sorry." Having entirely missed the significance of Linnet's words and Rhys's response, it was Alan who rushed in with an apology. "I wish I could speak your tongue, but . . ."

"Ah, pay me no mind." Owain ruffled the honey-hued hair of the boy at his side, grimacing in recognition of how clumsily he'd stumbled in his haste to alleviate the tension. "I meant only that choosing unfamiliar words may lead to misunderstandings."

Worries furrowed Alan's brow, but after he looked from Owain to David to Rhys and met their comforting smiles, it smoothed again.

Owain energetically slapped his large hands palm down upon the table, threatening to overturn bowls that, luckily, were empty, as he rose to his feet.

"Come, Rhys. Let David and me show you what progress we've made on the farm this early in the season." Casting a glance and a friendly grin back over his shoulder, Owain led the way out the door. The departing three spent several hours trooping through fields, examining cattle, pigs, and sheep, and taking stock of the goods stored in neighboring sheds while Linnet and her brother passed the time visiting quietly.

THE EAGLE'S SONG

BLACK SMOKE BILLOWED FROM A POT OF LARD LEFT SO
perilously near the hearth's flames it had caught
alight. Grannia rushed to suppress the fire beneath a
heavy lid while Linnet, choking from the noxious
fumes though holding a kitchen cloth's sizable square
against her face, rushed to tear the door open. Once it
was thrown wide, with each hand on a corner of the
cloth she energetically waved it in an attempt to
disperse the inky haze.

Leaving behind a pot too hot to move but no longer
emitting either flame or smoke, Grannia joined Linnet and added her efforts to the goal of fanning as
much of the acrid cloud from the Eagle's hall as
possible. When they'd accomplished what little they
could, they sagged against opposite sides of the door
frame to gratefully drag in deep breaths of sweet fresh
air. Neither imperiled their uneasy yet growing harmony by accusing the other of being responsible for
forgetting the lard's dangerous position and thus
allowing it to ignite.

Honestly unsure whether or not she was the culprit,
Linnet found Grannia's restraint an encouraging sign.
Although during the several days since Linnet's visit

to Newydd Farm Grannia hadn't apologized for her cold ways, she had made a grudging effort to establish peace between them by accepting Linnet's aid in household chores. A measure of satisfaction filled the amber gaze drifting over the peaceful view beyond wooden steps leading out from the Welsh prince's home.

The warmth of a welcome morning sun had begun to evaporate the ground fog's pale blue haze while earth drenched by the previous night's steady rainfall slowly dried. Wrinkling her nose, Linnet inhaled the pleasant pungent scent of newly washed earth and the aroma of herbs just sprouting in the small kitchen garden planted to one side of the door. Wrapped in a glow of contentment, almost she could have been lulled into forgetting the circumstances that had brought her here.

In truth, though weighted with the guilt of knowing 'twas a fact that made of her a traitor, she found it most difficult to rue the deed, particularly when the Eagle returned early enough of an evening to settle near the fire with both her and Grannia and talk of unimportant matters. Never before had a man, not even her indulgent father, actually listened to Linnet nor, of a certainty, been willing to seek her opinion on any subject. Yet the three of them had discussed everything from such mundane matters as the difficulty in acquiring certain spices to Rhys's contention that a Welsh longbow was superior to the Norman crossbow. Linnet had found the experience intoxicating. At the same time, Rhys and she had been careful not to touch upon sensitive topics raised during their journey to Newydd Farm, topics they had scrupulously avoided during their nearly silent return and every day since.

Linnet glanced toward her companion and followed the line of Grannia's discouraged gaze. The walls all around had been stained a dingy gray.

"No matter." Linnet shrugged and offered a cheerful solution. "The hall was in need of a fresh coat of whitewash even before our misadventure. And with two of us wielding brushes, 'twill be done in a trice."

Grannia's expression lightened—a little. "I wish David were here. He actually enjoys the task." She shook her head in exasperation while to her mouth came a smile as mocking as ever her brother's. "Although I cannot fathom what pleasure there is to be had in its doing."

Linnet's smile deepened. She felt gladdened by Grannia's failure to question her calm statement of intent to join in the task David was not there to perform. In her relief it never occurred to her to wonder at Grannia's knowledge of David's joy in the misliked task. To Linnet 'twas simply another example of how, since the day she'd first asked Grannia for tasks to busy idle hands, matters between them had settled into a smoother pace.

Not only had Linnet been permitted to help with household chores, but the past day Grannia had permitted her to prepare for the evening repast a fine dish of capon in milk and honey sauce. Although, when the meal was laid before him, the Eagle had given no verbal appreciation, the golden sparkle in the look he'd cast toward Linnet had wordlessly conveyed the sense of a secret shared. A response that had been more than enough recompense for the full day's toil required to see it prepared and cooked to perfection.

As if the thoughts in Linnet's mind had been spoken aloud, Grannia surprised her by turning to that very subject.

"The whitewashing can wait for the morrow . . ." The words firmly begun drifted off while an uncommon nervousness seemed to attack Grannia. She cleared her throat and gruffly started again. "I would have you teach me how to prepare the dish you served last eve."

Linnet blinked but restrained her surprise and evenly responded to a finer compliment than she'd ever thought to receive from this woman who, it was certain, only reluctantly sought instruction from her.

"Happily will I share the method for preparing a capon in that manner, but 'twould surely be of more use first to show you how to make a dish that is a little less difficult. One we can serve tonight." Near holding her breath, Linnet prayed Grannia would not be affronted by the alteration, made as diplomatically as possible, in the request granted.

The Welshwoman recognized both the ploy and the tact with which it had been phrased. Her initial frown slipped into a grimace. "You've the right of it—doubtless my brother would appreciate not being served the same dish for a second night."

An overabundance of ills had befallen Grannia in the past decade, leaving her prickly as a hedgehog and robbed of a smooth tongue. Though never would she have admitted it, Grannia greatly envied her brother's protective armor of smiling cynicism—and his easy charm. Aye, had she possessed either quality, it wouldn't be so difficult for her to form right words and have done with a necessary duty. Straightening her shoulders, Grannia gruffly embarked upon an apology owed but delayed until the shirked burden nagged mercilessly at her conscience.

"Although I once charged you with an inability to perform mundane chores, in actual fact 'tis I who lack the most basic skills of cookery." After passing over the highest hurdle, Grannia took a deep breath. The apology she'd made, but it wasn't enough. Linnet deserved a confession revealing her accuser as the one guilty of the very character flaws and lacks of which she'd been accused. Meeting the Norman damsel's gentle smile, Grannia wondered if the other would feel so sympathetic after having heard the whole. Taking a deep breath and donning an emotionless mask, Grannia went on.

"Ynid's mother first and then Ynid prepared the

meals in my father's hall. After his death, life continued unchanged as I shared that same hall—and Ynid's savory meals—with a husband. During the fourteen years that the spoiled girl I was spent in the prince's abode, never was I wise enough to yield to Ynid's constant urgings and lend attention to the lessons she sought to teach. Indeed, I learned nothing more of kitchen duties than the simple ingredients for a hearty stew and how to bake bread—which by some miracle I'd found interesting.

"In the four years after Lloyd carried me off to my dower lands, he allowed very few people to penetrate the borders of Abergele Farm." Grannia's eyes went to black ice under unpleasant memories revived. "I saw no other females and assuredly no one capable of teaching me the important skills I'd foolishly ignored."

After pausing to control the self-disgust threatening to curl her mouth downward, Grannia resolutely continued. "Warped by bitterness, Lloyd little cared what food he was served. It was I who soon tired of the same pitiful menu day after day. Though I attempted to teach myself, I won little success."

Hearing the resentment in Grannia's talk of Lloyd's bitterness, Linnet was struck by a curious question. Did she not realize how deeply she was afflicted with the same ailment?

"When Rhys summoned me to watch over you, I thought Ynid would be here. I came near to panic when she arrived that first morn only to announce her departure. Unwilling to risk revealing my ineptitude, and as stew is the only dish with which I've any certainty of success, stew is what I served. Still, I thought . . . Nay, I earnestly prayed that Ynid would soon return. Unfortunately the child's illness has spread to others, and you have proven to be our savior from a monotonous multitude of stews."

Grannia's grimace earned Linnet's understanding and a bright, encouraging smile. "Aye, well, if 'tis

cooking lessons you seek, I'll do my poor best to
oblige."

Amazed by the Norman damsel's generous response when she'd expected her to erupt with just
ridicule for a confessed incompetence in womanly
arts, Grannia felt a great burden lifted from her
shoulders and with its departure a spirit revitalized.

"Best we get started." Anxious to further dispel the
other's gloom, Linnet brought her palms together with
a single clap. "We've much to cover before the limits
your brother imposed on my time here expire."

"Time limit?" Grannia's brows rose in surprise.

In response, a slight frown puckered Linnet's forehead. "Did you not know of the message left for my
father?" The slight shake of a dark head was her
answer. "'Twas an oath promising to assure safe care
for me and Alan but only for the length of a fortnight."

The words brought both women a renewed awareness of the gulf between them and threatened to
unravel the tenuous threads of an accord so recently
woven.

"Mayhap we ought begin by washing the soot from
ourselves and the surfaces we shall need once your
first lesson commences." Determinedly putting bleak
thoughts aside, Linnet grinned. It was infectious and
won a tentative smile from Grannia.

Thankful that the smoke had nearly dissipated,
Linnet turned and went to the waist-high cupboard
upon which rested a bowl with a pile of clean cloth
squares inside. After lifting and placing stacked cloths
to one side, she handed one to Grannia and took
another herself before pouring water from a covered
ewer into the basin.

Attention first was given to the table, utensils, and
both of the benches stretching down the table's each
side. Dirtied water was repeatedly thrown out the
door and fresh water poured until, as a last chore
before washing hands further dirtied by their deeds,

they scrubbed seats near to the hearth and thus most begrimed. Once they stood with hands and face clean, a husky voice interrupted the exchanged smiles of satisfaction for a task well done.

"My traps were overblessed, and I thought to share my bounty with you."

Both women swung around to find Owain's broad form near blocking the open door's rectangle of light. From his uplifted hand dangled a plump pheasant.

"Ah, what a fine specimen and just what at the moment we need. 'Struth, Linnet?" As Grannia dropped her sullied cloth, she sent the hostage a pleading gaze. Linnet recognized this as a silent supplication for her willingness to make use of the unexpected gift. The fat braids falling near to her waist gleamed even through lingering smoke as she immediately nodded.

"Aye, 'twill be the perfect dish about which to build our evening meal." She ticked off a list of needed ingredients on the dainty fingers of one hand. "To make a fine course of stuffed pheasant we'll need only a few apples, some oats, and small portions of a few common herbs—rosemary, basil, and thyme."

"We've all of those items close to hand." Grannia fair beamed upon her appreciated confederate before turning back to the new arrival.

"'Twas wondrous kind of you to think of us, Owain." Grannia's words were harmless, but a softness in the dark depths of her eyes conveyed to Owain volumes more of a purely personal nature.

Nearly did Owain retreat under this dangerous welcome riddled with pitfalls, but instead justified remaining by telling himself he'd an important responsibility to see done. To prove—leastways to himself—that he was unfazed, Owain frowned and walked right past the blushing woman to lay the bird atop the table's bare planks. He lifted his chin as if in defiance when he turned to find the woman had followed and now stood too close.

"I'd another purpose in coming here, Grannia." He spoke with a coolness he could only wish he sincerely felt. "We must talk—in private." With the qualifier, he cast the hostage an uncomfortable glance.

Shrugging the silent and unnecessary apology aside, Linnet could not help but notice as, with surprising familiarity, the other woman stroked one of the powerful forearms crossed over Owain's wide chest.

"If 'tis privacy you seek, let us stroll through Rhys's tiny orchard. The apple trees' buds are fat and near to bursting into bloom." Without so much as a glance toward the woman whose presence she'd plainly forgotten, Grannia tugged the bearded bear to walk with her through the open door, which she absently pulled closed as they departed.

For a time they walked in silence, Owain glaring blindly into the same distance Grannia watched with dreamy admiration. But once they'd come to the orchard, near the only part of Prince Griffith's possessions to escape Lloyd's vindictive torch, Owain resolutely began.

"'Tis wrong of you to continue blaming Rhys for a deed not his choice."

This was the very last subject she'd expected her escort to broach, and as it had been discussed so many times before, it was surely not his true purpose.

"He knew of our father's death, and yet he chose not to return! Why must you keep at me on a matter you know we'll never agree upon?" All the harmony, rare in her life in recent years, which Linnet had invited her to share scattered beneath Owain's renewed attack.

"Because Rhys swears on his honor that he never received word of Prince Griffith's death, and only I can continue to urge you to believe it is so."

"How can I believe? How when with mine own eyes I saw the missive written and dispatched to Normandy? Do you think I am lying?" Her voice rose to an angry pitch and she stopped to face him, clenched hands on hips.

"Nay, I know you are not." Owain instantly soothed her growing ire with quiet words and huge hands rubbing her tensed arms with amazing gentleness. "But that it was written and sent does nothing to disprove the truth of Rhys's oath. Clearly something happened to the messenger. It never arrived!"

"Do you say that Ewais's report of having put it into Rhys's own hand is the lie?" With the words, Grannia's chin trembled and her gaze fell from cheery surroundings to the muddy ground beneath her feet. That the excitement of having Owain seek her company had come to this disappointing end summoned the tears she hadn't shed since her father's death. Welling up in her eyes, they were dangerously near to overbrimming.

"Ewais? Ewais was the messenger sent to Normandy?"

Owain's sharp question called back Grannia's gaze, but she refused to risk further embarrassment by speaking with an untrustworthy voice and merely nodded.

He hadn't known which man his father had ordered to carry the message, but while Owain felt the information offered a welcome step in tracking down the wretched misdeed that had brought about deeply rued consequences, he thrust aside further immediate consideration of the matter. Grannia was pained by the subject—a sight he couldn't bear, particularly when he knew himself in part to blame.

"Don't think on it more." Lifting gentle palms to rest against her cheeks, with his thumbs he lightly brushed aside the tears trembling on the tips of her lashes. "I'll find out where the truth lies and share it with you. Till then I pray you'll not brood on it, nor must you allow it to darken your days or disturb your nights."

Grannia bowed her head until her forehead rested

against Owain's chest. "'Tis not the reason for my gloom."

Her words were muffled, but Owain heard them well enough and found he hadn't the will to prevent himself from brushing his cheek across the top of her shiny black hair or sliding comforting hands to her back. "If not the rift between you and Rhys, then what is the source?"

"You. I thought you wanted to spend time with me. But, nay, you want no more of me than what I can tell you of the supposed miscommunication between your father and Rhys." Forehead still against him, she slowly shook her head. "I thought you wanted more of me."

"'Tis the problem." The statement was a low rumble from the chest beneath the cheek Grannia had shifted to lay full against him. "I want you too much."

Breath sighed from Grannia at this confirmation of what since childhood she'd waited to hear. Nothing could have prevented her from melting against him, wrapping her arms about his neck, and lifting an imploring mouth to his.

Owain fell to an undeniable sin. He claimed a devastating kiss. One kiss but no more.

When he pulled her arms from their embrace and held them to her side with hands that felt like a vise, Grannia moaned while her dark eyes wordlessly pleaded for a reprieve.

Owain shook his shaggy black mane. "This is why I welcomed my father's decision to take you to live at Abergele rather than join me at his hereditary home, Newydd Farm. 'Tis why I visited so seldom." Eyes hard as sapphires glittered remorselessly. "And why, since his death and your choice to move into Newydd, I rarely spend time at my own farm."

"But . . ." The single word ached with Grannia's resentment, pain, and regret.

* * *

With the couple's departure, Linnet was left standing alone beside the Eagle's cushioned chair with a damp rag hanging from her fingers. She smiled, quietly amused by the change Owain's appearance inevitably wrought in Grannia—as if someone had lit a bonfire in her center, putting a sparkle in her eyes and a gentle warmth upon her face. Knowing what dreadful misfortunes—lands seized and husband killed— had befallen Grannia at Earl Godfrey's hand, Linnet was relieved by the good portents of future happiness in the woman's response to Owain. Although it was near certain Grannia's recent widowhood would delay any remarriage, the vision of the pair in harmony pleased Linnet and with a lightened heart she turned her attention to plans for the requested cooking lesson.

If Ynid was as talented in the culinary arts as first Rhys's comments at Newydd and now Grannia's statements implied, then there must be a fine assortment of ingredients available. That being so, her first task was to hunt out those necessary to see the pheasant become a tasty meal. She would find and line them up in the proper order, ready for the lesson to commence once the couple returned and the bearded bear departed.

She went to shelves built against the wall behind the table. Salt, butter, and wine would surely present no difficulties. Thus she would waste no thought on their whereabouts. She instead leaned forward to peer at goods neatly stored until she found a bag filled with apples. The fact that they'd been harvested months past and were badly shriveled would make no difference to the taste of the dish. After selecting the largest three and placing them at the table's far end, she hunted for and easily located another bag, this one full of oats.

Linnet scooped into a bowl what she deemed an adequate amount for the size of the pheasant. Her next task, not so easily done, was the finding of necessary herbs. They would, of a certainty, have been dried from the previous year—if there were any at all. After looking without success into a multitude of vessels from tiny jars to monstrously big covered bowls, she nearly surrendered the quest. Then at last she found small earthen containers tucked inside a basket. Ynid must have feared for her supply of costly spices and herbs grown precious during the depths of winter when no more could be easily had. They'd been hidden in a basket and that basket had not been placed atop a shelf but rather rested in shadows on the floor under the lowest.

While setting out the appropriate choices, Linnet rued the earliness of the season, which prevented her from using fresh thyme and basil—tastier when recently picked. But—and she smiled for this redeeming fact—dried rosemary was best for the recipe she meant to employ on the pheasant, as it could be crushed into a fine powder. Humming absently, she located a small stone bowl. Into this she poured a measure of the rosemary and lifted the pestle to grind the dried leaves into mere dust.

Realizing of a sudden that she was alone in the house for the first time since her capture, Linnet spared only a fleeting thought to wonder why Pywell had not been sent to stand over her. She shrugged. Plainly Grannia had been too preoccupied with her companion to consider the supposed danger. A needless worry, as Linnet had no thought of escaping.

Glancing through a window half unshuttered, she caught a glimpse of Pywell's angular figure relaxed beneath a towering tree. Its spreading branches had likely protected the ground below from much of the drenching rain, which elsewhere had turned earth to mud. Pywell was leaning back against its broad trunk, and Linnet suspected he napped. No matter, his mere presence was a deterrent. And when added to the stout bars laid across the outside of the back wall's two windows, she was effectively confined, though in a remarkably comfortable, pleasant prison. Moreover, as she'd acknowledged the first day, her brother's absence was the most effective restraint that could be placed upon any dream of escape. Never would Linnet flee without Alan safely at her side.

She knew a moment of smug satisfaction that these were all fine and believable reasons for remaining where she was.

What a liar you are! Linnet mocked herself, but the smile accompanying the thought held no trace of regret. You wouldn't surrender a single moment in the Eagle's presence even were it in your power to walk with Alan safely free.

The dreamy smile of one moment in the next faded into a gloomy mask of shame. She was guilty of the worst of crimes against her own father. She had betrayed the honor he held so dear and felt herself shrinking under the knowledge that 'twas by her own wrongful deeds she'd fallen. 'Twas nowise the fault of the mighty warrior whose appearance in wicked visions she should have blocked from her daytime fantasies and nighttime dreams long, long ago. In truth, she should never have allowed them in the first instance! She was undeniably a sinner. The priests constantly warned against forbidden dreams— dreams of a lover of no substance—from which doubtless any good and virtuous lady would have recoiled.

Instead of carefully grinding the herbs, she pounded so viciously 'twas a wonder neither bowl nor pestle shattered. The steady smashing masked the sound of bars being carefully dislodged and shutters opened. Believing the worst had already befallen her, she had no reason to fear. When came the blow from behind she slumped forward never knowing she'd been struck.

Wearied by a day—nay, a sennight of unforeseen difficulties, with disputes breaking out between his supporters and renewed threats issued from both the east and the west—Rhys approached his home with relief. Though it was barely midday, he'd returned to retrieve a few needed instruments. Mayhap not actually needed but leastways useful—and a fine excuse for seeking a few quiet moments in his hostage's soothing company. The prospect lifted his spirits, and he paused at the door only long enough to stomp away as much of the thick mud from his boots as possible.

A resounding crash echoed from inside, and he momentarily froze. Then, after throwing the door open, Rhys flung himself halfway across the large chamber. Shutters spread wide framed a pair of disappearing legs. A low growl rumbled from the core of Rhys's being, and he crouched to launch himself after the unwelcome invader. But from the corner of his eyes he saw lying across his path a prone body fallen with limbs bent in awkward angles.

It was fortunate Linnet could not hear the vicious curse that roared from his depths as he dropped to his knees at her side. Fingertips laid against the side of her exposed throat established that her heart was still strongly beating. Golden brows drew into a fierce frown as he gently lifted her and rose to his feet.

"Lady Linnet!"

Rhys looked up from the poignantly small body in his arms to meet Pywell's horrified gaze. The guard he'd posted stood frozen in the doorway.

"An intruder entering through the back window did this." Later Rhys would comfort Pywell's self-blame for a deed he could never have foreseen from his position in front, but now was not the time. No moment must be lost. "Make haste. Track the despicable cur if you can!"

While Pywell rushed off to do as he was bidden, doubtless lent haste for knowing the perpetrator's vile deed had been wrought against Linnet, Rhys carried the injured damsel to his wide cushioned chair. He draped her upon its sturdy support as comfortably as possible. Moving to the table, he poured cool water into the waiting bowl and snatched up a square of coarse cloth plainly recently rinsed and still damp.

Bearing his negligible burdens, he returned to the small, unmoving figure. Carefully he stroked the cloth across her forehead and over cheeks robbed of their usual creamy color to become a fearful white.

For long moments heavy lashes futilely struggled to rise, and every failed attempt heightened Rhys's fears. But at last soft brown eyes blinked up at him in confusion.

Linnet gazed into the handsome face so near. This made no sense at all. One moment before she'd been alone crushing herbs and deriding herself for her wicked dreams, but now, in the next, their golden hero held her tenderly in his arms, radiating concern. Linnet nibbled her lips to a berry brightness the more vivid for the lingering paleness of her face. Like that first night in Radwell's tower, she wondered if her imagination had conjured up this bewildering scene.

Seeing the disorientation fogging her usual clear amber gaze, Rhys softly explained. "Someone, it seems, smote you over the head in an attempt to take you from me."

Linnet's frown deepened as she strove to find sense in facts where there was none. Who would want to take her from the Eagle? Her father? But . . .

"No matter his desire to see me returned, my father wouldn't allow me to be harmed." Linnet spoke her thoughts aloud while striving to school her thoughts into some semblance of order. Toward that goal, she pulled herself from the arms of the man whose closeness would assuredly make her success in that quest more difficult.

"I'm certain what you say is true." Rhys's quiet agreement was accompanied by a downward curl to one side of his mouth. Her father's minions would know better than to harm one hair of her head.

Moreover, they would surely have believed her anxious to escape, lending them no reason to start the rescue by knocking her senseless. Nonetheless, someone certainly had sneaked up behind her to deliver such a blow with the clear intent to take her away. But who?

6

"WHEN THE RABBIT TAKES THE BAIT, THE TRAP FALLS."
Alan slapped one palm against the other for emphasis,
and his eyes glowed with excitement. "Then, Linnet,
you've got him! No need for a blade of any sort! David
says it's more of a challenge to hunt unarmed." After a
quick glance toward the boy behind him, Alan bent
closer to his sister and with a mischievous grin loudly
whispered, "He's right. It was great fun!"

Amidst the cozy warmths of the Eagle's hall, Linnet's answering murmurs invited further details of
recent days from her animated brother. Firelight cast
shifting orange hues across his face, but the last rays of
dusk falling through an unshuttered window behind
him lent a pale outline to his figure.

Long hours had been spent laboring over various
dishes, which would be added to the multitude of
foodstuffs Cymer's women had much earlier begun
preparing. All this for what Linnet had been told was a
much anticipated annual event. Only after she and
Grannia had arranged the platters did they retreat
abovestairs to don more festive garb. Linnet possessed
only one alternative to borrowed homespun. But her
limited choice enabled her to make a quick exchange

of drab daywear for a cleansed and meticulously mended scarlet gown. Too, limited choice had allowed her time to brush her hair until it glowed near as bright as the golden ribbons Grannia had lent her to braid into glossy locks.

Once done, she'd descended to an empty hall. Deeming herself justified in seeking a brief rest after the morn's toil, she'd chosen a low stool well within the hearth's circle of warmth. From that perch, back presented to the fire's heat, she'd gazed through the open shutters of a front-facing window to watch the setting sun's brilliant colors paint the sky above the dark outline of not so distant hills. Though once pleasantly relaxed, Rhys's arrival with the two boys in tow had produced in her an unaccountable sense of guilty sloth.

Alan had rushed forward at finding his sister in a rare moment of idleness. Awkwardly folding a form lengthening too rapidly to allow for grace, he sat at her feet to regale her with a lively account of all the exciting diversions with which he and David had busied themselves during the few days since their last talk. While Alan recounted their adventures, David had followed the Norman boy's lead and settled down a short distance behind him.

Quietly marveling anew at the boys' easy relationship, Linnet gave them a gentle smile, encouraging them to continue their tales of recent escapades. It seemed the tender shoot of friendship budding betwixt Alan and the ebony-haired boy was flourishing.

She'd seen for herself that her brother had been well treated by those in whose charge he was, as well treated as she'd been by the Eagle and now even by Grannia. Her own experience lent understanding for Alan's response to people whom those at Radwell viewed as enemies. Despite her forcible abduction, she, too, found it difficult—nay, impossible—to see in their captors any shadow of the violent, inhuman monsters she'd been taught all of Welsh blood were. This inability to despise undeniable foes stabbed her with guilt for the betrayal to her father it must be. To deflect its blow, again she fell to an imprudent action become all too common to a heretofore circumspect woman. She spoke without forethought.

"Seems the days of your captivity have provided you with an exciting adventure." That Alan heard her comment as censure was clear by the stricken expression crossing his face. Linnet wished she'd bitten her tongue before speaking ill-considered words conveying a message far different from what was meant and hastened to repair the damage. "I'm glad your time was pleasantly filled. I, too, have learned much I would never elsewise have known."

Rhys's dark eyes chilled. He stood behind and slightly to one side of the seated woman. What could she have learned during early days spent near alone and more recent hours spent teaching his sister to cook? In their quiet evening talks, which he'd sought in large measure purely for the enjoyment of listening to the music of Linnet's voice, had he been lulled into an unwariness allowing the revelation of secrets best withheld from her father? Or . . . did she know something more of the attempted abduction than she had revealed when he asked? Her next words went some small way toward lessening the tension of his suspicions.

"Until this morn"—Linnet's grin sparkled— "never had I heard of Gwyn ap Nudd."

"The Wild Huntsman." David beamed at this woefully uninformed Norman lady. Anxious she should know the full measure of the mythical hero's greatness, he went on to extol both Gwyn and his extraordinary deeds and thus justify the rightfulness of honoring him.

"He fought a mighty battle with the dark forces of winter, and his victory freed summer to return. 'Tis why on the eve of May Day each year we light a *huge* bonfire." David flung his hands wide and then arched them up toward the heavily beamed ceiling.

"And celebrate with a feast of first fruits and abundant ale." Linnet laughed, repeating the description of the holiday, which an excited Grannia had told her more than once.

The melody of Linnet's laughter, sweet as her namesake's song, wrapped its gentle tendrils around Rhys. Certain that the boys held her interest, he felt free to study the tender damsel who was so different from what he'd first assumed. It was a boon infrequently granted. When not in direct conversation, she strove to keep her honeyed eyes averted, but whilst they shared the same abode he sensed the weight of her full attention ever upon him. Though more than a little irritated by repeatedly discovering himself prey to any woman's wiles, least of all those of this virginal captive, he seemed no more able to prevent their mutual attraction than she. A devastating admission from a man proud of his ability to meet and defeat any challenge.

Rhys frowned, hard pressed to still an urge to loosen the golden ribbons wound through her thick braids and free clouds of soft hair to his touch. Praise the saints, she seemed none the worse for the previous day's assault. His visual caress of unblemished creamy skin confirmed that fact.

While the boys fell into spirited talk of the coming event, Linnet slowly became aware of his dark gaze and glanced over her shoulder. An inaudible gasp escaped. What could she possibly have done to deserve so fierce a glare?

"Is something amiss?" Linnet asked the question quietly, intending only Rhys to hear.

Already familiar with the gentle nibbling of a lower lip as the sign of tension it was, now Rhys recognized shy bewilderment in her pansy-soft eyes.

"Only my concern that all be in readiness for the night's festivities."

With the excuse, his expression softened with a rare gentle smile. He knew his frown was the cause of her distress and intended to mend her fears. She should not be made to pay for a strong man's fall to her unintentional lures, nor could she be blamed for the temper roused by the bungled attempt to spirit her away.

Under his potent smile, Linnet's amber eyes filled with an unguarded warmth that threatened a further weakening of the practice-hardened armor closed about Rhys's cynical heart. As a shield against this danger, he looked toward the two youngsters. They were at an age when attention flitted from one subject to another, and they were now absorbed in plans for another hunting expedition. While appearing to listen to their schemes, he purposefully returned his thoughts to a puzzle that had dominated them since the attempted capture.

Though a failure, the attempt had left behind a mystery. One which, if allowed to go unsolved, could jeopardize the current course and more. Who was responsible and what had been his purpose? Those unanswered questions cast a haze of uncertainty over not just the present but the future as well.

The fact that Linnet had been physically assaulted made it improbable that the perpetrator was one of Earl Godfrey's supporters. If sent by the earl to rescue his children, the man would have found it exceedingly difficult to justify the harming of a damsel he could only believe would be anxious to cooperate in any escape. The likelihood that the mysterious intruder had not come from the earl raised the unwelcome possibility that the culprit was one of Rhys's own turned traitor. Someone who—as Grannia was fond of hinting—was not Rhys's loyal supporter and who deemed the taking of Norman hostages an ill-conceived and ill-fated strategy?

With the frustrated high spirits of anticipation for a soon coming event, the boys had fallen to wrestling at Linnet's feet, but she had no attention to spare for them. Rather, she surreptitiously peeked at Rhys. Though she chided herself for the wrong, it was a habit begun the first moment she'd seen the golden warrior, a habit become an addiction.

The smile he'd given her was reassurance that she was not the cause of the fierce scowl that had returned to eyes as dark and deep as midnight, but Linnet was concerned. Had his plan to barter his hostages gone awry? Had her father refused to bargain with an enemy? Slender shoulders lifted with the deep breath she took to steady a never strong courage and face her fear that the answers to these questions were the reason behind the past day's frightening events.

Aware of the apprehensive glances Linnet repeatedly sent his way, Rhys smoothed the frown from his brow but could not so easily push unpleasant possibilities from his thoughts. If the perpetrator had been one of his own, then tonight's traditional celebration of the Wild Huntsman's victory was a well-timed boon. The evening's festivities would offer him an excellent opportunity to view his people all gathered in one place and unaware that they were being watched with a purpose.

The previous day, once he had cared for Linnet's bruises, Rhys had examined the window through which her assailant had made his escape. On one broken shutter he'd discovered blood and beyond the open window an intermittent trail over uneven ground. Adding to his frustration over an unknown and unseen enemy striking so close, the trail had disappeared amid heavy undergrowth. Worse still, when put to the scent, the dogs had led their masters to the stream but there had lost the way. The only clue he had left to track the culprit was the crimson proof that the man had been injured. Tonight that injury might be apparent—a limp, a bound arm, a bandaged head, or someone absent who elsewise would have been present.

Hearing the sound of feet on the steep wooden

steps, Linnet glanced up. Grannia, garbed in sapphire blue, thick black braids piled atop her head while ringlets fell free to frame her lovely face, had begun to descend, but she paused at the sound of muddied feet stomping beyond a door next energetically thrust open.

"The fire roars, and the people have assembled!" Owain's announcement was cheery, and he rubbed his huge hands together in satisfaction. "Are you ready to join the merriment?" With the question he moved toward the hearth in the room's midst and bent to thump each boy's head. The lads scrambled to their feet in demonstration of a desire to depart straightaway for the site of promised fun.

Their immediate response earned a rumble of laughter from Rhys, and not until it faded into a grin shared with Owain was another voice heard.

"My harp?" The tension radiating from Grannia, hovering two stairsteps above the hall's rush-strewn floor, and cryptic words devoid of emotion made clear how important was the answer to her.

As Owain turned toward the corner stairway, his grin deepened while the laughter gleaming in his eyes softened to an intimate glow. "Aye, with my own hands I carefully bore it to our evening's destination."

Grannia's tightly controlled expression melted into a look of tenderness that wordlessly spoke of more than gratitude for a simple favor granted.

Linnet quietly watched the couple's visual exchange with warm approval. Having come to like the once aloof Welshwoman and wishing happiness for her, Linnet again spoke without thought.

"You are fortunate, Grannia, in having won the loyalty of a gallant champion such as every lady deserves and longs to win." Gentle merriment gleamed in Linnet's soft brown eyes.

Seeing the other woman's face go a ghastly white while Owain's turned beet red, Linnet realized that she'd once again taken a clumsy misstep.

"Aye, you are right. 'Tis what Grannia deserves, but until such a champion appears, her two stepsons will take up that charge." Owain's gaze, gone lifeless, shifted to the innocent face of his young brother. "Won't we, David?"

David, called to an honorable duty, squared his narrow shoulders and proudly nodded his pleasure in accepting the charge.

Now it was Linnet who felt the sweeping heat of embarrassment while a wild blush suffused her stricken face with bright color. Just as when she'd erred in thinking Grannia wife to Rhys, now another misunderstood relationship had led to rash words. Grannia's dead husband was the father of both Owain and David! Linnet had bumbled into a painful wound that plainly could never be healed. She had no doubt that Grannia loved Owain or that he felt the same emotion for her. As stepmother and stepson, however, their love was forever forbidden by church law. A match between individuals related within seven degrees, even through marriage, was forbidden.

Rhys was startled. Linnet's teasing words had peeled the scales from his eyes, and for the first time he saw the emotion flowing between his sister and his closest friend. How could he have been blind to what now was so clear? Had his vision been weakened by how little time he'd spent in Grannia's company during the five years since his return from Normandy?

He glanced toward Grannia and then Owain. Neither would meet his gaze. Instead they gazed forlornly down at the fresh rushes, which the day past Linnet had strewn over floor planks first swept clear of the old. Wrongly or rightly, he felt a silent accusation in their averted gazes.

A momentary flash of resentment hit Rhys. This estrangement between himself and his sister had been unavoidable and not by his wish. Had Grannia's husband not been determined to rule Cymer in her name, Rhys would have had the chance earlier to build a relationship with her. But, forced to end Lloyd's false claim, Rhys had deflated the older man's ambition. Shamed, Lloyd had thereafter avoided any contact with the victor and, too, had prevented his wife from seeing her brother.

Contact between Rhys and Grannia had been reestablished only in recent weeks. Rhys viewed that as the single positive result of the Norman earl's latest wretched deeds—the murder of Lloyd and seizure of Abergele Farm—despite the fact that his sister unaccountably blamed him for both actions. A crack in the barrier of silence between them had resulted from her compliance with Rhys's request that she serve as chaperon while a female hostage resided in his home. Leastways they were talking now, albeit most oft with harsh words.

The escalating tension between the four adults reached even the excited boys to hold them quiet and still. Apprehensive but curious, too, they glanced from the downcast Owain and Grannia to Linnet. Twisting scarlet cloth about her fingers as if she had not spent hours attempting to return it to as fine a condition as possible, Linnet looked as nervous as they. Finally, as if the two of them were of a single mind, they looked toward the Eagle, whose deep scowl gave even his golden visage the dark appearance of a building storm.

"Well, then"—Rhys fought against disheartening thoughts to break the strained hush—"if each of you young sirs will hoist a keg of the alewife's finest brew, we'll be off to the revels."

The two boys hastened to do as they were bidden and rushed to the barrels that had earlier been delivered and stacked beneath the windows. They waited to depart, however, until Owain, afflicted by an unusual awkwardness, hoisted a large wooden platter laden with an amazing assortment of foodstuffs prepared by the two women. The bearded bear then set off to lead a small procession. Following close behind

him were the youngsters, proud of being entrusted
with so important a task and pleased by the strange
conflict's end. Grannia, carrying a little tub of freshly
churned butter and a large chunk of bright orange
cheese, trailed after him . . . at a sedate distance.

Although he'd put the exodus in motion, Rhys held
back. Eyes as impenetrable as a cloudy midnight sky
watched the four move out through the open doorway.
Behind his emotionless facade lay an odd combination of relief and despair. In his recognition of the
couple's doomed emotions, and along with his sympathy for their pain, Rhys found a measure of relief. This
explained so much. Now he understood the reasoning
behind Grannia's resentment of him and his return a
year following their father's death. Rhys's reappearance had been months too late to save Grannia from
marriage to Lloyd and thus too late to prevent the
lowering of an immovable bar betwixt her and Owain.
Yet with the relief in knowing the source of Grannia's
bitterness came the despair in the near certainty that
his sister would never forgive him.

As dusk's growing dimness swallowed those who'd
already gone, Rhys forced his thoughts back to the
present. He lifted a brown cloak from a peg beside the
outer door and carefully draped it around Linnet's
shoulders.

His touch summoned Linnet from the melancholy
haze into which she'd been thrown by her blundering
words and her sadness for the pair's doomed love. She
felt that there must be some solution, some way to
alter their long, cold, and lonely course. She looked up
to the man who, leastways in her dreams, had been her
own valiant champion. Surely he could find the key to
unfasten the bar blocking his sister's happiness?

When amber eyes lifted questioningly to him,
Rhys's wry half-smile returned. He knew what Linnet
wordlessly sought, but he also knew too well the
impossibility of providing a welcome answer. Instead
of giving the only response he could, one dispiriting

albeit honest, he sought to lighten the mood and divert her thoughts to commonplace paths less fraught with rocks and stumble holes.

"Mayhap you deem this garment's warmth unnecessary on such a mild evening?" Rhys purposely misinterpreted her questioning frown, and when the question not honestly meant to elicit an answer received none, he immediately continued. "These are early hours, but as the night progresses, the shroud of darkness will lower its chill about you." As he spoke, Rhys swirled a black cloak around his own shoulders before positioning an ale keg in the crook of each arm and nodding his bright head in a silent request for her to precede him.

Accepting the irrationality of expecting Rhys to perform a miracle, Linnet gave him a resigned smile and then, for the first time since her visit to Newydd Farm, walked through the door and left the Eagle's aerie behind.

Rhys absently snapped a twig between clenched fists and tossed the two halves into a greedy blaze as his penetrating eyes turned from one member of the laughing crowd to another. Some stood while others lounged on bed furs and coverlets spread in a loose circle around the bonfire. He'd already closely examined each of the merry participants in the near consumed feast, but he'd discovered no evidence of the injury he sought, yet dreaded to find. 'Twas a failure perversely able to lift his spirits.

While her brother's brooding gaze settled upon the ever-shifting flames, Grannia settled herself atop an upended firewood round and pulled her graceful harp back against her shoulder. With eyes closed and cheek resting against its frame, she stroked a multitude of strings, coaxing from them the swirling sounds of a familiar and much loved ballad, which swept a hush across the crowd. Even the two boys, who'd been playfully wrestling, went quiet.

Clasped hands supported and provided a pillow for his head as Rhys settled back on furs shared with the small party come from his home. Firelight gleamed on golden hair, a stark contrast to the darkness all around, while fathomless eyes studied a view becoming too important.

Heavy lashes rested on Linnet's soft cheeks, and her tightly entwined fingers lay among the scarlet-hued folds covering her lap. Oblivious to any human, she surrendered to magical music carrying her spirits heavenward. Never before had she heard such sweet, rippling notes or a melody of such incredible beauty. Even moments after the last note, trembling like a fragile dewdrop on the tip of a twig, faded into silence Linnet remained lost in its lingering warmth.

"You enjoyed Grannia's harp playing?"

Rhys's low question summoned Linnet from mists of enchantment a moment before enthusiastic applause erupted. Blinking repeatedly, Linnet sought to focus on tentacles of towering flame reaching up from the blaze's base far into the black night sky. She struggled back to the present cheery celebration and the company of people she'd expected to resent her but who, though few spoke either French or Saxon, had instead been friendly and had accepted the hostage's presence without visible distaste.

Suddenly aware to her depths of the Eagle's steady gaze, Linnet turned toward him. Fortunately her dazed expression made her feelings clear, for she failed to find words sufficient to express her awed admiration of his sister's music. Rhys gifted her with an honest smile utterly lacking in its usual cynicism. That action, however, merely reinforced her sense of being lost in a realm of enchantment where existed not only heavenly melodies but fantasy heroes as well.

When amber eyes turned to molten honey, Rhys sat up and very nearly bent his head to taste the sweetness on her lips. The invisible bonds drawing him to a forbidden kiss were shattered by the first chords of a raucous tune played on the lute, wood pipes, and timbrels many had brought to these public festivities. Rhys abruptly pulled away while his smile took on a sharp edge, which, had Linnet but known it, was full of self-contempt for his repeated fall to temptations heightened by the impossible dreams recently invading the hours of his days and nights. To divert any attention drawn by his injudicious reaction, Rhys immediately blended his deep voice with those of his people already singing a tune he'd learned during long years in Normandy and later taught to them.

Beneath Rhys's sardonic smile Linnet felt doubly a fool—first, for her inability to express admiration of Grannia's harp playing and second, for her continuing wrongful response to him. Aye, Linnet silently confessed, she'd yearned upward toward a longed-for kiss and again had given the too attractive man excuse to charge her with pursuing him. Recent days of relative harmony made her the more loath to jeopardize their fragile accord. To repress the fears and anxieties aroused by the possibility, she too joined the repetitive chorus of a song often sung in Radwell's great hall.

Having been entranced by her voice since first he'd heard her speak, Rhys was not surprised that her singing flowed like a thread of pure gold through the dross of all the others. For inasmuch as Linnet had been enchanted by the melody of Grannia's harp, he and soon the whole of Cymer's people were held enthralled by her singing. 'Twas as true and lovely as ever the harp's music had been.

One voice after another fell silent until Linnet found herself singing alone and faltered to a halt. Embarrassment sent an inferno to burn her cheeks and twine her fingers so tightly together they were white against the bright gown. She was deeply uncomfortable as the center of attention.

Oh, aye, she'd had a lifetime of sitting, an insignificant extra, with her father at the high table, but the audience in Castle Radwell was composed of those she'd known since birth. Her only experiences in any way comparable to this distressing public spectacle were the occasions when she'd been called to serve as hostess while prospective mates covertly examined her. Plainly, the viewers had seen nothing to entice them into a longer relationship, for at the advanced age of eighteen, she was a still unwed though most maids were wed leastways by fifteen.

Linnet wanted to sink into the ground when an utterly unexpected mixture of clapping and cheers rang out. Failing that retreat, she buried her hot face in her open hands.

"We here in Wales have a deep appreciation for lyrical tales . . . and musical talents." Rhys explained the boisterous response to the self-conscious damsel. "When we meet in gatherings such as this, all of those present are encouraged to share their best efforts at whatever talent they possess."

"All paltry compared to the delight of your singing" —Owain, who had been half reclining on Linnet's left, rose up to offer the sincere compliment and then cast a sidelong glance at the woman on his other side—"and Grannia's harp playing."

From around Owain's broad shoulder, Grannia, blushing at the admiring words given her, smiled a warm echo of the man's appreciation for Linnet's sweet voice.

"'Struth." Rhys nodded, setting firelight rippling over his shining hair. "Pray accept our appreciation as the gift it is meant to be. Then we'll continue sharing our lesser abilities with you."

Naming herself a greater fool for a reaction drawing this further attention, Linnet forced herself to meet the eyes of the curiously watching crowd and give them a shy smile and soft thanks, which Rhys repeated in their language. Under the cover of another tune begun, she looked past the bearded bear to the wistful beauty sitting near her forbidden love.

"Grannia," Linnet began, determined to right the wrong in not giving praise much deserved, "the music you charm from your magical instrument is the sweetest ever I have heard." Linnet spoke not only to give a warranted compliment but, too, in hopes of showing her remorse for the earlier uncomfortable scene in the Eagle's home caused by her ill-informed tongue. "'Twas a joy—nay, more a privilege—to listen to you play."

Pleasure warmed Grannia's face as she wordlessly accepted both the praise for her music and the regret for an unintended hurt. Thought of the latter shifted her attention toward a companion in pain. Plainly Owain also had heard the oblique apology, for his fingertips were brushing through the short curls on his cheek and chin—a habit far more revealing than the emotionless expression on his face.

While the four adults in Prince Rhys's party were preoccupied with compliments and apologies, the second song ended. Then rose, in answer to rhythmic clapping and calls of "Ewais, Ewais," a tall, thin man all thick joints and awkward movements.

"Ewais is our most talented tale spinner," Rhys quietly told the two Norman hostages, explaining why the crowd had called for the man. "Each year 'tis he who recounts again the events we're here to honor."

Even before Rhys's brief explanation ended, the man began to move, and his gangling body seemed magically transformed. While Ewais's voice rose and fell with the drama of his tale, his body flowed in a reenactment of awesome feats, a dark silhouette against a flickering background of orange and yellow flames.

Rhys softly translated the Welsh words, but 'twas hardly necessary, as the speaker's pantomimed deeds and wildly exaggerated expressions were near enough to tell the story alone. At the last, Ewais crumpled to the ground, winter defeated. No sound save the crackling fire dared break the hush before, in an instant, he leapt triumphantly into the air with arms flung wide and a brilliant smile to proclaim summer's freedom and return to earth.

During the moment of peace following tumultuous applause, an excited David's young voice was piercing.

"Alan, show them *your* skill for mimicry."

The boy's face flushed a ruddy hue while about it whipped strands of honey-brown hair. "Nay, 'twould not be right."

"Oh, get on with you." David encouragingly thumped his friend's back and looked to Linnet, seeking added support. "But for his size, he'd make you think you were looking at Rhys himself. You shared your talent. Tell him he ought share his, too."

Rather than urging her brother to do the deed, Linnet fell into an anxious silence. She'd seen a goodly number of the impressions David had done of folks around Radwell. He was good at it, and they *were* funny . . . but his characterizations were most often wicked parodies of his targets' less admirable traits.

Without waiting for the lady's urgings, David spoke in the Welsh tongue to call for the entire company's attention. When with a flourish he waved toward Alan, it was too late to forestall the deed now promised.

Sensing Owain's sudden stillness, Linnet glanced sidelong and read his apprehension. Plainly he was as uncertain of the wisdom in this performance as she. Her head turned toward the golden man about to be mimicked. Rhys's head was tilted to one side, and curiosity gleamed in dark eyes.

Caught in a vise by the multitude of eyes boring into him, Alan felt he had no choice but to do what they awaited. First he placed his palms over his face and spread his fingers. When he lowered his hands, a replica of their prince's mocking half-smile looked back at them.

Only the sounds of breath caught and a few audible gasps broke the silence of an audience aghast and open-mouthed at both the boy and the man whose expression he'd mimicked.

Rhys threw his head back and with a roar of laughter shattered the tense moment. His reaction freed those watching so closely to join in his merriment. Their attention quickly turned to a new diversion, and people not too sotted rose with the intention of dancing to the rollicking music and happy beat of timbrels and pipes.

While dancers brave enough to risk trampled feet enthusiastically flung themselves into the hazardous whirl, Rhys leaned forward and laid his hand over the shoulder of the still uneasy boy. "You've an unusual talent, a fine accomplishment very few can claim. In one expression you captured me. How did you do it?"

A relieved Alan shook his head modestly but beamed nonetheless. "'Twas easy. Merely did I reproduce my brother Mark's expression—" For a moment his lips compressed. Then he made a sheepish admission. "I had to work at it a long time before I acquired the ability to imitate him. So, you see, mimicking you was not so fine an accomplishment after all."

"That you succeeded in the first instance makes it a fine accomplishment." The flash of Rhys's white smile was a renewal of his compliment, but he continued with a question in the words' inflection. "Your brother?" Although he knew the answer already, Rhys wanted to hear it and more from Alan's own lips.

"Wel-l-l." Alan shrugged and explained. "Mark is my *half* brother. He's older than me, older than Linnet, too. Moreover, we don't see him very often, as he is a part of Prince Henry's retinue." Soft brown eyes glowed with admiration, and he stated his brother's position so proudly 'twas almost a boast.

"I see." Rhys nodded, tempering his amusement into an indulgent smile. "Although I have none, by watching Owain and David I've learned how important brothers can be." Dark eyes shifted to the Norman damsel. "Is it the same for sisters?"

Linnet had been distracted by Alan's explanation of how he'd come to mimic Rhys. How had she failed to notice before that Rhys's smile was in truth much like Mark's? But the power of a penetrating gaze summoned her attention to his difficult question.

"Alan is assuredly important to me, but I hardly know Mark." Thought of the seldom-seen brother shadowed her gaze with faint puzzlement, and she nibbled at her lower lip while attempting to identify what position he inhabited in her world. On the few occasions when she'd been in Mark's company, he'd never spoken to her, but his silver-gray eyes surreptitiously glared at her as if she'd done him some ill.

Seeing what distress his probing had caused Linnet, and certain she truly knew little more, Rhys leaned closer, intending to keep her from falling back into gloom by inviting her to join the dancers.

"Would you . . ." Before he could finish, another spoke.

"Prince Rhys." Pywell's grimace accompanied his apology for interrupting. "Prithee pardon, but that which you've awaited has arrived."

On the folded parchment hastily thrust into Rhys's hands Linnet saw her father's seal. Her heart thudded uncomfortably as she watched Rhys break it open. With a restraint Linnet found maddening, he neatly unfolded the crackling sheet while she fervently wished for the ability to read the unknown marks scrawled across its pale surface. Had her father given in to the Eagle's demands? Did this mean she and Alan would soon be returned to Castle Radwell? Linnet imperceptibly shrank from the document as if its script contained some deadly poison.

Too soon her questions would have answers. The difficulty now lay in the chore of untangling wrongly mingled and terribly muddled emotions. That her father had responded within the time limit set brought relief . . . and regret. This seemingly innocent sheet meant the death knell to friendships just begun and a return to loneliness at the center of Radwell's many. But most disheartening, this was the end to hours spent in her fantasy hero's company. Struth, Prince Rhys of Cymer was her father's enemy and thus hers as well. Nonetheless, Linnet had seen and heard enough to be certain he was in reality all she'd dreamed he would be: honorable, loyal, courageous . . . and too much more.

After what to Linnet seemed hours, Rhys glanced her way. Though he immediately shifted his attention to Pywell, in one brief glimpse into his dark eyes she read the parchment's message as surely as if she'd been miraculously taught in an instant to decipher the meaningless marks.

"Pywell, go to Milo. Instruct him to have my steed and Owain's prepared and waiting with the dawn." As he spoke, Rhys passed the parchment across Linnet and into the waiting hands of his bearded friend.

As night shadows swallowed the retreating messenger's slender form, Rhys turned again to the damsel apprehensively watching through widened eyes of bruised-pansy brown.

"Come, I'll take you back to the house while Owain leads Alan to his farm." The voice, all of gentleness, made Linnet's heart ache the more.

The two boys sitting a small distance in front of the adults, giggling at the antics of people ale-robbed of whatever ability they might have possessed but nonetheless stumbling through intricate dance steps, heard only the talk of leaving. They turned in unison to protest an early departure. The forbidding grimness of the men's faces quashed their pleas unspoken.

"To be best prepared for the morn's long walk, you'll need rest." Rhys quietly answered Alan's silent confusion.

"We're going back to Radwell?" Alan's reed-brittle

voice hovered in a bewildering limbo between excitement and tears.

Feeling her own tears treacherously near to overbrimming, Linnet risked no words but rather rose from her position on the bed fur spread atop dewdamp grass with what grace she could manage—a task made difficult by hours spent sitting awkwardly curled on the cold ground.

"Grannia will help see the two boys home," Owain said, "and once they are settled for the night, I'll escort her back to you." Owain met the prince's dark eyes with a belligerence daring Rhys to refuse the offer.

Rhys blinked in surprise, but knowing how oversensitive his friend must surely be to the secret revealed by Linnet's too clear-sighted gaze and blundering words, he merely smiled and nodded agreement. Why should he deny Owain and Grannia the pleasure of each other's company when he would count as a gift this excuse for a last private hour with Linnet?

While the two men quietly talked of the morrow's plans, a discomfited Linnet kept her gaze demurely upon the flickering patterns cast by ever-moving flames. What would the people think to see their lord leave so early—and alone—with his female hostage?

Fool! What notice could those so far lost in drunken antics give the deed? Even had one been sane enough to limit his intake, he'd have no right to question his lord. Belike, Linnet ruefully acknowledged, such suspicions were no more than the product of her own wishful thoughts. Under a stab of self-disgust, rather than nibbling her lip she bit it—hard. But the resulting pain failed to stem the rising liquid threatening to lay shiny tracks down her cheeks.

"Come," Rhys whispered into the ear of a plainly upset damsel. "Owain will explain to others the need for our leave-taking."

Linnet obediently turned toward the shadowed forest. However, she had no notion how to retrace their path when even trampled grass and broken ferns were hidden by swirling ground fog and darkness intensified by the bright flames at her back.

Rhys lifted a small hand and laid it atop his uplifted forearm. When she glanced his way, the crystal brightness of her unshed tears smote his heart with regret equal to hers. Donning a charming smile and with the gallantry of any honorable knight escorting his lady-love into a royal court, he set off to lead her into misty shadows.

As an honorable knight in truth, Rhys admitted—leastways to himself—how he dreaded the looming moment when he must relinquish his sweet hostage. This return walk would be their last time alone. He moved slowly, Linnet gladly matched her step to his, and all the while the silence between them reverberated with aching awareness.

Despite their dawdling pace, they soon left the celebration's light and sound behind, lost unmourned in muffling mists and depths of a night faintly glowing with newly risen moonlight. As Linnet walked beside Rhys, her desperate pleasure increased by the knowledge that this was her last opportunity, Linnet reveled in his warmth and strength. Her handsome escort seemed in no haste to reach their destination. Was it possible that he regretted the end of her time in his hold as deeply as did she? Twining her free hand into scarlet linen, she mentally scoffed at the notion as merely more wishful thinking by a lovelorn maiden doomed by limited charms to dream in vain.

Preoccupied with bleak thoughts, she stumbled and surely would have fallen had her escort not wrapped a strong arm about her shoulders and pulled her close to his powerful form. Once in his hold, Linnet was determined not to forfeit this last opportunity to win memories to hoard as kindling for the fire of dreams that would have to last her a lifetime. She turned full into his embrace, wrapped her arms around his back, and mindlessly nestled against his broad chest. His muscles, flexing involuntarily beneath the crush of her abundant curves, were a revealing response and put a soft smile on the face she lifted to him.

He'd halted only to secure his tender hostage's balance and see her safe. Knocked off-balance by the feeling of her body melting hungrily into his, Rhys caught his breath and looked down into eyes of molten honey. His jaw went tight, as he recognized the deed for another grave mistake among the many that had littered his honorable path.

Fearful that the vexation threatening to squelch the desire burning in his dark gaze would see her set aside, Linnet lowered her lashes. Closed eyes left her free to drink in the delicious masculine scent beckoning her nearer still to the big body doing thrilling things to her senses.

Taking terrible pleasure in her willing surrender, though scorning himself for a fool, Rhys fell unrepentant to temptation. Surely, he thought, justifying an action he could not restrain, one final kiss, one last embrace, would be no threat to his honorable oath. On the morrow he would, as sworn, return her pure and unharmed to her father—after this further taste of forbidden fruit.

Sweeping one hand down the long arch of Linnet's back, Rhys pulled her deeper into his embrace and aligned her hips more intimately against his. The other hand yielded to an earlier temptation and gently pulled free the golden ribbons restraining her glossy tresses. Having loosened the braids, he combed his fingers through the luxuriant satin curtain before gently cradling the back of her head to hold her mouth steady while he took a kiss, long and slow and hard.

Linnet moaned beneath the sensuous assault, and at the wild sound Rhys deepened their contact to a sweet torment. Caught up in a whirlwind of fire, she clung to its steady center, instinctively savoring the strength of his broad back. When the hot pleasure of his mouth shifted to brush tantalizing kisses over her cheeks and find the sensitive hollows beneath her ears, Linnet's head fell back, laying her long, elegant throat vulnerable to a tongue tip trailing fire down to the dip at its base.

Rhys was no more able to resist this innocent invitation of a bared throat than he'd been able to reject her initial embrace. He savored skin like delicate rose petals and took pleasure in the wildly accelerated pulse beneath, pausing at the tie of her front-laced gown only long enough to loosen the restraints. His mouth then dipped down to nuzzle the tops of the lush breasts he longed to see, ached to taste.

Linnet gasped at hot sensations beyond bearing and, overcome by the liquid heat flowing through her veins, wound her fingers into his thick golden hair, urging him nearer to an intimate caress unknown but fervently sought. She clung to him, shivering beneath the fire of his mouth.

"Ohhh . . ." A feminine gasp and a stifled giggle effectively brought Rhys's head up although he held close the damsel trembling and too lost in passion's haze to safely stand alone. He glared at the young woman clinging to an equally young man. Plainly they'd slipped deep into the forest seeking privacy for a little love play and just as plainly thought they'd caught their prince and his hostage enjoying the same. Rhys's fierce scowl was directed as much at himself as at the intruders. Only by their timely interruption had their assumption been proven in error. No matter his fine intents, Rhys had very nearly forfeited his honor and forsworn his oath to claim the honey-sweet virgin.

"Pray pardon, milord." The boy-man's voice broke, and he turned a hue so amazingly bright it glowed even in moonlight. Never before had he seen such coldness on his prince's face. Even under the most difficult circumstances the strong warrior's smile was rarely absent, albeit too often either lacking in humor or filled with mockery.

While Rhys sent the pair a grim smile and lifted a hand to wave the awkward apology aside, Linnet became shockingly aware of just how complete had been her surrender to this man who embodied the contradiction of foe and hero. She would willingly—nay, gladly—have given him the one possession a well-born female was taught from birth to protect as her most precious possession—her virtue. She could only beg divine forgiveness and thank the saints that he had not succeeded in fully opening her gown and shamefully baring her not to his view alone but to that of the intruders as well.

Turned and firmly propelled down the homeward path by a man gone to solid ice, a confused and heartsore Linnet still could not truthfully claim she regretted their passionate interlude . . . too likely the last she would ever know.

7

As if in a last defiant display of its fading power, the slanted rays of a low-riding sun pierced the forest's green ceiling and dappled the ground to which Linnet had just been lowered. For long silent moments amber eyes gazed up at the extraordinary man still seated astride his steed, seeking to imprint in her memory the flesh-and-blood image of her fantasy hero—likely her last sight of him. Rhys truly was stunningly handsome with his charming, though constantly mocking half-smile, golden hair wind-brushed back over broad shoulders, ebony eyes so deep she would willingly have drowned in them. Once again she acknowledged that here in this forbidden Welsh prince was everything she dreamed her perfect hero would be—powerful and strong, gentle and just. Aye, these things and so much more that, though it might have been the act of a traitor, she had given him the unsought gift of her heart.

Behind his cynical mask, Rhys silently chided himself for the ache of knowing he would never again enjoy Linnet's company—in spite of his self-lectures on honor and duty to his people. Why, when he'd spent heated hours with a host of willing women and walked away with no twinge of regret, was there pain in watching this little virgin depart from his life? Hah! That question was all too easily answered. She'd proven to be so very different from what he had expected—a paradox in more than the discovery that an initial impression of plainness fell away to reveal a loveliness more real than any he'd ever known. Though an heiress, she was anything but pampered and, despite a basic reticence, quietly brave. Moreover, during their fireside talks she'd revealed a dreamer dwelling inside her dutiful, practical exterior. But, most tantalizing of all, when she was driven by either anger or passion, her fiery spirit burst into flames.

His jaw went hard with self-disgust. This foolish catalog of her many charms served only to deepen his regret at their parting. To combat it he reminded himself that this very regret reinforced a certain truth: the forlorn damsel's departure was a blessing. Elsewise he feared the forfeiture of his honor and her virtue would have been inevitable.

"Godspeed." He reached down to lightly brush a soft cheek robbed of color and gently tap a tension-nibbled lip. "Your anxious father doubtless awaits. Go, calm his fears with reassurances that I have kept my oath and held you safe."

Linnet's face involuntarily tilted into his touch while tears she'd sworn she would not shed suddenly brightened her eyes. "He'll see that verity for himself." With the strained words, she aimlessly motioned toward her scarlet-garbed self, but still she could not turn away.

These last touches and final words were precious. The more so as during the long journey, both on foot and ahorse, they had said little, although at the outset she'd tried to draw him into conversation. Other than brief responses to specific questions he'd hardly spoken at all, except when she had asked why he and his supporters kept their steeds so far distant from their homes. With wry laughter he'd explained.

"In thick forests and over steep countryside horses are of little value to us. Too big to slip silently through dense trees, they'd be more liability than aid and likely leave a trail where we would rather have none. Besides, on foot we can move with greater stealth—and more deadly force." At the memory of that last real conversation, far from personal, a single droplet crested the rim of one eye and slipped down a pale cheek.

Following that tear's path, Rhys's dark gaze flared with golden sparks of shared pain. Beneath his intense scrutiny, Linnet realized she could linger no longer. Taking a deep breath she resolutely turned away from the embodiment of impossible wishes and looked toward where, beyond a thin barrier of trees and bushes, stood Radwell Castle.

Inside its strong walls waited a loving father, Meara, and other friends. Friends? Were they really that? After a lifetime in their company, she couldn't claim to know any save the first two as well as, in less than a sennight, she'd come to know Rhys, Grannia, and the two brothers at Newydd Farm. Radwell's serfs and the men of its garrison offered her respect and aid in whatever she required—but never friendship. Only her dreams had provided comfort for the chill of a lonely heart, and now, with experience of both warm companionship and fiery delights, she worried that her flimsy visions would provide more distress than happiness. The prospect of a desolate future seemed to manacle leaden chains to the feet that must carry her away.

"Linnet, let's be off!" Already a few steps into the final strip of woodland, Alan was impatient. Despite the sadness he'd felt in bidding farewell to David, with the resilience of his age his thoughts had soon shifted to anticipation of the return home. His sister's apparent reluctance to depart with any haste was irritating.

Forcing a brittle smile to her lips and motion to heavy limbs, Linnet stepped forward to join her brother in breaking through the last shadowy barrier. She refused to glance behind her, as one more glimpse would only deepen the ache of loss already begun.

You hypocrite, she reprimanded herself. Spouting noble sentiments when in actual fact looking back with tears blurring your eyes you'd doubtless turn awkward—again. In truth, you haven't the courage to risk leaving him with a memory of you inelegantly fallen at his feet.

Earth freshly plowed but left fallow marked the way leading toward a steep hill and the forbidding tower at its summit. After leaving the unplanted ground, the pair strode through neat rows of new-sprouted crops while a sun very near the end of its day's journey peeked through a scattering of gauzy clouds to dapple their uneven path with light and shadow, a reflection of Linnet's unsettled emotions.

Though the journey to Rhys's home had taken most of a full night, their return to Radwell had occupied an even larger portion of daylight. Plainly, once ahorse, they'd been carried home by a most circuitous route to be certain their trail could not easily be retraced.

Alan sprinted the last short distance while the creaking of heavy chains heralded both the lowering of the drawbridge and the raising of the portcullis. That the defensive barriers had been left in place in the first instance deepened Linnet's frown. Seemed her father had feared the shrewd Welsh prince might seize the opportunity in the weak moment of an unguarded welcome to attack this nearly impregnable keep. Immediately Linnet spurned such reasoning. Firstly, 'twas an unjust insult to Rhys's honor; secondly, it was an irrational alarm. Attacking Radwell itself would be a foolish, useless action, and surely even her father knew the Eagle was too intelligent to contemplate such a futile assault when no goal would it win. The Eagle had promised to see Linnet and Alan safely returned in exchange for the return of Grannia's dower lands. Rhys had kept his part of the bargain, and so long as her father had done as demanded, he had nothing to fear. He *had* done what he'd sworn to do, he *had* summoned his mercenaries from the lands in question . . . hadn't he?

Once the drawbridge's thick planks lay across the wide moat and the iron grillwork had been lifted so high its sharp ends appeared to be teeth in the upper jaw of the gate's gaping mouth, Alan ran into his sire's open arms. Linnet's already slow pace nearly came to a stop. A peculiar array of people formed the front row of a crowd gathered to watch the hostages' return. Her father, having dropped to his knees to hug his precious heir, gave little attention to the damsel confused by the presence of the two men flanking him.

Her brooding half brother, Mark, stood proudly aloof on the earl's right. Earl Godfrey had never hesitated to show that his older son, though illegitimate, was as well beloved as either of his right-born children. How else, when Mark's darkly handsome image was so nearly a replica of the earl's own visage. Seven years Linnet's senior, Mark had rarely visited Radwell since he'd been sent to be fostered at the royal court in Normandy. She hardly knew the man he'd become as a member of Prince Henry's entourage, and she was startled to see him now.

The Saxon lord on her father's left was not such a surprise. Osric, as Alan's foster father and once her prospective mate, might be expected to show concern for the two who'd been taken by force. He was, leastways to Linnet's mind, near of an age with her father. Though his thinning hair was blond it was diluted by streaks of muddy brown and iron gray and nowise as bright as the Eagle's. Linnet gave her head a

brief shake to banish doomed comparisons able only
to remind her of what could never be hers.

When Godfrey rose to sweep his beloved daughter
into a hearty embrace, Alan turned to the half brother
he greatly admired. Linnet watched the older sibling's
eyes, a chill gray that had never warmed to her, glitter
down into the boy's upturned and openly adoring
face.

"Mark, we've had an adventure, and I've learned
amazing things!"

"Amazing things, hmmm?" Mark laughed and
rumpled his guileless sibling's hair. "Come, Mouse,
let's go and search out a quiet corner in the hall where
you can tell me about your adventure and everything
you've learned."

Grinning at his hero's affectionate name for him—
because as a babe he'd crawled about like a fat little
rodent—Alan trustingly laid his hand into the larger
one offered and began a rapid litany as they turned
toward the crowd, which parted for them.

A subdued Linnet followed, hand resting upon the
upraised forearm of the father who in public expected
demure quiet and downcast eyes from all well-bred
women and thus found nothing unusual in her less
than bubbling response to this return. 'Twas said by
the whole of Radwell that Earl Godfrey doted upon
his daughter, but they had not taken time to notice
that she'd earned his approval by unquestioning obedience.

They traversed a long tunnel through a thick stone
wall to enter the tower proper. No natural light
penetrated this huge chamber at ground level, but the
brightness of a roaring central fire nearly made useless
the tallow candles on iron stands behind the dais and
the resin-soaked torches placed at intervals along
opposite walls.

As Linnet stepped into the room, Meara bustled
forward to overwhelm the younger woman in a
smothering hug.

"You're home now." Meara leaned back and gave a

disgusted scowl at the linen gown begrimed by a day's travel. "So, my wee lamb, come, let me see you bathed and changed into fresh garb for the feast being laid to celebrate your safe return." The welcoming embrace shifted to an adamant tugging. "I've got your favorite cream gown in readiness and the forest-hued silk undergown that makes such a pretty contrast."

"Hold, there." Before Linnet could be hustled up the winding stairway built within the thickness of one corner wall, Earl Godfrey dropped a heavy restraining hand on the shoulder of his daughter's determined shepherd.

Meara cast the earl a glare, daring him to keep her from her self-appointed duty.

"'Tis important that another matter be addressed before we all are seated at table to enjoy the promised meal." Godfrey gave a disdainful smile to the woman who, on behalf of her charges, rarely hesitated to fight his control. "I command you to see Linnet join me and Lord Osric in my chamber as soon as she is bathed and dressed."

Meara huffily responded with a brisk nod before urging Linnet to ascend the steps, which were poorly lit by widely spaced firebrands braced in iron rings driven into the stone walls.

As she climbed, Linnet felt her already despondent heart sink even lower. A meeting with her father and the Saxon . . . alone. It could mean only one thing: an unpleasant and unwelcome bargain had been struck.

While Meara quickly prepared a bath in Linnet's bedchamber, Mark sat in the hall below with his young brother. He wore an unnatural smile upon his lips, but it could not forestall a deepening frown as he listened to Alan, like an irrepressible mountain spring, bubbling with the pure, clear tales of his recent days. The boy gave glowing descriptions of the marvels of wrestling, hunting without weapons, and the incredible celebration of Gwyn ap Nudd. But, most importantly, he proudly recounted how, under the

Eagle's tutelage, he'd succeeded in mastering a skill at which he'd had a previous lengthy record of failure.

During past visits to Radwell Mark had been vaguely annoyed by the boy's constant dogging of his every step, but to now hear such admiration of other men—and Welshmen at that—earned a fierce vexation.

"So, under the Welsh prince's tutelage you have mastered the art of swordsmanship?" A dark head tilted questioningly to one side, caught a white light as cold as the gleam in his gray eyes. "You must come to the practice yard with me one day soon and show me what you've learned."

Soft brown eyes glowed golden at the prospect of time willingly given him by the brother who seldom had time for him. "Tomorrow?" It was a breathless question full of hope.

Before Mark could answer, a servant who'd come close while Alan chattered without pause took the opportunity to clear his throat and interrupt the brothers' exchange. When icy gray eyes looked his way, the never brave Darrell fell a step back but remained determined to deliver the message, as his lord had bidden him.

"You are summoned to your father's chamber, Sir Mark. And he prays you will make haste to answer his summons."

Mark negligently shrugged and with inherent grace slowly rose to respond. But when he made to turn away, Alan piped up with a question, in truth more a plea.

"Shouldn't I go to our father, too?"

"Nay, young sir." Darrell's voice softened with affection as he refused the youngster's suggestion. "You are off to bathe and be fresh for the celebration of your homecoming."

Alan's open expression revealed an internal war between anticipation of the evening's festivities and disappointment at being excluded from the discussion of surely important matters. In the end he had no choice and accompanied Darrell to the bath awaiting him in his own small room while Mark continued on to the lord's chamber.

A single step into her father's chamber Linnet paused. Without glancing her way, Godfrey raised his hand and waved her to a small stool. She quietly closed the door and settled where he'd directed. Often enough before she'd come to hear his decision on matters regarding her only to be motioned to wait while he finished some item of estate business or military tactics. At no earlier time had she, as a female whose life revolved around the myriad small tasks required to see the castle smoothly run, been in any way interested in the topics her father discussed with the men of his garrison. She soon discovered this was different, very different.

"We are agreed, then?" Wasting no notice on his daughter's unimportant presence, Godfrey turned a penetrating stare from his raven-haired older son to the Saxon lord. "On the morrow when he arrives to retake the lands I justly seized by right of battle, we'll be waiting and put an end to his delusions—a final end." Lips grimly compressed echoed the determination revealed by the earl's tightly clenched fists.

Mark gave a brief nod while Osric's pleased smile would have frightened a man less focused. Indeed, it did frighten Linnet. But then, Linnet was horrified by the whole situation. No name had been spoken, but she had no doubt of whom they spoke, no doubt but that the father who had taught her the meaning of honor and whom she'd believed to be the epitome of all noble traits meant to forswear his oath, to trap and take revenge upon an enemy. Worse still, the blade of that revenge would plainly be aimed to deliver a mortal blow to Rhys.

She had to do something to forestall that wicked end. She must! But what? Blind to the other occupants of the chamber, she failed to notice as Mark departed, leaving his sister alone with her father and the Saxon.

"And now, Linnet." Godfrey's gentle smile failed to completely shield a distaste for what next he must do. "The time has come when I must renounce my selfishness in refusing offers of honorable alliances in order to keep you home and ever near."

Linnet frowned. Never had she been told of matches refused, but this news, which once might have gone some distance toward increasing her self-confidence, was of but momentary interest while serious dangers loomed. She steeled herself to hold her expression blank and shield her growing distress from her father's view. The clear-spoken threat to Rhys was near overwhelming of itself, but the announcement her father was doubtless about to make was the one raindrop too much that would cause a bucket filled with thousands to overflow. Feeling a suffocating panic rising, she curled her fingers into the pale ivory of the gown Meara had given her to don upon leaving the tub.

"Once the morn's distasteful business is finished, we will return here where Father Anselm will be waiting to bless the betrothal between you and our friend, Lord Osric." Godfrey waved toward the Saxon, and Linnet's gaze unwillingly followed the motion and fell victim to the disgustingly predatory gleam in Osric's narrowed gray eyes.

"Worry not." Osric chose to misinterpret the reason for brown eyes gone dark. "Our business with my foolish nephew will require little time and likely we'll return by the midday hour." Seeing the damsel's faint surprise at the title he'd given for the foe to be met, Osric relished explaining family relationships to her, who should have been told these important facts by her father years past. "My oldest sister, Emma, married Prince Griffith and bore first Rhys and then Grannia. My second sister, Morwena, is Mark's mother."

Welcoming even a brief respite from the unwelcome prospect of a repugnant bond, Linnet quickly assimilated Osric's account. This unpleasant creature had nothing in common with Mark save gray eyes. However, Osric's kinship claims also revealed her half brother and Rhys as cousins. Between those two, thanks to Alan's mimicry the past evening, she had already noted a similarity, leastwise in cynical smiles much alike.

"You'll have until next autumn to plan your wedding finery." Osric's gloating tone grated. "And, of course, to choose what you will bring with you to your new home in Northland Hall."

His words forced Linnet to face what she would rather have ignored. She wanted to scream a protest, to beg her father for a reprieve, but one glance in his direction revealed a glimpse of his own disgust for the matter. By recognition of the fact that her father was no more pleased than she, it became clear to her that somehow this Saxon had forced the choice upon the earl. Osric apparently held some power over her father, one doubtless of strength enough to disallow a positive response to any argument she might make against the union.

Attempting to block thoughts of the dreaded betrothal, Linnet stared down at the rush-strewn floor, absently noting that it needed to be swept and the rushes replaced. Even images of an unhappy future were knocked aside with ease by the hideous monster roused in her mind by a far more devastating and much nearer danger. She would waste not a moment more on thoughts of her own future until she had found some way to ensure Rhys would have one.

"The foodstuffs are growing cold, and our people cannot fall upon them until you appear, though they're almost certainly making free with barrels of ale." Linnet gave her father the best imitation of a teasing smile she could muster. "Surely we should descend to the hall and commence the meal before both a fine feast and the people's temper have soured?" She needed time to silently ponder fearsome challenges—and to find answers. Her best hope perversely lay in the crowd, the savory dishes, and the abundant drinks that would distract the men's attention and thus provide the female her father had trained to sit quiet and demure with the privacy she sought.

"Ah, you've the right of it, daughter." A widely smiling Godfrey offered his arm to Linnet. "Best we not permit clouds of impatience to darken this day of celebration."

Linnet laid her fingers atop the proffered forearm, but dropped her gaze to the floor, intending to prevent the men from seeing her bleak expression. For her the day had not begun as one of wholehearted celebration, and with this evening's news it had become as heavily overcast and stormy as any fierce North Sea gale.

8

THE STABLE, BUILT TO LEAN AGAINST THE TOWER'S STONE
wall, was dark and quiet. Resting horses barely stirred
when Linnet slipped from shadow to shadow. Fortunately even the stableboy was feasting upon his lord's
bounty, like every one of Radwell's people who'd
received and were physically able to answer their
lord's summons to a celebration for the safe return of
his own. 'Twas why the gates were still open. In fear of
a Welsh attack accompanying his children's return,
her father had ordered the cold greeting of portals
barred and guarded. But the lack of an assault then
had apparently eased his fears. Now the drawbridge
was down and the portcullis raised to welcome all who
would come to join the festivities. Aye, the portal was
open . . . but guarded.

Linnet looked regretfully from her gentle palfrey to
her father's massive warhorse. Never had she
mounted a steed so huge or attempted to control
something of such power, but tonight's task required
her to take extraordinary actions. Determined to right
the deadly consequences of her father's wrong in
reneging on his oath, she meant to mount Thunder,

a horse of far greater speed and stamina than her gentle mare, and ride out to warn Rhys of the danger.

She had slipped away from the feast when it began to grow rowdy, as any well-bred damsel ought, but hadn't retreated to her chamber as doubtless her father expected. Although wishing she could exchange her cream linen garb for clothing sturdier and of a hue less conspicuous, she feared the delay in any deed not absolutely necessary. Besides, Linnet knew that had anyone caught sight of her in garb different from what she'd worn at table, a dangerous curiosity might well have been incited, one possibly leading to a report given her sire in time to forestall her intent. Thus she'd been left to use her thick dark cloak as a shield for the ivory gown and silken undergown, which was deep green but shiny. Leastwise she'd been able to convince Meara of the right in arranging her hair in a single plait down the center of her back. Though held in place by a fine green ribbon, 'twould be the most practical style for this night's excursion.

Leaning against the central roof support, a tree trunk stripped of branches and bark, Linnet used thoughts of Rhys mortally injured by treachery to whip her never strong courage into a foment. Such bravery, rarely needed before her hero had appeared in the flesh, would be necessary to meet the challenges ahead. Afraid her bravado might fail were she to linger too long before putting it to use, her impatience grew with every moment she waited for Alan to appear. His aid she needed—to hoist a weighty saddle atop the fearsome beast and then to bait an all-important trap.

Early in the evening's festivities, she'd called for Alan to help her locate, in an upper-level storeroom, the additional goblets needed for a greater number of guests than had been anticipated—a task rightfully performed by serfs. Her brother had not appreciated being assigned such lowly duties, but by her ploy she'd gained moments to speak privately and had persuaded him to lend her support.

First, he would aid in preparing for her escape on an evening ride. She had chosen not to disillusion her young sibling with the news of their sire's wrongful intentions. Second, he would join in a "jest" to be played upon Edolf, the rotund guardsman tonight stationed at the gate. Often had the man unmercifully teased Alan for his lack of talent at elementary swordplay. To prevent being named the spineless, spoiled son of a nobleman and unable to face trouble alone, Alan had chosen not to complain of Edolf's misdeeds to their father.

By their actions this eve, Alan would be provided with a just revenge while she would secure an elsewise impossible opportunity to ride free and unseen from Radwell's hold. To set the plan in motion, Linnet had urged Alan to wait until the throng inside was thoroughly sotted and unlikely to notice or later recall when he slipped away. Having been witness to many ale-soaked feasts, Linnet had no doubt but that such a time would arrive. She spared a moment to wonder how her father could plan an attack and still, the night before, allow the free flow of wine and ale to the men of his garrison.

As Linnet reached this point in mentally repeating her plan for surely the hundredth time, Alan silently appeared at her side, a broad grin on his face. She pointed to an object constructed of metal, wood, and cloth, which had been neatly laid over a low bench. He promptly moved to grasp one end of the saddle, but when he saw which mount she'd chosen for her evening ride, he froze. In an earnest undertone Alan heartily questioned her sanity in making so dangerous a choice. Stifling resentment of precious time lost in the endeavor, Linnet at long last persuaded Alan to grant his *older* sister the right to select what horse she would. Once past that obstacle to the night's plan they set to the task at hand. After a difficult struggle they succeeded in the awkward task of lifting and placing atop the steed's broad back a saddle with an upright bow in front and equally high cantle behind. Giving due respect to the animal's latent power, Alan secured the single breast-band and girth before gingerly moving away.

To set the next and most vital step in motion, by the dim light of a moon barely cresting the horizon, and careful to make no sound, Linnet followed her brother up the wooden stairway built against a stone wall. Their goal was a small alcove within the width of the thick stone wall a few steps below the parapet walk at the castle's top. It was used to store weapons ready for use should an attack be made upon the castle proper.

Alan had long ago perfected his imitation of Meg, a voluptuous and particularly brazen peasant girl. Despite Meg's seemingly shameless ways and ability to keep a great many fellows panting for her attentions, she granted her favors only to those able to richly reward her efforts. Edolf was one of her most ardent admirers, but as a mere guardsman and neither lord nor knight, he pursued her in vain. Tonight Alan would exercise his talent for mimicry to good cause.

Linnet thanked her good fortune upon finding that the alcove door stood ajar. This prevented the unwelcome advance attention of a noisy opening involving creaky iron and leather hinges. Yet, even when they stood just within the complete darkness on either side of the narrow opening, it was far too soon to feel relief.

"Edolf, come to me, sweet Edolf." Alan uttered well-rehearsed lines in a husky feminine voice. "I'm here to give you what you seek, now while the whole company is too ale-fuddled to know what we do." The words slowed to an oozing, sticky syrup. "Come to me. Come to me now."

Despite his prodigious size, as an experienced warrior Edolf whirled with ease to peer toward where descending steps quickly dropped into the darkness beyond the ring of light cast by the castle summit's lone firebrand.

"I've brought tasty treats from the feast you've missed." The voice softly wheedled a man rapidly losing his will to forgo a much desired prize. "Come to me in the wee room where weapons are stored. 'Tis here I await your pleasure."

The breathy sigh accompanying these last words proved too much for Edolf to resist. What difference were he to take a few moments for himself while all others were enjoying so much more? Besides, the earl's enemies would be fools to attack a mighty fortress filled to the brim with experienced warriors. He hurried across the parapet and descended to the chamber in question while the prospect of savoring long-coveted delights crushed into nothing every vestige of prudent caution.

One step into the darkness brought a loud crash. Edolf had bumped into the first in a long line of weapons leaning against the wall.

Edolf muffled a curse. "Sweeting, surely you brought a candle to lend light to our tryst?" No answer, not even a stirring sound, answered his call. He straightened suspiciously . . . too late.

Someone or something landed hard against his back, throwing him to the floor in a heap. While he struggled to turn about, the door slammed shut. Next came an ominous scraping sound from beyond the closed portal—the noise of a metal bar passing through two rings driven into stone on either side of the oaken door. He was trapped!

"Let me out!" Edolf, furious with the female who'd done this to him, added a blistering and rich assortment of most colorful epithets, but ended with one simple and heartfelt. "God's curse upon you, you wretched bitch! *Let me out!*"

His demand fell on unyielding ears. Stifling laughter, which could have betrayed their identity, brother and sister rapidly descended the stairway together, but immediately parted at the bottom. Alan returned to the great hall and rejoined the crowd who'd no more noticed his departure than they noticed his return—not even those who had exercised a measure of restraint in their quaffing of plentiful ale.

Meanwhile, Linnet slipped back into the stable where Thunder awaited her tentative approach with baleful eyes. Taking a deep breath in a vain effort to calm her pounding pulse, Linnet dragged to the steed's side the bench atop which the saddle had rested. Before her craven nature could rob her of every shred of courage, she stepped upon it and launched herself into the saddle for the first and she hoped last time sitting astride. The stirrup leathers were too long for her to rest daintily slippered feet in the metal loops at their ends, and linen skirts settled in odd bunches both in front of and behind her, but she took up the reins and urged Thunder into action.

The mighty stallion remained motionless, plainly unimpressed by the less than imposing creature on his back. Though lacking spurs, Linnet copied an action she'd seen knights take and kicked her heels into the horse's sides. Thunder instantly leapt forward, catching Linnet unprepared. She was fortunate merely to remain ahorse as he raced from the stable and across the drawbridge, hooves pounding a rapid and heavy a beat on wooden planks as if to demonstrate the appropriateness of his name.

Hunched over the high arch of saddle front and clinging desperately to both reins and flowing mane, Linnet realized just how foolish she'd been to think this mode of transport in any way wise. Destriers were trained to obey their masters even amid the blood and clash of fierce battles, but she was in no way Thunder's master! Compared to a man in chain mail, her weight was insignificant, and her hold on reins previously caught in a man's iron grip meant little more to this warhorse than the annoyance of a pesky fly. The notion of controlling and pointing the beast to the path she wished to follow was a fool's jest! The most she could do now was beseech divine powers to see her safely to the ground once again.

Bounced mercilessly up and down while wind tore away the ribbon restraining hair in a single plait, eyes clenched shut in earnest prayer, Linnet had no idea in what direction this flying steed carried her. Nor was she prepared when Thunder abruptly halted. Nonetheless, she screamed as he jerked his mighty head down and tossed her in a tidy somersault right over his ears.

Thumped to the ground, which blessedly was layered with dead leaves and thick grasses, for long moments Linnet couldn't breathe. Finally, gasping for air, through sheer force of will she turned her head and by the light of a moon seemingly resting on treetops caught a fleeting glimpse of Thunder disappearing into the dense shadows of the forest beyond.

Her prayers had been answered, if not quite as she'd hoped. She *was* down and with relative safety. Leastwise she seemed to be all of a piece. Her adventure had only just begun, however. By the look of her surroundings she was deep into forested hills, a fact that surely meant Thunder had carried her into the Welsh princedom of Cymer.

Refusing to permit this hindrance to prevent the successful delivery of a warning to Rhys, Linnet allowed her lashes to fall again—just for a moment to gather thoughts scattered by her jarring fall and to plan what next she'd do. That question was really no question at all. What could she do save find someone, somewhere, able to lead her to Rhys—and with all possible haste! But what direction should she go? Up. The simple answer was "up." By her memory of the night he'd taken her to his home, she knew their path had followed an ever steeper incline. Linnet struggled until she was resting on her elbows, abundant hair loosed by the wild ride into a tangled cloud around her small face.

"How came you here? And why?" The low voice was laced with impatience and more than a little irritation. "Still intent on pursuing me?" The hint of amusement softening the last query was lost on its target.

As deeply shocked as she'd been at the first glimpse of her hero come to life, Linnet blinked against the apparent sorcery of her own wishes, for here stood the magnificent man, all muscle and power, with golden hair glowing in the moonlight. Aye, once again the man had magically appeared—in answer to her silent call?

"I've come seeking you. . . ." Her words faded into silence while she regrouped wildly tangled responses of relief, elation, embarrassment—and anger! His last question found and ignited the faint spark of her temper, and she started over with words spat through gritted teeth.

"I came to save your life, *not* because I have any interest in a pursuit of you." The first was a truth, but the last nearer to a bald-faced lie—and likely he knew it. Still, it saved a few tattered fragments of her pride. To further shift his attention, she turned the attack back upon the one whose sudden appearance was too great a coincidence to go uninvestigated. "How came *you* to the very spot where that wretched horse threw me?"

"A horse threw you?" As if he'd heard nothing but this last piece of news, Rhys dropped to his knees beside the fragile woman so harshly tumbled upon the ground that both her clothing and her hair were in wild disarray. "Are you hurt?" With a light, expert touch he ran his palms over her limbs while derision for his own untimely physical response to enticing glimpses of creamy flesh tilted one corner of his mouth.

"Only my dignity." Linnet's thoughts filled with self-contempt. Leave it to me, she thought, to be found by him while I lie in a graceless heap.

In his cynical smile a despairing Linnet witnessed

the demise of an earlier unacknowledged dream wherein she valiantly delivered a life-saving warning and was welcomed by a grateful and admiring prince. She should have known such a reward was impossible for one who appeared destined never to be more to the man than an occasional diversion and often an annoyance fallen at his feet.

Attempting to scatter that image, Linnet struggled to sit up and winced. Might be nothing was broken, but she would have some wicked bruises to show on the morrow. A wave of dizziness swept away her futile efforts, and she submitted to Rhys's insistence that she lie still a little longer. Nonetheless, she resented him for again looming over her while she lay like some female overcome by his allure . . . but then she very nearly was that. Not a thought to brighten her outlook. Get to the business that brought you here, she scolded herself.

"I came to warn you of a nasty scheme meant to see you dead." She was shamed by the admission of her father's dishonorable design and tightly compressed her lips into an unnaturally harsh line.

"Your father intends to catch me unprepared and lay me low when on the morrow I seek to resume control of Grannia's dower, hmm?"

Even as Rhys spoke he saw the distress in doe-soft eyes for this acceptance of dishonor in a father she'd admired her whole life. He ached for Linnet's pain, an emotion deepening his self-derision as it revealed a further weakening of his defenses against this lovely but forbidden foe turned friend.

Linnet gazed doubtfully at the mockery on his handsome face. Had someone already carried the news to him? How could that be when only her father, her half brother and the Saxon lord knew? 'Struth, the latter two were kin to Rhys, but which of them would willingly play traitor to her father? An instant later she fully recognized a fact that her concern for Rhys had pushed to the background. Her presence here made the title "traitor" properly her own. Despite the consternation caused by that revelation, Linnet was unrepentant. The wrong was in a father who, after years of preaching the all-important code of honor, planned to break a solemn oath.

"The price for my hostages' return unharmed I carefully chose in confident expectation of your sire's response." Expression gone to gentleness, to the one who would see him safe Rhys gave an explanation and oblique reassurance that he'd never intended to meet the earl's threat unprepared.

"But how could you have known? Why would you risk my father's retribution?" In his bewildering claim Linnet found further proof of how very dangerous was this golden Eagle . . . though a danger she was willing to tempt for even so small a reward as brief moments in his company.

Rhys's wry half-smile returned. "One day when we've the boon of unbespoken time I'll tell you an enlightening story which will make the matter clear, but now you must hastily return to Radwell." Though still on his knees, he reached out, intending to help her rise.

"No!" Linnet's cry was vehement, and she jerked from his hold, pressing back as if demanding that the very earth beneath her open and provide a safe haven. "I cannot. By taking my father's destrier and coming to you I have betrayed him."

Dark eyes widened. Rhys was too cynical to be often surprised, and yet Linnet repeatedly summoned that response—but never had he been more astonished than by the mental image of this small, feminine creature foolishly attempting to master a mighty warhorse. The wonder was not that she'd been thrown but that she'd stayed ahorse long enough to be carried this far into the forest. Quickly putting aside his amazement at her feat, he settled back on his heels and employed calm logic in seeking to alter her path.

"That very reason is why you must make the journey back immediately. My steed is near, and I'll see you to the edge of your father's lands. Go now before any can name you traitor with certainty."

"No! I won't go back!" Linnet shook her head emphatically. "If the dawn finds me in Castle Radwell, by dusk I'll be betrothed to that awful Saxon—committed to be wed with him when autumn arrives."

As the mocking expression left Rhys's face and his eyes went to black ice, Linnet crossed her arms over her midriff and twisted clenched fingers in creamy folds already wildly disarrayed by the force of her fall.

Fool! she berated herself. Once again I've proven what a witling I become whenever he is near—tripping over my own feet or my tongue or both! She'd spoken the ill-considered words without giving a moment's thought to the fact that they were a slight not only upon his uncle Osric, but upon the entire Saxon race—half of his blood heritage.

Though Rhys, as a boy, had barely known his uncle and had rarely seen the man since the end of his sojourn in Normandy, still he knew far too well precisely what manner of man was Osric. The prospect of this wee linnet wed with any other male was unpleasant, but the image of her forever bound to the overbearing, obnoxious Osric left Rhys not only unwilling to see the winsome damsel returned but determined to prevent the foul swine from ever claiming her as wife.

"He's not like you." Linnet was flustered and attempted to undo her blunder, unaware of the attention she was drawing to generous curves by twisting fingers into and tightening the cloth of her gown. Strained front laces gaped, and moonlight permitted enticing glimpses of creamy skin inadequately covered by near transparent green silk. "Not in the least like you." As she studied the man she had unintentionally maligned, regret lent a pansylike softness to her brown eyes.

"I fervently hope you are right." Her dismay warmed his dark gaze, but 'twas her firm, round flesh more clearly revealed than her modesty would knowingly permit that kindled the heat of golden sparks in the depths of his eyes. "Osric is the one man I most despise." Although sincere, the words were spoken by a man irresistibly drawn to the enticing vision he'd thought never to see again.

Rhys leaned forward, resting on hands placed on either side of this passionate virgin, her face lost in clouds of lustrous hair, helpless longing in velvet eyes and sweetness trembling on her lips. His gaze moved over her like a caress, lingering where the tight bodice gave an explicit glimpse of full breasts and their tight centers. Too vividly he remembered the stolen taste and feel of petal-smooth skin.

Filled with nameless wanting, Linnet stopped breathing beneath dark eyes glittering dangerously. Not even to save her soul from perdition could she have broken the visual bond with the source of lightning jolts flashing from his vibrant body to hers.

The damsel's fresh wildflower fragrance tantalized Rhys's senses near as much as did the view of her alluring curves. Beckoned by a temptation beyond his will to resist, the still kneeling man slowly stretched his long legs out beside her. He then lowered the unyielding wall of his chest against her soft heat.

Purposefully sinking into the realm of unthinking sensations, Linnet wrapped her arms about Rhys while at the devastating pleasure in this intimate contact a tiny, inarticulate sound welled up from her core. She welcomed the burning warmth of a powerful chest crushing aching breasts, and her hands slowly slid up the length of his muscular back to tangle in thick blond strands, tugging his mouth to hers. Tongue probing lightly between her lips, he kissed her with a slow, expert thoroughness. She counted her inhibitions well lost for these moments gone beyond reality into the sphere of impossible, forbidden dreams.

Though he was breathing hard and fast, the Eagle knew far better than this tender and too succulent songbird just what dangerous price would be required in exchange for the pleasures she innocently demanded. Unwilling to permit her the ultimate surrender, Rhys pulled gently away, if only so far as to rest on his forearms above the enticing damsel. He was certain the pleasures, no matter how urgently sought or deeply enjoyed, could never be adequate compensation for the loss of her virtue. And yet, despite his awareness of how near were the limits of his control, he fell to the same mistake he'd made too many times before. He gazed down into melting amber eyes and saw the trembling of passion-swollen lips silently pleading for the return of his. The sight drew forth an admission he'd never meant to speak.

"I lie awake at night and dream of seeing you, of tasting you like this." The velvet of Rhys's low voice was as potent a caress as any ardent touch.

After the multitude of fantasies Linnet had woven about him, though she was lost in mists of desire grown ever more dense, Linnet was dazed to learn he had dreamed of her. A faint moan escaped her tight throat as she looked up into the fires burning in the depths of dark eyes. Lured by swirling golden sparks, she tumbled into the blaze at their core, a willing sacrifice.

That further whimper won a slight, satisfied smile from lips that dipped again but only to move tantalizingly from eyelids to cheeks to chin and on to brush the corners of a mouth rosed by his passionate attentions. Whispery kisses aroused but failed to satisfy her, and Linnet clung to the hard-muscled shoulders above, holding his body determinedly separate from hers. She arched toward pleasure withheld, her pose unconsciously seductive while the brown eyes behind her half-closed lashes were stormy with need.

At the sight Rhys felt the end to his control perilously near and sought to drive back an almost ungovernable compulsion to accept the longed-for delights she offered. He abruptly dropped back upon a cushion of crushed grass, eyes clenched shut against further visual assaults on restraints only she could so thoroughly endanger.

Feeling suddenly bereft, Linnet helplessly followed. Like water flowing downhill she rolled toward his warmth, wanting the continuation of their devastating embrace, needing the feel of his fires to melt the cold loneliness of a lifetime. She buried her face in the curve between his throat and broad shoulder, nestling close against the rapid rise and fall of the wide chest her hands instinctively caressed. That contact merely increased her anguished hunger and because she was as interested in seeing him as their last forest encounter had proven him to be in seeing her, with reckless haste Linnet struggled to unfasten the thin leather cords of his tunic.

After succeeding in laying him near half bare, she shifted to stare shamelessly at the stunning view of a partially naked male torso—fascinating and frankly threatening, with its magnificent display of power at rest. Linnet plunged deeper into the seas of her own fantasies—nay, into an ocean of feelings and sensations far deeper than anything she'd imagined. Her inhibitions drowned by mighty waves, she daringly burrowed below what remained of the obstruction while gentle fingers brushed through a thicket of crisp curls to trace hard plains. Nothing existed but the feel of his skin, heat and iron thews beneath.

Under the tantalizing foray of her small fingers the blood in Rhys's veins turned to liquid flame, but he fought to lie motionless, yielding in this limited measure to her naive wiles. No use in justifying his inaction as some misguided attempt to stave off the effects of this remarkably passionate creature's dangerous advances. In truth, he feared any motion would frighten the curious songbird away, leaving him to ache for her return.

With the implicit permission granted by the lack of an immediate rejection of her tentative touches, Linnet nuzzled the dip at the base of his throat. Given this reprieve from endless loneliness, however short-lived, she moved to lay smiling lips over skin that seemed to take fire, and allowed the tip of her tongue to venture forth and taste.

Rhys caught his breath at this touch against his burning flesh. Beneath this onslaught of unruly, untutored caresses, he could no longer remain impassive. Now he would return the sweet torment. He rolled to his side and swept his hand, which had been buried beneath a wealth of tangled locks, from the nape of her neck to the base of her spine. Pressing her body closer, Rhys aligned her soft curves more intimately against the heated contours of his own, near welding them together with his ravenous fires.

Linnet's lashes fell beneath the weight of passion only to discover that in the darkness behind her eyelids, sensations intensified. As she slipped deeper into pleasure's fiery whirlwind, Linnet's heart went wild, loving the intimacy, the feel, the taste. With a small cry she mindlessly tightened her arms about him. Her world, spinning ever faster, began and ended with the man in her arms. Again his hands swept down the long arch of her back, but this time they settled at the tops of her thighs to urgently lift and pull her into the force of his need. Desperately wanting a closer contact, she arched against him, sensuously writhing against his powerful form.

As her soft breasts brushed across the hard muscles of his body, Rhys was achingly aware of her trembling hunger, and a rough groan tore from his tight throat while a shudder ran the length of him. He pushed her back against the forest's grassy floor. Then, with awkward haste, he tugged at her gown's laces and spread the bodice wide, exposing her to his hungry gaze. The gown's ivory hue was shamed by the delicate cream of her skin. The single barrier between him and sweet flesh, a layer of gossamer silk, was of no value as shield against probing eyes burning across a delicious sight for long moments before his mouth descended to find soft green silk and the even softer warmth of her breast.

Linnet gasped beneath the never before experienced delight as a seeking hand slid between loosened laces and fully caressed one swollen breast while the fire of his mouth opened over the taut, aching tip of the other. A strong shiver passed over her. She instinctively arched to invading lips and hands, spearing her fingers through thick golden hair and holding him to her body.

"Rhys, where are you?" The quiet call was barely more than a whisper but contained strains of both irritation and concern. "Are you all right?"

With a low growl Rhys instantly pulled away and sat up, thrusting behind his broad back the tempting damsel again unwillingly rescued from his weakness, a weakness he must admit in order to see it never again loosed.

"I'm here, Owain."

By stepping through the shadowy wall of vegetation with barely a sound, the bearded bear proved with what quickness and stealth an experienced warrior could move. The unexpected sight he found inside the small glade creased his brow with a perplexed frown, but he wisely forbore to question strange facts and instead awaited his friend's surely unavoidable explanation.

"Linnet valiantly came to warn me of a trick to be played upon my unwary head." Wry amusement overlaid but could not completely hide the rawness of a voice passion roughened.

"Did she, now?" Owain's head tilted curiously to

one side as his attention shifted to rest full upon the damsel sheltering behind his friend. "And how did you get here?"

A wickedly grinning Rhys answered while a blushing Linnet, shielded by the breadth of his back, fumbled to tighten laces recently undone.

"She rode her father's destrier."

Blue eyes widened and shot a quick glance to the golden prince. "'Struth?" Owain looked questioningly at the ever-reticent damsel with new respect—and a tinge of disbelief. "A destrier?"

Moonlight burnished a woman's slowly nodded head and rippled over waves of abundant hair flowing like a lustrous river about narrow shoulders and a lush form briefly glimpsed.

Owain shook his head in admiration of both her deed and her previously unsuspected charms but made a further comment. "Milady, I had not realized you knew where these disputed lands lay."

Now it was Linnet's turn to be surprised. *"These* are the lands where the battle will be fought?"

Feeling a faint suspicion had been confirmed, Owain spoke. "You took your father's destrier and came to warn his enemy—without so much as a specific destination?"

Her claim to have ridden a warhorse he had accepted because Rhys plainly did, but this second assertion was more than Owain could easily believe. Consequently distrust was as sharp as a bared blade in his skeptical words. "'Tis a miracle that you somehow stumbled upon our position."

"It would seem that Thunder, my father's steed, knows the path well, as it was his lead and not mine that we followed." Disgust for this truth coated Linnet's words and with front laces again neatly tied, she straightened to bravely meet the dark Welshman's clear skepticism.

Owain suffered grave doubts about the Norman lady's intent. Was her actual motive revenge for the affront of having been taken hostage? Had she come at her father's behest to disrupt any defense they raised? Still, no matter her intent, Owain could do naught but accept the fact that it was too late to attempt else than what had long been planned.

"Rhys, the eastern sky is rapidly growing lighter, and the hour of our confrontation is near. I feared you taken by one of the earl's mercenaries, although they seem to be peacefully passing the night in the ruins of Grannia's home, utterly unaware of our presence."

Linnet was surprised to learn that, despite his oath, her father hadn't so much as withdrawn his forces; he had not even taken that first step. At the same time it explained how he had thought to fight a battle though his men partook of a feast's abundant ale. Seemed certain that the warriors he meant to lead in the fight had never left their positions at all.

Caught up again in her disillusionment over the ease with which her father had chosen to forswear his honor, she failed to realize Rhys had risen until his strong hand came into sight. Without a moment's hesitation she trustingly placed her much littler hand in his and allowed him to gently aid her to her feet.

Wrapping his arm around the small maid and pulling her close to the strength of his side, Rhys looked at his longtime supporter with a silent but crystal-clear rebuke for unspoken suspicion.

"The time, then, has come and best we be prepared. Rouse our men and see them take up the positions we earlier discussed while I find a haven wherein our lady guest will safely wait out the battle."

9

ALTHOUGH THE PREDAWN SKY HAD THE DULL HUE OF IRON
and seemed as heavily forbidding, the surprise awaiting Godfrey outside the castle swept such unimportant omens from his thoughts.

Thunder stood already saddled a few strides this
side of the still lowered drawbridge, sides heaving as if
he'd only just returned from a wild ride. Thick
iron-gray brows met in a fierce frown as the earl left
his older son and his Saxon guest on the stairs leading
down into the dew-muddied courtyard. Anxiety
warred with irritation in the man who strode toward
his destrier and reached out to calm this beast more
prized than most humans in his domain.

What fool had dared misuse Thunder? Had the
stableboy been witless enough to mount a mighty
warhorse? Nay, Arn cowered at the edge of the group
of men assembled for the morning's adventure and
looked to be more amazed by this unwelcome sight
than he, though the lad was plainly terrified of being
blamed for the wrong. Godfrey next wondered if his
squire was to blame. However, of that accusation
Bevin was assuredly innocent. Bleary-eyed and much
tousled, the young man gaped in confusion at a steed

he had not saddled, though 'twas his duty to see it done. In Bevin's appearance Godfrey found proof of two facts. First, it seemed clear that he was unequal to the night of hard drinking just past; the lanky youth had yet to learn the art of restraint and of pacing his consumption for the meeting of responsibilities. Second, but by that same token, 'twas clear he was incapable of climbing atop his lord's stallion and riding madly across the countryside.

But then who had? Who? The earl's heavy frown grew even fiercer. Surely the gate guard must have seen the miscreant. Brown eyes, like caldrons filled with muddy disgust on the boil, shifted from favored steed to heavy chains winch-released and thick planks of a lowered drawbridge. Another misdeed. Godfrey twisted about and glared at men gathered in unquestioning response to his previous day's oblique command, men both disturbed by the mysteriously saddled horse and apprehensive of their lord's increasing ire.

"Bring Edolf to me!" No one moved. "Curse you, you spineless worms! Bring him to me now!"

"He's gone missing, milord." With proudly tilted chin, narrow shoulders back, and spine straight, Sir Basil, the guard captain, took one step forward to meet a just reprimand. To answer was his duty, though one that would reveal a further duty at which he had failed. The open portal and its absent guard were proof of that. Leastwise in this instance he lacked the required control over and knowledge of the location of every man in Radwell's garrison. Despite earnest attempts to rectify his error, Basil had no notion where the guardsman assigned to a deserted post now sheltered. But of a certainty Edolf would pay more dearly than he for that wrong.

"Missing? *Missing!*" Under the ferocious ire in the earl's words even his well-trained destrier, taught to stand impervious amid the violence of war, flinched.

"Aye," Sir Basil bravely continued. "I discovered

Edolf's absence a short time past. Immediately I turned to men awake and, by your command, clear-headed enough to aid in successfully winning your objective. These men I set to hunting the missing guardsman. But knowing the need for a timely return, they were unable to execute a complete search and came back with no news of Edolf's whereabouts."

These ill omens were so obvious even Godfrey found them impossible to discount. Nonetheless, the moment to begin a more important task had arrived and could not be postponed, weary horse and missing gate guard or no. Men he'd carefully selected to accompany him were waiting for news of their day's mission, and he must put the painstakingly created plan into motion. First, however, he would ensure that the search for an Edolf worthy of punishment would continue.

"Sir Basil, wake the garrison—douse the men with icy water if need be—and see that the whole take up the chore of locating our 'friend' Edolf. Allow no slacking until he is found, and have him ready to meet my judgment for his wrong when I return."

The guard captain nodded immediate obedience even as his lord's attention shifted from a destrier near calmed to normal breathing to those awaiting his command. "Get you to your steeds and carts."

Even this close to the outset of their scheme, Godfrey gave his older son and the disliked but necessary Saxon lord no moment's attention more than that given to those of lesser station. Mark's company was always welcome, but Osric's presence he had far rather do without, though Godfrey was not fool enough to do less than ensure that the man was seen to be as culpable in this questionable deed as he himself. Too oft and for too long he'd been held captive to the whims of others. Now he was free, or almost so, and would never again knowingly submit.

"Lose no moment more in obeying my command for this morning we will mete out retribution upon the contemptible Welshman who ever hides from honest battle."

Men impatient for the promised fray rapidly turned to do as they were bidden. Some fetched horses and harnessed them to crude wagons to carry unmounted troops while knights, and a fortunate few others, saw to the saddling of their steeds. Little time passed before the courtyard filled with men prepared to depart.

"Let's be to the task at hand." As he spoke, Godfrey swung up into the saddle. His supporters made haste to follow his lead. The thunderous cadence of many hooves pounding the planks of a drawbridge which wrongly remained lowered drove every consideration from Godfrey's mind save the long anticipated and imminent deadly confrontation with the infamous Welsh prince some wretch had dubbed the Eagle.

Even as the earl and his small army departed to join others still posted at their destination, those rudely awakened by a snarling Sir Basil undertook the quest left to their resentful hands. They began searching every possible corner and crevice while heartily cursing the fellow guardsman whose disappearance had forced them to lift pounding heads from the beds earlier than elsewise would have been required.

Their commotion roused all within Radwell. The only one of noble blood left behind hurried from his chamber and out from the castle to curiously seek its explanation from the guard captain standing in the courtyard, clenched fists on hips, staring at the rapidly disappearing force.

"What's afoot?" Alan stared curiously toward figures diminished by distance but easily identified both by the rippling of his father's banner and by the unmistakable black steed. Surely Thunder's presence meant Linnet, too, had safely returned? Alan was relieved.

Basil forced to his mouth a smile of welcome for the earl's young son. "Your father has set forth to lead a force into disputed lands and seek revenge for the capture of you and your sister."

"But . . ." As Radwell's loyal heir, Alan was confused by the certain wrong in his concern for the Eagle's safety, and by another and even more troubling point, which settled a bleak shroud over shoulders that drooped. Alan remembered too clearly the terms Rhys had set for his hostages' release. Never would the powerful prince have released them had he not received the oath demanded of Earl Godfrey to yield and leave the disputed lands secure from either trespass or assault. How was it that the father who'd ever stressed the importance of untainted honor thought to justify breaking his sworn word by descending on the area?

As if Alan's unspoken thoughts had been heard, the dutiful guard captain answered the question—but with a response that raised a further distressing issue and question of honor: Alan's honor.

"Your father intends to seek vengeance for the insult done his family, and that quest is as just as the punishment he will wreak upon the wretched Edolf for failing in his important duty."

To Basil the comparison was glaringly obvious, for his thoughts couldn't be long waylaid from the serious misdeed for which he knew himself to be partly at fault. He was Edolf's superior, the leader of all men in the garrison and responsible for overseeing every guardsman's assigned tasks.

The news that Edolf was to be punished struck Alan like an unfairly landed blow. This, he knew beyond doubt, was the result of his playacting the past night. Deeply disliking the man, he'd fallen to an urge to pay him back for hurtful taunts, but never had he meant Edolf to truly suffer . . . and suffer it seemed he would do. Alan turned away from a man too caught up in his own concerns to notice. After slipping back into the castle, he climbed up to the second level and his own small bedchamber. He disconsolately sank down onto a mattress stuffed with straw, impervious to its lumps and the stems poking uncomfortably through rough ticking, while he desperately sought an answer for the quandary of what he ought do to set the matter straight.

At some point between midmorn and noon Linnet lay curled in the haven Rhys had created for her hours gone by. 'Twas in a hollow between three close-grown trees cloaked in the fresh green of new leaves and padded with soft grasses and ferns. And despite its relative comfort, tension wrapped its icy band ever more firmly about Linnet's heart, leaving her blind to woodland beauty and impervious to the soft, elusive scent of nearby wildflowers. In the joust for her attention these gentle surroundings were no match against powerful mental images roused by the deadly intent she'd recognized at the base of her father's resolve to wreak his vengeance upon Rhys.

More fearsome still was the fact that no matter the winner of the battle whose clashing blades she could hear though not see beyond the slight rise at her back, she would lose. She had absently stripped the leaves and bark from a small branch, plainly fallen in a recent windstorm, and now it abruptly snapped between hands clenched tight. Painful loss threatened to follow whether the victor was her father or the man she loved. Though the seed of that emotion had been sown in fantasies, it was not as their insubstantial hero that she loved Rhys but rather as the flesh-and-blood man of honor she'd come to know during her days in his company.

Of a sudden Linnet thrust aside idle worries and rose. She could not, would not, simply hide here in safety and agonizing fear while the two men most important to her met in mortal combat. She must *do* something! Unwilling to remain here like a wild creature trapped and forced to await its fate at the hands of men, she would go to the site of the struggle and watch events certain to alter the course of her life.

Though she was naught but a woman utterly lacking in military skills, mayhap even her meager talents would be of some use in preventing the tragedy she feared. A plain brown linnet herself, she might well be able to serve as important a part as had the wee bird in the folk tale that had staved off the devastation of an entire village by plucking the seeds of destruction from an ogre's hand.

Mind set on her course, Linnet nimbly stepped around the uprooted bushes Rhys had carefully placed as a shield across the mouth of her haven. Though not high, the hill behind her hiding place was densely covered by an array of vegetation and so steep Linnet had perforce to use her hands to gain its summit. During her struggling climb, she strengthened the weak threads of her courage with the stout cords of her certainty that only by seeing these events with her own eyes could she prevent others from seeking to tell her of the fray while remolding facts to suit their own purposes. And surely reality could be no worse than the horrible scenes supplied by her fertile imagination.

Linnet, upon reaching the hilltop, instinctively began brushing damp earth and broken pieces of foliage from her hands. Then she froze, unable even to breathe. She gazed down an equally steep descent to the point where a small valley broadened into tilled fields left fallow. There, fearfully near, broadswords flashed in the grim light of a heavily overcast day.

The terrifying sight bore no resemblance to the gallant adventures of her fantasies wherein her hero stood unharmed and victorious against an inhuman monster. An innocent riverlet flowed through the valley's center, its cheery rippling as sadly misplaced alongside the charred remains of Grannia's home as was Linnet's past joy in dreams of unreal battles—

dreams here proven truly a fool's game. Now all she wanted of those dreams was their happy ending, a resolution that would see both Rhys and her father walk free and unscathed from the conflict.

Clutching her dark cloak tightly closed to hide a creamy gown threatening to act as a beacon amid forest shadows, Linnet carefully picked her way a short distance farther down the treacherous slope. But all the while her horrified attention remained on the magnificent form of the golden-haired prince. He had dismounted, and every mighty angle of his body was tensed as he did battle against two of her father's most renowned warriors.

Knee-length black cloak thrown back but swirling with every thrust and clashing contact blade to blade, Rhys moved with the grace and assurance of superior skill. Linnet spared a brief thought for the lesson this would be to men she'd heard deride the Eagle for his tactic of striking unexpectedly from forest gloom rather than meeting his enemy on an open field of battle. They'd cherished the plainly inaccurate belief that the Welshman's strategy was proof that he was incapable of successfully meeting them face to face. She had no sympathy for the arrogant pair learning their folly.

Though continuing her litany of earnest prayers for the safety of both Rhys and her father, Linnet found herself unable to close wide amber eyes focused on honed blades. Flashing steel sang an eerie tune as the men moved through the charred ruins on the tiny stream's far side in a dance of chilling intent. Although wounds had been inflicted upon men of both factions, the mortal combat went on until, at long last and almost simultaneously, a number of those dressed in her father's colors found an end to their battle at the point of a Welshman's sword.

As lifeless bodies crumpled to blackened earth, their compatriots broke ranks. In spite of Earl Godfrey's intermingled curses and commands to remain, the loss of so many in so brief a time put the remaining Norman guardsmen to flight. Mounted warriors fled while foot soldiers dashed wildly into the forest, abandoning carts that were too slow when pursued by Welshmen ahorse.

Fighting on with only Mark at his side, Godfrey was left no choice but to signal the retreat already begun. However, he resolved that the craven fools who'd deserted him would pay a higher price for their cowardly actions than that threatened by the Eagle and his supporters. Death by the sword was swift and at the cost of naught but a moment's piercing sting. The penalty he planned to exact would be neither quick nor painless.

Standing in the limited shelter provided by several tall flowering bushes heavily laden with blooms, Linnet watched as her father turned Thunder about and raced through the opposite forest wall with mounted Welshmen at his heels. But for the steepness of the slope beneath her feet, she'd have sunk to her knees in relief. Her pleas for divine intervention had been answered; though she regretted the loss of other lives, leastwise neither the earl nor Rhys had been harmed.

In the next moment Linnet discovered her prayer of gratitude had been too soon begun. For some inexplicable reason—a gift for which she swore to offer many prayers of thanks—she saw a horrifying sight.

The men of Cymer, afoot and mounted, chased fleeing adversaries, leaving only Rhys on the battlefield. While his beacon-bright head tilted over a fallen Norman another of her father's men crept from forest shadows and stealthily approached him from behind, vicious dagger upheld in joined hands.

"Rhys!" Linnet screamed. "Beware!"

The prince's black cloak swirled like the wings of a mighty eagle as Rhys simultaneously turned toward the sound and ducked from the descending blade. The intended deathblow fell short of its mark yet still it struck flesh. Without a moment's thought wasted on his wounded inner thigh, Rhys returned the attack with greater success. The Norman doubled over and dropped face down upon ground rapidly soaked by his blood.

Linnet started running toward the injured prince, but stumble holes hidden amid lush grasses and a near vertical descent conspired to steal solid ground from 'neath her feet. With a gasp she fell back and slid on her derriere down the remaining length of the hill.

Gown bunched awkwardly about her thighs, clumps of dirt and twigs tangled in loose tresses, she again— as she had too many times before—looked up into the half-amused, half-annoyed, and totally mocking expression of the man at whose feet she constantly found herself lying.

"What of your oath to remain safely where I put you?" A fighting man used to the minor wounds of battle, Rhys gave no thought to an unimportant injury to be dealt with only once other matters had been resolved.

"I gave no oath." Stung by the unexpected assault of a man whose life she had just saved, Linnet's rarely lit temper flashed for the second time within the span of a single night and day. "You asked it of me but I did *not* give it."

"Nonetheless, you should have stayed put." Rhys was amused by this uncommon fire so soon reignited in the damsel he'd come to believe practical in all things. Aye, practical but also quietly courageous and generous with warmth and kindness. Against her other attributes, the physical charms again temptingly revealed by the disarray of a fall, he purposefully closed his thoughts. Attention given where best it not be would too likely lead into a repetition of the dangerous responses and actions no more justified now than when she'd been his hostage.

"'Struth?" Linnet's tone held at least as much scorn as ever had his. "Had I done as you asked, you'd be dead!"

Rhys's smile held its usual cynical tilt, but a gentleness lay in its depths as he reached down to help her rise, unmindful of the fleeting grimace brought by a stinging in his thigh.

Burningly aware of her dishevelment, the woman feeling wrongly abused muttered sotto voce, "Proves linnets are more useful than peacocks." Then, as she took his extended hand, her gaze fell on the gap between the dagger-sundered edges of his chausses and lingered on the gash beneath.

"What?" Rhys had caught the damsel's odd words and suspected their meaning but was curious to hear her explanation.

As Linnet regained her balance she shook her head to brush aside words rendered meaningless by the much more important fact that Rhys stood before her wounded.

"Your thigh must soon be treated. Elsewise it may fester and spread poison enough to finish your attacker's deadly chore." Linnet glanced up at him with a concern that melted her wild honey eyes and silenced the faint moans of the other wounded men lying nearby.

Striving to block the flow of warm emotion weakening the barricade about his heart, Rhys spoke more harshly than he'd intended to. "Treated? Here? Do you see materials that I do not?"

Linnet swallowed hard but instantly bent to lift her cream linen skirt well above her ankles. Placing the sharp edge of her own dainty dagger against her undergown's lower edge, she cut free a broad strip of green silk.

"Now I do." She held up flimsy cloth that rippled on the breeze like a warrior's pennant.

Through narrowed eyes Rhys dubiously viewed her trophy but promptly settled on the trunk of an uprooted tree. "I yield." He was coming to realize that, quiet as Linnet might be, her determination was a force to be reckoned with.

Some few of his warriors would soon return to carry

their wounded fellows to a neighboring home where Ynid waited to treat them. And, as Rhys had no wish to distract the woman, who would be occupied by far more serious injuries, it was an easy thing to bend to Linnet's insistence. Yet how, he wondered, did she think to treat a man fully dressed?

Unaware of his wry amusement, Linnet moved to the stream bank. First she severed and then soaked one-quarter of the precious cloth willingly donated to meet his need. With the unused portion draped over her shoulders and again wafting on a gentle wind, she returned to Rhys. Linnet knelt before him and leaned forward to more closely examine his injury while folding the wet cloth into a neat square. Like all ladies trained to become mistress of a castle, she'd been taught the methods of caring for those ailing or maimed. Although Rhys was right in saying there was little to be done before returning to where better supplies might be had, Linnet was confident that she also was right in stating the need for immediate binding.

Linnet gently pulled apart the blade-split edges of the tear in his chausses and applied the damp cloth directly to the wound. Next she wrapped the remaining silk in a neat bandage about his thigh and over the pad she'd created.

Rhys gazed down at the masses of warm brown hair covering a bent head and the dainty hands working efficiently to bind his injured flesh. Their touch was cool but spread a path of flame that roused in him a dangerous predator. He shifted uncomfortably as his body responded all too readily.

From her position between his knees Linnet looked up to meet an intent black gaze burning with golden embers revived. His face was stiffly controlled, but an erratic pulse beat in his throat. Linnet's thick lashes dropped to shield her from the power of a gaze she feared would read her unsought love.

Firmly taking one ministering hand in each of his

own, Rhys pulled Linnet to her feet as he himself rose. "The battle is won and now is the time to withdraw."

Withdraw, Rhys thought, mocking his own words, from Abergele's ruins and the scene of temptations resisted by virtue of a fight near as difficult.

While the limited light of a cloudy day began fading in the west, Castle Radwell's great hall swarmed with curious folk of every station from the lowliest stable and kitchen serfs to guardsmen and even a Saxon lord. They'd gathered to see a spectacle, the public punishment of a guardsman. Waved back by others of the garrison, the serfs pressed against inside walls while others of greater import stood in front. The center was left open. In moments the focus of this event was roughly thrown into its midst.

"Well?" Earl Godfrey boomed, driving all other sounds to silence. "Give your excuse if you dare believe 'tis possible one exists." While waiting for the wretch to speak, he silently acknowledged pride in a daughter too wise to be seen here showing coarse interest in such matters.

Arms bound behind and on his knees before the earl, who was seated at the high table, Edolf whined his excuse as his pride fell to ashes.

"Had Meg not locked me inside the weapons storeroom on the rampart wall, I'da been gone little more'n an hour and no harm done."

"Such is your excuse for dereliction of duty? The irresistible call of some slattern?" Disgust coated the earl's words while the watching guardsmen snickered their disdain first for Edolf's wrong and second for his expectation of so brief a sojourn in the buxom woman's arms.

"Fetch Meg." Godfrey was determined to drag into the open the full measure of wrongs done him. The craven guardsmen who'd deserted their lord's fight already languished in the dungeon below and on the morrow would face the full measure of his wrath. He only wished he could demand a like penalty from Osric, but the Saxon would too likely shift his support to the Eagle and see his earl publicly shamed for a forsworn oath.

No matter his frustration with a cowardice to go unpunished, this night Godfrey meant to devote to the offenses that had opened the morning with foreboding and dark omens. As for the too willing maidservant who seemed at its core . . .

Though oddly uncomfortable, Sir Basil wordlessly turned to appoint a minion to carry out the earl's command. While avidly watching house serfs and guardsmen shifted to allow the leave-taking of the chosen man, Alan stood in the shadows on the crowd's outer edges, his guilt burning deeper with an acid that ate into his middle. He spared no thought for the whispers filling this momentary interruption in the proceedings or for the two men standing on either side of him—his half brother, Mark, on the right and his foster father, Osric, on the left.

"If Edolf's claim is true," Godfrey said, continuing his harangue after the briefest of pauses to ensure his will would be carried out, "Meg called a gate guard to break his duty to me. That was a dangerous deed in itself, but she added to that wrong by locking him away from his post, thus leaving Radwell vulnerable to attack for the whole of a night in an action beyond forgiveness."

In what, to Alan, seemed like an amazingly short time, into the opening earlier cleared in the hall's center for these proceedings Meg was thrust so roughly that she near tripped over the kneeling man awaiting the earl's judgment.

Edolf glared at Meg with hate overbrimming in his eyes. "You did this to me, bitch. And now you'll share the blame . . . and the price for misdeeds."

Sneering at the guardsman of whose transgression

she'd heard, Meg pulled herself together and boldly turned to meet the earl's gaze with righteous indignation in her own. "I am guilty of *no* wrong!"

"Our friend"—the word dripped with acid— "swears you summoned him to a tryst in the weapons storeroom last night. Then, rather than welcoming his arrival, he contends that you locked him within its unyielding hold."

"A tryst . . . with *him?*" Meg drew back from the claimant, disdain in every generous curve. "Rather than endure his embrace I might be tempted to see him confined, but I had no part in the deed of which he accuses me. Indeed I had far livelier games to entertain me the length of the night's dark hours." Meg's eyes narrowed, and she turned a sultry gaze upon an uncomfortably shifting Basil. "A companion not so foolish as to waste either time or vigor in drinking too heartily of abundant ale."

Hardly hearing the words, Alan, fair to bursting with guilt, could no longer allow others to take the blame for his misdeed. He pushed his way between much taller companions to stand alone before his father.

"Sire, for the sake of the honor you've always cautioned me to hold most dear, I must confess my part in this deed."

The earl was inwardly shamed by his heir's talk of honor so close upon an action calling his own into question. Godfrey's frown softened to one less fierce than puzzled. "What part could you possibly have played?"

Gray eyes glittered with the unhealthy enjoyment Osric found in seeing the earl squirm under the unknowingly wielded lash of his son's honesty. That the father feared the son's discovery of his own iniquity convinced the Saxon that the time had come to truly accelerate the course of revenge. A cold smile twisted thin lips but had nothing to do with the words Alan next spoke.

"'Twas I who summoned Edolf to the storeroom."
As verification of the claim, Alan repeated his performance in a voice perfectly mimicked.

Laughter rolled through the room, a fine relief from growing tensions, and the loudest guffaws came from the woman whose voice Alan had imitated. Edolf's eyes burned with hate. Aside from the offender, Godfrey alone was unamused. In words that acted upon listeners like a dousing of water over weak flames struggling to life, he pointed out unchanged wrongs.

"Meg is exonerated by your confession, Alan, but only she. It matters little whether her call or yours lay at the root, the foul fruit remains the same—Edolf's abandonment of a critical post." Godfrey's attention moved from Alan to the bowed head of the guilty man. "In consideration of the Eagle's devious assault, once for a like failure I absolved you of wrongdoing. But, Edolf, for this serious offense you've no excuse."

The crowd was utterly silent, waiting for judgment to be levied upon the trembling culprit, now a hulking mass of fear.

"The price for your wrong begins with a fortnight in my dungeon and naught but gruel for sustenance. Then in fourteen days' time your sword will be broken and you'll be forever banished from Radwell."

A sigh whooshed through the crowd like the ill wind presaging storm. Though the earl could have claimed Edolf's life, he'd chosen a punishment more severe. After being reviled and sent from one lord's garrison for wrongdoing, never would the man be welcome in another's lands, far less into another's army. Thus, Edolf would have no honest method of obtaining the necessities of survival, and though free, he'd possess not even so much as the lowliest serfs who leastways had their lords' protection and a place where they belonged. Likely Edolf would be driven into some large city there to lose himself among its dank mazes and become naught but another homeless beggar.

"You did this to me, you dirty little rotter!" Somehow Edolf had gained his feet to swing around toward Alan with a glare sharper than any dagger. "I swear on the Body of Christ that I will see *you* pay an even higher price!" Despite bound hands and legs cramped by hours of kneeling, the huge man staggered toward the boy with deadly intent.

The shocked immobility of Edolf's gaolers broke under the vicious threat. They launched themselves at his staggering form, bringing him down with a bone-crunching slam against unyielding floor planks.

Pinned beneath the crushing weight of several men, Edolf lay with his mouth and nose amid stale rushes rapidly going fetid, not having been changed since Linnet had spread them afore being taken hostage. And still the curses and threats poured forth from the prisoner like poison from a festering wound.

10

LINNET SAT DEMURELY UPON A THREE-LEGGED STOOL
drawn near the fire Rhys had revived in his hall's
central hearth. Her plainly reluctant host strode in
silence from a window shuttered against deepening
twilight to the hearth and back again while her wide
amber eyes apprehensively watched him. A calm
demeanor, experience-honed, hid any sign of her
dread of Rhys's further reaction to her flight into
Cymer. It seemed clearer with each passing moment
and each completed circuit from window to hearth
that his honest response to her desperate deed—long
delayed by her bruising falls, his injury, and a battle
fiercely fought—would be else than the grateful pleasure of her hopeless dreams.

Sensing her serene facade's imminent collapse, she
lowered her gaze to the ivory linen covering her lap
and fingers, which were tightly entwined to still their
tense motions. Between this moment and the same
time on the previous day she'd been through a whirl-
pool of events and emotions more widely varied than
during the whole of her life, and she felt near to
dissolving into humiliating tears. In a desperate attempt to waylay their flow, Linnet took careful note of

her pale dress's cleanliness, despite horse rides and awkward falls. Here was proof of the amazing shielding powers provided by the brown cloak now hanging on a peg beside the outer door.

The battle had commenced at midmorn had ended shortly after the nooning hour. It had required all the time betwixt its end and the arrival of dusk to reach this abode. Since the door had closed them inside the house gone empty for a day and grown chill, Rhys had busied himself either stoking the fire or restlessly pacing while mentally seeking some gentle method to say what he must. At the end of a fruitless search he was forced to admit it a quest doomed to failure from the outset.

Though Rhys would far rather have swept the increasingly forlorn damsel into his arms and passionately demonstrated his gratitude for her timely intervention, he instead gifted Linnet with cold words, opening the way for a necessary smothering of hopeless fires . . . his own.

"'Tis impossible."

It had begun, as Linnet had known it would since the dark hours of the night past when he'd initially greeted her warning with little welcome and urgings for her immediate return to Radwell. Aye, here was the rejection of her unworthy self which, in the depths of her honest soul, she'd known was the inevitable result of a plain brown linnet's fantasy to be chosen as mate by a mighty golden eagle.

"Your warning call while I foolishly stood unprepared for the attacker creeping from behind to strike me down granted me the boon of continued life. 'Tis a blessing for which I will be forever grateful . . . but more than gratitude between us is impossible." Rhys had near to grit his teeth to speak the last, deeply regretted half of his statement. Regret the impossibility of more betwixt himself and this sweet songbird he assuredly did. She, of all the females in his not inconsiderable experience, was the only woman he desired to know better—not physically alone but also her mind and emotions, which were, he'd become certain, a treasure worth any price.

Rhys's face went as cold and hard as an unyielding stone monolith. No matter his own desires, he could never turn away from the unavoidable truth that a pursuit of this prize was a forbidden one entangled in chains forged by duties owed the people of Cymer. *Their* health and well-being must ever and always be his first responsibility. He had fought for that right and, before failing his people, he would willingly forfeit his own happiness, surrender his very life.

While dreaded words echoed in her mind like a bell tolling doom, Linnet inwardly watched her fragile dreams evaporate. Her shoulders slumped. She seemed almost to shrink, diminished by their loss. Despite the passionate embraces that had been so important to Linnet, her beloved's emotionless assertion rendered indisputable proof that her precious fantasies had been formed of nothing more substantial than smoke and cobwebs. Driven beyond her will to prevent it, Linnet lifted her gaze to the chill face of the man who'd moved to tower above where she huddled, helpless, beneath his rejection.

The hurt turning her eyes near as dark as his own forced Rhys to give a useless explanation that would not alter unpleasant realities.

"In the first instance, our respective heritages put us at odds with each other. Both the Welsh and the Saxons have ever been foes to those of Norman blood."

Her acceptance was silent despite an anguish so sharp it drove a barb into his heart. Still Rhys met the demands of honor and duty by determinedly continuing this necessary task.

"But, going deeper than that, an unabated emnity lies between your father and me, between his people and mine. Moreover, I am all but bound by important commitments vital to Cymer's future peace and prosperity." He spread his hands wide, palms upward, in an oddly vulnerable motion. "Thus, you surely see that too many barriers lie between us."

"You mean, then, to return a traitorous daughter to meet her father's wrath." His reasoning was indisputable, and Linnet's response was not a question but an unemotionally stated fact. Her gaze fell again, settling on weak flames that seemed as unequal to the struggle of heating the cold hall as she was of changing the Eagle's decision. Believing her cause hopeless, she chose not to humble herself with futile pleas.

"Nay." The quiet growl contained a tightly withheld pain. "Never would I force you to any unwelcome destination." Nor, Rhys privately acknowledged, would he ever permit Earl Godfrey to sacrifice the tender songbird to his Saxon uncle's cruel talons. There were other possibilities, though they were no more welcome. "The Abbey of Saint Anne is not far distant and would offer you its protection—from any man who meant you harm."

Small hands gripped ivory linen so tightly they threatened to leave permanent creases in fine cloth while a startled Linnet looked up to meet the unspoken entreaty in dark eyes. An abbey? He asked her to retreat into a life of quiet toil and prayer? Though initially struck by how alien was this option never before considered, on a moment's closer scrutiny she realized it would be little different from the years spent in Castle Radwell. What in all her life had she done but work on her father's behalf, merely passing through the mundane motions of days begun and ended with prayers in the chapel?

Her sole relief from practical chores had been secret fantasies, and only see what penance of anguish had been assessed upon her for that folly. Aye, a future withdrawn from the world would be an appropriate end to traitorous dreams and actions. Moreover, if Rhys was to remain forever beyond her reach, she deemed it better to seek the solitary life of a nun than to submit to another male's hold.

"I'll go." The quiet words ached with unhappy resignation.

Gazing down upon tresses flowing like thick, warm honey from the woman's bowed head, Rhys was disconcerted to find she had seemingly retreated so far from him as to have already entered that cloistered sphere. Though irrational, considering all the fine arguments he'd presented and the suggestion he'd offered in an attempt to see it so, he resented her emotional withdrawal. No amount of sane and logical reasoning urging him to the contrary could prevent his next words from being spoken as much to summon her back to him as to communicate what more needed to be understood.

"As your visit is unexpected, there is no female presently near and available to lend propriety to these hours alone." When she raised her desolate eyes to him, Rhys realized how easily this unarmed woman could strike a blow more painful than any delivered by even the fiercest of his foes. A lance of guilt, formed by his demand that she accept unpleasant realities and honed by the dutiful words his honor had demanded be spoken, smote him more sharply than ever had a steel blade. It pierced his armor and struck a well-guarded heart.

"Even Ynid's energies are needed elsewhere. Those who were wounded during this morn's battle require her healing skills to see them recovered." To defeat an urge to confess his feelings, even to himself, Rhys turned slightly and concentrated with considerable force on the window's blameless shutters. Not a single faint gleam shone through tiny cracks between their joined planks. The day was at an end. Refusing to risk the recently acknowledged chink in the armor of his willpower by inviting another of the woman's unwitting visual assaults, Rhys continued without looking back. "I did, however, send for my sister when we arrived."

Linnet had heard him talk with one of the older men who'd met them as they descended the slope to this abode. But Rhys had naturally spoken Welsh, and she'd had no way of knowing what he had said.

"If you remember the length of time required for our journey to and from Newydd Farm," Rhys went on, "you'll understand why it will be a considerable time before she arrives."

"Newydd?" Linnet studied Rhys's averted face, puzzled first by his apparent distress and second by facts in which even she recognized hazards to Grannia and Owain, who shared a wayward love. "The place where you took me to visit Alan—Owain and David's home?" Her questions probed tentatively, leaving the way open for him to brush them aside did he wish to do so.

"Aye. Her dead husband's home farm." Rhys knew precisely in what direction Linnet's thoughts led her. But, as she was responsible for rousing the couple's embarrassment and revealing their shared emotions to him, he saw no purpose in pretending those emotions did not exist.

"Grannia moved to Newydd, claiming her right to share the home with her stepsons." His attention, evading well-intended restraints, returned to exchange a knowing look with the watching damsel. "'Tis undeniably her right—though doubtless we both see how unwise was the choice. Indeed, I and Owain attempted to dissuade her, but she has a will as inflexible as iron."

Linnet smiled wryly at the frustration in the depths of a dark velvet voice. "It seems a trait common to your family." The subtle barb hit its mark and eased a measure of the tension betwixt them while at the same time shifting the subject of their conversation.

Rhys laughed, relieved at this proof that he'd not so thoroughly crushed the small Linnet's spirit as to have permanently robbed her of humor. "'Struth, but where it is expected of a man, it is less welcome in a woman."

"Why?" Linnet calmly tilted her head to one side while her eyes turned to topaz under the glow of a temper roused more often in the past few weeks than in the whole of the previous eighteen years. "Are we poor females forbidden to reason for ourselves?" Her melodious voice deepened to include a thread of sarcasm worthy of Rhys himself as again, by reminding him of her valuable intercession, she struck back at words in which she heard an insult.

"Indeed you are fortunate—as am I—that I pride myself on possessing sharp wits, for had I merely submitted to my father's will, though safe in Radwell, I would now be betrothed to a man I despise and you would be lying lifeless on a charred field."

Her mercurial shift in mood startled another burst of laughter from Rhys. Its deep and unrestrained rumble filled the large chamber. As the reverberations faded, he gazed at her with amused eyes gone gentle.

"As a seasoned warrior I know when 'tis best to yield the field and regroup to return of a piece on another day." Linnet had once more proven a fact he'd spent hours trying to deny since the night he had brought her to Cymer as hostage—her company would be a never-ending delight.

"As already I have said, I am thankful for the warning that saved my life. Moreover, I'm most willing to concede that I am fortunate you possess both sharp wits and the courage to employ them."

Shy pleasure washed the defiance from the quiet loveliness of Linnet's face, a sight that warmed Rhys's expression with a gentle smile even as black eyes narrowed with penetrating intensity on her soft mouth. Despite bells ringing in his mind, warning of danger looming over the path of his thoughts, he remembered how her lips felt like rose petals kissed by the sun and tasted of honey-sweetened wine. Rhys's hands abruptly clenched as if to fight back forbidden memories even as he withdrew deep into himself.

Turning his back on tender and too tempting prey, the Eagle strode irritably to the window, opened a shutter and glared into the anonymous darkness beyond. He could see little of the landscape over which heavy clouds gathered in increasing numbers, threatening to brew up a storm.

Linnet was confused by the grimace that had crossed his face for a brief moment before he again become unapproachable. Was its source pain? Foolish question. Linnet's guilty attention fell to the silken and inappropriately beautiful bandage wrapped about his thigh. For hours she'd been selfishly caught up in her own concerns while he stood before her doubtless pained by a wound assuredly in need of more thorough tending than simple bandaging.

"Where are your medicinal supplies stored?" An unswerving amber gaze steadily watched the broad back turned to her.

Rhys was tilted off stride by the abrupt shift in both subject and emotion. Glancing over his shoulder, from beneath scowling brows of dark gold, he looked directly into Linnet's determined eyes.

"Surely"—Linnet was impatient to do what she had shamefully allowed be waylaid by her heedless self-absorption—"you do have a supply of your own?" Still he didn't answer but rather stared at her enigmatically. To ward off this wordless refusal of her aid, with cool logic she relentlessly insisted. "I know you would prefer that Ynid treat your injury, but as you've said, she is elsewise occupied and you need closer attention—now."

Choosing not to insult the damsel further than had by necessity already been done, Rhys pointed to a chest tucked into the gloom beneath the stairway.

Linnet made her way to the trunk. She sank to her knees and threw back the iron-bound lid to begin sorting through the wooden box's contents. Within she found an adequate supply of bandages and a small pot of salve, which she recognized by the odor as an unguent able to stave off infection and aid healing. Even while selecting appropriate lengths of cloth to bind the gash once treated, she felt the weight of dark eyes and glanced sidelong to find in them a curiously uncertain shadow.

"I realize that you mean to treat my wound, but what would you have me do to facilitate the deed? Boldly rid myself of my nether garments?" The half-smile accompanying these questions, though it was his customary expression, contained an unusually strong dose of cynicism. "'Twould be an action much less likely to embarrass me than you."

In spite of his certainty that what he claimed was true, Rhys was conscious of the fact that such an action would also reveal to her the physical proof of his intense desire. Desire roused at the prospect of the repeated close touch demonstrated during her earlier treatment of his injury. Such a revelation threatened to negate all his fine attempts to convince her that seeking more between them was hopeless.

Linnet's hands, holding the small container of thick salve and clean strips of cloth, dropped aimlessly to her lap while she named herself a dolt ten times over. 'Struth, she would be mortified if he removed his clothing. For the first time she questioned her father's refusal to permit her to perform one of a castle mistress's duties—supervising the bathing of all newly arrived guests, female and male. Never had she seen an unclothed man.

The next instant Linnet recognized her folly in thinking that viewing a multitude of nude men—skinny or fat, young or old—would have prepared her for, let alone made her impervious to, the sight of Rhys's overwhelming masculinity. By their previous night's heated play and her intimate exploration of his chest, she knew enough to realize nothing would lessen the impact. Of a sudden she greatly feared that the task she'd insisted upon performing might be beyond her ability to calmly accomplish. Nonetheless, her practical side warned, the wound needed seeing to and seeing to now. If for Rhys's sake she could steal her father's destrier and ride alone into the dangerous night forest, surely for the sake of his health she was capable of performing this feat.

"Whatever is necessary to see the deed done, I'll do." With the determined words and a brave facade of calmness, Linnet rose to her feet while meeting his penetrating gaze full on.

Rhys drew a deep breath. Here was another glimpse of the seldom revealed inner strength at her core, a strength beyond and more enduring than her infrequent flashes of angry fire. After closing and securely fastening the shutter, he squarely faced her to unemotionally offer a compromise.

"If you demand I comply with your wishes, pray first permit me to withdraw for a brief time to my chamber. There will I remove these garments and replace them with a fresh tunic able leastwise to cover me from shoulder to mid-thigh and thus spare a measure of your innocent blushes." Aye, he silently admitted, her innocent blushes and his own fragile hope for successfully navigating the ship of his honor untouched through desire's stormy seas.

Linnet refused to let Rhys see the depth of her relief as she nodded agreement. Fine intentions were all well and good, but she was none too certain of her ability to deal with the full effect of his superb power and blatant masculinity laid bare to what she feared would likely be a revealing gaze, as awed as it was embarrassed.

Suiting actions to words, Rhys quickly retreated to his chamber, unfastened the silken bandage, stripped off his clothing, and returned to the hall garbed in the abundant folds of a rough homespun shirt. Although it was unlaced at his throat, a belt rode about his narrow hips. Before pouring himself a goblet full of deep red wine, with lifted vessel and upraised brow, he silently offered Linnet the same. Her response was a slight shake of shiny tresses.

Back momentarily turned to her, he completed the task, thankful for an additional blessing. 'Twas a stroke of great good fortune that it had apparently not occurred to her to insist upon caring for the wound while he reclined in his chamber. Ynid would have done so, but motherly Ynid would have presented no temptation. Whereas Rhys very much doubted that his famed iron control was equal to overcoming the enticement of Linnet's soft form in close proximity to the inviting cavern of his high, heavily draped bed.

As Linnet approached the man who'd lowered himself onto a bench with back resting against the table behind him, he tilted his head and took a long drink from the sturdy vessel filled near to the brim. White light from a small pyramid of candles on the table top glowed over his shining hair. Waves of wrongful awareness washed over her, waves she knew emanated from the man who shared their power. That potent knowledge contained a greater peril, as she was certain Rhys would never forgive her for testing him beyond the limits imposed by his honor, not when he'd been at pains to warn her about those limits. To divert the aching tide, she forced a distant lightness to her voice.

"If you will arrange the tunic so as to lay bare the wound, I'll set to the task at hand and have it done in a trice." Even these innocuous words brought a rosy glow to Linnet's cheeks.

Rhys was amused by the blush emphasizing her creamy complexion. Here was proof to allay any lingering doubt he might have had about her inexperience, for this was a further demonstration of how unaccustomed she was to all things intimate. Plainly she found it embarrassing to so much as say the word "bare," let alone move the garment herself. It was just as well, for a touch, inadvertently too adventurous, would have been—as he'd first feared—a fearsome revelation to such an innocent.

"Does this answer your needs?" Rhys asked with a mockery he knew she would not understand, while pulling the edge of his long homespun shirt safely up to a point just above the top end of the bright gash in his flesh.

Linnet nodded, taking a deep breath before bravely lowering the gaze she'd kept upon his fully covered and thus somewhat less threatening chest. The view of Rhys's heavily muscled thigh was so close that, despite her determination that it would not happen, an even brighter hue burned her face. The alarming proximity between herself and this beloved yet frightening man made her heart stop and skip wildly.

Thank the saints I am sitting, Linnet fervently told herself. Elsewise, like the fool I become when he's near, I'd doubtless fall again at his feet.

"Aye, well"—Linnet audibly gulped, much to her observer's secret delight. "I—I'd best treat this wound afore you freeze."

Dark gold brows rose in mock surprise while a sardonic smile curled his mouth. Him—freeze? 'Twas the very last danger she ought fear.

"This unguent will sting, but only for a moment." With the fingertips of one hand Linnet scooped out a small portion of the creamy salve, then leaned forward to gently apply it so as to cause him the least possible discomfort.

The hand touching Rhys spread fire in its path, but not the fire of the salve, though in truth it hurt not a little. Too aware of an unaccustomed vulnerability to this woman's innocent wiles and the strain put upon his honorable intentions by unconsciously caressing fingers, self-disgust hardened his handsome face into a mask of cool cynicism.

Once she'd finished smoothing the salve where needed, Linnet's fingers remained on hair-roughened skin just beyond the outer edge of an already closing gash. She'd found a wrongful pleasure in the feel of his flesh and the way hard muscles tightened beneath her touch.

"Be quick about your binding of the wound." Rhys's words were curt, and his face was rigid with frustration.

The mingled irritation and impatience in his voice told Linnet she'd exposed her helpless response to his sensual lures. She was shamed by that fact. Although assuredly unwise, her gaze rose to meet the intensity of eyes blacker than midnight. Confused by the fire in their depths, she looked away. Whether its source was anger or desire mattered little when she'd earlier acknowledged that he would never forgive her were she to cost him his honor.

Linnet pulled together the ragged edges of pride savaged by a vulnerability repeatedly exposed and rejected as she hastened to fold a pad for covering the wound. Without risking another upward glance she fastened it in place by neatly wrapping strips about the hard contours of a powerful thigh. But when she had fastened the end, she went motionless, unsure what next to do.

Feeling like the Wicked Troll of Pontfaen, whose name mothers wielded to frighten small children into right ways, Rhys caught the hands twisting a cream linen skirt into tortured folds. To forestall an insane urge to put them where he must not, Rhys meant to rise and lift Linnet to her feet. Instead he made the dire mistake of looking down into a piquant face dominated by wide amber eyes near matched in hue by clouds of lustrous hair.

Beneath his potent gaze Linnet melted to pure honey, unable to look away from the warm smile gently curving hard lips with a rare sweetness and the same welcome he'd shown in her fantasies. The impact of this attention sent through her a wave of strangled pleasure. It drove all else beyond the edge of her consciousness, narrowing her world to a dark and private place filled with the slow, hot stirring of anticipation.

Just as Rhys bent his head toward forbidden lips, the door burst open. The howling winds of the threatened night storm seemed to blow a dark figure into the hall.

A black cloak swirled around Grannia as she dropped its hood back to stare with accusing eyes at the scene before her: Rhys half dressed while the Norman damsel rested on her knees at his feet, clearly naught but a heartbeat from surrendering to his passion. Her gaze remained steady on the pair while she grasped the door, thrust it closed with a loud thud, and leaned back against its solid planks.

"Sister, welcome." Feeling an unaccustomed heat flood his cheeks, Rhys silently ridiculed himself for blushing like a guilty child. "As Ynid has gone to care for my injured warriors, our guest has exercised her healing talents to see this wound of mine treated and bound." As he had first intended, Rhys rose and pulled Linnet to her feet.

Grannia nodded but made no comment, although she gave her brother a glare both skeptical and accusing.

Rhys's jaw went taut; he felt even more like a small boy caught in wrongdoing by a disapproving mother. "For the sake of that wound and responsibilities to be met on the morrow, I mean now to retreat and seek needed rest." Without further word or so much as a glance toward Linnet, he stalked toward the corner stairway.

The two women watched until he'd climbed wooden steps and disappeared into the shadowed hallway at the top. Indeed, not until the click of a door latch falling closed had been heard did Linnet sink down upon the bench he'd vacated.

Grannia divested herself of her cloak and hung it from one of the pegs driven into the wall beside the door. Moving to the table's far side, she took a seat on the bench opposite this woman whose quiet courage, willingness to toil, and ability to calmly handle whatever challenges life dealt she'd come to admire. Even before Linnet's departure, Grannia had realized the wrong in blaming her for the sins of her father. And the words she'd realized must be said, facts this gentle damsel had best know, were not meant to cause anguish but rather to forestall a larger measure.

"Rhys and I are but half Welsh." Grannia awkwardly began a warning well intended.

Linnet nodded, a faint frown creasing her brow. What reason was there for Grannia to repeat a known fact?

"Therefore"—Grannia saw the other's puzzlement but could not allow it to deter her from the objective of giving information that might prevent harm to both Linnet's virtue and Rhys's future—"any child he might give you would be but a quarter Welsh and, if a son, of bloodline so weak that the people of Cymer would never accept him as prince. No matter Rhys's feelings for you or yours for him, by this reasoning alone an honorable union between you is impossible."

Linnet's smile was forlorn, but her chin tilted bravely upward. She was already facing a multilayered wall of the many restraints Rhys had earlier named; this further barrier was unnecessary.

Before Linnet could respond, Grannia spoke again. "Truly, I tell you this only to see you forewarned of the deed's price. Whether or not you go to Rhys is none of my concern, made even less so by the choice I've made." She shared Linnet's obvious pain and wished it were one possible to cure, but she knew all too well that no remedy existed for the malady of love.

"I thank you for caring what comes of the love I bear your brother—an emotion I know 'twould be useless to deny." In Grannia's dark eyes Linnet read sincere concern and smiled, although it accomplished no more than a slight lifting of lips. "But, as my love is not returned and Rhys has spent the better part of this night and many times afore telling me that *any* bond betwixt us would be impossible, your worries would seem to be needless."

A skeptical gleam returned to Grannia's eyes. Linnet was plainly too blinded by her own emotion to recognize Rhys's response was more than the mere physical enthrallment Grannia's fortuitous arrival had sundered. Nay, Grannia had seen the tenderness softening his gaze and the warmth in smiles losing their cynicism when turned upon the Norman damsel. Still, it was best Linnet fail to know Rhys's actual feelings. Certainly Grannia would not be the cause of additional hurt by insisting that Linnet know how tantalizingly near was a forbidden happiness.

Grannia reached out to lightly squeeze the fingers distress had tightly entwined. "Seems we are more alike than I'd once thought possible."

Amber eyes met black in complete understanding. "Aye, impossible loves are our lot. But to give final end to mine, I've agreed to Prince Rhys's suggestion that I retire to the Abbey of Saint Anne and join the sisters there."

11

IT MIGHT HAVE BEEN THOUGHT THAT EARL GODFREY'S glare could attain no fiercer heat than had the burning glower earned by the previous day's discovery of a gate guard's failure to fulfill an honorable command or the furious scowl he gave to cowards in battle. Yet, this morn's frozen expression proved it horribly untrue. That it was merely a dangerously thin layer atop roiling sparks on the verge of erupting was clear. Every moment withheld increased the savagery of flames threatening to burst their restraints and rain tongues of flame upon them.

Godfrey abruptly rose from the high table, leaving the day's first meal behind untasted. His disquieted men rose immediately to follow him, despite longing glances cast at food but half eaten.

Linnet hadn't, as Godfrey had assumed the previous night, remained demurely secluded during the execution of justice upon unworthy heads. Nay, rather she was not in the castle at all! His pale brown eyes threatened to throw fiery bolts of ire upon any who dared cross his path as, flanked by Osric and Mark, he strode from the hall with a large contingent of warriors at his back.

Mark sent an oblique glance toward his father. Though the earl had refused even to contemplate such a possibility, it seemed clear to Mark—likely to Osric as well—that, at least a day gone by, Linnet had slipped from the castle and warned the Eagle of yestermorn's strategy and goal. How else could the Welsh prince have been waiting, prepared for battle? Only she, aside from Mark, his uncle, and his father, had known of the plan before the day of battle began.

While Godfrey fumed and Mark silently questioned recent events, Osric stifled a gratified grin, although cruel pleasure still gleamed in his gaze. First Godfrey's young heir had unknowingly called his father to task for honor tainted, and now the earl's beloved daughter, plainly disillusioned by his actions, had fled from Castle Radwell to warn an intended victim. Osric felt he couldn't have planned a punishment more fitting—or satisfying. And he would take great delight in watching Godfrey squirm.

Upon entering a courtyard filled with destriers readied and awaiting riders whose day's chore was a search, the group split into quiet clusters talking in undertones while they checked saddles, girths, and reins.

"Nephew." The word was quiet and drew the attention of none but its target. "You know why you were summoned home?" Osric's question was not really a question, for after years of planning why else would the young man have returned? Nonetheless, one bushy brow lifted above unwavering eyes demanding answer.

Osric quickly grew impatient awaiting some reaction from the unmoving Mark. Why the hesitation, if hesitation be the source? For all that since the age of ten Mark had rarely been with Morwena, it was certain that during those initial years he'd been thoroughly indoctrinated with the wickedness of the conduct by which his father had robbed him of a position rightfully his. Too, the boy now man had been repeatedly lectured on the one method of putting right the wrong done him.

Face impassive, Mark at last nodded toward his uncle Osric.

"Aye, well, then . . ." Osric was uncomfortable under Mark's silent and expressionless response. He distinctly disliked the feeling and continued in a tone dangerously louder and harsher. "The day of retribution has arrived. See you to the task required."

This command was met by the steadiness of an icy gaze from a younger man gone utterly motionless.

"Once we're off, likely we'll be divided to more quickly cover larger stretches of ground." Osric doggedly continued, determined Mark should not fail for lack of understanding a scheme surely as clear as spring water. "Thus none will notice if you double back and entice our prey to join you in the search."

Mark glanced over his shoulder toward the glum lad standing among shadows at the top of the castle steps, plainly disgusted that he was to be left at home with the women while the men of Radwell set off on an exciting quest. Narrowed silver eyes returned to the Saxon but only for a moment before Mark wordlessly turned to the task at hand.

Osric's irritation with his nephew's attitude increased, and only with difficulty did he suppress his ire. Here, surrounded by a hushed and focused group, he could hardly press the point with more force. Besides, 'twould surely be unnecessary. Over the whole of Mark's lifetime Morwena had been sowing in him the seeds of bitterness and jealousy. Her sole purpose had been to see grow within him a crop of discontent healthy enough to sustain him through any action necessary to reap the future of which he'd been cheated. This long-awaited harvest could be secured by the deed that Osric urged he take this day.

Osric knew where Linnet must be—as, doubtless, did Godfrey. Fortunately, it would take time before Godfrey was able to admit his beloved daughter had defected to the enemy. This fact made it possible for actions, if taken quickly, to hasten the arrival of Osric's lifelong goal—to see Godfrey robbed of everything of any importance to him and subjugated beneath a Saxon's unsympathetic heel. Osric meant to see Godfrey suffer as had his own father with everything taken from him, then left to die a shamed man. Since the moment dishonorable oaths had been spoken decades gone by, Osric had schemed and worked to see the Norman earl come to this end. Osric's goal was almost in his grasp, but knowing that haste might act like butter on his fingers and cause the prize to slip from his hold, he tamped down a dangerous fever to instantly pounce atop it.

Realizing the earl was mounted, Osric turned and swung atop his own great steed, but not even the drizzle quickly becoming a steady rainfall could dampen the fires of his anticipation.

The dreariness of a relentless rainfall was merely a reflection of the gloomy attitudes of the unspeaking four within Rhys's hall. Seated at one end of the table, golden brows knit with concentration, Rhys diligently moved the sharpened point of a hollow quill across a sheet of parchment while Owain stood before a window whose shutters he had opened to the bleak view. Impatiently waiting for Rhys to finish his task, Owain was still wearing the cloak he'd refused to remove upon entering a brief time earlier. He wanted it clear to *all* within that this was not a social visit but an answer to a summons. With this reaffirmed decision, he cast a quick frown toward Grannia.

Two women hustled about the far end of the table where Rhys worked. Into the large basket opened to receive it, Grannia carefully placed a small earthen pot of the thick and savory-smelling stew she'd set to simmering the night past. Linnet added to the basket slices of carved venison, rounds of dark rye bread, and a large portion of deep orange cheese. Once the wicker lid had been closed upon goods ready for carrying to their proposed destination and recipients, Grannia resolutely moved to stand beside the bearded bear.

"When you leave on my brother's errand"— determination further firmed the well-defined line of her jaw—"I will walk with you as far as Ynid's cottage. While she toils to heal the wounds of others, we would not have her family suffer for the lack of her presence. Linnet and I have prepared these foodstuffs to see them properly fed through this time without her." She waved toward the sturdy hamper, which bulged with bounty.

Firelight from behind Owain gleamed over coal black curls as he grudgingly nodded. Still, he refused to glance toward the temptation he must struggle to reject. When Grannia slipped her hand into the crook created by a mighty arm bent to rest fingers on sill, Owain went rigid. Refusing to allow his attitude to deflect her intent, in quiet words she wheedled for even a faint easing of his restraint, and her dark eyes softened with a potent inducement to yield, which he stubbornly refused to meet.

While the pair by the window talked in low tones, Linnet drifted helplessly nearer to Rhys, as if she were naught but inconsequential iron shavings drawn to the lodestone he was. She idly glanced over his shoulder with mild curiosity.

Although aware of Linnet's nearness with every fiber of his being, Rhys looked up with feigned surprise. "Can you read these words?"

Linnet answered with a wistful smile of regret for her inability to give meaning to black marks laid atop creamy vellum. Then, as a clearer response, she gave a slight shake of abundant tresses washed free of the twigs and dirt of her adventures but brushed and left unbound to dry in the relative privacy of this abode.

"As a well-born Norman damsel I'd have thought you able." Although a statement, Rhys's last words ended on an upward note, which made of them a question. He meant to elicit verbal reinforcement of her silent response's clear meaning. Though unnecessary for him, he had seen the suspicious look Owain cast toward Linnet.

"Nay. In truth, I know very few men, save priests, who possess that ability." The intensity of a gentle smile sweetly curling soft berry-bright lips went beyond the polite acknowledgment of acquaintances. "And never have I heard of a woman able to decipher the meaning of the mysterious symbols you've made."

"I am fortunate that in my Norman foster father's castle dwelt a most learned man who deemed the ability to read and write to be as important as the skilled wielding of a sword."

"'Struth." Linnet nodded without hesitation. "An unusual man."

The pleasure-pain in having Linnet so close put Rhys in a purgatory all his own, caught between the heaven of her nearness and the fires of despair in knowing she could never be his.

"I am also fortunate he was willing to fill the winter's long, empty hours first teaching me the secrets to written languages and later lending me his precious scripts to read."

"I have heard priests entice prospective novices with talk of the worlds to be found in such scripts—the stories of the ancients as well as the teachings of God." Sincerity softly rang in Linnet's next words. "Would that I were offered the key to such treasures."

Rhys was surprised to hear any well-born damsel speak with such fervor of matters holding little enough interest for the men of his acquaintance and none for the women.

"Were we to be together for any length of time, I would share the knowledge with you."

"Then, when you were absent for any length of time," Linnet replied, "you could send missives from which I could read news of your mission's progress and reassurances of your health to those left behind."

Warm amber eyes glowed with quiet dreams although thick lashes shyly fell as she added, "And I could send mundane news of hearth and home to you." Eyes bright but an instant before went a dull brown.

Her talk of impossible deeds and his reference to limited time together returned them both to face the harsh facts of their present. While Linnet took an involuntary step back, Rhys withdrew into the impassive fortress built long ago to hold his true reactions safe from the prying of others.

Blinded by their own distress, neither of the two so near an all-important document noticed the further distrustful glance Owain cast Linnet. Yielding to the demands of his own suspicions, he turned from Grannia and strode toward the table. Might be the Norman damsel spoke true of her inability to read, but might also be she did not. And, if she was possessed of that skill, her purpose in approaching Rhys could well have been to secure knowledge of the Eagle's plans with the intent of warning her father.

"I see you are done with the deed." Not waiting for an answer, Owain swept up the sheet of parchment covered with characters in ink now fortunately dry. This he neatly folded until no glimpse of black marks could be seen. He placed the pristine square atop wooden planks, ready for closure by the Eagle's distinctive seal. It then would remain unopened until King William Rufus himself broke the seal.

With wry amusement, Rhys looked up into a steady blue gaze. Owain had already spoken to him privately of his distrust of the earl's daughter and her "oh, so opportune" flight to Abergele. But having naught to wield against his friend's concerns but an inner certainty of Linnet's trustworthiness, Rhys could hardly battle the man's doubts, although they were equally nebulous. In truth, any statement of personal trust would likely rouse in Owain naught but a deeper despair by convincing him that his leader had fallen weak to a feminine adversary's wiles. Nay, time will out, and in the end nothing Rhys could say would speed that revelation.

"Send it off to the destination we've discussed. Then we will wait upon the response it wins and see for ourselves to what lengths a lord's duty to his people extends."

Linnet was confused by this talk of lords and their people—on this isle surely a topic of importance only to the Norman baronage and their serfs. Rhys had earlier taken pains to explain that in Wales all men were free and only for the common good of the people would they answer even a prince's summons.

"We should have answer to our petition within a fortnight." Owain's words were directed to Rhys but his attention was heavy upon Linnet.

At last shifting the glare, which its object entirely failed to understand, Owain turned toward the outer door. Grannia hastened to don her own cloak, then paused to speak to the two who would remain.

"While off to do your bidding, Owain will see me safe to Ynid's door." Grannia announced it as a fact and not one open to dispute. "Pywell can walk me home after."

Rhys absently nodded, preoccupied with thoughts of how best to proceed in the days before a response to his missive could be reasonably expected.

Owain lifted the heavy basket in one hand and reluctantly offered his free forearm to Grannia. Resting slender fingers lightly atop the grudgingly offered arm, Grannia gave her unwilling escort a blindingly brilliant smile. Owain caught his breath and then glared off into the gloomy distance as he led from the abode a female demanding more than either dared give. 'Twas Grannia who reached back to see the door closed with a snap.

Through steady rainfall the hooded pair walked in complete silence. A determined Owain scowled into the rain-darkened view ahead while Grannia refused to dwell upon her companion's tight-lipped displeasure. Their destination was an old but sturdy cottage closed against the dreary day while golden light from the hearth within slipped through every crevice in the daub and wattle walls and shone between cracks about the frames of windows and doors. As they approached, Grannia came to a halt beneath the marginal protection of a spreading elm's abundant leaves.

Feeling Grannia's hand slip from his arm, Owain had perforce to turn and see what was amiss. Nothing. Black brows fiercely frowned. 'Twas as he'd suspected. Merely did she stand, hair hood-sheltered from the rain and in shadow while her beguiling face was tilted to one side and lent a warm glow by the faint illumination from the cottage.

"You intend to invite Ynid's family to picnic with you here?" Owain was in no mood for her antics, and his tightly restrained vexation fair smothered the words.

Never one to be so easily deflected, certainly not by Owain's irritation, where her goal was so important, Grannia glided forward to rest both palms against the man's broad chest. "As besiegers take even a well-fortified castle by outwaiting their foes, with my patient but relentless pursuit I shall win what I seek." In accompaniment to that oblique declaration, she rose on tiptoe, wrapped her arms about his neck, and laid her mouth squarely atop his.

A growl rumbled from Owain. His free hand lifted to push Grannia away, but turning traitor to his will, it instead crushed her closer while his lips parted in demand for a much deeper kiss. When she accepted— nay, welcomed—his demand, Owain felt his control slipping away. He desperately wanted to taste her full measure, to swallow her whole, but in a remote corner of his mind sanity survived and shrieked the warning that this embrace could never, must never, be! Whatever the pain required, he must see that Grannia lose this war whose victory would cost her even more than the price he would pay.

Owain jerked his head up; and, while regaining steady breath and again locking an inflexible control over his emotions, he gazed into the leafy branches above where lurked a green darkness seemingly filled with condemnation.

"Halt your attempts to see me fall victim to your wiles! End your dangerous game now!" He pulled from her embrace and held her at arm's length. "Victory in your pursuit will only bring us both greater pain—and shame. I warn you, the day you return to Newydd Farm will be the day that I leave it behind."

Without waiting for her response, Owain marched toward the cottage door. She could either follow or remain behind. He refused to glance her way to discover which choice she'd made. After setting the basket on the ground, he rapped sharply on thick oaken planks. He meant there to be no time for his delicious opponent to prolong this skirmish.

Grannia hurried after the angry man, but before she reached his side, the door was opening—and Owain was disappearing down the path. Though she cheerfully returned the greetings of excited children clustered in an open portal, an unaltered determination burned in Grannia's gaze.

After the door sharply shut behind the couple, Linnet uncomfortably shifted from one foot to the other while unblinking eyes of pure obsidian studied the hearth's low-burning flames.

"Methinks Owain had rather not play the gallant to your sister." Hoping to distract Rhys from his plainly bleak thoughts, Linnet sought to make light of the tension in the pair's departure—and failed so miserably that she instantly regretted her sorry whim.

"Owain is not and never can be Grannia's gallant— as you learned once before." Rhys's tone was a low rumble, as tightly controlled as his impassive face. "He is her stepson, and that, as we both know, is the crux of the matter and the underlying source of his attitude." Dark eyes drifted over a too lovely form with a show of disdain. "For the sake of his honor as well as hers, he cannot give what she seeks."

Folly. Pure, witless folly! Linnet wrapped her arms about her waist and tangled her fingers in the abundant cloth there. She ought not to have resurrected a topic best left lying safely untouched. Linnet earnestly wished she could simply melt into nothingness beneath the golden sparks of a black gaze's steady heat. Worse still, his penetrating scrutiny left her in no doubt but that his last words were directed as much toward their unsought proximity as toward the departing couple.

Despite her regret for having raised the subject in the first instance, Linnet blundered onward, wanting him to understand his sister's actions. "Aye, their love is impossible, but that fact can no more end the emotion than either you or I can halt the rain falling without." Caught up in the fervor of her own words, Linnet loosed clenched cloth to wave toward the storm beyond sheltering walls. "Nor," she continued, heedless of either the consequences or the pride-crushing secret her words revealed, "can what I feel for you be halted simply because you order it so."

The sparks in the Eagle's eyes exploded into a fire threatening to consume its tender prey. This was dangerous. This was wrong. And, God forgive him, this openly offered love was also what he hopelessly wanted beyond all reason. The passion of an impossible love returned quickly incinerated his good sense and honorable intents.

Although shaking his head against a wrong he could not stop, in one fluid motion Rhys rose and stepped over the bench to sweep the trembling damsel into his arms. Her flesh seemed to melt at his touch. While she pressed luscious curves against him without thought of denial, he tangled his fingers into warm tresses that enveloped his hands like a living caress.

Linnet's breath caught on pleasures unexpectedly given, and heavy lids fell over eyes of molten honey. With every sense atuned, she felt the approach of his kiss and yearned upward while searing, exciting images of their last embrace filled her thoughts.

Mouth closing over her sigh-parted lips, Rhys claimed delicious forbidden fruit. Aye, forbidden but too sweet to easily relinquish. He closed his eyes tightly as if to blot out warnings of wrongs done and the prices to be paid. Large hands beneath a mass of dark honey silk slid slowly down a slender back. Beneath the caress Linnet instinctively arched while shudders of wild excitement shook her. Loving the feel, the taste, the intimacy, she was aware that her heart thudded a heavy beat. She tightened her arms about his neck, crushing herself against him, wanting to be closer still.

The damsel's action brought Rhys potent memories of her tender and generous flesh against his own tough skin with only the flimsiest barrier betwixt, and a small satisfied smile curled lips laying a path of teasing fire from Linnet's mouth down the arch of her throat. Then a soft whimper escaped the damsel's tight throat. That vulnerable sound smote Rhys with guilt, and the headlong surrender of a plainly innocent damsel struck a blow deep into his conscience. Rhys immediately lifted his head and tucked her face beneath the chin he rested atop a cloud of amber tresses.

The realization that she'd been rejected once again unceremoniously dropped Linnet from the heights of passion.

To lessen the anguish emanating from his gentle beloved, Rhys spoke, his words a husky thunder. "I could nearly forfeit everything to accept that which you'd have willingly surrendered now—and times before. Aye, to claim that and all that you are, would I give anything—save my honor. And my honor is the price I would be required to forfeit for taking you as my own."

Linnet was stunned, caught between the heaven of the admission he'd made and the glimpse of hell to be found in the rejection blocking any future between them and taking away her every hope of happiness.

"Seems we've arrived at an inopportune moment, sister."

Rhys went rigid, thankful his back was to the door and broad enough to shield the sight of Linnet's too open expression. Keeping the damsel behind him, Rhys sharply turned about to send the speaker—a small, dark, and wiry man little older than he was—a fierce glare near able to pin any foe to the floor.

"A man stationed outside told us not only that you were here but that you'd recently been injured. We knocked but when no answer came, fearing some complication of the wound had incapacitated you, we let ourselves inside."

Purred words came from a stunningly beautiful woman whose clear blue eyes were narrowed with spite. Masses of curly dark hair, only nominally restrained by the loose braids that fell over her shoulders, outlined a softly feminine and very elegant form.

Linnet, peeking around Rhys's broad shoulder, felt herself already shrinking beneath the inevitable comparison between her inadequate charms and this . . . She refused to put the demoralizing comparison into words, even in her own thoughts.

"Indeed, as you see, I am in fine health. And, as my guest has expertly treated the injury, I've no need of your aid." Rhys paused, letting his gaze slowly measure both his male guest and the two husky men, plainly his guards, who had crowded in behind him.

"Lady Linnet, meet here another Welshman of importance." Rhys reached around and wrapped his arm around his guest, pulling her forward to stand at his side. "Prince Cawdr of Dyfi—and his lovely sister, Gwendellyn."

While the female's narrowed sapphire eyes measured her with disdain, Linnet wanted nothing so much as to hide once more in Rhys's shadow. But, determined to never again flinch before and expose her pigeonhearted nature to this woman, she restrained the urge. The one blessing lent Linnet by Gwendellyn's gaze was that she had no attention to spare for the prince of Dyfi's far crueler scrutiny.

"Cawdr," Rhys continued. "If you've come to see Grannia, you have arrived moments too late. She has only just left to take a basket of foodstuffs to a family in need of it."

"Nay." A dark head prematurely streaked with gray shook, but its owner's eyes never left Linnet's winsome face. "I have not come so much to see Grannia as Gwendellyn has come to see you. She pesters me incessantly to visit and urge you to lend haste to the promised deed."

Gwendellyn's heavy lashes fell in an apparent modesty, which Linnet didn't for a moment believe, an opinion reinforced as the woman advanced to within a mere whisper of Rhys. She easily insinuated herself between Linnet and the golden prince to run her forefinger teasingly across the full distance of his broad chest.

While glaring so heatedly at trespassing fingers 'twas a miracle they were not burned, Linnet suspiciously wondered what claim this woman had upon Rhys.

"Don't make me wait too long, Rhys." The coy voice was seductively low while sapphire eyes peeked up through flirtatiously half-lowered lashes. "Already you've postponed the betrothal ceremony too many times."

Cawdr caught a glimpse of the unmistakable, if immediately hidden, jealousy on the Norman damsel's face. "Aye, Rhys, 'twould be dangerous to make Gwendellyn wait too long." With the veiled threat he sent the prince of Cymer a level, accusing glance.

Rhys met the other's oblique warning with no visible response beyond arms firmly crossed over a broad chest.

A smile nearer a sneer bent Cawdr's lips as he took a step closer to his host and increased the stakes. "Moreover, the possibility you've raised of an alliance between our lands made doubly strong by virtue of a like bond between me and Grannia is a matter that should soon be discussed."

"At a later time." Rhys's reactions were hidden behind his habitual mocking smile, although inwardly he cursed himself for a defense too hastily wielded. By the ill-thought ploy he'd opened a subject he wanted to discuss even less than the possibility of his own betrothal.

"'Struth. A bond between our peoples would be invaluable—to us both." Rhys gave a slight shrug and a brief nod. "As I've said again and again, however, I cannot take on this or any other responsibility until I have overcome more immediate threats and met other challenges."

He'd been putting off the inevitable for months, and now a postponement was even more earnestly desired. The prospect of being bound to the haughty, self-centered, and demanding woman standing too near was a hundredfold more distasteful after his recent taste of an Eagle's perfect mate: a soft and gentle Linnet with a honey-sweet voice . . . and the defensive talons of a hawk.

"As for Grannia's future," Rhys continued, realizing he'd paused and sent too long and intent a look to the woman preferred, "she is a newly made widow and will need time to heal." Again he idly shrugged. "Mayhap when sufficient time has passed for her sorrow to fade, I too will be free to forge firm links betwixt our lands." Or mayhap, Rhys would fervently pray, other more permanent paths could be found to circumvent the distasteful bond.

Linnet had felt the touch of the Eagle's gaze and knew, too, when it shifted away. She was certain he'd found a much more pleasing sight in the beauty whose fingers toyed with the laces at his throat as if on the verge of pulling them loose for a more intimate touch. Refusing to allow the betrayal in the fall of despicably plentiful tears rosing cheeks and brightening eyes, Linnet stared down at the hem of a borrowed home-spun gown. Its roughness and dull hue seemed a reminder that, for all that a plain linnet might on occasion be a more valuable defender for an eagle, 'twas clear a humble brown bird could never compete for attention against a peacock's bright plumage.

"You speak of dangers and challenges to *first* be met, but, fellow prince, I trust you'll not forget that the alliance betwixt our families and our peoples is one meant to prevent even greater difficulties." Cawdr's deep gray eyes were as hard and threatening as flint the moment before fire is struck from its surface.

"Were you forced to meet enemies attacking from the west as well as from the east," he continued, "your forces would be split—greatly increasing your vulner-ability." No tactful verbiage lent its cushioning shield to this unmistakable warning while charcoal eyes measured Linnet as would an executioner his victim for the ax. "You'd probably lose everything you mean to save."

"'Struth, and a rationale I am unlikely to allow to be either forgotten or forgone." Rhys remained im-mobile beneath the caressing and increasingly inti-mate touch of the woman he had far rather push from him. "Would you care to join us for a midday meal? I believe we've some savory stew to share."

The question gave Rhys an excuse to step free of

Gwendellyn. He moved toward the central hearth and lifted a ladleful of the tasty concoction, holding it encouragingly toward unwelcome guests.

"Nay. Though we thank you for the invitation, we've other matters awaiting our coming and needs must be off." Cawdr signaled for his guardsmen to step aside, opening the way for him to escort his sister out.

"Remember, Rhys." Gwendellyn paused and glanced coyly over her shoulder. "There are limits to my patience, limits to Cawdr's restraints."

Even after the visitors were gone, Gwendellyn's cooing voice grated over Linnet's nerves, but unbeknownst to her, it grated over Rhys's even more seriously. Linnet's distress deepened with the memory of that beautiful woman possessively touching the golden man she loved, and with the memory came an ache that passed beyond jealousy into the despair of hopeless inadequacy. With the cold, clear vision lent by time, his sweet declaration of willingness to pay any price to claim her seemed merely a sop given to lessen her shame in offering herself to him so oft it must seem like the refrain of a common song difficult to drive from one's thoughts.

As if it were a living thing, Linnet's anguish reached out toward Rhys. Gazing down at a piquant face whose eyes were downcast and lower lip was nibbled, he wished he could comfort her. However, with the recent repeated demonstrations of how very thin was his control where this one woman was concerned, he dared not.

Linnet felt the concentrated warmth of Rhys's attention but interpreted it as pity. She resented the fact her emotions were apparently clear to him, and that resentment kindled in her a courage strong enough to straighten her spine, lift her chin, and enable an amber gaze to meet the dangerous darkness of his eyes directly. After first banishing all expression from her face, in an attempt to erect a shield as impenetrable as his mocking smile, she threw out the one completely irrelevant subject that came to mind.

"When I arrived to warn you of my father's intent to be waiting at Abergele Farm, you promised that one day, when we had adequate time alone, you'd tell me an enlightening tale, which would explain how it was that you already knew his plan."

Dark gold brows rose in surprise at the unexpected topic she'd raised. Rhys hadn't forgotten his promise to reveal the whole of her father's wrongs—only had he made the promise with no expectation that it would ever be called forfeit.

"Surely," Linnet persisted, "we've adequate time now."

"Aye, we have, but it's a truth I am sure you'd be happier not knowing." He hesitated to be the agent through which Linnet heard the disturbing facts she demanded be told.

"Why? Because by that truth my father's honor is tainted? How could it possibly hurt me more than seeing proof of his *dis*honor in the battle I watched?"

Skepticism made Rhys's eyes completely black. Although, unlike Owain, Rhys trusted the innocence of Linnet and believed her truly uninformed about these secrets, he was not convinced that the full details of the earl's wrongful deeds ought be shared with the man's daughter. Still, he'd made the unwise promise and could not now refuse.

"How much do you know of the time when your father first came to Radwell as the lord chosen by the conqueror to take it under Norman rule?"

"Only that he fought bravely at William's side and was rewarded with the fiefdom of Radwell." Her chosen diversion proved more successful than expected as thoughts of her unimportant woes faded beneath what obviously would be a sobering revelation.

"That and no more?"

Linnet nodded, firelight gleaming on waves of amber hair.

It was true, then. Rhys's lips firmed into a grim line. Linnet knew only the whitewashed shell of past events, a fact that made the task ahead more daunting. He tugged her down to sit across from him at the table.

"Godfrey was cautioned by his duke to consider the need for healthy serfs to till the soil. Thus he was urged to treat with the Saxon master of Radwell rather than press for a one-sided fight certain to end in a killing, which would decimate his own possessions."

Linnet nodded. This much she'd concluded from idle talk of castle serfs but the steady light in dark eyes told her there was more.

"The young Godfrey did as directed but failed to take into account the age and experience of his rival. Radwell's Saxon lord, Siward, negotiated with his Norman conqueror. In exchange for the bloodless claiming of Radwell, Siward wrung from your father three oaths sworn upon the Holy Cross." Rhys paused to see what effect this news had on the wide-eyed damsel who, while awaiting what further he had to say, remained perfectly still.

"Of the three oaths the first was Godfrey's promise to honor and hold inviolate the Welsh border dowry lands of Siward's older daughter, Emma, my mother." Rhys sent his listener a faint half-smile and slight nod. "They'd been given several years earlier upon her marriage to Prince Griffith of Cymer, my father.

"The second oath was a pledge to bestow upon Siward's only surviving son the subfief of Northland." Rhys squarely met unblinking doe-brown eyes. "To this, too, your father agreed—so long as Osric swore homage to him."

While Linnet met Rhys's penetrating gaze unflinching, the onslaught of facts disclosed and apprehension over further revelations saw small fingers join so tightly together their tips turned white. Oh, aye,

Osric's talk of kinship as uncle to both Rhys and Mark had forewarned her of leastways that part of this tangle. And of course she'd always known that the man who held a subfief from her father was the son of the old Saxon lord, though amazingly powerful for one of lesser standing. But never had anyone hinted to Linnet that her father's subjugation of Radwell had been won by ceding major concessions.

Rhys saw tangled fingers and a gentle crease laid between delicate brows, but before she could put words into a question, he went on to finish what he'd begun.

"Third—and by the knowledge of subsequent events it would seem the most difficult for Godfrey to keep, as 'twas the first to be broken—he gave his oath to wed Siward's younger daughter, Morwena. Along with that vow he promised to name the southern borderlands as dower for her and her children."

"Mark's mother?" Linnet's response was not so much an honest question as a plea for rebuttal of a darker truth than could be easily accepted, as it foreshadowed unpleasant truths about her own background.

Candlelight flickered over blond hair as Rhys nodded. He took her hands into his and gently calmed their desperate twisting. "Morwena lived in Castle Radwell as Godfrey's wife in practice, though their union was never blessed by a priest. She was in residence there with her five-year-old son when your father left to answer a royal summons and journey to William's court in Normandy. Nearly a year passed before Godfrey returned . . . with a pregnant Norman wife."

"Me!" Linnet wanted to bury burning cheeks in her hands and would have, had Rhys not refused to allow her to pull them from his grasp. Looking up with desperation clear on her stricken face, she met the solace in eyes gone a gentle, cloudy black. "That's when my father brought my mother and Meara to Radwell. I was the expected babe."

The desolation in her gaze was an unconscious appeal for denial. Rhys wished he could say it was not so, fervently wished he'd never made the foolish promise to tell her this sorry tale.

Linnet read the answer in regretful eyes and gentle hold, an answer this truthful man couldn't deny. "Small wonder Mark has never been comfortable with me. I am the one who sent him from his home."

"Nay, you did not do that." Rhys was pleased there was some little detail he could refute and use to ease Linnet's pain. "Although Morwena was immediately consigned to the lands of her dowry on the southern border—where she lives today—Mark remained at the castle until your mother's distress over her seeming inability to bear a living son led her to believe many superstitions. Worried that Mark's presence doomed her childbearing goals, she begged your father to send the boy elsewhere. Bending to her wishes was convenient for Godfrey, as Mark was of an age to begin training for knighthood, and he sent the boy off to be fostered at his king's Norman court."

Although this first concern had been explained, Linnet's mind still whirled with all the unforeseen consequences of facts newly given.

"Now you see why when I came to Radwell and claimed you as hostage I had no need to specify which lands I demanded be returned. Your father knew I sought the dower he'd sworn to hold inviolate for my mother and her heirs. And now you can understand why I expected he would no more respect that oath made to me than he'd kept those given Siward many years past."

In admitting her father's wrongful intentions against Rhys, Linnet had already accepted his lack of honor, and though the notion hurt, it failed to divert her attention from another curious question.

"I don't understand why my father easily shirked the pledge to Mark's mother but waited so long to break the oath concerning your mother's lands."

"The Saxon lord was no fool. Once your father verbally gave these oaths before Siward and his three children, the aging man brought in a priest, who put them into written words. Your father had little option but to sign the document, though he doubtless thought it would be a small matter to see the parchment later destroyed.

"Siward, however, had planned for that likely threat as well. He gave the signed document to a young Osric with instructions to hide it in a secret place from which it could be retrieved should Godfrey fail in holding his oaths dear. Were the worst to happen, this evidence was to be sent to the Norman king, who valued the honoring of oaths."

"Then why was it not exercised on Morwena and Mark's behalf?" Having succeeded in pulling this tangled skein of past events into the light, Linnet wanted to untangle each knot and see the thread fully revealed from end to end.

"To what purpose, when the marriage was a fact and a child was on the way?" Rhys's smile was cynical. "I have vague memories of urgent messages arriving from a distraught Morwena, but they received scant attention as only a sennight earlier my mother had died bearing Grannia.

"My father had flouted Welsh tradition by wedding a Saxon, and under the best of circumstances there'd have been little possibility of him intervening on behalf of his sister-in-law. Grief-stricken . . ." Rhys slowly shook his head at the impossibility of such a deed, but then he continued.

"Nor could he apply to the Norman king for relief. There was no physical proof of a sundered oath, only rumors of that document. Even had it had been produced, the king couldn't have undone a church-blessed union. Moreover, a dissolution granted by

Rome would have left one child or the other illegitimate. No one of Welsh or Saxon blood believed the Norman king would choose to protect a Saxon child over the unborn babe of a noble Norman damsel. Nay, only did your father's marriage increase the power of the threat Osric effectively wielded over your father's head like a sharp blade."

Linnet grimaced as she nodded comprehension. "'Tis why Alan was not sent to foster with my father's overlord, the king, but rather to a nobleman of lesser standing—to Osric himself."

Rhys gave a humorless smile of agreement.

"It answers many questions I never dared ask. . . ." Linnet's words were soft but in the room's stillness clearly heard. "It even explains why and to whom my father has agreed to see me betrothed."

Rhys slowly shook his head. "Although it at first seems true, I doubt that it is. Leastways the worth of the original document as a weapon lasted only so long as the priest who wrote it lived. Father Bertrand died in the waning days of winter. His death is, I believe, what freed Godfrey to attack Abergele Farm and, too, why Alan was summoned home . . . in time for me to take him hostage along with you. Your father, I think, had decided that the old threat was no longer valid. Who would believe such a claim made by a Saxon alone after lo, these many years?"

"But my father *did* intend to see me betrothed to Osric. Of that I am certain." A cloud of confusion put a slight crease on Linnet's brow.

"I don't doubt that he meant to do so." Holding mockery at bay, Rhys smiled soothingly. "Merely do I doubt that the original document was the price."

His explanation increased Linnet's puzzlement, and she frowned in earnest.

"I saw Osric on the fringes of the battle at Abergele Farm," Rhys said, "but he took no part in the fight. I suspect the promise of marriage with you was the price for my uncle's support in a battle against his nephew—me. Your father couldn't elsewise be certain of having it despite the oath of fealty Osric had given him as liege lord—not after having delivered dual insults to Osric by summoning Alan home with the intention of sending him off to the king and by earlier refusing his suit for you."

In the long silence that followed, Rhys watched Linnet's solemn face while new facts tilted the even surface of her world, shifting images of people and events. He wanted to remain and offer comfort, but that wish was a danger in itself. Nay, he dared not linger to answer more questions or spend more moments alone with this temptation to a wrong he'd come too near to seizing too often. He released her hands and in continuation of the same movement rose to his feet.

"I must go to check with men who stand guard along the eastern border." It was a cryptic excuse, and he turned sharply from wounded eyes to stride out of the house without a backward glance.

After the Eagle had flown from his aerie, Linnet was overcome by fears for Rhys, who apparently intended to fly into areas where continuing perils waited. She knew her father would, by his defeat the previous day, be even more determined to see dead the enemy who'd foiled him.

Finding herself caught in the same trap she'd evaded when deserting the haven Rhys had created for her to watch the battle and in the end save his life, Linnet grew even more anxious. This time she had no choice but to helplessly wait.

12

"WE MAKE A FINE PAIR."

Linnet's comment was as mocking as any Rhys had
ever uttered. Again wearing a practical homespun
gown, she scooted to the middle of one bench to sit
across the bare table from a droop-shouldered
Grannia, who was gloomier and far less energetic than
her usual vital self.

The new day had barely begun, but already Owain
had come to summon Rhys. A rash of small assaults
had been launched at various points along the border
between Radwell and Cymer. Remembering too well
her father's scheme to kill Rhys and having no doubt
that he would continue trying until the deed was done,
Linnet knew she must either block thoughts of dangers to be faced by the two men who'd departed early
or surrender to useless panic. The long, lonely night
hours had been fraught not only with fears for the
men's safety but also with thoughts of impossible
love.

"I admire your determination and courage in returning to Newydd Farm in spite of Rhys's and even
Owain's attempts to dissuade you." Linnet shifted her
attention into the single path enticing enough to

waylay bleak specters. She marveled at Grannia's strength of will in pursuing one beloved, no matter the towering walls blocking their relationship, walls even more formidable than those between her and Rhys.

Initially Linnet had wondered why the pair hadn't simply sought a papal dispensation to wed, but further consideration of the matter revealed their reasoning. First, they hadn't the wealth required to buy such a dispensation. Second, the pope's word hadn't the weight among Welshmen that it carried for her Norman peers. Thus, despite an exception granted by Rome, likely the people of Cymer would still look askance upon the union between a woman and her stepson.

Grannia's dark gaze lifted but revealed neither a hint of warmth nor a spark of energy. During his brief morning appearance, the bearded man had held his cold blue eyes as determinedly averted as they'd been almost every hour since the day Grannia had flouted his will and claimed her right to reside in her dead husband's home.

"Owain swears that if I return to Newydd, he'll leave. He has nearly done so already. Oh, he hasn't moved his belongings elsewhere, but neither does he truly live in the house with David and me. He leaves before I arise and returns only after I'm abed—no matter how long I wait by the fire."

Empathy darkened amber eyes. Linnet had suffered the same cold rejection from Rhys. Most recently a few hours past when she'd rushed to see him off in the purple haze of predawn. Idly fingering the lone iron candlestick placed in the table's center, against its black swirls she saw the scene wherein Rhys had refused to cast even one glance in her direction.

"Still . . ." Linnet focused again on Grannia and continued in a quiet, admiring tone that went far toward bolstering the other's resolve. "In seeking your goal you've shown a courage I covet. Would that I possessed the bravery to seek what I desire from Rhys."

Grannia turned to her companion a dark gaze so uncannily like her brother's that Linnet was startled. "I haven't won my goal."

"But you will." Linnet nodded firmly.

"'Struth. I have a plan." Grannia promptly agreed while staring fiercely at fingers flattened and pressed hard against the unyielding planks of the table top. "If Owain persists in returning home only to sleep—and rumpled bedcovers prove that he does—then that's where I'll be waiting—in his darkened bedchamber and in his bed."

Grannia knew such a tactic wouldn't achieve the end goal. Rather, it would be the first step in her battle to win the victory she sought. Glancing up at the other woman's pensive face, she realized how important it was for the Norman lady to be aware that any triumph would not be without cost.

"My choice I made knowing the wrong in what I seek—and its price. So long as Owain does not wed with me—and marriage would be a sin I would never allow him to commit—his honor will not be tainted, nor will he be blamed for giving what I boldly seek. I am certain that the stubborn fool loves me as much as I do him, and I'll gladly forfeit my good name to share that love."

"Aye." Linnet directly met the other woman's searching gaze. "'Tis a rationale I understand, for after spending the greater share of dark hours in impossible dreams, I came to a like decision." Reacting to Grannia's slowly shaking head, Linnet leaned forward and earnestly restated her decision. "Aye, I would welcome an opportunity such as the one this night will bring to you. Happily would I surrender my virtue to Rhys for the memory of one night in his arms before he delivers me into the abbey—one night to warm me through a lifetime of cold loneliness."

Grannia recognized a heartfelt commitment as deep as her own and grew determined to lend what little support she could to the other's cause.

"Even your warning that any son I might bear your brother would never be heir to his lands seems no impossible barrier," Linnet continued. "The babe would not lack for love, and I'm certain Rhys's child would be strong and prove himself capable enough to win, as my half brother has done, a place of honor for himself."

Amber eyes that had begun to sparkle went bleak. "Such fine resolutions are of little use to me, however. I lack your clear advantage. Whereas Owain loves you, putting you a giant's step nearer your goal, to Rhys I am more an irritant complicating his life than a valued companion, even less a woman beloved."

"There you are wrong. Rhys is very good at hiding his emotions—a talent that held him safe from torment while hostage in the land of his foes. Now this ability has made it possible for him to prevent you from seeing what is plain to an outside observer."

Linnet looked to Grannia with the faint stirrings of a hope she hesitated to test against the dangerous light of truth.

Grannia shook her head and grinned. "He watches you when you do not see, watches you with a tender fire in his dark eyes, which he gives no other."

"Then you think my cause not hopeless at the outset?"

Having already seen Linnet demonstrate an ability to calmly face and overcome life's challenges, in response to the desperate, fearful hope on her solemn face, Grannia smiled encouragingly.

"Best we lay plans to see our goals won."

Silver eyes squinted up into a sun hazed by lingering fog, though it was past midday. The nooning meal ought to have been consumed, Mark reasoned. 'Twas

218

the best time to reappear and embark upon the deed his mother and uncle demanded he perform.

He spurred his gray stallion into a canter so as to more quickly cover the ground between forest edge and the lowered drawbridge. Once across thick wooden planks and into the courtyard, he swung down. He wasted no time entering the hall. From his position a single pace within he caught sight of his quarry.

"Mark!" Alan's gloomy frown lifted into bright welcome. He dashed across the room and in a flurry of rushes skidded to a halt at his older brother's side. "You came back. Have you found Linnet?"

Affection melted Mark's icy eyes as with an exaggerated pout of despair he slowly shook his head.

"But you mean to resume the search? Will you take me with you, *please?*" Alan asked the questions without pausing for answers while at the same time taking one of Mark's hands in both of his as if to squeeze from it an agreement.

"That's why I've returned, Mouse. I thought it unfair you remained behind when all other males set off on a quest. Although, between you and me"—his voice dropped to a whisper—"I don't believe Linnet's been abducted or become lost. If my suspicions are true, she doesn't wish to be found, and thus no amount of searching will discover her."

Alan grimaced and made an admission which, when confessing his part in seeing Edolf locked in the storeroom, he'd told not even his father.

"Father didn't ask, though I expected he would, and I didn't offer the news that Linnet planned her departure. She told me her intention was merely a late ride. Should've smelled an untruth when she insisted on riding Thunder!"

Dark brows arched. "Thunder?" Mark hadn't put the hard-ridden destrier together with Linnet's disappearance. Even if he had connected the two facts, he'd have expected some male accomplice to have ridden the warhorse, carrying her as well. If truly she'd taken Thunder out alone, his opinion of her was greatly enhanced. It would take a brave, or leastwise determined, woman to risk mounting so powerful a steed. A foolish one as well.

Alan nodded. "When the next morn I saw our father riding away on the black beast, I thought Linnet, too, must again be safely home."

A frown replaced Mark's surprise. Was it possible he'd misjudged the situation? Had his half sister really gone for a midnight ride only to be thrown somewhere in the woods? Was she now lying somewhere sorely injured . . . or dead?

"What's wrong?" Alan's young voice squeaked with alarm revived.

"Nary a thing, Mouse." Mark ruffled the boy's amber locks and grinned a reassurance for them both. Surely if ill had befallen Linnet, the multitude of searchers would locate her. After all, they'd loosed hunting dogs to find and follow her trail. He shrugged away his concern for the female he'd never been able to like.

"I wonder if we dare slip into the forest where you can demonstrate for me this new method of hunting without weapons."

A gurgle of laughter escaped Alan's throat, revealing his utter faith in Mark's judgments. "Oh, can we? Please, please. Say we can."

The sight of the excited boy hopping from foot to foot won a laugh from Mark. "If you'll forgo that very interesting dance, we can set out right now."

In the forest naught but a small distance from where Alan was setting his trap to show off a new skill for his older brother, the man who'd ordered Mark to take the boy into the woods with ill intent met with another conspirator. Unnoticed by either group, a second young boy moved silently through dense green shadows and curiously watched a portion of both meetings although he heard the words of neither.

"You'll agree that I have provided you with valuable information." Osric's smile was as insincere as that of the man he faced.

"Valuable information have you given me—but of even greater benefit to you." A sneer played about the corners of Cawdr's mouth.

"Willingly conceded." The Saxon's face settled into smug lines. "What manner of weakling would it make of me to have aided you elsewise?"

Cawdr's laughter, muffled by thick vegetation and towering trees, was not a pleasant sound.

Osric continued unaffected. "I am pleased that you agree 'tis best we be honest and admit we assist each other only to gain what is best for ourselves."

Fog-diffused sunlight burnished the gray streaking a dark head tilted in interest, but still Cawdr said nothing.

"I have a plan with which, by joining our talents and forces, we will win a goal mutually sought. A goal providing more than enough fine booty for us both."

While the Saxon lord spoke, the Welsh prince listened. Then the bargaining began. Their bartering continued until shadows deepened under a low-riding sun painting the western horizon's hazy sky with a vivid rose shading into an even more brilliant orange.

When Osric rode from the site, satisfaction gleamed in his pale eyes. His goal was near, so near he could taste its sweetness on his tongue. The seeds of one assault had been planted and the ground for a second plowed. He would find it hard to be patient until their fruition, but the end would be well worth the wait. Meanwhile he would savor their blooms in the sight of Godfrey's growing discomfort.

Nothing could lessen Osric's bitter enjoyment of his day's work . . . until he strode into Radwell's great hall. There, already seated at the high table, were both

Mark *and* Alan! He glared at them both. Mark had lost the perfect opportunity to permanently remove what Morwena had taught him was the only barrier between himself and the earldom of Radwell. Aye, Mark had forfeited the chance to remove the brat and see the deed blamed upon Osric's other wretched nephew, the prince of Cymer. He must find his sister and see that she spoke strongly with her foolish son.

13

WITH TREMBLING HANDS LINNET EASED THE DOOR CLOSED
and then leaned back to rest against its support. She
peered into the velvet darkness of the Eagle's chamber
but gave no attention to its rich furnishings. That the
intricately carved high bed was draped in costly
brocaded silks, looped back on one side, held no
interest when between their parted edges lay revealed
the source of a treasure she'd come in the dead of
night to steal.

Pale moonlight fell through shutters opened wide,
and Linnet gazed in fascination at a broad male chest
completely bared to her for the first time by covers
pushed down to narrow hips. Dark gold hair spread
across a wide expanse of sun-bronzed skin. Rose lips
fell open, her gaze was drawn uncontrollably to the
V's arrowing path downward until it reached a cloth
impediment—and clenched shut. She gulped but
determinedly approached the sleeping man.

Grannia's intent to seduce an Owain made unwary
by deep slumber seemed to Linnet a fine plan. Hazy
possibilities had first begun to form this morn while
the other woman talked of her plan, but they'd been

refined and Linnet's intent firmed when the two of them had joined forces to plot similar though separate campaigns. Linnet felt certain this was her only hope for securing even a brief taste of the forbidden fruit, which would be a sin more wicked once she'd joined the nuns of Saint Anne. Thought of the abbey and the prospect of a barren future reinforced her determination to seize sufficient memories to live on for a lonely lifetime.

Linnet had been sincere in what she'd told Grannia. She *was* willing to forfeit her virtue in return for the memory of one night filled with secret joys and sweet delights in the love she could give no other and which no other could give to her. Thus, with unbound hair and loosened gown, she'd come prepared to this battlefield of last chances. Here in the privacy of his chamber, in his bed, she meant to launch a tender assault and seize a night of memories begun with this stunning view of his strongly muscled body's blatant power.

She drank in the sight, unable to look away even if she'd wished it. And having already relinquished the inhibitions of a lifetime to come this far, she shamelessly had no such desire. Despite her inexperience in such intimate forays, she hoped the strategy of coming upon a foe unexpectedly would provide her the same advantage similar tactics had lent Rhys the night he'd taken her captive.

Only one fact, the same fact that earlier had given her pause, held her back now. Where the Welsh pair's obviously mutual devotion would aid Grannia in securing her goal, Linnet was not fool enough to believe the other woman's well-meant but assuredly unfounded claim that Rhys returned her love. Though a dreamer within, she'd been raised to think in practical, realistic terms and saw too plainly that Rhys's feelings for her were no more than a simple physical response doubtless born of the proximity enforced by sharing a house.

No matter. Linnet shoved away from the door. Rhys's response to her was the single weak link she'd found in his defenses and lent power to her only weapon in this gentle assault—his desire. Exercising more courage than had been required even to mount a fierce black destrier, she shrugged out of the gown, lifted the corner of a rich coverlet, and slid into the Eagle's bed.

Rhys shifted slightly. Linnet froze, heart pounding, until it was clear that, despite his ragged breathing, he had not awakened. Uncertain what to do next to win the goal desperately sought and soon to be forever barred from her by abbey walls, she unconsciously nibbled a full lower lip and turned her head toward a breath-stealing sight.

She called upon vivid memories of every moment she'd spent in Rhys's arms, from the mocking kiss in Radwell's tower to the intoxicating embrace amid the forest—all kept fresh and embellished by dreams she could no more stop than she could draw her last breath and still live. This night she was determined to see those dreams fulfilled. Taking her cue from lessons his earlier restrained lovemaking had taught, she slid closer.

Pressing her body's lush curves against his side, she extended one hand to tentatively caress the hard, cool planes of his massive chest. Her fascination with the erotic combination of rough satin skin, abrasive hair, and steely muscles beneath overwhelmed her last hesitation. She touched more firmly, moving her fingers up to stroke the breadth of wide shoulders and felt his every line and curve begin to burn.

Rhys dreamed, as he had near every night since the moment he'd come upon the Norman damsel in her bath, of tempting, forbidden embraces he'd wrongfully reveled in only to be haunted by hot fantasies of anguished hungers impossible to appease. Now slumbering amid sleep-visions of honeyed delights, when dreams became a very real feminine shape moving against the aching heat of an aroused form, his sleep-fogged mind refused the call to unwelcome wakefulness with its unpleasant realities. Rather, at the feel of soft flesh melded to the hard muscle of his body, he groaned and suddenly rolled over, trapping her yielding form beneath his own.

Linnet's gasp faded into a sigh of welcome as his mouth descended and found hers with unerring accuracy. She lay motionless, savoring a first taste of the victory feast in this contact with his body pressed exactly over hers, hard chest against soft breasts, hip to hip, thigh to thigh. The heady intimacy elicited a faint whimper from her. Clinging to him, she felt the heavy pounding of his heart, an echo of her own. Drowning in blazing sensations, she sank deeper into burning dreams and, tempted by his, Linnet's tongue ventured forth to taste him.

Rhys responded immediately, crushing the gentle songbird even closer to his power, both giving and taking the devastating kiss he craved. Whether his strong need had given substance to his dream or she was of flesh and blood, lost in the red haze of passion Rhys had no will to question the gift. Already the fire in his blood blazed too fiercely to be quenched.

His mouth left hers. Resting on his forearms, Rhys gazed down into a beguiling face and eyes of molten honey. Pillowed on thick amber hair glowing in moonlight, her warm cream and deep rose flesh embodied the only tender emotion, completely unsullied by distrust, that Rhys had ever experienced. With the release of this dangerous admission went his last hope of putting safely aside the only woman he desired, the woman who was openly, trustingly, surrendering herself to him.

Beneath the golden fires in the depths of his dark eyes, Linnet gave a quiet cry of protest, fearing he'd come awake angered by her invasion of his bed and determined to reject her again. Then one masculine hand gradually laid a searing path up her side, over her hip and narrow waist to the sensitive flesh beneath one of the arms still clinging to his broad shoulders.

Slowly, slowly, Rhys let his outspread hand glide over skin whose velvety texture felt like rose petals and found the first gentle swell of her breast. He watched with satisfaction as wild shudders of excitement shook the enticing woman who'd invaded his bed. There could be no question what the forbidden innocent had come seeking. Nor, in spite of the many barriers he'd attempted to raise between them, was there any doubt but that the man caught off guard by a temptation too potent would give all that she sought . . . and more than a virgin could have reason to expect.

Heat-thickened blood had slowed Linnet's pulse to a dragging and uncertain rhythm. Now it blazed and sang. Though once the aggressor, she lay beneath him vulnerable and utterly, willingly defenseless as he reversed the roles she'd thought they would play. Incapable of restraining the revealing action, Linnet twisted sensuously under his touch. Rhys watched her respond to the pleasure of his caress, watched her drag in deep breaths as his palms returned to move more firmly against the outer edges of aching mounds. Helpless to prevent the action, she reached up to clasp his hand to needful flesh. He lightly pressed the warm softness, and she gasped. Linnet succumbed to a smoldering need while his hand cupped the full weight of her breast and mindlessly tangled her fingers into cool golden strands, urging him to renew the shocking pleasure he'd given her once before.

Yielding, Rhys bent his golden head to nuzzle her breasts slowly, cherishing her softness until she trembled under flashes of wildfire. He savored the addictive delicacy of creamy skin, and yet that caress was not enough for either of them. Linnet tugged him closer and at last came the whisper-light brush of his lips across the peak, driving her deeper into the fire's depths, teasing her senses mercilessly. Even then she wanted more and arched against his mouth, wordlessly demanding the surrender of a pleasure withheld until his lips opened and drew the tip into a starving cavern.

Linnet was overwhelmed by blazing sensations; another sweet moan rose and escaped her tight throat, earning a further small, satisfied smile from the tormenting lips of a man intoxicated by the sound. She plunged deeper into the dark fires of wicked sensations and wandered through the smoke of desire. Writhing against his hard body in shattering intimacy, she reveled in the searing heat of their embrace and the liquid blaze in her veins.

Rhys couldn't hold his body from moving against hers in a rhythm as old as time, and when she instinctively met the motion, he knew the end of his control was perilously near. Aching moments past, he'd conceded to the inevitabity of the culmination demanded by her irresistible lures, but still he wanted her memory of their joining to be one of a piercingly sweet satisfaction unmarred by pain. Fighting for a moment's mastery over his desire, in spite of his urgent need to merge their forms completely, he again pulled a short distance away from the forbidden delights contained in her dainty form.

"No-o-o!" When she saw his eyes clenched shut against her, as they had been too many times before, Linnet's whispered cry was a refusal to accept another rejection. Determined to entice him beyond his control, she wrapped her arms more tightly about his strong neck and recklessly arched up to brush generous curves across the width of his torso, reveling in the sweet rasp of its wiry curls across tender tips.

The deep velvet growl coming from the Eagle's throat sent a shiver of desire through Linnet. Rhys gazed down at the exquisite creature whose actions had driven from his hold the last hope for any measure of restraint. Beyond rational thinking, he came down fully atop her slender length. Knowing she'd shattered his strained control and glorying in that unsuspected power, Linnet pressed even closer, shaking in an agony of need.

Rhys slid both hands, palms flat, down to her hips and then under to cup the perfect curve of her derriere, tilting it to ease their slow joining. Feeling as if she were flying up into the golden fires nearly obscuring the black of his eyes and incinerated by hungry flames stoked to an ever-building heat, Linnet barely felt the moment of pain. She twined silken limbs about him in welcome and clung desperately to this burning source of delicious torment while he rocked her higher into a sky ablaze.

"Linnet . . ." The name was a cry of longing more potent to her than the most passionate caress.

Her arms contracted about him. She whispered her love on an aching sigh and surrendered totally to the unimagined pleasure of this most intimate embrace, giving herself as tinder to feed a hotter blaze. Rhys yielded to the strength of erotic dreams too long gone unfulfilled. With a rhythm that grew wilder and wilder, he swept his naive temptress up into the fiery heights at the very center of a fire storm.

With the Eagle, Linnet soared ever nearer to the pinnacle of flame only to repeatedly discover it rose still higher. Fearing it impossible to reach the summit, she yearned toward the unknown goal just beyond her reach. Then, her feverish cry blending with his deep growl, at last they crested the whirling blaze of incredible sensations just as it exploded, scattering a glittering shower of sparks to ripple through every nerve in her body.

Uncounted moments later she drifted on the billowing smoke of blissful contentment, stunned still by the beauty of the Eagle's flight. She clung to him until finally overtaken by dreams that could never match the reality of him.

While the sweet, wanton virgin who'd provoked him into a wrong that could never be undone snuggled close, Rhys fought the call to satisfaction's slumbers. Now what he'd suspected, even feared, had been proven true. She was the embodiment of a passion and sweet joy he had previously not thought could exist . . . and he had wrongfully taken it. Although she had come to him, she'd come as an innocent, while he was a man fourteen years her senior, a man who should have had restraint enough to refuse the too precious gift of her chastity. Purposefully shifting his gaze, he stared into the gloom left by the moon's departure and accepted the darkness as an appropriate setting for his fall from grace.

Rising, he bent to carefully wrap the coverlet about a damsel who in her sleep seemed little more than a toddler. Gently he carried her into her own chamber and deposited her atop the humble bed that had been hers since the day he'd abducted her. Without waking she turned on her side, curling up with a cheek pillowed against joined hands—an innocent pose that smote him with guilt for taking the symbol of that purity from her. Then, feeling as if the action had ripped the heart from his body, he left her there alone and returned to a big bed gone cold.

Owain raked his fingers through black curls and shrugged his shoulders in a vain attempt to dislodge the weight of day-long weariness. After glancing toward the hearth to be certain David had properly banked its fires, he began moving up the corner stairway. Anticipation lent haste to slow feet anxious to reach the wished-for rest awaiting in his bedchamber on the level above.

He frowned. The latch had unaccountably been left loose, and a candle flickered in a far corner. His frown melted into a fond smile for the boy who must've left these symbols of welcome for an exhausted brother. He closed the door, careful to see the latch fall into its proper place. Grasping the hem of his tunic, preparing to rid himself of its rain-damp folds, he turned . . .

and froze at an unexpected, unwelcome sight.
Grannia lay half-reclining atop his bed.

"What are you doing here?"

The question was a low rumble as ominous as
thunder, but Grannia refused to shift from her painstakingly contrived position. Her gown was loosened to
reveal tantalizing glimpses of silken flesh emphasized
by a rich tangle of ebony curls brushed to a shiny
luster. The black cloud also framed the oval of her
face and brushed the chin tilted with a determination
at odds with her seductive expression. Often during
the afternoon she'd gazed at her reflection in a basin
filled with still water and practiced both the sensuous
smile and the best method to half-lower thick lashes
over dark, slumberous eyes.

Owain was not, definitely not, immune, but neither
would he willingly submit to the woman striving to
lead them both to ruin. Blue eyes narrowed, he firmly
resolved to reject her transparent invitation. She was
a potent temptation but one to which he would never
surrender.

"No matter." He shrugged as if her invasion of his
bedchamber truly was of little interest to him. "Your
presence here may be a boon." Shifting his gaze from
the danger too near, Owain promptly began speaking
on a subject certain to reinforce the barrier between
them. "I needn't wait till the morrow to show you
what I've taken pains to uncover. Here is irrefutable
proof of Rhys's innocence in the wrong for which
you've unjustly blamed him."

Owain spread a crumpled sheet of vellum across the
flat top of a bedside trunk and glanced at her. His
scowl deepened. Grannia had not stirred.

"Here!" Owain forcefully jabbed his forefinger at
the center of a document in danger of disintegrating.
"I sought out Ewais. He was relieved to be rid of this
burden and of the guilt he was left to carry alone."

Grannia reluctantly rose and moved to look down
at the pale cream rectangle bright against the trunk's

dark wood. Though she was unable to read the black script marching boldly across the page, its identity was clear.

"Just as you've repeatedly stated, you saw my father write this message and give it into Ewais's hand." Owain turned toward her and glared at the face gone mutinous against words yet to be spoken. "You saw the deed but were not privy to the directions accompanying it.

"My father, your husband, commanded Ewais to take the sealed missive not to Normandy but far into the forest and to bury it so deep it could never be found. Ewais was instructed that, once his task was done, he was to journey on for a lengthy visit with his mother's family in Prince Cawdr's lands. Then, my father ordered that when Ewais returned, he was to speak only of your brother's derision of all things Welsh."

In honesty, Grannia was inclined to accept the document's authenticity. But, faced with Owain's belligerent attitude, rather than admit it she'd have preferred to spend a dark forest night in the company of Puck and his dangerous elfin kind—reputedly able to steal human souls.

"The mere fact that the letter he was commanded to bury was still in Ewais's possession surely shows he is not to be trusted," she said. "Why are you so quick to accept what Ewais says now? What makes this tale more believable than his first report of a prince's preference for Norman friends and ways?" As she spoke, Grannia unthinkingly curled her fingers about one of the forearms crossed over his broad chest.

A growl of disgust rumbled from Owain. He pulled free and turned his back on the alluring female who ought to have known better than to come to *any* man's room in the midst of night!

"The truth is right there before your eyes and disproves the flimsy excuses you've wielded to reject a brother's care." Grannia was too near! He gritted out a command of his own. "Put yourself to rights!" The glare he cast behind him brushed a visual accusation over laces temptingly, wrongly loosened. "I'll escort you back to Rhys's home, back into his charge. Pray God he soon finds you a suitable second husband." His teeth clenched over the final two incredibly unpleasant words.

"I will not submit to Rhys's custody." Grannia again stepped around to boldly face the huge man who ought to have known he couldn't so easily put her aside. "Nor will I return to Rhys's home this night, when Linnet is surely winning more success in her foray into his bedchamber than I have found in yours."

Though Grannia had no trouble refusing to obey Owain's commands, she found it difficult to ignore the vision his mention of a second spouse summoned. A too vivid, repugnant picture of Cawdr forcing her into the marital bed had haunted her since this morning when Linnet had told her of the conversation between her brother and the disgusting prince of Dyfi.

Owain's blue eyes narrowed incredulously. "The Norman damsel means to seduce my friend . . . tonight? Steal into his bed though the deed threatens to cost him the honor he prizes above all else? She means to go to a man unguarded, vulnerable in sleep?"

Owain slowly shook his head, and black curls caught the limited light of the chamber's single candle. "We both know Rhys will attempt to bleach the stain from his honor by wedding his archenemy's daughter, thereby risking the loss of the princedom he fought to keep." His expression hardened. "And you schemed with her to see it done." This was not a question but an outraged reproach.

"Rhys intends to consign Linnet to the abstinent, lonely life of a nun at the Abbey of Saint Anne." Grannia's anger and dread had faded beneath concern for a friend. She moved closer to her beloved and stroked soothing hands over his still crossed arms and clenched fists. "Only does she mean to claim a single night's joys and would no more allow him to pay the price of marriage than I'd permit you to bear the stigma of wedding the stepmother whose love is yours for the taking."

Owain fair ground his teeth against tempting images inspired by her blatant offer and immediately sought to divert the focus of her words.

"I worry for more than Rhys's honor," he said. "I fear the Norman damsel may not be what she appears."

Dark eyes flashed with gold sparks as Grannia opened her mouth to make an emphatic rebuttal, but his upraised hand forestalled the words.

"Her miraculous reappearance, with a wild tale of having ridden a destrier to just the right destination, is difficult to believe. Nay, I suspect the seemingly innocent Linnet is a spy flown into the eagle's otherwise hidden aerie."

"Hah!" Grannia's hoot of derision left no doubt as to her opinion of his suspicions, but still she continued. "No one could have been more distrustful of Linnet than I; and no one among the people of Cymer, save Rhys, has come to know her better. I would stake my life on the fact that she is precisely the disaffected daughter of a Norman earl she seems to be."

After having firmly defended her comrade in love's warfare, Grannia pushed aside every subject but the one most important to her. "Even were Linnet not with Rhys now, I wouldn't return to the brother who has already begun discussing a wedding bond between me and Prince Cawdr."

Owain felt unexpectedly punched by a mighty fist, and his ruddy face went an unnatural pasty white. His rash talk of her remarriage had been an ill-considered and foolish tactic to punish the woman—first, for attempting to entice him into a sweet but wicked sin, and second, for thinking him so uncaring that he would allow her to bear its shame alone. In reality he'd long dreaded the possibility of her being wed to *any* other man. Now a blow had been dealt by the prospect of his forbidden love bound to the odious prince of Dyfi.

Eyes gone to black ice, Grannia made a flat statement of refusal. "I despise the man and will never submit to another forced marriage."

Although it was her brother's right to choose a mate for her, Owain felt betrayed by a friend who had never mentioned the plan to him who—as Grannia's stepson, if naught else—deserved to have been told.

Desperate for the dark solitude, which would provide a chance to sort through dangerously chaotic emotions, Owain swept Grannia off her feet. Before she could recover her wits from the surprise and organize a protest, he deposited her in the corridor on the far side of a door he immediately closed against her.

14

FROM HIS SEAT AT THE HIGH TABLE'S CENTER A MOROSE Godfrey glared at the company assembled for the day's first meal. He and his men had searched every corner of Radwell's lands and a goodly portion of those across the Welsh border. Linnet was nowhere to be found. Yet he bitterly resented the sly whispers that had reached even his ears, whispers suggesting his daughter had returned to the arms of his most hated enemy.

Never would his quiet, submissive Linnet do such a dastardly thing! Never! He'd instead grown certain it was the wretched Edolf's fault. Edolf had been posted as guard on both of the occasions when she'd been abducted—and Godfrey refused to believe her disappearance anything but an abduction. To Godfrey it seemed plain that Edolf was in league with the Eagle and had assisted the Welshman in his dastardly schemes.

Once the duties required of a lord had been met, he would go and "question" the man already in his prison. Aye, once he'd finished standing in judgment over his vassals' disputes and dealt with the petty problems of his serfs, he would be free. Then he'd demand that Edolf, first, explain the reasons for his treachery and, second, give a detailed description of where Linnet was forcibly held. If the man was unwilling to answer these simple questions, the dungeons contained a variety of instruments, from whip to rack, each more than capable of squeezing a confession from an overfed body.

All in the earl's hall shrank from sulfurous fires banked but burning in his pale brown eyes, fires that raised tensions in even the sons seated on his right.

"Alan"—Mark leaned down to speak softly near the ear of a boy shifting uncomfortably on the high-backed chair—"what say we go early this morning to the practice yards, before they're needed for the training of the boys being fostered here. You can show me the tricks of swordsmanship, as you promised the day of your return."

Mark's offer of his company for an unprecedented second day eased Alan's troubles and lit his face with a brilliant grin.

"I'm done." With the impulsiveness of tender years, he shoved his platter back and gave his older brother a pleading gaze. "Can we go now?"

Mark laughed, and that sound amid the huge chamber's heavy gloom summoned the curious attention of many to the darkly handsome son of their lord as he nodded his assent to a brother's appeal.

"If our sire will permit us to leave afore he has finished with his meal." Light gray eyes narrowed on the glum father just beyond Alan.

Godfrey felt a pang of guilt for permitting his distress over Linnet's disappearance to cloud this rare opportunity to spend time with both his sons. But, deeply aware of duties owed his people, which no responsible lord would set aside for personal wishes, he accepted the impossibility of doing anything with them at the moment. That fact made his approval of their request important.

"Aye, Mark, take your young brother out and enjoy

a day that bodes bright despite the night's dreary rain." He attempted, with limited success, to give an honest smile to the pair rising to their feet.

Mark felt a moment of regretful pity for the man whose permission sanctioned a deed he would deeply rue. Stepping down from the dais behind Alan, he laid a hand atop amber locks still baby fine and led the boy in the right direction. Mark had heard enough and too much of his mother's rantings, had endured too long his Saxon uncle's cold glares and vicious words. He had no choice but to act.

Still seated at Godfrey's left, Osric was sorely strained to repress a triumphant grin. Mark would see the necessary deed done, and an important step in Osric's near lifelong scheme would be complete. Soon —very soon, if another held true to his word—a further step would be well in hand. Under the pretext of brushing bread crumbs from his fingers, Osric rubbed his hands together in barely restrained glee. The next step was his to perform.

Osric took perverse joy in Godfrey's distress but hid a smile as the disheartened earl pushed back his chair and stood. Those seated at the lower tables instantly followed suit. The men of the garrison set off to resume tasks delayed by two days of fruitless—and, most thought, useless—searching while others turned to the pattern of set routines.

Anxious to begin and more anxious to conclude a nobleman's jealously guarded but often tiresome duty to preside over the lord's court, Godfrey ordered serfs to hastily clear the hall. A small army of homespun-clad minions immediately began disassembling trestle tables, leaning table tops against parallel walls and neatly stacking trestles in shadowed corners.

In the temporary chaos required to speedily establish a new order, Osric found slipping unnoticed into the stairwell an easy task. Stepping inside the poorly lit passageway cut within the thickness of a stone wall, he descended to the dungeon level. Osric paused in the opening between last step and dark chamber, waiting for his eyes to grow accustomed to the single resin-soaked torch's flickering orange light. It was nowise equal to the challenge of clearly illuminating so vast an area.

Guardsmen proven cowardly by their flight from battle had been so sorely lashed that many would forever bear scars as testament to their shame. But chastened men had then been returned to the guardroom and to duties they'd know better than to fail at again. Thus, only Edolf remained locked in a cell with the dank odors of moldy straw, filthy human flesh and wastes.

Osric's face wrinkled against the stench, but he relentlessly moved to within an arm's length of iron bars.

"I come bearing a gift." The silky words were a threat in themselves, and rather than approach his visitor, Edolf retreated to the cell's farthest corner.

"Were I to believe that, I'd make of myself a bigger fool than that little brat has already done."

"Aye, a fool you are, but a bigger one you'd be to reject the freedom I offer." From Osric's lifted hand dangled a key taken from the earl who, to soothe his previous night's despair, had drunk himself senseless.

Edolf took two suspicious steps forward but halted again. "What is there in this 'gift' for you?"

"Ah, a fool indeed, but a wise one as well." Osric's smile was a sneer. "You've the right of it. I would do nothing for you—or any other—but that it do even more for me."

Edolf's suspicion was paradoxically eased by this admission, and he moved closer still.

"The earl's daughter has been missing since the night of your misdeed. Of course her father blames the Eagle. But now I fear a lamentable accident is about to befall your friend, the young heir. His father will doubtless blame the Eagle for this ill as well. But should the first scapegoat be proven inadequate, my intention is to ensure that a second exists."

"And I am to be that scapegoat?" Edolf lifted his chin against the formless assault of words.

Osric nodded, and orange torchlight glowed as clearly on the scalp beneath as on his thinning hair. "In the end you will be blamed, whether you remain here or flee elsewhere. It's only a matter of time before Earl Godfrey comes to blame you for all that is wrong in his world.

"I am an honest man and to prove my trustworthiness choose to speak openly of both unpleasant facts and my own purposes." Osric spread his hands wide in an apparent plea for the other's confidence, but as expected, it was the dull gleam of metal in one palm that held the prisoner's attention.

The width and brightness of the Saxon's smile left Edolf too aware of his deceitful nature.

"My purpose in coming is to see you safe from the earl's vengeance." The Saxon's voice was quiet but intense. "Accept my gift and with it my offer of secret transport to and guarantee of safe shelter at Northland."

Never would Edolf trust the smooth words and likely lies of this treacherous man, but to be free of iron bars was an enticement too strong to refuse. Surely, once out of this malodorous gloom he could find firm footing and take care of himself.

When Edolf had nodded his shaggy head, Osric inserted and turned the key. Once the unfastened door swung wide, key abandoned in the lock, Osric motioned his new cohort toward the dark stairwell. He followed the man's bulky figure into the gloom, whispering details of the plan for an unseen escape from Radwell's formidable walls.

At midmorn the prince's hall was lit by sunlight flowing through shutters opened to welcome a bright day at odds with the dark expressions of two men and a child.

"Don't know what it means or even if'n it's important, but Owain thought you ought be told." An earnest David met Rhys's dark gaze.

David had described for his brother all that he'd seen in the forest the previous afternoon. And, without once questioning his words, Owain had gone in search of their prince. After finding the man, Owain had returned to accompany David here so that he might personally repeat the tale for the Eagle in private. That David had done and, too, he'd answered what questions he could.

"You did right, and I thank you for the warning." Leaning across an empty table, Rhys offered his arm to the solemn boy.

David recognized the honor bestowed by this gesture and promptly joined his forearm to the much larger one extended.

Owain stood behind the boy and after a quiet moment cleared his throat to gruffly speak. "Then come, lad. Best we get back to chores undone."

David promptly rose and stepped over the bench to stand at his brother's side.

Rhys gave a grim smile to the man who early this morn had found him again checking with guards along a surprisingly quiet border. They'd shared a private and sometimes heated discussion of women too tempting and too persistent, of betrothals, and of endangered honor before Owain had repeated his brother's report of an ominous meeting.

The steady gaze Rhys sent his friend was meant to encourage a man whose "chore" for the day was to find Grannia. Rhys empathized with Owain's frustration. For, although he'd won the battle Rhys had lost, on rising this morning Owain had discovered the woman absent. She'd plainly fled to avoid the threatened return to her brother's hold. Rhys was uncertain whether his headstrong sister's action was born of her determination not to yield a lost cause or her obstinate refusal to believe the proof Owain had given of a brother's innocence.

Hovering quietly on the hearth's far side with fingers extended toward cheery flames, Linnet had openly watched the exchange. At first sight of the bearded bear, she'd wondered if Grannia had succeeded in her quest. Close examination of the man had yielded no answer, but the question itself brought warm thoughts of her own sweet victory in winning a treasure of memories. Only the strange news imparted by David had been interesting enough to call her from those potent memories of intimate delights and rouse in her a curiosity likely matched by the other three.

Filled with the misgivings and alarming questions raised by revelation of possible intrigue between Osric and Prince Cawdr, she was in no way prepared for the brief but blatant suspicion—or was it an accusation?—in the bearded bear's expression. Linnet looked toward Rhys, seeking an explanation for Owain's silent distrust, but found the golden man had turned his back on her to follow the brothers to the door.

"Pywell." Clear as a deep-toned bell the call rang across fields tended by the young man and others of his family. Rhys waited in the open doorway while Pywell hastened to answer.

Linnet had awakened to an empty bed, an empty chamber, but heated memories had forestalled the initial chill of loneliness. A single night in his arms she'd sought and won. But later, after she had descended to the hall and found him already gone, the cold truth she had sought to hold back forced upon her a fact earlier blocked to ease the selfish seeking of her heart's desire. She had taken what Rhys had not wanted to give. That certainty was reinforced by the black granite expression of the man who'd escorted the brothers into his home a short time past.

Linnet had known before stealing her night of love that Rhys would never forgive her that success. Expecting the proud man's reaction, she had barricaded her heart against both the pain of unrequited love and his anger over the victory she'd secured by catching him in his weakest, most ill-defended moments. The tactics she'd employed might have been laudable in a great warrior, but in a woman they would assuredly be despised as wicked feminine schemes. Indeed, now Rhys could justifiably scorn her for the relentless pursuit of him she'd so oft denied.

That confession was too dreary to silently bear. Linnet bit back a despairing moan and resolutely moved to the shelves on the room's far side. There were meals to be planned and preparations to begin. She would keep bleak thoughts at bay by putting practical skills to use.

Lifting down a large bowl, she turned to place it on the table's bare planks and saw Rhys step outside to speak in undertones with Pywell. The younger man cast furtive glances her way, leaving her to wonder if Rhys, as well as Owain, had come to view her with suspicion. Surely he didn't—couldn't—think her purpose for returning to Cymer had been to aid her father's cause against him? Nay, not after she'd saved his life with her warning of a killing blow's descent. But if not, why was he whispering to Pywell and why did what he said have the young man looking strangely at her? Although she'd spent hours preparing to endure Rhys's resentment of her night actions, she was utterly unready for this apparent distrust.

When Rhys faced her again, Linnet studied his stern expression with pain-filled eyes. Was his displeasure's source mistrust, or had she merely proven how hopelessly inadequate was a linnet in comparison with the throng of stunning peacocks who'd given him his undoubted experience?

Rhys sent Linnet a grim smile. Despite a small chin uptilted in a wordless refusal to regret what had passed between them, her anxiety was clear and put an ache in his heart. He dared not speak with her of wrongs committed in the night, not now when looming dangers had so recently increased twofold. Yet it required the full measure of his much-vaunted willpower to keep his hands safely at his side instead of reaching out to cradle her in solace for shared pain.

"Early this morn I met with men guarding the security of Cymer's eastern border and found that your father and his men have chosen to leave them in peace—leastways for now."

She took several steps toward him, and he cursed a poorly formed statement when hope flared in amber eyes. To block temptation, he immediately continued laying necessary groundwork.

"This unexpected break in hostilities provides me a chance to survey the damage wrought thus far. I'm off and may not return before well into night. But if Owain has his way—and I don't doubt that he will—Grannia will soon be here."

What did he mean, "if Owain has his way"? And what did that imply about Grannia's plans of yestereve? These questions were washed from Linnet's mind by the accusing look accompanying words she heard as reproach for her own actions during the night's darkest hours. She nodded, but Rhys had already turned away and the door closed behind his broad back even before joined gleams of bright sunlight and golden firelight had finished rippling over her dark-honey hair.

Having half crossed the room only to bid him farewell, Linnet sank forlornly atop the fire pit's wide stone ledge. Though expected, his silent rejection wrapped her in a dismal cloud while in the same moment anger flashed against the injustice of the possibility that he might blame her for the very actions from which she'd come to save him.

While Linnet labored under the weight of bleak thoughts and quiet crystal drops slid unnoticed from fawn-brown eyes, time marched inexorably onward. Enough and too much! Linnet abruptly stood. The

sun had reached and dropped a distance below its
zenith. Resolutely she strode toward the rough homespun sacks neatly arranged beneath the lowest shelf.
From one she carefully selected crisp onions. These
she laid atop the table. What she needed now was
fresh, cool spring water rather than the tepid liquid
remaining in the bucket beside the outer door.

Determined to waste no moment more on useless,
selfish thoughts, Linnet lifted the bucket by its strap.
She stepped outside and closed the door behind her.
Catching a glimpse of Pywell, who for some obscure
reason was laboring on ground already tilled, she gave
him a cheerful wave. She rounded the side of the
house and entered a small thicket of trees.

Lush greenery sheltered a bubbling spring. Linnet
crouched down and lowered her bucket into the clear
pool at its edge, careful to hold the hem of her skirts
safe from its moss- and pebble-lined edge. As she
stood, off-balance from the weight of the bucket, a
strange gleam caught her attention. She glanced to the
side and gasped. A man rapidly approached, the silver
of a glittering blade extending like a gruesome claw
from his curled and upraised fist.

Without a moment's hesitation or thought to cry
out, Linnet swung the heavy bucket and its liquid load
in an arc that ended against the side of her assailant's
head. With the thudding contact, water splashed over
the man falling unconscious—and over the man a
mere pace behind.

Water dripped from Rhys's nose and chin and
darkened the gold of his drenched hair. Nonetheless,
his low laughter echoed through the glade. He opened
his mouth to speak, but another sight jerked his head
to one side.

A second assailant had rounded the corner of the
house with broadsword at the ready. Rhys's own sang
as he smoothly pulled it from the scabbard at his
waist—another unnecessary action, for Pywell had
launched himself at the man's back. The foolish

attacker fell face down upon the ground. Pywell squarely straddled the prone man, wrenched the weapon from his grip, and tossed it into thick undergrowth, all while holding his dagger to a vulnerable throat.

"Thank you, Pywell." Linnet's quiet voice and sweet smile earned a bashful grin from the recipient of her gratitude.

Pywell felt that by this brave deed he'd restored the pride stolen from him by the initial assault made upon Linnet while he was assigned as her protector . . . well, as a guard against her escape, but he should have been able to forestall an enemy's attack.

"Linnet, go fetch a pile of kitchen cloths and also, from the largest chest beneath the stairway, a deal of stout rope. My friend"—Rhys cast Pywell a wry smile—"and I will ensure our unwelcome visitors remain to accept our hospitality."

Linnet instantly hastened to do as she was bidden and returned with fine speed. Rhys soon had both men—the one lost in unnatural sleep and the one sprawled beneath a young man's weight—gagged with kitchen cloths and bound hand and foot.

When Rhys shouldered the deadweight of the lifeless body, Pywell did the same with the second assailant, although it was a difficult chore for one of slighter build. Linnet was pleased that his prince knew better than to insult his abilities by suggesting he wait until either Rhys could return or a donkey be brought to bear the load. She gathered up the sturdy bucket unharmed by its fearsome task, quickly refilled it, and trailed along behind the two men and their burdens.

Rhys halted at the small stone bakehouse not far from one side of his home and half turned toward the woman behind him. "We've work to do with these two, so please go back inside the house and bar both the door and the window shutters. Open to none save me." He paused and grimaced at thought of a possible complication. "Or to Owain should he and Grannia arrive."

Although trembling inwardly with delayed reaction to the attempted assault, Linnet reluctantly obeyed. Her feet felt near as heavy as the bucket bending her so far to one side it fair dragged upon the ground. Still she cast many regretful glances back at the men depositing assailants inside the windowless stone structure.

15

ONCE INSIDE THE EAGLE'S HOME, LINNET DID AS RHYS HAD commanded and put a stout bar into place across the heavy planks of the iron-bound door. From window to window she went, swinging shutters together, blocking natural light out with similar bars. The resulting gloom was a just setting for the tenor of thoughts brightened only by the certainty that this assault must leastwise prove to Rhys that she'd had no part in wicked schemes against him.

Linnet had recognized the assailant she'd struck as one of the men who'd accompanied Prince Cawdr on his recent visit here. Apparently Cawdr meant to leave no chance that his sister might be set aside in preference for a Norman wife. A groundless fear. Yet it meant Rhys had not only her father for foe but Cawdr as well. And Rhys's Saxon uncle, too! For proof she had only to think of this morn's revelation of the meeting between Cawdr and Osric.

Resuming her earlier intent, Linnet set out to divert useless but increasing fears over the many further evils assuredly awaiting her beloved and to waylay her curiosity about Grannia's mission. First, to brighten the room, she lit a pyramid of candles in each of two tall brass stands placed in corners and others grouped on a tabletop platter and then returned to tasks begun hours before.

Unlike the tapers special made and notched to mark the passing of hours, which at Radwell were nightly lit, one in the great hall and one in the lord's chamber, those she'd lighted here burned unevenly and were an unreliable measure of time. Moreover, in this tightly closed chamber neither could Linnet use the sun's position as a marker of passing hours. Nonetheless, by the time a loud knocking at long last broke the tense silence, a meal of unusual variety awaited.

"Who's there?" She called into the cracks between the tightly joined planks. Naught but two simple words yet given a lilting melody by hopeful anticipation.

"Rhys."

The dark velvet voice was unmistakable. Linnet's heart soared. After hastily sliding the heavy bar from metal loops driven into the wall beside the door frame, she moved back for him to enter. The opening permitted a brief glimpse of the sky and revealed twilight's lavender mists quickly descending.

With the fluid grace natural to him, Rhys stepped inside, took the bar from her, and blocked the portal again.

"Your evening meal awaits." Amber eyes carefully studied the man to be certain he'd returned uninjured as, without glancing away, she waved toward the waiting repast.

Rhys's gaze followed her gesture, and dark gold brows arched in surprise. Flavorsome aromas wafted up from a table laden with an uncommonly fine array of dishes for a simple evening meal. In truth it was a small feast and all the more amazing for the fact that it had been prepared in the afternoon hours since the assault. She must have toiled like a demon!

Linnet had indeed worked very hard to prepare what she suddenly realized was a frightful overabundance for two people. Her attempt at distraction from worry had been so successful she'd ceased to think rationally! Gasping silently, with held breath she watched Rhys survey her offering.

There was a long platter of venison twice boiled to leach its preserving salt, then thinly sliced and covered with a thick gravy. And a rabbit spit-roasted to golden perfection now rested on its own platter. These meat courses held primary attention but were accompanied by three lesser dishes: first, a large pot of thick pea and barley soup; second, cheese melted and, with cream, butter, and spices, cooled and re-formed into an array of small cakes in imaginative shapes; and third, two loaves of bread baked days earlier but now sliced in half, their extracted centers reduced to crumbs and stirred with butter and fennel seeds before being replaced. To finish the meal she'd fried apples in ale batter. In fact, she'd kept herself busy preparing everything she knew Rhys enjoyed or thought he might.

"Did you take me seriously when I said we'd be hosting this afternoon's assailants? Nay, there's too much here for even three men and a damsel." Rhys tried to look at her severely, but the gleam in dark eyes betrayed his amusement as he wryly added, "Mayhap I've missed news of a descending horde?"

Linnet blushed, relief flooding through her at his teasing. "I knew you were weary of simple stews and believed variety would not go amiss." A lame excuse for the excess prompted by anxiety but the only one she had, and if his potent smile was a true indication, it was adequate.

Rhys moved to lift the lid from a pot suspended above glowing coals and a savory steam rewarded him. He recognized this lightly spiced sauce and knew it was intended to accompany the rabbit. Pleasure that the sweet songbird had given such thought to his preferences overwhelmed and buried the cold, stern rebuke for the night past, which he'd meant to speak immediately upon his return.

"I am not a small man and have a healthy appetite, but I fear there is far, far more than enough here to satisfy me. And I know you are no glutton and alone could never eat all that remains."

Linnet worried the full curve of her lower lip for a moment and then made a brave suggestion. "I thought mayhap, after we've taken our portions, you might be willing to summon Pywell and allow him to carry what's left to his family."

In reality, she'd thought no such thing in advance of this moment of need, but she deemed it a fine excuse and squarely met his curious gaze.

"Surely Pywell and the rest of Ynid's family will appreciate this generosity as much as they did the foodstuffs Grannia and I prepared two night's past."

"I congratulate you on a fine and generous plan." Rhys's smile was mocking but his compliment sincerely meant, although the goods she'd generously prepared and now offered to others were his.

With little space left on the table to comfortably place his trencher, Rhys rearranged the platters until the smallest, once bearing only cakes of cheese, held a sampling of each dish. As Linnet ladled sauce from the pot steaming above the fire onto the portion of rabbit on his trencher, he drank in the sight of the damsel whose seductive curves could not be hidden even 'neath an overabundance of homespun. The hearth's flames lent a rosy hue to the pure cream of her complexion and added luster to amber hair that matched her eyes and provided a perfect frame for her winsome face. When the color in her cheeks went several shades brighter, he realized how long he'd been gawking at her like a foolish boy. He abruptly stepped back and with his meal quickly settled into the fireside chair.

Heart wildly pounding from the heady power of his

closeness, Linnet retreated to the overburdened table, from which safe distance she unobtrusively studied the man, golden head tilted as he lifted a bread raston to firm lips. She remembered how that warm mouth had joined hers with the heat of fire, how it burned across her skin. Shaking her head to put aside poorly timed memories, she stared down at the platters heaped upon bare planks.

Stomach uneasy under the tensions of a long day, Linnet dared not attempt to swallow a single bite of the food she'd labored to see both tasty and tempting. Thankful that Rhys hadn't insisted she try, Linnet found an unused basket and several empty bowls. Then she dug through the small trunk for even more of the near depleted supply of kitchen cloths. These she used to pack food for Ynid's large family while also neatly storing away portions of what dishes could be served at later meals.

She was tucking the last towel over the top of the filled basket when Rhys finished his meal. In answer to his prince's call Pywell appeared almost immediately. By the haste of his response Linnet realized he'd been stationed nearby. Was he guarding her, even while Rhys was in residence? Nay, it would be useless when they were barred inside the house. Besides, on a moment's closer thought it was plain to her that he stood watch over the bakehouse and the prisoners lodged within.

Pywell summoned his father who, Linnet had learned, spent most days patrolling the eastern border. Soon the man, an older version of his cheerful son, appeared with news that Ynid would return to her home on the morrow. He gave Linnet profuse gratitude for her toil and thanks to his prince whose bounty had supplied the wherewithal to see it done.

When only the meal's lingering aroma remained, Linnet sensed the time had come for Rhys to speak with her of matters assiduously avoided till now.

"On the morrow I'll accompany you to Saint

Anne's. There you'll be safe from your father and any other man who wishes you ill." The sight of Linnet's courageously lifted chin further softened the dark eyes of a man already filled with aching regret for this necessary deed.

He chose, leastways, not to burden one who already this day had faced too many woes with news of more complications. He would not tell her of the message received from Cawdr warning of two brothers abducted. No, he would simply deal with the danger. After seeing Linnet to safety, he was to meet Owain. They would then go directly to negotiate with the culprit . . . doubtless a dangerous endeavor.

"You need not give it a pretty face." Linnet steadily met Rhys's gaze. "I told you before of my willingness to join the sisters at Saint Anne's."

Rhys scowled against the flat statement of an end apparently more unpleasant to him than to her.

Linnet momentarily faltered beneath his abruptly cold expression, assuming it a precursor to the rebuke for her wanton invasion of his bed and a reminder of his advance warning that nothing could come of her deed. Now is no time for you to fall pigeonhearted, she firmly chided her faint heart. This far you have come, so follow it through to the end.

"I expect nothing more from you, Rhys. I came to your bed last evening seeking only a single happy memory to take with me into the loneliness of life within abbey walls." Linnet lifted and held her hands out with vulnerable palms exposed.

This response to his opening of the subject Rhys had not expected. He had known better than to think her likely to demand what he'd told her couldn't be given, but he had expected her honest nature to seek answers he was not prepared to give to questions whose asking should never have been possible. Her future and his had been forever altered during dark hours by barriers sundered and forbidden deeds done but too sweet to regret. Nevertheless, he couldn't speak to her of the future while their path was cluttered by additional blocks and shadowed by looming dangers. What might happen next was too uncertain to allow firm answers. The best he could give her now was protection from further harm. Leastwise 'twas what he thought until she spoke again.

"'Tis the abbey I choose, for I had rather forsake all worldly goods than accept for spouse Osric . . . or any man save you." As if for visible proof of her claimed willingness to separate herself from him, Linnet began to pull back her outstretched hands.

Eyes blacker than midnight, Rhys moved two paces forward and caught dainty fingers in his powerful hands. He'd lost the will to fool himself that there could be any end to their song but this. Gently he tugged her nearer and then swallowed her in his embrace.

Marveling at the faint tremor of arms cherishing her close to a broad chest, for one precious moment Linnet permitted her cheek to rest against the strong wall above a heart whose strong beat she could hear. She was certain Rhys would soon regret this action, a certainty shaken by words that caught her breath with happiness . . . and put clouds of anguish in her eyes.

"You would *join* a nunnery?" Rhys's plan called for her to spend naught but a few days within its protection. "Nay! I'd sooner surrender my life than see you resigned to an abbey's cold cot when the fire of my bed will fade into ashes without you to feed its flame. The eagle has been trapped by a linnet's lures.

"I love you and must have you in my life to survive." The rough velvet of Rhys's voice stroked like passion against Linnet's ear.

Having confessed to himself, the night past, his all-consuming emotion for this sweet songbird, Rhys knew no greater pain existed than the prospect of a future without her to lend it warmth and joy. Nothing, not even wedding an enemy's daughter without her father's leave, could be more dishonorable than taking his beloved's innocence and then leaving her to face the consequences alone. Dark eyes gleamed with mockery for this poor excuse to justify a deed he would see done at any cost. His tender wee linnet was worth any price demanded of him. And the promise that she would be his alone once he'd overcome hazards and defeated those who threatened them was a protective amulet powerful enough to see him safely through a dragon's lair.

"No!" Linnet pulled away but only the scant distance he permitted. "Grannia and I swore we would not allow the men we love to pay the price for a treasure we stole in the night."

Rhys offered the paradise of her fantasies, but . . . Linnet had sworn an oath. Moreover, by the recently told tale of her father's past, she'd learned enough of broken oaths to be certain that forswearing her own would lead not to bright dreams fulfilled but instead to others dark and fearsome. Were she to break her pledge, her beloved would be in danger of losing what he most prized—his honor and his princedom. That fact reinforced her decision. She would prove to him that her stubborn will was equal to his and Grannia's. Toward that end, Linnet pressed as far back as she could and courageously lifted her face to him.

"I *will* join the abbey and leave your honor unstained!" Though the deed's pain drained all light from doe brown eyes, determination wove a thread of steel through her words.

"Shhh." Again Rhys swept the innocent temptress he'd claimed as his into a possessive embrace, rubbing his lips across the top of lustrous, flower-scented hair. He wouldn't argue with her, and neither would he permit her to sacrifice their future happiness.

Linnet suspected his strategy but had one of her own. He would take her to Saint Anne's on the morrow, and before he returned, her commitment to the abbey would be made. But between this moment and that hour there would be hours of dark solitude.

She melted against him, wax to candle flame. For this night she would willingly close her thoughts to the future and the past, willingly pay the price of hell in a lifetime without him for the heaven of this unexpected embrace. Savoring the feel of his big, hard body and nuzzling her cheek against his chest, she felt the rumble of his groan before it reached his throat, and she smiled.

Rhys settled her more intimately against the changing contours of his body, urged her closer. Reveling in the strength of the hold binding her to him, Linnet yielded eagerly and without hesitation wrapped her hands about his back, smoothing its hard planes.

Burying his fingers in her thick mane, Rhys urged her face to tilt upward, revealing it to a hot and glittery gaze while his mouth slowly bent to within a whisper of hers.

"You're mine." The words were a darkly textured growl while he nibbled teasingly at the corner of lips that followed his. "And never another man's."

Linnet helplessly nodded, legs trembling while resting against his strength. His breath mingled with hers, and the light touch of his lips was a torment. She tangled her fingers into bright strands, pulling until he fit his mouth over hers with exquisite care and deepened the kiss with a devastating slowness and a hungry ferocity.

Sinking fast into the hazy smoke of desire, she felt the heavy thudding of his heart and the changing tension in powerful muscles. If this was to be their last taste of paradise, she wanted it to be the most shattering, unforgettable experience of passion he would ever know. Surely her unstinting love for him would outweigh her lack of experience in the ways of intimacy. As an ever-increasing hunger smothered her doubts, she sensuously twisted against him, determined to draw him into the same unmanageable depths of need into which he so easily summoned her.

Rhys released her mouth, head falling back as a

deep moan escaped his tight throat. Linnet smiled. Tugging a leather cord to untie the laces at his throat, she rose on tiptoe and rained teasing kisses over the wedge of bronze skin thus revealed. Readily yielding to her unspoken request, he stepped back and stripped off the annoying tunic in one quick, smooth motion that set muscles to rippling. Her exquisite face was flushed with desire, wide melting eyes saying more of her admiration than words ever could.

In silent praise her hands reached out to slowly roam up his powerful arms, over the breadth of wide shoulders and across the hard muscle and abrasive hair on his chest. His breath went harsh and uneven while his blood boiled with need.

Of a sudden Rhys pushed her a short distance away.

Linnet was in despair, fearing he meant to end this final dream so soon, and a soundless moan of protest parted her mouth. She tried to press close to him, but gentle hands held her a whisper from that goal.

Heavy lids half fell over golden sparks smoldering in dark eyes. Rhys recognized her fear and smiled with passion-stiff lips. No matter what was wise, with wildfire flowing through his veins, uncontrollable and unstoppable, it was far too late for him to douse the flames or set her aside. Though he'd first viewed a repetition of this wrong as a weakness that might endanger Linnet, now he recognized in it the source of strength that would allow him to defeat other dangers and clear the way for his return to forever claim her—and any child she might bear him. With trembling hands he brushed the borrowed gown from her shoulders. It fell unmourned into a circle about her feet.

Too far into the irrational realm of passion, she couldn't form thoughts to wonder at the magic that had seen the rough garment come undone. Nor could she feel shame or a need to cover herself, not while the wild excitement of his gaze blazed over soft flesh like a physical caress. Her labored breathing caught on a cry of longing lodged in her throat, and she arched slightly toward the source of promised pleasures.

Shaken by her headlong response, he let his hand follow the path his eyes had taken, stroking a welcome torment over her body while his other arm cradled her against his side. Widespread fingertips teasingly brushed a full breast and explored its textures with exquisite gentleness.

"So perfect, like the rest of you. A hidden delight all mine."

Surrendering to a temptation beyond words, he bent to envelop a hard peak in his mouth. But only for a moment, and Linnet's fingers clenched in golden hair, trying to draw the sweet suction of his mouth nearer even as he pulled away.

Linnet gazed upward, stunned by the pleasure given by the passion on his tense face and the scorching flames in the depths of dark eyes. Rhys, with a hand gently curled over each shoulder, gradually drew her closer, watching as rose tips disappeared into the hair covering his chest before he rubbed her soft breasts back and forth across his hard muscles.

Near overcome by a wall of flame that seemed to dissolve her bones, Linnet trembled and melted into arms that welcomed her. At the shocking feel of her delicious bounty surrendered to him, Rhys shuddered, and his large hands swept down a satin back to grip her smooth, perfectly rounded derriere, press her into his urgent need, and move her against it.

An anguished whimper escaped her throat as incredible sensations trembled through her. That soft cry, added to the feeling of her melded to his every angle and curve, was more than Rhys could longer resist. With his great strength he lifted her clear of the floor. His long strides quickly carried them across the hall and up narrow steps to the lord's chamber and the heavily draped bed.

Once the eagle's tender prey lay in the depths of that dark cavern, he drank in the sight of her cream and rose flesh in his bed while, with the speed and efficiency of a fighting man trained never to waste precious time, stripping off his remaining garments.

Beyond inhibitions, Linnet watched as he approached the bed. Then, sitting up, once again she reached out to trace the ridges and planes beneath a pelt of shining curls. Leaning forward, she let her lips follow their path. Rhys's fingers speared through the thick masses of her hair, and he laid her back with the descent of his hard, muscular body. In the time that followed, with pleasure hot and wild he taught her that their previous lovemaking had been but a flight through summer skies tamed for a novice's sake. This time together they soared through the center of the sun itself.

Owain was worried. Very worried! And angry, too. Grannia was acting like a child, a spoiled child! He glared into a near formless darkness. And when he found her, he would . . . Nay, furious as he was over her foolishness, if . . . when he found her safe and all of a piece, likely he'd fall on his knees and thank God for mercy shown one undeserving.

In his anger taking no care to go quietly, he stomped through thick undergrowth, ducked under tree limbs, and kicked at any small impediment foolish enough to be found in his path. He should have allowed Rhys to assign men to aid in this search, but Rhys had few to spare with two borders now on alert. Besides, having struggled to see Grannia's name remain unstained, Owain had been unwilling to see her foolish flight jeopardize it now. But if he did not find her by dawn . . .

Before the sun set on the morrow, he and Rhys would have to meet with a dangerous antagonist. It was not a prospect to sweeten Owain's dispostion. He couldn't understand why his friend should care a damn that the two sons of Radwell had been taken captive. Oh, all right. One of them was Rhys's cousin.

But that one was a man and surely able to fend for himself. If not, he deserved what he got. Rhys was not responsible for him! Rhys had enough to worry about without adding the earl's sons to the list!

Owain kicked what in the gloom appeared to be a rock of inconsequential size. It proved to be a partially exposed root well buried in dirt and immovable. His foot hurt, he nearly fell, and in the process of recovering his balance blundered into a low-hanging branch and loosed a long, loud line of heartfelt curses.

Even though her brother was the prince of this land, Grannia was no safer than any other woman in the forest during the depths of night. A night? Or was it two? Was she still somewhere in the woodland? Had she found someone to take her in? He gasped with disgust for the thought. No one would take the prince's sister in without telling Rhys of the deed. Nay, if she was not here, then either she'd been abducted or . . .

Owain growled. These questions without answers must end! He'd find her; he would. Mentally repeating that resolution like a litany, he forced back fearsome questions and thoughts of threatening realities.

"You sound like a big, awkward bear stumbling around. You near scared the life out of me!"

Owain fell back. The very one he sought suddenly stood less than a single arm's length from him, long black hair as neatly braided and clothes as fresh as if she'd just descended for a new day.

The next instant Grannia discovered Owain not only sounded like a bear but felt like one, too, when he swept her into a crushing embrace. She didn't protest, but rather cuddled nearer.

"Don't do it again." The bear growled. "Swear you won't run off again."

To Grannia's loving ears the wealth of repressed emotion in his gruff demand was blessedly clear. With arms wrapped as tightly about him as his were about her, she leaned back just far enough to look up into his stern expression.

"You'll have my oath the moment you swear you'll never again so much as threaten to force me to go back to Rhys or to live anywhere but Newydd or to leave your own home there."

Owain clicked his tongue with disgust. "I asked only one oath, but you would have me give three to earn it."

"Not really, for all three sift down to the same result." Grannia steadily met his gaze while he took in her meaning.

"And that I cannot do."

"It's what you must do if you'd rather I not spend my life in the forest like a wild animal."

Owain shook his shaggy head. "You *are* a wild animal."

"Then so are you, for we are two of a kind—fated to be together but robbed of our destiny by a greedy man."

"My father . . ." Owain's eyes went hard while the respect owed a sire warred with the truth as he'd known it all his life.

"My husband." Bitterness soured the word she spoke.

Owain pulled Grannia close, tucked her head under his chin, and rocked her quietly in his arms. "We can't. Not ever."

Grannia let him repeat what he sincerely believed over and over, but all the while her hands were burrowing under his cloak, smoothing over his back, and then winnowing up under his tunic. She was stroking his skin with temptation before he realized what she was about.

Owain growled again when he felt her teasing fingers tangling with the hair on his chest. He took an unwise step back, tripped over the same exposed root that had caused his recent problems, and fell. Fortu-

nately he landed on the thick blades of grass and lush
ferns between two trees. Slightly disoriented, he failed
to immediately regain his feet and in the next moment
discovered himself in a most vulnerable position
while the one woman he couldn't have but most
wanted leaned over him. She efficiently pushed his
tunic up under his arms and laid dangerous kisses
over forbidden flesh.

Her husband had not been her choice, nor had she
found anything but discomfort and disgust in his bed,
but she was not a shrinking virgin. Though she hadn't
planned this hunt, never would she lose what could be
her last chance to capture her prey. Wielding the
unwanted knowledge her marriage had taught,
Grannia shocked her quarry. With bold caresses of
hands and lips and even more wanton actions, she
soon roused in Owain a potent hunger that burned his
restraints to ashes and turned his reluctance into a
desperate need that demanded to be satisfied.

Thus, there atop discarded cloak and clothes and
amid the warm spring night's wildflower-scented air,
Grannia won her heart's delight and an overmeasure
of sweet ecstasy.

16

FROM ATOP A MONOTONOUSLY PLODDING DONKEY, LINNET steadily watched the powerful figure leading her mount while his swirling black cloak disturbed luminous mists drifting across the mountain path. The limited light of predawn surrounded them with a magical blue between the indigo of night and the brightness of summer sky. It stole color from the trees reaching their limbs out above and the flowers below poking innocent blooms through thick undergrowth on either side. It stole even the gold from the mane brushing the broad shoulders of the man who during a near sleepless night had given her a treasure of memories—fiery delights and sweet contentment.

Rhys felt the weight of amber eyes and glanced behind him to give her a smile of piercing sweetness. He saw her catch her breath, and as he turned his attention back to the path, he began absently humming a haunting song of love he hadn't thought of since his departure from Normandy.

"What tune is that?" Linnet was accustomed to the martial songs of valor and defeat ever performed in Radwell's great hall. This was a melody she'd never heard, one even more unusual than the merry tune she'd heard at the feast of Gwyn ap Nudd. "Does it have words?"

Rhys was startled. He hadn't realized he was humming, let alone what song he'd randomly chosen—or was it random? No matter, he identified both it and its source.

"'Tis the song of a roaming minstrel who sang in my foster father's castle." Wrapping the donkey's reins about his hand, he fell back to walk beside the damsel who held his heart in her hands. "The man claimed its story was his own."

Linnet's soft gaze never left his handsome face as Rhys sang for her an eerie tale of love in peril. His low voice gave it a beauty, and a fire to match the flame glowing in the depths of his eyes.

In response to the forlorn expression on his beloved's winsome face at the verse's sad close, he strung together words that gave the tale a new and happy ending.

"It's wonderful." The awed approval in her voice said more than the words as, without thought, she reached out to run a forefinger down the line of his cheek. "Teach it to me?"

Rhys's jaw went hard beneath her touch, and the flame in his eyes flashed brighter as he nodded. He'd give her what she now desired just as he had during the hours of night. One line at a time, he led her through the tune and its words. And as her incredible voice melded with his, he was aware that likely there was nothing he would fail to give her should she ask. That prospect which once would have struck him with terror. But having come to trust as well as love this tender linnet, it now held no fear.

Nay, the fear was all on his side—fear for what would happen to her should he fail to win the fight ahead. He'd said she would be safe in the abbey. But when a woman's father had not agreed beforehand to let his daughter enter a convent, by Norman law he could drag her out of the abbey if he chose. Indeed, even if he'd arranged to have her enter sanctified walls, if enough wealth passed between him and the church, he would assuredly win what he sought. The image of Linnet wed to the despicable Osric—or to any other man—hardened Rhys's determination to forestall that possibility and by wedding her himself erect a permanent block to the deed.

Rhys dropped into morose silence, and Linnet, too, fell quiet. While a bleak future loomed too near, she gazed at the beloved man who so soon would forever disappear from the view of a woman whose determination had never wavered. She *would* commit herself to a nun's life and free him from a price she'd sworn he would not pay for her misdeed—nay, misdeeds.

All too soon the thick wooden gates of the abbey appeared amid fog dissipating under the growing daylight of midmorn.

"Ah, you're here at last." The words were a growl.

Surprised, Linnet looked to one side and found the unexpected sight of Owain stepping into their path from woodland shadows.

"As you see." Dark eyes narrowed on the impatient man. And as Rhys stepped nearer, he flicked several crushed leaves from the other's shoulder. "Were you in such haste to meet me that you slept in the forest?"

Owain's face went instantly red with a blush of such brightness it couldn't be hidden by even the black curls of his beard.

"I see." Rhys grinned. "You found Grannia."

Growling again, Owain huffily whirled and stomped back into the forest. "I'll be here waiting for you to finish your business." Irrationally vexed by the amusement of this friend he'd feared would be angered at even the suspicion that his sister had been intimate with a man forbidden, Owain stood with his back turned to the pair steadily moving nearer the abbey.

Towering trees parted to make room for Saint Anne's. The sunlight in the clearing gleamed over a still broadly smiling Rhys as, at the gate, he reached out to lift Linnet from her angular mount.

When he wrapped his strong hands near completely about her small waist, Linnet clasped his broad shoulders for steady anchor. Though by their night's play she was familiar with the feel of iron-hard muscle rippling beneath her touch, familiarity had not weakened the shock of pleasure the contact brought. Indeed, having experienced the feel of hot satin skin and the power below only made this unintentional caress the more potent.

Hearing her breath catch, Rhys looked up into a melting amber gaze. She was as light as thistledown. He easily held her suspended above him, much aware of lush curves so near. But the time was purely wrong for him to fall prey to her undeniably tempting charms. Nonetheless, their eyes remained bonded all through her slow descent to earth.

Rhys abruptly looked away. The immediate response to his knock on thick oak planks proved that, as he'd suspected, a nun had been watching them.

"We welcome you, Prince Rhys, to our humble abbey." The speaker was a plump woman of quiet smile and soft words. "The abbess is waiting for you in the common room. Come, I'll lead you and your companion there."

Although Linnet didn't understand the Welsh words the woman had spoken, when the nun took a step back and motioned them to come inside, her meaning was clear enough.

The nun permitted the two visitors to enter before closing and barring the gate once more. Then, palms clasped and fingertips resting beneath her chin, she turned and moved toward a long building on one side of a small garden where young sprouts lent the brown of fertile earth a green fur.

Rhys offered Linnet his arm, and she lightly rested the fingertips of one hand atop. In silence they followed the gently swaying nun to a door that quietly opened as they approached. Their guide stepped back, nodding to indicate that they should enter.

On a raised dais at the long, empty room's far end a tiny woman sat stiffly upright in a chair whose high back seemed to further diminish her size. Moving nearer, Linnet saw a face so wreathed in a multitude of wrinkles it appeared that she, like a fine woolen garment wrongly washed in boiling water, had shrunk. A silly thought, but it had the fortunate effect of relieving a measure of the despair threatening to bury Linnet during these final moments in Rhys's company.

"Ah, the Eagle. Come closer, boy. I've not seen you since before you were packed off to Normandy." Her voice was as frail as her body. The woman had spoken English, proving that she had been forewarned of her feminine guest's identity.

"I think my eyes are even older than the rest of me." Her smile added another layer of wrinkles, and she shrugged. "Mayhap they've merely seen too much."

Rhys let Linnet's hand fall as he moved forward to drop down on one knee before the abbess and kiss her hand.

"You have the look of your mother, that kind woman. You certainly must have inherited your size from her family." The abbess's small head was tilted against the chair back behind her, as even a kneeling Rhys towered over her. "But, too, you resemble your father. With those eyes, it would be impossible not to see that you are of my brother's line."

Linnet was startled to learn of this family relationship and looked closer, searching for a family resemblance. It was difficult to find until the woman shifted her attention to her female guest.

"Ah . . ." The golden sparkle of amusement in dark eyes was strikingly familiar. "The little birdling you would see me protect. Bring her closer."

Rhys smoothly rose and twisted around to hold his hand out to Linnet. She unhesitatingly stepped forward to lay her fingers in the palm of his hand.

"Linnet, here meet my Aunt Tayled, the abbess of Saint Anne's."

While Rhys told his aunt Linnet's name and a brief history of her reason for seeking shelter, Linnet sank to her knees before the tiny woman.

"I'm not his aunt, you know." These were the first words the abbess had spoken directly to Linnet. "Honesty is my trade, and I must confess that in truth I was aunt to his father, sister to his grandsire."

Linnet was unsure what response was called for and merely nodded.

A surprisingly girlish giggle bubbled from the tiny body. "I've lived more than four score years, can't walk, can barely move, and am nearly blind." She shook her head. "And I don't recommend living so long to anyone. But I've surrendered myself to God's will and can only assume I'm paying penance for my sins here on earth and pray that when He brings an end to my mortal stay I'll be permitted to enter heaven directly.

"So go on with you, Rhys." She made a weak shooing motion with one frail hand. "I'll see your birdling safe."

Rhys didn't move. "Aunt, I've another request to make of you before I depart."

The abbess's eyes narrowed until only the faintest glimmer appeared between folds of skin.

Rhys lifted his chin proudly. "When I return, and I soon will, I pray that you'll summon a priest to bless my union with Lady Linnet of Castle Radwell . . . no matter the response for good or ill which our alliance may bring from others."

Eyes now completely closed, for long moments the abbess remained silent.

Linnet soundlessly gasped. She ought speak against Rhys's request now if she meant to do so at all, but somehow the words couldn't find their way through a throat blocked with tension and tears. Was Rhys to be refused by his blood kin?

When at last heavy lids rose, the abbess's gaze blazed near completely gold.

Linnet's attention flew from this possibly fearful view to Rhys, whose face looked to be carved of emotionless granite while his eyes were flat black.

"You are your father's son. A rebel against traditional ways." The abbess's words held a pleased satisfaction that calmed the fears of both visitors. "I'll wait until you return. Then I shall do all I can to see your request fulfilled." Her face split with a smile that was youthful despite the lines of age wrapped about it. "But, Rhys, make it soon, as surely God will not ask me to live for too many more weeks."

Rhys dropped to his knees beside Linnet and wrapped one arm about her shoulders while again kissing his aunt's fingers. "Not long, Aunt, I swear it."

With his wish granted, Rhys soon rose and departed. Linnet was still gazing at the door through which he'd disappeared when an ineffably light touch on her shoulder summoned her attention.

"I will give you my good wishes now, aware as I am of my uncertain days. I am thankful that Rhys has chosen to ask for a priest and has not been so impatient as the fool who sought to supplant him as prince."

Linnet's eyes widened, and the speaker thought her surprise born of the condemnation in her words.

"Aye, as a woman of God, I ought leave the man and his sins for the Almighty to judge. But that he 'claimed' my niece, Rhys's sister, with rites that were an abomination to all things sacred revives a temper I've fought for eighty years to subdue."

Was it possible? Linnet wondered. Was there hope for Grannia and Owain after all? She took a deep, calming breath and tried to put her wild hopes into sane questions.

"You speak of Grannia's dead husband, Lloyd? Was their marriage not church-blessed?"

The abbess clicked her tongue in obvious disgust. "Lloyd was a fool—a fool to think he could rule Cymer, a fool to snare the first stranger who appeared and bribe him to perform sham rites to sanctify the marriage." She went on to describe the method and perpetrator of the deed, ending with a simple statement. "A sin."

"Nay, not a sin," Linnet quickly countered, taking the abbess's frail hands in hers without advance thought. "A miracle it is. A miracle that will prevent far greater sins and an unjust punishment from being wreaked upon Grannia."

Seeing the puzzled tilt and intensely curious gaze bent upon her, Linnet explained precisely what awful wrongs had been perpetrated upon an innocent woman by the false marriage. And when she had done, it was the abbess who squeezed her hands.

"A miracle," Tayled said. "Aye, a miracle, and one I am glad I was permitted to live long enough to see. Now I understand that God allowed me to remain on this earth long enough to carry out his will by undoing a wickedness."

Linnet was alarmed when the woman who'd sat so stiffly upright for so long suddenly sagged back against her chair. She leaned forward, heart pounding in her concern.

"I tire easily," the abbess said, "and would rest now if you would be so kind as to summon Sister Martha. I'm certain she'll be hovering just beyond the door."

Linnet did as requested and found the same woman who'd led her and Rhys to this room waiting in the bright sunshine outside. The abbess was soon ensconced in her own bed and peacefully resting. The lady guest was hospitably invited to share a plain but filling meal. And after its conclusion, feeling both grateful for the answer to Grannia's woe and fearful for Rhys, she accompanied the small group of sweetly smiling nuns to the chapel where she joined them in quiet prayers.

Osric unobtrusively watched the only other person seated at the high table for the day's first meal. Godfrey had plainly passed beyond anger to bewildered grief and bleak fear. All three of the earl's children were missing . . . vanished, gone.

Although he took joy in Godfrey's anguish, one fact was a blight on his enjoyment, a very serious blight. Mark had so far not appeared at his mother's home, although both Osric and Morwena had repeatedly urged Mark to use that site for the necessary task. At Morwena's house the deed could best be done and hidden. No matter; Osric felt he understood Mark's choice to act alone. The fewer who knew specific facts, the safer he would be.

At the prospect of this end, Osric leaned forward until a thin curtain of hair fell about his face to shield the satisfied smile it was growing harder every day to conceal.

He'd escorted Edolf to Northland the day past but had hastened back to Radwell, anxious to miss no moment of the pleasure to be had in these scenes building to a long-awaited conclusion. Thus, to remain near, he'd sympathized with Godfrey, assured him that he ached for his pain, and offered to lend both his company and his support while the wretch responsible for the abductions was found and punished. After savoring the pleasure for one instant more, he loosed another bolt from his crossbow of destruction.

"After you were abed last night, my lord, I sent out a message."

An uninterested Godfrey glanced toward his guest with lackluster eyes.

"I sent it deep into Wales and received answer this morning."

The message's destination won Godfrey's honest

attention, although he didn't move, afraid that to do so would disperse faint wisps of hope. He had searched long and uselessly for Linnet, cursing the Welsh villain who'd taken her. Then when his sons, too, had disappeared, he'd been furious, so furious he'd stormed down to the dungeons intending to force answers out of Edolf, only to receive a third blow. Even his suspect, his one link, one hope, had been secreted away. The black-hearted Eagle was a conjuror. Must be! Godfrey had blamed Edolf for making possible the man's seemingly incredible trick of scaling a stone wall, but Godfrey had no one to blame for stealing Edolf from his hands.

Seeing a world of anguish and anger pass through the earl's pale brown eyes, Osric tamed his satisfaction into a tight smile of mock comfort as he continued. "I believe this message offers an end to all the ills that have befallen Radwell."

The earl sat fully upright, though he was still wary of disappointment.

The words Osric had spoken were true, but their meaning was different from what Godfrey thought he understood. While the earl saw a vision of his children returned and happiness descending upon Radwell again, Osric awaited the end to the overwhelming wrong that had seen his inheritance seized by another a score and more years gone past.

"My urgent message I sent to Prince Cawdr of Dyfi, whose Welsh princedom lies to the west of Cymer."

Godfrey nodded, fear of disappointment fading with every word Osric spoke until, by the last uttered, his vigor was restored.

"Cawdr will lend us his aid," Osric said, "for a price. Nothing is without price. But if you are willing to share with him the spoils of our task—divide with him the lands which Cymer comprises—Cawdr will join in our endeavors. Knowing the love you bear your children, I assured him in the missive I sent that for the safe return of your children you would pay his price."

"I will!" Godfrey emphatically agreed. Indeed, he would happily give up all claim to the lands to win that reward.

Osric allowed his smile to widen as brightly as it had for days sought to do.

"I was certain you'd welcome the chance not only to win back your children but also to punish the culprit and further stretch your borders with lands seized from the villain. Cawdr has already baited a trap to tempt the Eagle to his ruin—today."

"Today?" In combined shock and anticipation, Godfrey slapped a heavy hand palm down on the table top, splattering crimson drops from his overfull wine vessel and bouncing bread crusts across his trencher. "Quick"—he bent nearer to Osric, fires again burning in pale brown eyes—"tell me what we must do so that I will have sufficient time to summon my warriors and see them better prepared to meet our enemy this time."

"Aye, you'll need to act immediately, for no later than the nooning hour, we should cross the border from the lands of Morwena's dowery into Cymer. Within the forest just beyond, our men will hide among the trees and green shadows to wait." Osric hesitated for a moment, thinking he'd failed to earlier appreciate the pleasure to be had in reviving his prey's hope before increasing his own joy by taking it away again.

"And then?" Godfrey was too impatient to permit Osric even a momentary pause.

"Then? Then the fellow prince, Rhys of Cymer, whom Cawdr has summoned to meet with him there, will appear—doubtless with Owain, his most important ally, by his side and a cadre of warriors. But once the three Welsh men are talking—while the Eagle and his brethren are still unaware of our presence—we'll swoop down and take Prince Rhys and his ally, Owain, leaving his soldiers leaderless."

"You mean to leave the Eagle's warriors behind?" Godfrey was skeptical of such a scheme.

"If we take them with us, all we shall have are more mouths to feed and no one left to bargain with for the return of your children."

Godfrey saw a vague wisdom in the plan, although he thought permitting one—at most, two—Welshmen to return would be sufficient. Still, with victory so near he could almost feel the Eagle's throat in his hands, he chose not to challenge the plan already under way.

"With the Eagle and his friend as our captives," Osric said in an attempt to soothe the earl's doubts, "we'll be able to negotiate with the far less effective men we've left behind for the return of your children."

"They will demand their prince's return for the spared lives of my children." Now that Godfrey had been assured of a viable way to restore order to his world, his wits began functioning with their usual attention to possible future dangers and the methods of defeating them.

"Undoubtedly." Osric felt secure in the certainty that the earl could do little to upset his carefully laid plans.

Godfrey nodded readily enough, but his eyes narrowed as he made one stipulation to the scheme plotted by others.

"For my children's safe return, we'll give them Owain, the prince's ally. Then you and Cawdr may divide Cymer between you however you choose, but I personally claim the pleasure of taking the Eagle's life."

"I'll guarantee you that pleasure, Godfrey." Osric was more than pleased at having been given the very thing he most wanted—the tool with which to bargain for a further concession. "If you'll take the first step toward fulfilling a promise earlier made."

Godfrey leaned back to study more completely the one seeking to turn the deal around. "What promise have I made you?"

"You promised Linnet as my wife." Near colorless gray eyes steadily met pale brown.

Uncomfortably reminded of the deeply rued pledge he'd purposely put from his mind, Godfrey blustered. "But she's not here."

"Not yet." Osric's wispy hair brushed heavy shoulders as he nodded agreement. "But if you want me to agree to the boon you seek, I ask that you send for a priest now. Have him waiting here in Castle Radwell to perform the marriage the moment she appears— not a fortnight or even a sennight later but the very day of her return."

Godfrey felt as trapped as doubtless the Eagle soon would. With no choice close to hand, he reluctantly gritted out his agreement. "For your promise to give me the pleasure of causing the Eagle's death, I'll send for the priest before we depart on our mission. *But* I will *not* see you wed with her before the Welshman is dead."

17

LINNET BRUSHED BACK TANGLED AMBER HAIR WITH ONE hand, while the sturdy shoes Rhys had ordered made for her dangled by their long laces from the other. She had been fast asleep on a narrow, comfortless cot in the cramped cell allotted her, until a silent nun insistently shook her to wakefulness and rushed her along the abbey's corridors. It must be very late, Linnet thought, or very early in the morning. The moon, face almost fully turned away from the earth and toward night darkness, had near disappeared behind the horizon's ridge of trees.

Awkward fingers had barely finished tugging her front-closing gown tight before she was ushered into an austere chamber lit by a single malodorous tallow taper. Linnet squinted through the dim light to where Tayled, the abbess, sat in her bed propped up against the whitewashed wall.

"Distressing news has arrived." Though Tayled spoke quietly, her words rang like a bell tolling doom.

A faint cry escaped the hands Linnet clapped over her mouth while through her mind flashed horrible visions of Rhys wounded . . . dying.

"Just tell me he's alive!" Linnet threw herself to her

knees beside the bed, fingers desperately gripping its blanket. So long as he drew breath, there was hope. "Tell me he lives—" The plea was strangled by a sob rising in her throat. She'd spent near the whole day imploring God to lend His protection to her beloved. And only with faith in divine power had she been able to fall into a dreamless sleep. Only see how wrong she'd been not to continue her prayers throughout the night.

"So far as is known," the abbess spoke immediately to calm the anguished damsel's fears, "Rhys has suffered no injuries."

Linnet took a deep breath and consciously relaxed her hold on the other woman's bed. "Then what news has come?"

"Rhys hasn't been injured." The abbess repeated. "But he has been taken captive, as has been his friend Owain."

Linnet's hands came together and tightly clenched as if their pressure would in some way force her fears to abate and lend her the strength necessary to see wicked deeds undone.

"A young man who says his name is Pywell was sent by Grannia to fetch you back to our captured prince's home. She's waiting for you there and most anxious that you answer her call."

Linnet scrambled to her feet, but Tayled's hand, remarkably strong for fingers so frail, held her back.

"Child, consider carefully. Rhys brought you to me with a plea that I hold you safe for him. I cannot keep the promise I gave to do so if you leave my abbey. My powers do not extend beyond its walls."

Dark eyes glittered, but Linnet couldn't read in them the answer she sought. What response did the abbess seek from her? No matter, there was only one she could give.

"I must go and join Grannia, Reverend Mother." Determination drove Linnet's fear into abeyance, and her expression was filled with calm purpose. Knowing how unwavering was her father's resolve to destroy Rhys, she assumed without question that he was responsible for this action.

"Between my knowledge of Norman practices and of my father's habits and the loyalty Grannia is surely owed by others of Welsh heritage, she and I will find an undefeatable strategy with which to win freedom for the men we love."

"I thought you would say some such thing." The abbess's voice held all the support that Linnet had hoped to find in her eyes. "'Tis why the donkey Rhys left behind in preparation for his return already waits with young Pywell at the gate."

Linnet was suddenly very aware that the abbess could simply have refused Pywell's supplication—could, without reproach, have turned him away—but she hadn't. She hadn't because she wanted to see her nephew freed as badly as did the woman whom he'd consigned to her safekeeping.

Linnet bent to fervently kiss fingers that had released their hold on her. "Thank you, Abbess, thank you!"

"Godspeed and my endless prayers go with you."

Casting the tiny woman a last grateful smile, Linnet rushed from the chamber and hastened to the gate, where the nun who'd roused her stood waiting to unbar the portal.

"We will pray for a happy . . . resolution to your mission." The nun softly spoke in halting English to the woman slipping beyond the abbey's encircling wall. "And for contentment in your future as well."

The bar fell with the last statement of earnest good wishes, and Linnet was heartened. She smiled encouragement to the waiting and clearly troubled Pywell, who was holding the donkey's reins. So troubled was he that the ever-talkative soul rarely spoke as they hurried through the darkness toward the far valley that was their destination. And certain Pywell's silence proclaimed his lack of useful information, Linnet chose not to increase his woe by questioning him.

Linnet had departed from Rhys's home in the gloom of predawn. Now, in the same dim light one day later, she returned.

One pace inside the cold, dark hall of Rhys's home a weeping Grannia fell upon her, sobbing near incoherently at the fickleness of mortal life.

"I'd just won him and now he's been snatched from me." The despairing words ended on a wail.

Holding the devastated woman close, patting her back in solace, Linnet came to a surprising discovery. Grannia, like many a sturdy structure able to stand strong against nature's many whims from blistering sun to pounding hail, teetered beneath a blizzard's unexpected force. At the same time, Linnet, who had rarely been exposed to life's battering weather, found that the vicious storm had bared a core of inflexible steel. This she wielded to reinforce her friend's sorrow-weakened will.

"No matter who has taken them or where, we'll bring them home again." Linnet's words held such calm assurance that Grannia stepped away and gazed up into steady amber eyes.

"How?" From dark, red-rimmed eyes tears flowed down puffy cheeks, but desperate hope had begun slowing Grannia's gasping breath into a more normal pattern.

"We'll find a way. We shall devise a strategy that will set them free." Linnet squarely met Grannia's silently imploring eyes. "We both have too much at stake to concede failure and bow to defeat."

Linnet lifted one of Grannia's icy hands and turned to lead her to the big chair beside a hearth whose untended fire was nearly dead.

"Pywell?" Linnet called over her shoulder to the young man hovering anxiously near the door. "This cold will dull the wits we'd best hone to their sharpest if we're to have any hope of defeating our adversaries and winning success in our attempt to free Rhys and Owain. Might you revive a cheering blaze?"

Without a moment's hesitation Pywell hastened to do as he was bidden while Linnet settled a shivering woman into the limited comfort of the prince's chair. Soon he had flames soaring into the gray shadows of a hall almost in darkness.

Linnet worked quickly, fetching a bed fur to tuck about the chilled woman and then replacing candles that had long since guttered out. In the restored candlelight and the welcome heat, the hall's dismal atmosphere was vanquished and replaced by Linnet's bright determination.

While Pywell retreated to a bench on one side of the table, Linnet sat atop a stool beside her friend, who had regained her composure but not her spirit. Certain she had the precise spur needed to revive that spirit, Linnet leaned closer and whispered all-important news into an ear buried in black curls.

"The abbess, your Aunt Tayled, chose not to shame you by making known a fact I've assured her will bring you only joy: in the church's eyes you were never wed to Lloyd. There is not now, nor ever has there been, a bar to your union with Owain."

Golden sparks flashed in dark eyes as Grannia abruptly sat upright. Then, dreading disappointment, she questioned the mere possibility. "How could it be? Lloyd claimed me as wife before a priest, and that priest blessed our bond."

"Nay." Shifting orange lights cast by the fire very near flickered over one side of Linnet's firmly shaken head. "Not a priest, merely an unlanded freeman passing through Cymer who was bribed to don religious robes and mislead everyone."

Grannia's eyes widened.

Linnet earnestly repeated every word that Tayled had spoken to her. "The abbess said that Lloyd was too impatient, too fearful that others might prevent the marriage, to wait for the arrival of a true man of God."

Grannia leaned back in the chair again, a slow smile warming her expression as thoroughly as the fire had warmed her flesh.

Thankful for this gift, though she regretted the time taken to give it—time better devoted to saving Owain and her brother—Grannia lost not a moment more in pursuing that goal.

"What initial step need we take to bring our heroes home?"

"We'll devise a plan together." A bright smile lit Linnet's face. "I would know first all that you can tell me about the way they were stolen from us."

Grimacing, Grannia made an admission. "Once the meaning of words reporting the deed came clear in a mind shocked to feeble mush, in my anger and pain I heard little and asked nothing."

Linnet lightly touched the other's clenched hand with sympathetic understanding, and Grannia quickly provided a partial solution to their problem.

"Summoning the one who brought the ill tidings to me will be no difficult thing. It was Taff, Pywell's father." Even as she spoke to Linnet, Grannia twisted around to face the young man seated at the table and with an imploring smile made a request.

Pywell hustled off to carry the summons to his home. He soon returned—accompanied by others besides his father. Pywell led into the hall his father, his older brothers, and several neighbors, all of whom had been at Taff's cottage discussing the wicked wrong done their prince and weighing wild, impossible schemes to see it undone.

Pywell interpreted for Linnet as Taff began a report of how he, his older sons, and a few other armed men of Cymer had accompanied the Eagle on a short trip to meet with the Prince of Dyfi.

"Why were they meeting?" Grannia demanded, voice strained. She could think only of negotiations supposedly under way between Rhys and Cawdr with the intent of arranging her marriage to the man. How could Rhys take Owain to witness such a discussion? More to the point, would Owain meekly go— particularly so soon after their night of passion?

"Don't know." Taff shook a head of thick gray hair. "We weren't told afore we set off, and once we'd arrived it didn't matter."

Grannia opened her mouth to challenge the odd statement, but Taff lifted a big hand to forestall useless words.

"The two princes had barely greeted each other when the forest came alive with armed men. They descended upon our far smaller band and quickly overmastered us all, wresting weapons from our hold and flinging them far into the forest."

"How many were killed?" Grannia's face hardened against the near certainty of a gruesome answer, since the men of Cymer had been so badly outnumbered.

"None."

Puzzled, Linnet bit at her lips while Grannia sent her a look of like confusion. No part of these tactics made sense. Why had the assailants not laid waste to their foes? And why had they not held tight to confiscated weapons, the very booty over whose possession many battles were fought? Unspoken questions were thrust aside as the women's attention was summoned once more by the man continuing his account.

"When we men of Cymer lay unarmed beneath the Normans' threat, a big Saxon who speaks our tongue appeared." Taff's face went harsh with disgust. "Though it has been many years since last I saw him, I believe the man to be brother to our dead prince's wife."

"My Uncle Osric?" Grannia's initial surprise was immediately replaced by disgust. "My contemptible uncle."

Taff met her dark gaze unflinching and immediately

continued. "Osric thanked Cawdr for his aid while two of his supporters hoisted the bound Rhys and Owain over their shoulders and disappeared into the forest. He then ordered that those of us remaining be herded into a tight clump and forced to lie shamefully weaponless and prone at our conquerors' feet."

Again Taff paused, mouth working to hold back the blistering curses burning on his tongue, which had best not be spoken before these two females. "Osric told us that they would exchange Owain for the safe restoration of the earl's three children."

Linnet frowned. *"Three* children?"

"I can only report what was said." Taff shrugged defensively and, thinking her question born of an odd detail he'd noticed himself, hastened to add, "Though I saw no sign of the earl himself, many of those who burst upon us from the forest bore his shield and colors."

Accepting the strange demand for the return of three children as merely another odd, unanswerable question, and anxious to reach what was for her the most important point, Linnet asked the question her informant dreaded. "But what of Rhys? What did they demand in exchange for his return?"

"Cymer." The answer was a single word, but plainly the women demanded a further explanation. "A Cymer humbled and resigned to its division between the Saxon and the prince of Dyfi."

Grannia hissed the fiery curse that, moments past, had burned on Taff's tongue. He gave a humorless grin but hurried on to finish his sorry narrative.

"Hurling ridicule at us, our 'masters' calmly departed. And by the time we'd retrieved our weapons from the trees, bushes, and roaring streams where they'd been thrown, Osric and our foes had completely disappeared."

Taff's expression reflected both shame and frustrated rage. But it was a sense of lingering helplessness that weighted down his drooping shoulders.

Linnet rose to her feet, chin bravely lifted as she resolutely stated her intention. "I will return to Radwell and assure my father that he has no justification for holding your prince." It seemed a frustratingly feeble gesture but the only action she could immediately see that offered any chance of success. "We can pray that when I've confessed my preference for the Eagle's company and told my father of my unaided escape into Cymer . . ." Linnet shook her head, then continued in despair. "Surely when I've told Father of my disgust for all the oaths he's forsworn, he'll understand the wrong is in him and no longer blame Rhys for the results of his own failings."

While Pywell repeated her words for fellow Welshmen, amazed by her statement, Grannia stood, firmly clasped Linnet's slender arms, and sought to gently shake sense into a mind seemingly gone daft.

"What good would your sacrifice accomplish? You've admitted your father is without honor. Why should he care that imprisoning Rhys is unjust? Once he has you back, he's far more likely simply to call his enemy's life forfeit."

Linnet went white. There was undeniable truth in Grannia's words. 'Twas what her father was almost certain to do.

"But if I'm there," she argued, unwilling to surrender their only hope, "I may be able to free Rhys and Owain before harm befalls them. Leastwise it's a chance I must take."

Grannia shook her head. The two women stood silently within the fire's circle of warmth while the male audience hovered uncomfortably on its outer edge. At length Grannia gave words to a fact that had reared up like a deadly fire-breathing dragon ready to incinerate any flimsy defense waged against its fiery breath.

"That's our most difficult problem. *Where* are Rhys and Owain being held? At Radwell? That seems unlikely when your father had no visible part in the taking. On my uncle's lands? Or in Dyfi?" In a room where only the crackling of the fire competed for attention, Grannia's words sounded unnaturally loud and alarmingly clear. "This puzzle is at the center of an already confusing maze of questions. The trail begins with why our men were left alive and continues with why their weapons were thrown into the forest rather than being taken as booty. But the question of where Rhys and Owain are being held is the one for which we must have answer, as that is the key to open the door for any successful liberation."

"I've brought you that key—leastways I think I have." The high-pitched voice ringing from the open door immediately won the surprised attention of all.

Only on seeing David standing there did Grannia realize she'd completely forgotten about her second stepson in the horror of the grave news she'd learned hours past.

David proudly stepped farther into the room and looked behind him to motion others to follow. "I saw them in the forest two days past and figured they'd be somewhere about the area." He nearly crowed his success. "I was right!"

Another youngster of roughly the same size, along with a dark-haired man with piercing gray eyes, came through the door behind David.

"Alan! Mark!" Linnet rushed across the hall to give her younger brother a crushing hug before being swept into one even stronger by her taller half brother.

Linnet looked up into Mark's gray eyes, bewildered by this first sign of affection from an ever-aloof sibling.

Mark released her with a slightly awkward shrug. "Before Alan and I left Radwell, we knew you were missing and have spent more than a few hours worrying for your health."

"I'm fine," Linnet promptly assured them. "And, as

Alan knows, I left by my own choice." With the mention of his name, she turned a faint frown upon the boy who was her replica in coloring. "But why did you two leave?"

"Mark couldn't kill me, though his uncle Osric insisted that he must. His mother, too." Alan gazed adoringly up at his brother. "So we decided to live off the forest until the conflict between our father and his uncle is past. Mark says it will be soon."

"Our guide insists that you've a desperate need for aid from us." Mark, uncomfortable with this open admission that his fondness for Alan was so strong that he'd gone against both uncle and mother, effectively shifted to a subject of more immediate urgency. "Is it true that my cousin Rhys was snatched from Cymer by men who claimed to be holding us two?" Mark motioned to himself and Alan.

David had heard clearly the report which during its first telling horror had muffled in Grannia's ears. He'd understood the demand for an exchange of Radwell's three children for his brother. But, certain the men giving the account would not take seriously a child's claim to know the whereabouts of Radwell's missing sons, he'd merely slipped away and gone to find David and Mark. And once he found his friend Alan, he'd pleaded for their aid in seeing both Owain and their prince freed.

Before his arrival at Rhys's home, Mark had been cautioned by both boys to speak English. Linnet had spoken nothing else while in Welsh lands and, though excited by the unexpected appearance of her brothers, had instinctively continued to do so even when speaking with two whose native language was the Norman tongue.

One hand resting on Alan's head and the other wrapped about Mark's arm, she hastily repeated the story she'd just learned, adding her intention to return to Radwell to locate and free the captives—and

Grannia's objection to her plan. All the while Pywell stumbled over his tongue trying to keep up with his translation of their conversation for the roomful of observers.

"I agree that your return to Radwell would be unwise. Osric would never allow a pawn of this import to slip from his hands for a single moment before whatever price he has demanded for his cooperation is delivered."

"Me." Linnet quietly stated.

"What?" Mark's dark brows crashed fiercely together.

His was a reaction no sharper than Grannia's. The revelation of a planned union between Linnet and the Saxon wretch whom Grannia could not bear to name uncle made her friend's choice to enter the abbey all the easier to understand.

"I am the payment father promised for Osric's aid," Linnet calmly explained, unaware of Grannia's surprise. "Leastwise I was the price for his acquiescence to the battle at Abergele. Rhys was meant to be killed that morning, and after the feat was accomplished I was to be betrothed to Osric."

"I'd wondered what Father gave for my uncle's willingness to see the deed done, though it meant the breaking of another oath given to the last Saxon lord."

Grannia had waited patiently for the conclusion of this exchange, had been interested in its disclosures, but could endure the wait no longer. "If not at Castle Radwell, then where are the captives held?"

"As I said"—Mark turned toward the speaker, and the familiar look of mockery, which Alan had captured so well to imitate both his brother and the Eagle, was stunningly apparent—"my Uncle Osric holds Prince Rhys and Owain, but not, I think, in his own lands. The danger would be too great, as my father—staunch in his determination to see the Eagle dead—would certainly seek him there first."

"Then where?" Grannia's growing anxiety brooked no further delay in laying firm plans to win release for those wrongly seized.

Mark looked to the tall, gray-haired man who was clearly the leader of the others and who was almost certainly present to give the account of a firsthand witness. He took a step toward the man to ask of him a single question. "Where did you meet with the prince of Dyfi?"

Taff glanced to his son. Pywell quickly translated the question and then restated the immediate answer for Mark, an answer that deepened Mark's cynical smile.

"'Tis as I thought. The lands of my mother's dowry lie directly across the border in Radwell. It's there that the men you seek will be confined."

"Then we'll take an army and besiege the hall." Grannia only wished they didn't have to wait for armed Welshmen to be summoned.

Mark laughed, but it held little humor. "The task will not be quite so simple as that. There is no large, defended hall. Oh, there's a building larger than others, but 'tis unlikely Osric would lodge his prisoners in so obvious a place. Nay, they'll be in one of a number of small cottages scattered through a valley near as long, steep, and rugged as this one." Gray eyes met the unshifting intensity in Grannia's black stare.

"Then what had we best do to reclaim them?" Linnet calmly demanded while Grannia sputtered with frustration.

"Is that truly what you wish to be done?" Mark quietly asked his sister, gaze shifting to narrow on her solemn face.

"More than my life."

Mark's lips barely curled in a smile of both agreement with and recognition of the depth of emotion revealed in those few words. "Then for you, and because I believe it may be the only hope of sparing our father as well, I will help you see the deed done.

"But first, so that all is clear before we seek a firm strategy, let me explain the tactics you found so strange in Cawdr and Osric's capture of unwary prey." Mark looked from the group of men clustered about their leader to Grannia and then toward his sister.

"The prince's men were allowed to live for the same reason that our father, Earl Godfrey, negotiated with Lord Siward when claiming conquered lands. He bargained to prevent damage to his new property— the serfs he needed to work for him. Likewise, Osric and Cawdr will need the men of Cymer."

Even as bitter smiles were exchanged for what should have been an obvious answer to their question, Mark embarked upon an explanation for the second action they'd found puzzling.

"Weapons were not seized but rather thrown wide to delay the Welshmen, who elsewise would assuredly have pursued those who were hauling such booty away and possibly slowed by that task."

Once it was clear they'd accepted his solutions to the maze of questions Grannia had outlined during the moments he'd hovered just beyond the door, Mark motioned the two women and the one who'd spoken for the gathered men to join him at the table.

Linnet wanted an explanation for Mark's reference to their only hope of sparing their father, but felt it could wait till after a strategy offering hope for victory had been devised and preparations put into motion. Thus she and Grannia followed Mark to the table where Taff sat with his interpreter-son very near. The remaining men listened intently, while Alan and David, proving boys their age could remain utterly still, settled unobtrusively on the floor.

To aid in the attainment of their goal, Mark reported further and previously unsuspected treacheries, which answered Linnet's question. A strategy was discussed, revised, and refined, but in its final form Linnet saw a glimmer of hope for everyone important to her. Success in this endeavor truly would free not only Rhys but her father as well. She regretted only that her deep concern over the earl's threat to her beloved had held her attention so fully she'd failed to recognize a greater danger overshadowing the whole.

Their desperate scheme, it had been decided, would best be initiated at dusk. Anxious to see every detail of their advance arrangements carefully completed, the group at the table arose. Determination was a steady glow in their eyes in spite of the fact that their success would depend upon many difficult deeds that would have to be flawlessly performed to allow for comfort or easy expectation of victory. In the full light of midmorning, Taff dispatched his men to the far corners of Cymer, carrying a call to arms on behalf of Prince Rhys.

To ensure that all would be in readiness Linnet, too, turned her attention toward necessary preparations. She was content with their planned maneuvers, although the part she'd insisted on playing in them was far more dangerous than her first poor plan involving a mere return to her father and a possible forced marriage to Osric. This one might well cost many lives . . . including her own.

18

A STREAM BABBLED SOMEWHERE NEARBY, BUT DEEPENING twilight and the need to watch her step on a sharp descent prevented Linnet from catching so much as a glimpse of its rushing waters. Upon cresting the last hill, she and Mark had gazed sharply down into a long, narrow valley. Her brother had informed her that before them lay the lands of his mother's dowry. The valley was beautiful—fertile and dotted with whitewashed cottages that in the distance she'd thought looked like blossoms scattered by a faerie's hand.

In truth, Linnet acknowledged while cautiously stepping over an unfortunate sapling earlier uprooted and dropped across their path, the valley below had seemed a lush and peaceful vale. The notion earned a rueful smile. Peaceful? An inappropriate site, then, for the night's coming conflict. But she'd believed much the same of Abergele Farm. Keeping her eyes on grasses parted by her brother's footfalls, Linnet slowly shook her head. Men's battles were no respecters of either beauty or peace.

They'd chosen not to ride Mark's destrier on the journey, as a single horse would have been more a liability than an aid in the escape of three men and a woman. Besides, their route was steep and wound through trees grown so close together their progress was further dimmed by overhanging branches. Linnet's courage did not falter. The fear and tension of waiting had been calmed by the physical actions of the actual attempt begun. Her concern for Rhys and Owain had not lessened, but knowing she was doing everything possible gave her composure and cool thinking. For that Linnet was thankful. Any untoward nervousness might smell of trickery, warning Osric and his cohorts of things to come.

Linnet carefully followed Mark's lead down a path only someone familiar with its location would have been able to find. Though overgrown with long blades of grass, ferns, and an abundance of wildflowers whose scent under other circumstances she would have savored, it provided a direct route to their goal.

As they approached a structure perched near the bottom of the steep slope, Mark's pace quickened. Unlike the many daub-and-wattle cottages dimly seen in light reflected by a clear sky that had yet to be fully claimed by night, this building was wood-framed, sturdy, and twice their size. Still, Linnet silently acknowledged that the many smaller structures confirmed Mark's claim that without a method to identify the building in which Rhys was confined, finding him would require more time than they had.

After mounting stone steps made treacherous by dew-damp moss, they reached a heavy oak door warped by age and harsh weather. As son of the house, Mark opened the door without knocking. He was surprised Osric had failed to post guards at the approach. But then, his uncle was prone to overconfidence.

"Mark!" The dry cackle came from the throat of a woman hastening forward, back bent and leaning heavily on a knotted stick.

"Mother, I've returned, as you urged." Mark stood

patient and firm beneath her unsteady embrace. "And I've brought a surprise for my uncle, which I know he will welcome."

Having caught a glimpse of Osric, frozen with a drink halfway to his lips, Mark turned toward the man. He sat on the floor against the far wall of a chamber narrow and not overly large when compared to the hall at Radwell or even the one in the Eagle's aerie. And its size was further shrunk by the clutter of a daunting number of other people.

"Uncle Osric, when the opportunity arose for me to save my sister from another's hands, I took it . . . and her." Mark reached behind him and jerked Linnet forward by the long, loose end of the rope binding her wrists together.

Delight with this unanticipated gift flared in Osric's eyes as he rose and moved toward his nephew with more haste than his size suggested possible. He impatiently wound his way through the many human obstructions while rubbing his hands together—a habitual manifestation of satisfaction recognized by both Mark and his sister.

"You are much appreciated, nephew." The words were for Mark, but the older man's gaze never left the curving lines of Linnet's bountiful charms. As soon as he was close enough, Osric took her bound wrists between his hands.

"Come, my dear." He inexorably drew her against his well-fed body. "I would have my allies meet the bride who will soon, very soon, be mine."

Letting thick lashes fall as if in feminine modesty, Linnet hid her disgust and apprehension of Osric's unexpected haste. She refused to look up as he dragged her through a crooked path of men to what must surely have been the place from which he'd set out. At their destination, she was pushed down onto a rough plank floor unsoftened by rushes, and the next moment Osric's heavy body thudded down beside her.

While the ill-matched pair settled, Morwena irritably hissed. She had no interest in her brother's lust and no patience to waste on matters of minor import compared to the one she'd long waited to see finished. Tugging at Mark's sleeve, Morwena demanded his attention.

"Have you taken care of the Norman brat?"

Had anyone of less sodden wits than most in the hall bothered to observe the young man's face, he would have caught a clearer glimpse of Mark's honest emotions than anyone had seen since the days of a childhood preceding his father's marriage—a strange mixture of pity, love . . . and distaste for Morwena.

"Aye, Mother. I've taken care of Alan."

A cackle of glee rasped from Morwena's throat. "Did you hear, Osric? Mark has done the deed!" Her voice held a sharpness that sliced through the dull roar of the many speaking in at least two different languages. "It leaves him the earl's only son. A son the arrogant cur will have to see legitimized to have an heir."

Lifting his head, Osric gave his sister a contemptuous smile before turning to exchange a meaningful look with the prince of Dyfi, who was lounging beside him.

Cawdr's contempt was more subtle and directed at a host too self-satisfied to recognize it. The Saxon was a disgusting swine but a man whose company he was willing to endure for the prize of more Welsh lands to greatly widen the boundaries of his own.

Speaking in an undertone not meant to be heard by any save the slender Welsh prince whose dark hair was marked by broad streaks of gray, Osric gloated.

"In the space of precious few hours our plans have leapt forward and fallen into place with a haste that proves us heaven-blessed."

A smug Osric was gratified by the many prizes long sought which of a sudden were flowing with ease into his hands. He and Cawdr had earlier agreed it was near certain to require a minimum of two days, and likely a sennight or more, for leaderless but stubborn Welshmen to accept their defeat and the inevitability of surrender to the control of new lords. Osric had been undaunted by the prospect of a paltry few additional days when he'd already waited a score of years. Moreover, as the first bargain offered had involved Linnet's return, he had been certain that the men of Cymer would attempt to barter for time—and a leader—by delivering her to the earl. Hence, Osric's demand that Godfrey have a priest on hand and that a marriage take place immediately upon her return.

Osric lifted a thick amber braid, admiring its soft contrast to the callused flesh of his hand. With Linnet in his hold and Alan dead, he need wait no longer either to claim her or to dispatch the only remaining impediment to his ultimate triumph. It seemed the earl's cooperation was no longer needed . . . leastways not beyond the enjoyment to be derived from watching him lose everything. But at the moment he could safely put Godfrey from his mind completely.

Aware of Osric's smug expression and his hold on her, through thick lashes Linnet peeked at Mark and in the depths of his ice gray eyes saw encouragement for the ordeal likely to worsen afore it came right. When she'd insisted on performing this part in their plan, her brother had tried earnestly to dissuade her. He'd warned her of precisely what Osric was likely to demand of her; he'd warned her that his hands would be tied as any interference by him would shred the fragile fabric of their painstakingly woven strategy. Thus, forewarned but undeterred, Linnet had come to undertake a simple but vital role that no one else could have performed. Oh, there were other possible methods of winning the same goal, but none so promising or so likely to fit within the limited time frame.

Less than an hour after they arrived, a feast was heaped upon a table in the center of the crowded hall.

From this the crowd of men, most already half sotted, took what they pleased. Carrying both food and tankards from which a measure of dark ale inevitably slopped, drink-befuddled men wandered aimlessly about until they found an open space to claim. Groggy, stumbling men were the reason their two leaders had chosen positions safely back against a wall and the reason they meant to remain where they were throughout the night.

Although Linnet refused to look up and risk meeting the direct gaze of any of the many men whose eyes she felt crawling over her, one fact became clear: half spoke English and the other half Welsh. Apparently only the Welsh prince spoke both languages.

Throughout the noisy meal, in Linnet's opinion more like a slopping of pigs, she sat with eyes downcast, tethered to the man who had claimed her. Osric was not drunk, but with each long draft of potent ale he became more boisterous, and what had begun as a light patting of her back became a revolting pawing of her throat. His touch then roamed over her shoulders and dared dip even lower. This Linnet felt justified in defending herself against, as no well-born woman would permit a groping so public.

Osric laughed heartily when Linnet pulled away. "Ah, the fine lady—so serene, so remote—has a fiery spirit after all."

Winding the loose end of her rope about his hand, he slowly pulled her resisting body nearer until it was pressed tight against his own.

"One whose taming will add to my enjoyment." The free hand returned to endlessly stroking her throat, then began a deliberate, taunting descent.

Repulsed by the fetid breath issuing from a wet mouth too near, Linnet wielded her proximity to Osric like a weapon. Abruptly and with force she brought her knee up toward the apex of his thighs.

"Uwrgh!" Osric's guttural gasp was not so loud as to summon the attention of most, but he was intensely aware of completely sober Cawdr's amused gaze. He compelled a smile to stiff lips. "Spirit. It adds to the pleasure."

Cawdr nodded but watched as a released Linnet warily settled as far distant from her prospective mate as the rope allowed.

Anxious to divert the attention of Cawdr and any other who might have seen a claimed bride's rejection of his favors, Osric proposed an entertainment.

"My bride has a wondrous voice. Sings like . . . Nay, sings better than her namesake." He laughed at his own wit. "Ought to, she gives words to the tunes."

At a sudden rough jerk of the rope, Linnet sprawled across the floor at his feet. Lying prone, palms flat on thick plank flooring, Linnet failed to see the glitter of revenge in her would-be master's eyes. Rather, she turned her head to exchange a brief look of triumph with Mark.

"Sing!" Osric demanded, jerking the rope again, enjoying his power over the earl's daughter. "Sing!"

Linnet made as much distracting noise as possible as she gathered herself up to rest on her knees. Meanwhile, unnoticed by men too lost in their revels to take note, Mark slipped out the door, then braced it open a handbreadth.

Once her brother was in position, without need for further prompting, Linnet began to sing the sweet, sad song the Eagle had taught her during their journey to the abbey. Her very real sorrow for their parting and distress for his present danger added depth to a powerful voice of surpassing beauty. Even men near lost in drunken stupor held silent while thrice she slowly sang the first verse.

"Father, redeem your honor!" Alan's initial earnest but quiet pleas had become desperate supplications and nearly shrill. He stood bravely, a small figure in the open space below the dais where his father was seated alone at the high table. Alan's arrival had been timed to see him enter Radwell's hall as the evening meal began.

Intensely conscious of a sea of staring eyes, a glowering Godfrey again hissed his wordless rejection.

"Order the Eagle's release," Alan said. "*Please,* Father! You've no just reason to hold him captive."

"Hah!" Godfrey growled his derision. "Have I not? He *stole* my children from me. No lord must endure such insult without revenge."

"He took Linnet and me but treated us kindly and returned us just as he swore he would. 'Twas you who broke the oath you gave to win our return, the pledge you made to leave Abergele free."

So enraged was Godfrey by this naming of secret wrongs by his own son 'twas a miracle black steam did not billow from his ears.

With the heedlessness of youth, Alan continued his rebuke. "Only that once did the Eagle 'steal' anyone from you!" Intense emotion put flags of bright color on the boy's cheeks. "Rhys did not seize Linnet a second time. 'Tis only that you taught both Linnet and me the importance of honor." He paused and even Godfrey, filled with dread, took no breath until his son spoke again. "She left Radwell of her own accord to prevent you from staining your honor with foul murder."

Godfrey had heard enough and too much, as had all in his hall. The boy must be stopped!

"Sir Basil, take my plainly misled offspring to his chamber and keep him within until he admits the wretched Welsh source of these wild tales and recants them."

Basil instantly rose from his seat at a lower table and hastened to do as commanded, despite distaste for the unhappy chore. He, along with most on the demesne, had suspected facts this boy alone was brave enough to boldly, publicly throw before the earl.

Just as the guard captain reached for him, Alan dipped to one side with the lightness of foot Rhys had taught him to use in swordplay. He spun about, agilely leapt up onto the dais, and leaned forward to make a final plea.

"One thing more you've got to be told, Father. Mark and I hid in the forest to frustrate the plot of your ally. The Saxon swine, Osric, demanded I be killed. Is my death the price you're willing to pay to see the Eagle fall?"

Basil had rushed forward and stretched out his arm to catch the slippery heir, but the question froze him mid-motion. Utter silence echoed in the large chamber like an omen of doom. Neither cough nor rustle of floor rushes disturbed the stillness. Even the dogs chained near the fire seemed struck to stone.

A door was abruptly thrown wide, shattering the unnatural quiet and breaking the spell.

Instead of seizing Alan, Basil turned toward the sound. In the portal stood a stranger bearing the king's arms. His presence commanded the attention of all. Without glancing behind him, he deliberately pushed the door closed and purposefully strode between two long rows of tables filled with a stunned audience to whom he gave no moment's notice. Ignoring the small impediment between him and his goal, he bent a steady stare upon the lone man seated at the high table.

Once the newcomer stood where he'd so recently been, Alan stepped down from the dais but remained near the father he loved no matter the man's folly.

"I am Sir Walter Tirel and have come to Castle Radwell by command of King William Rufus."

Godfrey nervously nodded. He'd had very little contact with this son of the Conqueror, and what he'd heard of the man had convinced Godfrey he preferred it that way. Nonetheless, his sovereign was his sovereign, and those who represented the Crown were due hospitality and respect. Having heard more than one tale of young Walter Tirel and his skills as both huntsman and warrior, he was loath to offend him.

"Won't you join me for the evening meal? I fear it is a simple one, for we were not expecting to host a royal envoy."

The knight's smile was cold. "Perhaps later, after I fulfill my charge." He pulled a roll of parchment from the leather pouch tied at his waist.

Thinking it his copy of a royal writ such as those which were on occasion delivered to all of the king's vassals, Godfrey leaned forward and reached for the pale cream sheet.

Had the disdain in Sir Walter's eyes failed to quell the earl, the words accompanying it would surely have done so.

"I am commanded to publicly read this censure and warning." Amusement utterly lacking in humor did nothing to warm the speaker's chill expression as he began reading: "'Proofs have been delivered of an affront to the Crown's sovereignty over the kingdom's whole. You have committed a wrong outlawed since the Conqueror's reign.'"

"No-o-o!" Godfrey was stricken, and his protest came out as a pitiful whine. "Nothing would I do to offend my liege lord."

Was this a fulfillment of Osric's threat? A blow from the ominous blade that had hovered over Godfrey's head for more than two decades? His face gone ashy white, Godfrey struggled to meet the knight's condemning glare and to assemble a believable defense. Never mind the absurdity of an action taken when joined goals were so near to hand, what proof could Osric possibly have presented? Surely, Godfrey reassured himself, he needed only to challenge a parchment signed long, long past. King William Rufus couldn't place serious store in a document that could be verified only by the two men whose futures rested so heavily upon it. He would be forced to decide in favor of a fellow Norman.

Though Tirel's gaze narrowed on the shaken transgressor, no flicker of emotion crossed his unyielding face, and he continued from where the untoward interruption had halted the words: "'Within the span of a single day and night you forswore your signed and sealed oath to respect the lands of my loyal vassal, Rhys of Cymer.'"

As the knight read further, Godfrey was dazed by this further unexpected blow, and his eyes widened so completely that white could be seen all the way around brown irises.

Tirel went on reading: "'The bearer of this message will investigate the Prince of Cymer's accusation. If it proves to be true, as laid down in royal statutes, the lands of Radwell will be held forfeit to the Crown.'"

Godfrey pressed back against the impressively high back of his chair, a buttress to prevent him from physically crumpling beneath the weight of this latest disaster. He barely heard Tirel's steady reading of the king's message continue . . . until the warning of the final provision drove a disorienting fog of distress from his thoughts.

"'Should anything untoward happen to the king's lieutenant or to the vassal lodging this complaint, the matter will be decided in the Welsh prince's favor.'"

Desperate to prevent such a hideous punishment, Godfrey leapt to his feet, surprising even the knight. To keep his lands he *must* stop Osric's schemes, *must* do the very thing Alan had fought to win from him. He would fight to free the Welshman he loathed. An unpleasant prospect but much more welcome than the imminent loss of everything that made him the powerful noble he was.

"How soon?" In a voice little above a whisper, Osric responded to Cawdr's question. "Very soon." The words were heavy with meaning. "As son of the house, Mark sleeps in his own chamber just through there." Osric nodded toward a curtained opening a few paces away. The wall they leaned against separated the great hall from two smaller chambers.

Mark's room lies across a narrow corridor from where his gift to me is tethered to a bed and guarded by Morwena. By now doubtless both women have fallen into dreams."

Even as he spoke the words, an uncomfortable sense of being watched pricked at his neck. Osric's gray eyes, now narrowed with suspicion, darted about the hall filled with men lost in drunken stupor. The only sound was the tuneless cadence of a multitude of hoarse snores and wheezing snorts. Shrugging to dislodge a plainly unfounded anxiety, he glanced back to the emotionless Cawdr.

"I deem the hour just before dawn the best suited for my intention. By then Mark will surely lie in deepest slumber. He will not likely waken afore the killing blow provides him with eternal rest."

Cawdr gave the heavy man a grim smile of acknowledgment. Though not a man of principle, Cawdr could never have coldly planned the murder of any member of his family. Osric's deed, however, was none of his concern, so he settled back on the cloak he'd bunched against the wall and closed his eyes to seek his own rest.

Having no one left to whom he could crow over the victory that seemed so near, a sullen Osric followed the example of the multitude of warriors. Because these men by heritage had been enemies for generations, Osric and Cawdr had chosen not to risk leaving them unwatched in Morwena's hall.

When at last it seemed all were lost to wakefulness, the bent figure of a woman cautiously moved back from the folds of heavy draperies and, in amazing silence despite a necessary staff, hobbled down the short corridor dividing two chambers.

"Mark!" Morwena's call was little more than a stirring of air, but it drew the immediate attention of the man standing fully dressed just beyond the opening whose curtain Morwena had carefully lifted aside.

Focused on her goal, Morwena was aware of nothing save the one whose arms she hurried to take in bony hands.

"You must flee!" she said. The intensity of her nearly colorless eyes lent an emphasis she dared not risk with sound. "Elsewise by the dawn you will be dead."

"We mean to depart." Mark quietly sought to soothe his mother's distress. "Already we are garbed for the deed." He motioned to his cloak fastened on one shoulder with an enameled ring and pin.

"I'll help." Mark's use of "we"—to include Linnet—meant nothing to Morwena as she urgently tugged at the sleeve covering his strong forearm. "Look! My secret will help you."

With difficulty Mark calmed his impatience at this unexpected delay of a deed requiring immediate action. A most dangerous feat lay ahead. He was anxious to undertake and have done with the challenge of seeing both himself and Linnet safely through a vast chamber crowded with men he prayed were so drink-sodden they slept like the dead. Still his attention followed the motion of his mother's hand.

Morwena ran her fingers down a crevice between the wall planks on Mark's left, then paused. When she touched a hidden latch, one panel silently sprang back, allowing a draft of fresh night air to enter the room and giving Mark a view of a brief drop to the ground below.

"Help I can." In a mannerism curiously her own, Morwena tilted her head, and her bird-bright eyes met her son's surprise with a childish glee. "'Tis a secret all my own."

And a welcome answer, Mark silently acknowledged, to a difficult problem. "We'll be gone before any can possibly know of our escape. Thank you, Mother." He brushed his lips across her papery cheek. "Likely you've saved my life."

He began to turn, but his mother reached up and laid a frail hand on his shoulder, an insistent demand for his attention.

"Aye, go. Go to the second cottage down the slope. Lander's been set to guard those locked within. Go, free the Eagle and his companion. But first demand they promise a boon in gratitude for that deed. The Welsh prince must promise you safe haven."

Mark smiled. His mother was a strange composite of odd habits and misarranged wits but with flashes of brilliance matched by penetrating logic. And for once she wielded it to his honest benefit rather than to advance wild schemes slanted by her hatred of the earl. Again he tried to leave, but again she urgently recalled his attention.

"I'll lead you to the hidden store of weapons Osric and Cawdr took from their men."

Linnet, who'd held back not wishing to intrude, recognized both the advantages and the disadvantages of this offer. She stepped nearer her brother to speak.

"Although you carry your weapons, I'm certain the men we seek to rescue would appreciate blades to protect themselves." A slight lift of her shoulders said as much as her next words. "More weapons than we need I fear would only hamper our flight."

Linnet had as well have been a stone statue for all the notice earlier given her by Morwena, but her words broke the spell. The older woman's glare was vicious, and in an instant she stood with arms widespread as a bar between door and Norman damsel.

"She can't use my secret. It's not for her!" The last word was a dangerously loud hiss.

Mark firmly, slowly shook his dark head to reject the demand.

With a sly gleam in her strange light eyes, and in what for all its whispered tone was a conciliatory voice, Morwena sought to cajole Mark into what she deemed right reasoning. "If go she must, leave her tied up on the path. Finding her will waylay Osric and be consolation for his fury."

"Nay, Mother." Mark met his mother's angry gaze steadily. "The choice is yours. Either we both depart or we both remain to face whatever end your brother metes out."

Morwena's scowl deepened. For long moments she stood unmoving, but Mark also remained motionless. In the end she dropped impeding arms, though her face twisted with an impotent rage that imbued her nearly soundless words with hatred.

"Then go. Free the Eagle. I'll fetch the swords and daggers, then meet you at the gnarled tree above Elbert's cottage. From there I will lead you from the valley by a southwesterly route unknown to Osric."

Never for a moment believing his mother could be so easily defeated, Mark was suspicious of her intent to join their flight into a land whose inhabitants she despised. Still he had no alternative but to accept this uneasy alliance. He lowered Linnet out through the opening and down to the ground below, but before he could offer the same service to his mother, the bent and gnarled woman had hopped down of her own strength. Again her odd ways caught him unprepared, and Mark saw a look of similar amazement widen Linnet's eyes.

Once all three stood on solid ground, Morwena located a latch and sent the panel silently back into place.

Unwilling to leave Linnet's back exposed to his mother, Mark put a hand at the nape of her neck and urged her through the featureless dark of moonless night toward a cottage's darker shadow. When he uneasily glanced behind him once to be certain they hadn't been followed, he saw that his mother was making steady progress in another direction. Putting a finger to his lips, he released Linnet and with his free hand motioned toward a peculiar shadow on the ground a short distance ahead.

Linnet's eyes had become accustomed to the dark, and she was able to discern what it was. On the earth at the bottom of the cottage door a man lay sleeping on his back with the pale shape of a sword resting nearby. While she tangled her fingers together and pressed them against her chest, Mark swooped forward and with a single clean motion brought his sword down. The guard's already relaxed body went utterly slack. Mark leaned across it and threw wide the door.

"Wake up, Owain. We've company."

The forceful nudging of one tightly bound pair of feet against another did more to see the task done than had the quiet call.

"What?" An irritable bear grumbled as Owain awkwardly struggled into a sitting position, despite being tied at wrists and ankles. "You can't secure rest enough to sweeten your disposition and now you've got to steal mine as well?" The growled complaint died away at the sight of a door opened to the night.

Although even faint hope was welcome, Rhys was wary as he turned an impassive face toward a night visitor who might be either foe or friend. The matter was settled when a smaller figure forced its way past the barrier.

"Rhys, we've come to free you." Linnet dropped to her knees beside the man she loved, but despite her words, instead of sundering his bonds, she threw her arms about one physically unable to deny her even if he wanted to, which he didn't.

Though startled by this development, Rhys welcomed the kiss tasting of the honey he knew lay in eyes he couldn't clearly see. Only after winning this response and with it assurance that Rhys truly was found and unharmed did Linnet draw back to accept the dagger her brother offered, along with a statement of what he planned.

"I'll step outside to deal more carefully with the guard and temporarily take on his duty myself."

A slight frown appeared above Linnet's eyes. What more could or needed to be done to the man? No matter, she had a more important task to do, and in spite of the difficulty darkness lent, she carefully put the dagger to good use. Soon her beloved was rubbing his wrists to restore long limited circulation. He spoke while she bent to sunder the rope about his ankles.

"Seems to have become an unbreakable pattern." Rhys lightly brushed his fingertips down the satin curve of her cheek. "Danger looms and I comfort myself that leastwise I've left you safe from harm— only to find you willfully barging into the midst of it."

"Aye, seems a pattern." Bonds sundered, Linnet grinned up at him, dropping the dagger to lift a hand and press his nearer. "I come to save you from harm and you inevitably blame *me!*"

Rhys met the feigned despair with a loving laugh and pulled her up with him as he rose to his feet. She instantly melted against his powerful form, drinking in the warm strength of him with thankfulness that the dangerous actions she and Mark had taken had won her leastways these moments.

Arms firmly wrapped about his sweet rescuer, Rhys leaned away, and mockery gleamed in his eyes as he made a mournful complaint. "I only pray the gods of war will someday allow me to save *you*. This being ever rescued by a dainty woman plays havoc with a warrior's pride."

Linnet softly gasped. Never had such an issue occurred to her, but then, before Rhys appeared in her life never had she thought plain and practical Linnet might ever be called to do such a thing.

She stepped back, lifting her hands palms up in a gesture pleading for forgiveness. "I . . . I . . ." What could she say? I'm sorry? She wasn't, not when the alternative was injury or even death to him.

"Nay, sweeting." Rhys took her hands and pulled her close again. "I but jest with you. I've fought too hard and in too many battles to have doubt of my own abilities. I thank you now, as I have thanked you before, for risking so much on my behalf."

Filled with relief, Linnet burrowed deeper into the embrace of his mighty arms.

"Hah! Forget me, why don't you!" Owain's quietly spoken words held a wealth of mock-disgust.

Rhys grinned down at his still bound friend. "You are not forgot. Merely have I matters of more import which needs must be settled firstly."

Dark eyes gone soft brushed love over a winsome face before returning a gleaming gaze to the bear whose bantering he repaid in kind. "'Tis only right that the one proven most efficient in the quest to preserve my health and freedom receive first attentions."

Again Owain snorted his disgust. In an exaggerated show of deep regret Rhys set aside the tender songbird who had used her talons once again. Before he could kneel to free his friend, however, Mark slipped back inside, recovered the dagger, and accomplished the deed.

Mark met the other men's curious eyes. He saw no reason to be less than open and gave a succinct account of the past few days, particularly those actions following David's delivery of both him and Alan to Rhys's home.

"Seems you and your sister have left little for Owain and me to do save join you in departing these unpleasant environs."

"I pray it will be that simple," Mark answered. "I've discovered that things which seem simple seldom are in the end."

"'Struth," Rhys agreed, his face going impassive. "A fact made more certain by every moment we linger here." With the words he waved toward the open portal.

As they left the building, carefully closing the door, Linnet saw what her brother had meant by his stated intent to deal with the guard. They had perforce to step over the man's body, which Mark had arranged to give the illusion of one sleeping.

Once again Linnet followed as Mark led the way to a destination only he knew, a destination his mother had chosen. Her discomfort with that fact was lessened by the company of the two freed captives.

They passed another darkened cottage and climbed some little way up the steep slope before Mark motioned toward the stark silhouette of a dead tree stretching its barren branches to a sky somewhat lightened by a still distant dawn. At its base a bent figure waited, weapons cradled like children in her arms.

Osric came awake with a start. Irritated with himself for sleeping at all, he scrambled to his feet. Still, he took care not to disturb the morass of deeply sleeping men as he made his way to heavy draperies and slipped beyond them.

Anticipation swelled in his heart and lit fiendish fires in his eyes. After moving a short distance down the corridor, he quietly pushed aside a second and final curtain between himself and his goal. Osric stopped in shock. Kicking a stool from his path to crash against a wall, he stalked toward a vacant bed. A bed clearly undisturbed by anyone this night.

He stormed from the room and crossed the corridor to one opposite. Empty! Both were empty! No Mark. No Linnet. Someone would pay!

Striding back down the corridor, wildly shoving the curtain aside, he bellowed, "Arise, you fools! We've been betrayed!"

Cawdr, a light sleeper and restrained drinker, sat up immediately, the first to answer the Saxon's shouting.

"Betrayed?" He questioned, reaching Osric's side in three long strides. "How have we been betrayed?"

"I went to do as I said I would only to find Mark gone. And not Mark alone but Linnet, too!"

Cawdr's disgust was so thick even Osric saw it

clearly. "Then, friend, *you* have been betrayed, not I. Our pact does not demand that I involve myself and my men in your problems with an errant nephew and fleeing bride." In truth, Cawdr thought those two were wise to have done with Osric; he wished he could as easily copy their action.

Sputtering, but only for a moment, Osric narrowed his eyes as he coldly spat out a fact certain to reverse his questionable cohort's perspective. "If they are gone, you fool, they've not gone alone."

Cawdr's chin jerked up as if it'd been struck by this man who was too free with his invective. Without speaking he whirled and marched so quickly toward the outer door that those in his path either moved or were stepped upon. Osric followed.

No sign of the sun touched the horizon, but the sky, once black, was now charcoal gray and provided sufficient light for the marching men to soon approach their goal. Cawdr shot Osric a sneer at sight of a sleeping guardsman still curled up before the cottage door.

Osric's frown returned, and he strode ahead of the Welshman to kick at the prone man.

"Wake up." No response. He kicked again and so viciously that any breathing man would leastways have groaned in pain. Instead, the body rolled over to reveal a dark stain across its chest.

Wasting no time on a man whose use to him was done, Osric barged into the small cottage—as empty as the chambers earlier inspected. Feeling vindicated, he turned toward the other man with a cold announcement.

"My prediction was accurate."

"I'll force our men to their senses while you throw open the cellar where their weapons are stored."

Though resenting the order issued to him, whose scheme had seen the Eagle taken in the first instance, Osric did the deed with as little wasted motion as Cawdr in performing the task he'd chosen for himself.

Soon men dripping with cold water thrown over them were roughly searching through the hoard of weapons, each attempting to locate his own. Once the soldiers were armed, they turned as one toward the Saxon lord in unspoken expectation of a command that would point the direction of their pursuit.

Osric's face closed. In his anger over the escape, and focused on speeding through the turmoil of necessary preparations, this was a question he hadn't considered. This, was *the* question of supreme importance whose answer would justify all that had gone before.

He didn't have one.

19

THE SMALL PARTY OF TWO WOMEN AND THREE MEN HAD climbed rather more than halfway up the steep incline toward the hill's brow when a sharp moan broke the silence, followed by the sound of a body crumpling. Fortunately, Morwena sagged sideways and landed amid a particularly lush patch of spring-fresh vegetation.

Mark dropped to his knees at her side, and those behind him peered over his shoulder in concern for their guide.

"Let me rest." Morwena's voice was faint, and her pleading eyes glistened with weary tears. "For just a short while?"

Her weak condition eased Mark's suspicion of a ploy to delay the escape, and he glanced anxiously over his shoulder seeking the others' reaction. Answering for them all, Rhys immediately nodded a willingness to grant the frail woman this boon. She was his aunt, but when, two days past, he'd been delivered to her lands, it had been their first meeting in decades, and he'd been disconcerted to find that she appeared easily twice or thrice the age he knew her to be.

After Mark released the pin fastening of his cloak and swirled the garment around his mother's frail form, Rhys gave his attention to the comfort of his gentle ladylove. Gentle, aye, Linnet was that but also brave enough to boldly face danger for the sake of protecting those she loved.

Realizing that she was likely as weary as his aunt, for Linnet Rhys spread his own black cloak upon ground between the older woman and the massive trunk of an oak that would spread its shielding limbs over them both. He took Linnet's small hand, led her to the pallet he'd created, and settled her atop its comfort.

While the two women rested, the three men stood close together in hushed conversation. This was Rhys's first opportunity to question his cousin more thoroughly about what dangers might yet remain. Reluctant to admit a distrust of his mother, Mark had taken care not to speak openly of plans she might take back to their foes. With the gift of these moments of relative privacy he detailed for Rhys and Owain the risky roles being played in a confrontation they would seek to avoid but whose probability they could not discount.

There was one unknown, the most menacing of all, that could easily destroy the whole: no one could be certain of the earl's response to the desperate plea Alan had been dispatched to lay before him. Would Godfrey simply refuse to entertain the matter at all? That was his response to most unpleasant facts. Or would he be so enraged that he'd lead his large force of skilled warriors on a raid intended to end in the destruction of his foe? Another believable choice, something that couldn't be said of the alternative Alan had gone to beg of his father: the admission of wrong and, by way of penance, a foray into Morwena's lands to subdue his Saxon vassal and free the Eagle. It was dangerous, this unknown response, and a threat hovering at the edge of any success they might think to win.

While the men were engrossed in their murmured discussion, a smiling Linnet relaxed atop the cloak holding Rhys's scent. She permitted heavy lashes to drop while unthinkingly rolling on her side and curling into a ball as she did every night to summon sleep. Sleep . . . she'd had none since being awakened at the abbey. Her fears eased by the success of their plan thus far, she dozed in exhaustion.

Covered to the chin by her son's fine cloak, Morwena surreptitiously watched the men, heads bent together in quiet conversation. The opportunity she'd sought by her feigned collapse was hers now. Godfrey had broken the oath given her father, had stolen her son's inheritance from him. Godfrey's heir, young Alan, was dead—Mark had said so—but that was too small a punishment for all the pain he'd wreaked upon her. She would never permit him any comfort she could steal, and steal the comfort of the earl's beloved daughter she would. Furtively moving a hand to the bag ever tied at her waist, she withdrew from it an object she had secreted there while locating the weapons belonging to the two escaping Welshmen.

A movement caught Rhys's attention. He glanced to one side. In the blink of an eye his body followed the line of his gaze. His powerful hand encircled a frail wrist and stayed it from its goal.

"No! You won't stop me! You won't!" Morwena's screeches pierced the peaceful silence preceding dawn. "I'll have her life!" She writhed wildly, desperately attempting to break free. "I'll kill her, I will!"

Rhys forced the woman once bending over Linnet's exposed back to lie flat on the ground even while he twisted a glittering dagger from the hand that moment's earlier had lifted it threateningly above his beloved.

Springing forward, Mark helped Rhys restrain the woman who'd given him birth. He was distressed to find no recognizable sign of his mother in eyes glazed with madness, which lent such inhuman strength to a frail creature that it required two mighty men to subdue her.

Although held physically immobile, still Morwena screamed incoherent words punctuated by language of a foulness few men could have matched. Then as suddenly as the bout of hysteria had overtaken her, she went limp and began sobbing piteously.

While the other two men were subduing the aging woman, Owain had quickly sliced his own cloak into long strips for use as more permanent restraints. These he extended to Mark, in the belief that only her son should be allowed to wrap them about the woman. These Mark accepted. Gently but firmly, he bound Morwena's hands behind her back and covered her mouth to prevent further outbursts.

Rhys pulled away from the pair and, patiently waiting for Mark to perform his sorry but necessary task, sat with forehead atop crossed arms resting on updrawn knees. He sought the quiet moment to steady the pulse still pounding in response to the near success of the woman's ghastly deed.

Linnet's light touch on Rhys's shoulder drew his attention to where she knelt at his side. "Seems the gods of war heard your plea. Now you've saved my life." Behind her impish smile lay earnest gratitude for his lightning speed and protection. Doe-soft eyes caressed his handsome face while her hand brushed back blond hair tangled by the struggle. "We're even."

Her assertion surprised a short laugh from Rhys. The thought furthest from his mind had been the silly jest he'd made. "Nay, you've thrice saved me." A white smile flashed. "So, by my reckoning, I owe you the same duty two times more."

"Ah, but you've not counted your rescue of me from a lifetime of drudgery at best, a lifetime bound to a man I despise at worst." Her smile deepened as his brows skeptically rose. Expression sliding into tenderness, she huskily whispered, "Oh, aye, 'tis a rescue worth far more than the debt you think owed." With that praise she leaned forward and pressed soft lips to his cheek.

From the corner of his eye, Rhys saw that Mark had finished his task. It was important that they resume their flight immediately, for the hag's screams had doubtless served as a beacon to draw their pursuers to them. But first Rhys turned his head and claimed a sweet kiss to prove the one he would willingly have given his life to keep safe was alive and well.

A sound, one small sound, brought a golden head up just as the woodland on the path's far side erupted with scores of men, weapons at the ready. Giving a warning call for his cohorts, Rhys instantly rolled sideways, knocking two assailants flat. Then he leapt to his feet, bared blade in hand, and fought off another.

Shock drove breath from Linnet's body. Rhys, Owain, and Mark stood facing three different directions, each wielding his broadsword with great efficiency. But for all her fantasies of heroic deeds, by years of training in sensible thinking she knew where dreams ended and reality began. The reinforcements were doubtless anxiously waiting at the valley's far end. Still on her knees near the bound Morwena, Linnet felt struck to stone by an awful truth. It was inevitable that the force of greater numbers would prevail over three no matter how courageous, brilliant, or expert in swordplay they were.

The lifeless body of an assailant fell near atop Linnet, freeing her from immobilizing terror. She scrambled to her feet, courage revived. Defeat might be inevitable, but Osric's men would not seize it without paying a fierce price.

She attempted to take up the dead soldier's broadsword, but it was far heavier than ever she'd dreamed such a weapon would be. Moreover, it was of such a length that were its tip at her toes, its hilt would have reached well above her waist. Useless. She hissed in disgust. The sword was useless to her. If it required such strength to lift, never could she swing it to good purpose. Wasting no further effort on the large blade, she instead took the long dagger from a scabbard buckled at the man's waist. But by the time she had the smaller weapon in hand and looked up in search of a target, a welcome sight had appeared.

Taff and the warriors of Cymer, spoiling for the opportunity to avenge the taking of their prince and to restore pride lost in that ambush, swarmed down the hillside. They infused fresh spirit into the fray against men impaired by a night of heavy drinking.

Linnet realized that with so many skilled at the art of war now on the scene any paltry contribution she might offer was likely to be a hindrance. Intending to avoid being a distraction, she tossed the unneeded dagger aside and stepped back into the oak's shadows.

"A fearsome sight. We can do naught but watch." Grannia ducked under a low-hanging branch to take up a position at Linnet's side. Together in grim fascination they watched for what seemed an eternity as, with arcs of shining steel and clashing blades, the men they loved waged mortal combat. For fear of it being a dangerous distraction, Grannia strangled a moan summoned by the sight of an alarming blow.

Linnet, who was the only one close enough to hear the tiny sound, was rendered deaf by an amazing scene that drove everything else from her consciousness. Rhys, hair glowing in the rapidly increasing light of coming day, had pressed the tip of his sword to the vulnerable base of a fallen Cawdr's throat. From that same throat poured a torrent of Welsh words of which Linnet understood only a repeated "Dyfi." Those words, she noticed, caused the larger portion of Rhys's adversaries to drop their weapons and step back.

"Cawdr has surrendered and ordered his men to follow his example if they would see him live." An anxious Grannia gave Linnet this likely needless interpretation of the defeated prince's words.

Confused by this strange turn of events, Osric's apparently leaderless men fell into disorder. Most turned to run while others remained, following the example of Dyfi's warriors and dropping their weapons.

The men of Cymer lost no moment in confiscating abandoned weapons and turning the screw full about; those who had humiliated them now became the ones lying prone, faces in dirt trampled by battle.

The moment success was ensured and enemies subdued, Grannia rushed to the man whose shoulder she'd seen take the point of a blade. "Owain, you're injured."

Startled blue eyes blinked several times at the unexpected sight. No one had told him that there was even a possibility of Grannia accompanying Cymer's army on its rescue mission.

"Nay." He shrugged and absently answered. "'Tis little more than the pricking of a pin."

"Come, let me examine it to be sure." Grannia took one of his huge hands and pulled him to one of the few open spaces on the wayside somewhat higher on the trail.

Not having caught his balance from the reeling blow her presence had delivered, Owain followed her like a lamb. Grannia gently pushed him down to sit while she knelt and bent over his shoulder.

"I have news," she softly announced while unlacing his tunic far enough so that she could push it aside and lay the wound bare to her view. "The abbess told Linnet of a fact she had long held in confidence." Grannia peered at the wound, which was truly not serious, before settling back on her heels and meeting Owain's curious blue eyes directly. "My father's Aunt Tayled shrouded this truth in secrecy to spare me the shame of knowing my marriage to your father was, in truth, no marriage at all."

"Explain!" The soft, fervent growl brooked no hesitation, and Owain twisted around to subject her to a more piercing scrutiny.

"That priest your father found to bless the union was no priest but rather an itinerant freeman passing through Cymer."

Owain's expression hardened with fury for the wicked act his father had committed. It required no more than the briefest of moments for him to realize that the fruit of that evil seed was the sweetest of blooms. He swept Grannia into a hug of such strength it threatened to crush her bones . . . and she welcomed it full well.

Though a warm smile curled Linnet's lips as she watched the couple embrace, she felt like an intruder and purposefully glanced away to where Rhys's men were fastening cords about the joined wrists and ankles of their prostrate foes. After the fear and labor required to see it so, Linnet was pleased, but an odd fact shook her complacency. One who should have been here was absent, while another was present who should not have been. The guardsman, Edolf, whom she and Alan had locked in a storeroom on Radwell's parapet wall, lay amid the other defeated men, but Osric, who was responsible for this and for many other wrongs, was nowhere in sight. Indeed, though she had watched the battle with fervent attention, never had she caught even a glimpse of the Saxon lord.

While Welshmen finished seeing their enemies firmly bound, a triumphantly grinning Taff approached his prince with rope enough to restrain his prey. Once at Rhys's side, he glanced from Pywell, striding past with an armload of seized weapons to heap on a growing pile, to the defeated Cawdr with a derisive smile.

"*We* won't leave this booty lying about for you to reclaim." Taff's satisfaction fair sang with contempt.

The remark, which Pywell repeated in English, won a bark of laughter from Mark as the pair of them approached on the Eagle's other side. Rhys joined with all of his men in this appropriate climax for their victory.

A short-lived celebration.

The day had begun, and although no cloud marred a sky rosed by dawn, thunder reverberated from the brow of the hill, demanding and winning apprehensive attention.

Linnet gasped. There atop the hill her father's standard rippled on a faint breeze, and a multitude of armed men garbed in chain mail stood bold beneath it.

"Send to me my son!" Standing in his stirrups, Godfrey glared down the slope. With a gauntleted hand he imperiously motioned toward Mark to reinforce the words he'd spoken in English to be certain Osric's Saxon force would understand.

Before anyone could move, a howl of cruel laughter echoed from behind Linnet. The crowd, already shocked by one unexpected appearance, twisted toward the sound that issued from the forest shadows through which Osric stepped.

"All that fine swordsmanship for naught. The Eagle is dead." Without giving notice to his bound and gagged sister as he passed her, Osric moved to stand at Linnet's back. As she made to duck away, he wrapped a meaty arm around her, pinning arms to her sides.

"To harm me," Osric sneered at the golden prince advancing with sword raised, "you must first damage the pretty songbird."

Rhys froze while his black ice gaze threatened to freeze an uncle surely as demented as his sister.

"You would no more harm Linnet than I mean to harm you," Osric said.

Linnet clamped her lips together to keep from crying out her disgust for the deceitful speaker and a warning for her love not to believe him.

The Eagle's glare deepened at this seeming reversal of the man's first claim.

"Truly, I've no intention of killing you." Osric chortled. "That pleasure I have promised to the earl, who in turn promised me this tender birdling." Osric swept his hand down his prize's soft bounty. Having been so near utter defeat, he found this reprieve surely sweeter than even the fabled nectar from the faerie realm.

Though she'd known of her father's intent to see Rhys dead, still Linnet flinched on hearing it announced with such glee.

Mark feared Osric's claim would be fulfilled and while across his shackled sister the two men faced each other unmoving, he rushed up the hill to the side of his mounted father.

"There are facts you *must* be told, Father. I beg you will do nothing until you've heard me speak of them."

Godfrey stared at his older son. How was it that his two sons had been enticed into an alliance with his worst enemy? The fact hadn't been lessened but rather reinforced by the dangerous charges the Eagle had lodged with the king.

"I told him, Mark." Alan peeked from behind Basil and wiggled until the guard captain lowered him to the ground so he could rush to his older brother. "Father has come to free Rhys."

Looking into the earl's set expression Mark saw that this was an unwelcome fact but a fact nonetheless.

It was a fact Osric recognized as well. He'd been betrayed! Betrayed by Godfrey and the whole of his brood! The appearance of the supposedly dead heir, Alan, was confirmation of that infuriating fact.

"We made a pact, Godfrey!" The rage in Osric's voice was so thick it near smothered every listener and sent icicles of dread down Linnet's spine. "I've delivered the Eagle for you to kill, and now I claim Linnet as mine."

For these damning words spoken before one specific observer, Godfrey's anger flared as fiercely as Osric's —so fiercely he found himself unable to force words beyond the block in his throat. No need. It was that observer who spoke the truth for him and in the tongue Osric could not fail to understand.

"If *any* harm befalls Prince Rhys," Sir Walter Tirel succinctly announced, "the king will call Radwell forfeit to the Crown."

Rhys's attention had not once shifted from the unbalanced man holding Linnet captive, but at the sound of this voice he glanced toward a former comrade-in-arms from his days in Normandy. Plainly the king had dispatched Sir Walter to Radwell in response to the message Rhys had sent. Tirel met Rhys's gaze and gave a brief salute, which was interrupted by Osric's heightened ire.

In frustration over this stranger's news, Osric snarled a filthy oath. An end to the Eagle's life would mean an end to Godfrey's tenure as earl? If only that, he would have cheered. But to Osric it meant worse! The threat alone was death to any hope that he might claim Radwell for himself.

Godfrey found his voice again in an unpleasant laugh for the Saxon. "Disappointed, Osric?" He met the Saxon's burning eyes with disdain. "Aye, I know your intent to see my heir and even my firstborn dead. Moreover, I know you foolishly thought that by marriage to my daughter you could carry Radwell back into Saxon hands."

Osric's fury increased until Linnet could feel him trembling with it. She looked to Rhys. He'd seen the reaction, too. Every muscle in Rhys's body tightened in preparation to foil whatever insane deed threatened the small damsel standing remarkably brave in a madman's hold.

Shaking his head in disdain, Godfrey heightened the danger with further scorn. "Fool! Be it I die without a male heir, Radwell would rest in the king's hands. It is a fief held and bestowed only by his goodwill."

Unarmed but standing free, Cawdr softly snorted at

hearing his erstwhile cohort's favorite epithet used against him. The sound was soft, but it drew Godfrey's attention.

"You've well and truly lost," the earl said, addressing Cawdr. "Neither you nor your Saxon ally will have any part of Cymer, for if need be, I'll add the force of my garrison to its protection."

While even Linnet's attention was focused on the prince of Dyfi, Osric furtively dropped his free hand and with stealth pulled a dagger from its scabbard. Godfrey's sons lived, but the unsuspecting daughter he owed to Osric would not!

A low grunt startled Linnet. Then the ponderous weight slumping against her back knocked her to her knees.

Rhys hauled Osric's body aside and lifted completely into his gentle arms the one who a moment before had been in even greater danger than he'd realized. A dagger was still clasped in the fallen Osric's hand. While cradling her near and burying his lips in the amber silk at her temple, for the first time Rhys saw that a blade had been driven to the hilt in Osric's back. His gaze shifted to a dazed youngster standing over his handiwork and trembling.

"Thank you, David." The few words were quiet but so heartfelt they called the boy from the shock of his first experience in the realm of real conflict.

David beamed with pride. The next moment he was swept up into the burly arms of his brother.

"You were splendid!" Owain was unstinting in his praise. "You did something no man dared."

"Hidden in the forest, I've been watching since first we of Cymer arrived," David explained. Now that he'd recovered from his momentary paralysis, he was eager to tell his story. "Linnet dropped a dagger just after our warriors joined the battle. I had always wanted a man-size blade, so I picked it up."

David leaned back a bit in Owain's arms, chin lifted defensively as if he was worried that the action might earn censure, but Owain gave him only a fond smile. And from Owain's side Grannia murmured that she ought be upset with David for following the men to the site of a battle rather than staying put, but she couldn't upbraid him, for his wrong's result was a right.

Reassured, David continued his tale. "When from behind I saw that man draw his dagger, it seemed certain sure he meant to see Linnet dead. I aimed the point of mine and threw myself against him as hard as I could."

"You saved my life." Linnet understood nothing of what the younger brother had told the older, nor did she grasp what Grannia had said, but she had no doubt of this fact. And along with her English words, she held a hand out to the boy. "Never can I repay you."

David sheepishly shrugged, but his beaming smile said volumes more.

Intended victim, miniature savior, and the men who held them were soon surrounded by a multitude of well-wishers. The earl dismounted and led his warriors down to his daughter, and they joined their voices to those of the Eagle's supporters. The result was such a confusion of words that Linnet thought herself somehow transported to the biblical Tower of Babel. Surrendering to the impossibility of sorting out the tangled morass of Norman, English, and Welsh words, Linnet contented herself with a sweet smile of gratitude for all and rested her head in the crook between Rhys's throat and shoulder.

Once the initial uproar died down, Rhys tempered a likely too mocking smile and spoke to the earl, who stood very near the daughter lying in a position to which he plainly objected.

"I thank you for your earlier offer of support in the protection of Cymer, although I doubt it will be needed."

Godfrey answered with a stiff nod.

"However," Rhys calmly went on, "I do seek an alliance between us." Linnet buried her mouth against his strong throat to muffle a gasp of pleasure.

Godfrey straightened to his full height—a distressing handbreadth below that of the other man—his suspicious frown lowering over narrowed eyes as the Eagle continued undisturbed.

"Understand, whether or not you lend the deed your blessing, I will see it done."

This was clearly a warning, and Godfrey did not take kindly to warnings. Too many life-altering events had shattered the calm tenor of his life in too brief a time. More he did not need, and he scowled at the Welsh prince.

"Alliance? The only alliance we will have is one forced upon me to keep Radwell safely in my hands."

Golden hair caught and reflected the rising sun's fiery gleams as Rhys slowly shook his head while strong arms cradled his wee linnet even closer.

"I mean to wed your daughter and with all possible haste."

These words, like those before, rumbled from the chest beneath Linnet's ear. Rhys's public claim of her thrilled her. Vaguely aware of her brothers' bright grins and ignoring her father's frown, she tilted her head to gaze up at Rhys with love unhidden.

Meeting the melting warmth of pansy-soft eyes, Rhys finished what he'd begun to say. "I will wed Linnet no matter the objections of any." This last was meant as much for the many of Cymer crowded behind him as for the earl, and he turned to defiantly repeat the statement in his people's language.

The immediate tide of their murmured delight quashed Rhys's last lingering concern over their welcome of his Norman bride. Clearly, by so oft risking her life in protection of him, the linnet had proven herself to be what he already knew—the perfect mate to an eagle. He raised his chin in pride as his supporters loosed their approval in unrestrained cheers.

The sweet smile that bloomed on Linnet's lips contained warmth enough to near outshine the sun. Reveling in the approval that even foreign words couldn't mask, Linnet reached up and wrapped her arms about the golden focus of all her fantasies come true.

"Never!" Godfrey blustered, dismayed by this further defection by one of his own. That seemingly all others on his demesne had believed it true for so long only made the reality harder to bear. Added to that irritation was the need to repeat his rejection once and once again before anyone paid the least attention to a father's decision.

Rhys drew a deep breath, preparing to reinforce his unyielding intention, but before he could speak another did.

Linnet lifted her head to gaze directly into her father's glower. "If you refuse to sanction the bond, I shall be forced to run again into a land you dare not wreak violence upon." She smiled serenely, pleased by the king's unknowing support of her cause.

Once more gazing down into honey-soft eyes, Rhys backed her daring defiance. "Aye, my lord, if you refuse to give your daughter to me, I'll abduct her— again."

After a long moment of silence Rhys looked up into the face of a man realizing himself well and truly trapped. "Whatever we must do, we will do. And marry, with or without your blessing, we *will.*"

While a large audience watched in growing amusement, Godfrey continued blustering, but when his supply of wind ran low, he irritably shrugged and gave in.

"Leastways my grandchildren will be close to hand." Not a man to do things by half measures, once he'd yielded this far, he made a generous offer to see the deed done in good order.

"Might as well put to his intended use the priest already at Radwell to see Linnet wed to Osric."

Linnet managed a fair replica of her father's glare at this disclosure of how near she'd come to being forever bound to the swine whose touch had revolted her the night past.

At Linnet's glare Godfrey shrugged. "It wasn't a prospect I welcomed either, but summoning the priest was a necessary evil."

Both Linnet and Rhys much doubted that, but since the man was giving them what they sought, they were inclined to be generous.

Godfrey looked to Rhys with a slight grimace. "Even will I admit I prefer an alliance with you rather than see Linnet wed to the cur who near killed her."

Of a sudden finding herself blessed with a reality far better than any fantasy, Linnet turned her thoughts to friends deserving of the same happiness. With that goal in mind, she spoke to her father.

"So long as a priest is waiting, pray let us employ his powers to their fullest measure."

Both Godfrey and Rhys looked at her as if she'd gone daft, what with repeating a plan already laid as if never spoke afore.

When had faded the trill of laughter sweet as birdsong, which had increased the men's confusion, Linnet tilted her head to whisper into Rhys's ear.

"Are you willing that there be not one wedding but two?" Rhys solemnly asked the question of Earl Godfrey. Once he had received a puzzled nod of agreement, Rhys lowered Linnet to her feet although he wrapped an arm about her shoulders to hold her near. Then, with the flash of a white smile, he turned with her to face his gathered supporters while he made public the secret she'd whispered to him.

Welshmen, already delighted by the prospect of their prince's near immediate wedding and coming happiness, were equally pleased for his sister and Owain once they heard words dissolving the bar to their happiness. Few there were who hadn't known of the forbidden love, though it was never spoken of.

Begun with good wishes given by Mark and added to by two young boys, friends for life, further congratulations were heaped upon the two couples by an amazingly intermingled throng of former enemies.

Then, while Rhys grinned and Owain blushed bright red, both brides cuddled near their grooms as plans were laid for a gathering of families from Radwell and Cymer. Everyone was to join on the morrow for a wedding and feast of celebration.

And in the warm excitement no one noticed or later cared that a never restrained Cawdr had freed his men and all of Dyfi had slunk back to their own land.

20

Radwell's great hall was a festive sight. In addition to the usual torches burning along the walls, the central hearth leapt with uncommonly cheery flames. The many branches of the tall iron stands behind the dais had been supplied with fine wax tapers, while at intervals down the long rows of lower tables, candles were massed atop silver platters that enhanced and reflected their glow. In truth, so brightly lit was the vast chamber that it seemed to Linnet as if a sun night-driven from the sky had been beckoned inside to join the celebration under way.

With a priest on one end, an abbess on the other, and a Norman earl in the center, the high table hosted a unique combination of characters. Godfrey, mellowed by flavorsome foods and plentiful wine, was flanked on the left by his daughter, a Welsh prince, the prince's sister, her new husband, and the abbess. On the right side sat Godfrey's older son, his younger son, a Welsh boy, and the priest.

From her seat, Linnet gazed with pleasure over the scene below. The usual number of tables, running in long diagonal rows from the dais, had been doubled and were interrupted only by the hearth. But what brought a quiet delight to brown eyes was the odd intermingling of guardsmen, Radwell vassals and serfs, knights, and free people of Cymer.

To minimize the language barriers she'd arranged for interpreters to occupy seats in strategic positions. It had unexpectedly become a game for men like Pywell and Milo to translate Welsh words into English and then for castle serfs who spoke both tongues to shift them from English into Norman French. The oft garbled translations earned bouts of hearty laughter, which punctuated the chamber's merriment and camaraderie.

Their sumptuous feast had included everything from whole pit-roasted boar and pheasants with golden-brown skin refeathered to steaming pasty pies. A remarkable feast considering how near two women had come to blows over the subject of what would be served. Fortunately the apple-cheeked Ynid and Meara, who believed that any meal served at Radwell was her province alone, had found a simple solution. They'd decided to serve everything either could concoct, and in the preparations, despite their lack of a common language, the two women had become confidantes.

Linnet was happy. Leastwise for this day people who had been enemies for generations came together as friends. She could hope and work to see that this alliance, confirmed by the bond betwixt Rhys and her, would become a permanent condition.

"Have I any part in whatever has put such a smile of sweet contentment upon your lips?" Rhys whispered the question into the ear at which he paused to nibble.

Linnet glanced up into the golden glow in the depths of his dark eyes, and her cheeks warmed under its heat. "I was thinking of the blessings peace will surely bring to your people and mine. What we see below is proof we are more alike than different."

Rhys smiled down into the openly loving expression of this soft, sweet woman whose courage was as

330

enduring as her compassion. Hers was a philosophy that only months earlier he and assuredly the earl would have staunchly rejected. But by virtue of the ease with which this Norman damsel had pierced a Welsh prince's armor and firmly lodged herself within his heart, it seemed not only possible and desirable but probable.

While two new-wedded couples drifted on mists of satisfaction for the enchantment that in less than two full days had transformed their lives, Earl Godfrey came to an abrupt realization. The last in a parade of savory dishes, all offered by pages on bended knee, had been consumed, and musicians were gathering. Either he must seize this moment or likely it would be too late.

The earl reached for a silver chalice and rose to his feet. Priding himself on the evenhanded if sometimes harsh justice he wielded in dealing with the people of Radwell, he could not longer ignore the admiration all three of his children bore the Eagle. And having resigned himself to the inevitable alliance, he must express his ungrudging acceptance of this new family member. He glanced down at Rhys and caught a glimpse of the pair beyond. All right, Godfrey inwardly groused, family members.

Godfrey's booming voice demanded attention. When it was given, he gruffly toasted first his daughter and the princely mate she'd chosen for herself and then his new son-in-law's sister and her bridegroom.

The deed won hearty congratulations for both couples—and rousing cheers for this demonstration of the earl's unexpected willingness to adapt and accept.

A decade in Normandy had taught Rhys the ceremony's proper next step, one he'd gladly take. He rose with goblet in hand.

"Join me in a toast of gratitude to the earl feting us with his bounty and to the many who had part in both the victory and the peace won yestermorn."

As the toast was drunk, Rhys met the eyes of Pywell, Taff, and the brave men they'd led into the fight on his behalf. And once the toast was finished, Rhys sent a special nod of appreciation to his sister. He only regretted that Sir Walter Tirel had been unable to remain for these festivities. Shortly after their arrival at Radwell the previous day, another royal messenger had appeared with news of fresh fighting on the Scottish border and a summons for Tirel's immediate return to the king's side.

Rhys remained standing and again lifted his goblet, this time toward the amber-haired bride to whom he gave a potent but gentle smile. "Lastly, join me in honoring the wee linnet whose courage and sweet song went far to see me freed and whose soothing spirit not only tamed an eagle but would see two peoples bound by peace."

Linnet's creamy cheeks went pink when she gazed steadily at the hero of her fantasies, now miraculously hers, as he resumed his seat at her side. The flickering lights of the many candles on the iron stands behind them combined to lend his hair a shining halo. Still, it was no brighter than the tender golden blaze in the black depths of his eyes as he lifted his goblet toward her and softly added a personal salute.

"To the songbird this eagle will soon carry off and hold safe in his mountain aerie."

Rhys's smile slid into one so sensuous Linnet felt as if her bones were melting. Beneath its power the realities of time and place faded while she was drawn forward, tilted chin lifting her lips toward his.

"Hrmm." Grannia's gently cleared throat broke the visual bond, but when Linnet glanced toward her friend her smile was warm. She and Rhys had a lifetime to savor such delights and could be generous with their attention.

"Only did Owain and I want to thank you one more time for the opportunity you've given David." Grannia sent Owain a glare, its supposed intent foiled by the love glowing on her face. "It was left to me to interrupt your . . ." The words trailed away. "Because the big oaf who could bash down a house feared to do the deed."

"I was not afraid," Owain growled while black brows met in a heavy frown. His fierceness, however, was no more effective than hers had been, as betraying gleams of laughter sparkled in blue eyes. "I am merely too well mannered to bash into private matters."

Owain turned his attention from the merry bride at his side to look between his new brother and sister-in-law. "But 'tis true that I, too, appreciate the generous arrangements made to see my young brother off to Normandy with his friend Alan."

Grinning, Linnet gave a slight shake of her head at the other couple's foolery. "David will be good company for my little brother.

"Despite Alan's years of training, never has he been so far from Radwell," Linnet continued, turning her attention to the other side and meeting her father's pleased smile. With the end of Alan's tutelage under Lord Osric, the earl was free to do as he should have done before and send his son to foster with an equal or superior lord—in this instance, to join a royal household.

Looking beyond the earl, Linnet met Mark's pale gray gaze. "Although there'll be a sea between us, we've none of us any reason to worry about the boys, as Mark will be near to watch over them."

With a flashing white smile, Mark wordlessly thanked his sister for her confidence. "As I'm returning to my position with Prince Henry, escorting the boys on their journey to his court will be a simple enough task. Moreover, watching over them during their years of training will be a chore far less worrisome than that of caring for Alan's safety these days since my return to Radwell." The last truth stole the humor from his smile, although it did not fade.

Once the wedding rites had been concluded and the

far more interesting mountains of food had arrived, the boys had given little attention to the adults seated at the table—until was raised this subject of a thrilling event soon to alter their young lives.

"I'll miss my brother and Grannia, but Alan and I will have such adventures!" David's excitement over a decision made only this morn got the better of him. From near the end of the table he burst into the conversation. "Alan says there'll be lots of others our age; and Alan says I'll learn all manner of new things most Welsh boys don't."

Rhys only absently listened to the chattering boys as he observed the fond amusement of the earl's older son. He'd initially viewed Mark's return to Radwell with suspicion, fearing his intent. But then the younger man had risked much to keep his half brother safe and had responded to his sister's plea for aid in her struggle to set an erstwhile enemy free. Now Rhys no longer questioned Mark's honor. Moreover . . . Rhys's lips tilted into their old mocking half-smile, but this one was lacking disdain. Mark's willingness to immediately escort the boys to Normandy would provide Owain with the privacy a new-wedded husband most desired. And when Owain was elsewise occupied, Rhys would be blessed with the same privacy.

That pleasant thought was followed by one far less so. Along with the boys, Mark would take to Normandy the mother who was his responsibility. Rhys had watched Mark deal with Morwena as gently as he'd dealt with Alan. Mark had carried the unspeaking woman from the site of yestermorn's hillside battle to the spot where Milo had been waiting with his destrier and the steeds of Cymer. Morwena now lay, guarded, in a chamber above.

Golden sparks were doused from Rhys's dark eyes by thoughts of the conversation that had passed between him and Mark early this morning. As cousins by virtue of Saxon mothers who were sisters, and as brothers-in-law by virtue of Mark's Norman sister, Mark had seen fit to discuss with Rhys the plans he'd made for Morwena.

"Mother," Mark had told him, "stares blindly at the wall, and no longer seems capable of caring for herself. Nor, considering the questionable state of her sanity, would I be wise to leave her alone. She's spoken to me only once and that immediately after I'd deposited her inside my bedchamber. She accused me of lying to her about the killing of Godfrey's heir.

"I reminded her that I claimed only to have 'taken care of' Alan. It was the truth. Although freely I admitted that I love both my brother and our father, I assured mother that I loved her as well. But it seems the bitterness she's poured into my ears at every opportunity, her frustrated determination to see me earl of Radwell—even at the price of Alan's life—has driven her into a world beyond my reach."

At the too vivid memory of this sad admission, Rhys shook his bright head. He regretted the burden to be borne by a young knight who'd earnestly stated his satisfaction with life as a respected member of Prince Henry's entourage. Heartily Rhys had endorsed the plan to settle Morwena on the Norman lands Mark held as fief from the English prince. Rhys had promised to join his prayers to the younger man's with the hope that the complete change of scene and company would have a beneficial effect upon Morwena.

While those at the high table were discussing the boys' coming adventure, timbrels, pipes, and lutes had begun a soft rhythm, urging haste in the clearing of a large open space below the dais. Emptied trestle tables were disassembled and soon leaning against the walls while benches were pushed back against them.

It was traditional for a bridegroom to lead his bride into the first dance. Rhys had turned to urge Owain to claim Grannia and join him and Linnet in performing that gallant deed when a soft chant began. It grew louder, the gentle but insistent chant demanding that Linnet sing for them all the song that had played so important a role in winning the prince's freedom.

Linnet felt heat tingling in her cheeks, but remembered the lesson of sharing one's talents, which she'd learned at the Feast of Gwyn ap Nudd. Besides, after she'd sung for Osric's coarse crowd, repeating the performance for these friends would be more of a joy.

Rhys saw amber eyes darken with determination as she took a deep breath and nodded her willingness—with a single condition.

"I will sing the Eagle's song . . . but only if Grannia accompanies the tune on her harp." Much earlier, as people were finding seats at lower tables, Linnet had seen Taff placing the graceful harp in a crowded corner where other instruments were stored.

"But I don't . . ." Grannia began to argue, having no notion of Taff's deed. But at the amazing appearance of her precious harp, her protesting words halted. Used to such public performances, she wasted no moment further in denials and stepped down from the dais to move around the high table and into the opening below.

Linnet went with her friend, comforted that leastways she need not stand alone as the center of attention. Once Linnet had taken her place beside the seated Welshwoman, Grannia started to coax magic from taut strings while Linnet lifted her chin and began to sing. The words flowed forth on a melody like liquid silver. 'Twas a song so near a mirror of her heart that Linnet's nervousness dissipated, leaving only the strength and wild sweetness of her voice. She sang the first melancholy verse, then the second, which Rhys had created. It no longer ended there. Linnet added a new final verse—one of soaring triumph over treachery and welcoming depths of endless happiness.

As the notes faded, the very stones of the castle walls seemed to catch their breath, and the silence

ached with an acclaim more fervent than even the
wild applause that followed. Through the thunder of
clapping hands Linnet and Grannia moved to rejoin
their bridegrooms.

A sturdy woman blocked their path. "Come, lady-
bird." Meara's voice was as soft as her saucy smile.
"And tell your fellow bride 'tis time."

Glancing in Grannia's direction, Linnet found she
had no need to speak. Grannia had already begun
briskly walking toward the stairway.

Linnet moved forward just as promptly, little caring
what construction their closely watching audience
would place upon the unmaidenly haste of two brides.
The teasing calls trailing the women were accompanied by nothing more hurtful than kindly smiles and
pleased grins. Although Linnet no longer feared for
the possible ill opinions of others, still she was relieved that, as three of the wedding party's four were
Welsh, the embarrassing Norman bedding ceremony
would not take place.

At the foot of the circular stone stairway, Ynid
waited to escort Grannia into one bridal chamber
while Meara led Linnet into another. Both rooms
were decorated with spring flowers and sweetly
scented with herbs and spices. Ensconced in intimate
shadows of heavily draped beds, freed hair brushed to
lustrous beauty and eyes glowing with love each bride
would welcome the man for whom she had fought—
first to claim him over his objections and second to
free him from the hands of his foes.

The soft rose lips of a sleeping damsel curved
upward as a large hand slowly caressed the satin skin
of her back. Linnet arched against a warm and solid
pillow, slowly becoming aware of the source of this
welcome heat. She nestled closer.

"My sweet beauty, you sleep a deal too much." The
rough velvet grumble was nearer to being a purr of
satisfaction.

Thick lashes still rested in crescents on creamy cheeks as smiling lips shifted to press tiny kisses against a massive chest and whisper, "You make me feel like the beautiful peacock I've always longed to be."

The pillow shifted to rise above and honey-brown eyes struggled to open and gaze up in mild rebuke. They discovered an unexpected mockery on a stunningly handsome face.

"I thank God a peacock you are not!" Rhys remembered an earlier murmured reference to the superiority of linnets over peacocks made by this dainty creature of lush amber hair, silky skin, and surprisingly generous curves—all his. Rhys's grin widened.

The insecurity Linnet thought she'd left behind suddenly struck anew. Did Rhys find the notion of her as a truly beautiful creature so difficult to accept?

"Nay, sweeting." A bright head dipped, and brief but passionate kisses sought to smother her fears. "In my eyes you are the most beautiful woman in the whole of Christendom." He stroked the elegant line from brow down high cheekbones to chin, then dropped his fingers over her graceful throat—and teasingly lower.

"Your beauty is more rare for the fact that it radiates from the inside out. Too many beauties have I known, like Gwendellyn, are like shiny red apples— beautiful on the outside but so rotten at the core they make ill any man unwise enough to taste their bitter fruit."

Another, longer and hungrier kiss lifted Linnet's spirits higher, although still the lips that gave it were curved in the old one-sided smile.

"'Tis only," Rhys continued, "that I wonder if ever you have seen a pea*hen*?"

Delicate brows came together in a suspicious frown. Rhys was very clearly suppressing a wicked grin, but it escaped in the golden lights flashing from dark eyes.

"I'll arrange for you to view one. The hen is very

plain in appearance—and is mate to a peacock, the male of the species."

A multitude of expressions crossed Linnet's face in little more than the space of a single moment and ended in a small gale of delighted laughter.

"Ah, now I see." A mischievous grin taunted a man beloved. "*You* are a peacock, an incredibly beautiful male, while I am the plain peahen."

It was Rhys's turn to frown. "That was *not* my point! And I am no peacock but rather an eagle."

"But it *is* my point, and whether peacock or eagle, you are beautiful. Men *can* be . . . at least you are. So beautiful that I invented an entire flock of fantasies, and you were the hero of them all. So many were there that when you suddenly appeared in my chamber I thought I'd lost my wits. In actual truth I'd only lost my heart." Linnet gazed up into eyes gone to pure golden fires.

"And in retribution," Rhys said, continuing her metaphor while laying heated kisses into the curve of her throat, "the songbird stole the eagle's heart."

Like the fierce predator for which he'd been named, Rhys swooped down to again claim the tenderest of prey and in turn freely gave himself into her gentle hands. On the wings of an eagle, Linnet glided ever higher into passion's heavens until together they again soared into the consuming pleasures of a fiery sun.

Pocket Books
Proudly Announces

THE KEEPSAKE
Marylyle Rogers

Coming from
Pocket Books
Spring 1993

The following
is a preview of
The Keepsake . . .

Spring 1882

"Papa!" Liz dropped to her knees beside her father's bed and clasped between her palms the hand she remembered as big and strong but that now seemed frail. Heavy drapes were drawn across the windows, blocking late afternoon sun and leaving the bedroom so dark its fine furnishings were little more than ominous shadows.

"Ah, Miss Elizabeth, thank the good Lord you've arrived at last . . . and in time."

Piercing blue eyes shifted to the portly physician standing at the foot of the bed. Always a mild, self-effacing man, Dr. Farrell looked alarmingly anxious. *In time?* What, precisely, did that mean? Was Samuel H. Hughes's end so near?

Heart threatening to suffocate her with its urgent

pounding, Liz again peered through the gloom at the indistinct figure buried in quilts. It was terrifying to think that this weak, bed-ridden man was the same ruddy-complexioned father, hardy as a horse, she'd known all her life. As worried as she'd been by the telegram summoning her from the ranch in Wyoming to his New York bedside, this sight increased her fears fourfold.

Admittedly headstrong by nature, she was never one to sit idle when taking action, any action, offered even slim hope for a speedier conclusion. In meeting this serious illness that trait collided with something she had no power to change. The inability to *do* anything added further layers of frustration to her escalating alarm.

"Oooph!" Liz gasped as Marnie, once her nurse-maid but now her father's housekeeper, yanked the cords of her corset one last time. To recover her poise she took several shallow breaths while the ends were neatly tied at her back.

The beastly corset was a symbol of all Liz found detestable about city life—so tightly constraining it threatened to suffocate her. She grimaced with self-disgust. Little over one full day in New York and already she longed for the wide-open spaces of the Double H and the freedom to rule her own life. But not now. Not now. How could she be so selfish as to think of her own wishes when her father was so sick. If he could put himself to what must surely be far greater pains to welcome a foreign guest, how dare she complain about this comparatively mild discomfort.

"For Father's sake. Only for Father." Liz twisted about to roughly jerk a gown from the polished cherry wardrobe with no concern for which among the many her hand had fallen upon.

"Did you bring nothing more suitable, Miss Lizzy?"

Liz looked from the white folds of a half-donned gown to Marnie and shook her head.

"Not with Papa sick. I gathered up only enough to get me here. Besides, I thought I'd be taking care of him, not entertaining guests." Her nose wrinkled in irritation. Designed for a schoolgirl, the frilly gown was inappropriate for a twenty-year-old. But no matter, Liz thrust her arms into place. Never before had she bothered with what was or wasn't fashionable and this was no time to start.

Upon reaching the ground-level parlor, Liz went immediately to where her father waited, sitting propped up by a mass of chintz-covered pillows.

"Papa." On her knees at his side Liz tentatively broached a subject she feared might dangerously waken his temper and, as the doctor had warned, put his fragile heart at risk. "Are you certain it's wise to attempt a social engagement under these circumstances?"

"More certain than I've been of anything in many years." His enigmatic answer and the gleam in eyes as blue as her own roused further questions in Liz, but there was no opportunity to seek explanations as at that moment their butler, Davis, announced their evening guest's arrival.

"His Grace, the Duke of Ashleigh."

Expecting an ancient, withered nobleman but knowing it her duty to greet him politely, Liz rose and took several steps toward the door only to stop abruptly.

The duke was stunningly handsome with raven black hair emphasized by wings of silver at each temple that matched the silver frost of his eyes. Her defenses leapt to life. Liz didn't trust exceptionally handsome men. The few she'd observed, from the safe distance of adolescence, during her father's business-related social gatherings had been too practiced, too certain of their own exaggerated importance. She'd watched while they proved themselves a danger to the hearts, even virtue, of foolishly susceptible females. This man was by far the most attractive she'd ever seen. And the most dangerous.

"Grayson, allow me to introduce my daughter, Elizabeth." The seated man's voice was faint but steady.

"Samuel, are you ill?"

Liz watched as the visitor strode past her with amazing grace for one of his exceptional height. The man settled on his heels beside his host.

"You should have sent me a message," the dark guest gently chided. "Our dinner could have been postponed until a more convenient time."

"Pshaw." Samuel faintly waved a limp hand. "There may never be a more convenient time for me. And, too, I am aware of the limits placed upon your visit to our land and the need to conclude our business posthaste."

"Daughter—" Lifting his face, Samuel sent Liz a fond smile as he continued. "Meet Grayson Brandt, eighth Duke of Ashleigh."

The quiet "Pshaw" from a man whose epithets generally ran along saltier lines had sparked Liz's ready humor. And, as their guest rose to his formidable height, barely restrained laughter danced in the depths of a blue gaze directly meeting one of silver.

Gray moved to take his hostess's hand while taking close inventory of the woman for whose New York arrival he'd been waiting. The suspicion of impish amusement lurking behind the carefully correct lines of her face so intrigued him that it pushed aside his initial shock over her startlingly vivid figure. Samuel had told him of her red hair, but he'd thought to meet a woman with locks either the golden rose of sunrise or the deep, rich red of a fine brandy. But, no, hers were as bright as newly harvested carrots. And even more surprising, her skin was tanned to a golden tone, a condition which would've put the women of his acquaintance into a strategic decline until all traces could be eradicated. Her eyes, however, were beautiful—large, widely spaced and a startlingly brilliant turquoise . . . if a good deal too direct for maidenly decorum.

"I'm delighted to meet you, Miss Hughes." As Gray bent to brush a light kiss to her fingers he wondered if by wearing the virginal white garb of a schoolroom miss she thought to mislead him about her age.

Liz blinked, gazing down at the back of the dark head, unwillingly becoming disgustingly aware of his magnetism.

Releasing his hold but still standing near, Gray met her unflinchingly honest gaze and dismissed the possibility that she'd meant to fool him about her age or about anything else.

Gray mentally shrugged aside the faint sense of having been deceived. Although in no way was Miss Elizabeth Hughes what he'd expected, he hadn't been misled. Instead, he had been frankly, if rather off-handedly, informed of her age, red hair and spirited nature. Looking at her now, he feared that the term "spirited nature" might be as complete an understatement as the bland mention of red hair. Signed already were the all-important documents by which the American railroad magnate parted with a sizeable sum of money to see his daughter become a duchess. The self-mockery curving his lips compressed in acknowledgment of a solemn fact. Even had the papers not been signed, Gray had given his word, and never did a gentleman—much less a duke—renege on an oath.

Discomfort intensified by their guest's penetrating scrutiny, Liz's eyes narrowed with what she hoped he'd recognize as an unspoken warning not to waste his time attempting to charm her. She was wary of men, didn't want to be subjugated to a husband's control. She needed no man beyond a foreman to oversee the hard labor which kept the ranch running smoothly. And, of course, her father. The thought of Samuel Hughes brought Liz back to the present with a thump. Her attention abruptly shifted to the speculative gleam in the older man's gaze. Rats! Apparently she'd watched the wretched duke too long. So long that her father had mistaken warning for interest.

"Papa, perhaps I should leave the two of you to—"

"Dinner is served." Davis's sonorous announcement interrupted the offer. He next stepped back, leaving the door open for the parlor's company to enter the dining room.

"Permit me." Gray offered his arm to the woman plainly caught between worry for her ailing father and irritation with the situation . . . and, likely, him.

Liz had no option but to place her fingers lightly in the crook of his arm, yet as they moved forward she lifted her chin while proud disdain radiated from every line.

As the younger two moved toward the dining room, Davis stepped behind his master. In their wake he pushed the wicker chair which even Miss Elizabeth had failed to realize was equipped with wheels.

"Have you traveled to the Continent, Miss Hughes?" Gray politely asked once they'd been seated and the first course of trout in a light wine sauce had been served by a dark-suited, white-gloved footman.

"No." The briefest of glances accompanied Liz's single-word answer. She didn't add that there was little to interest her across the Atlantic. The fact that it would've been rude had nothing to do with her restraint. Rather, its source was a determination for her father to quickly realize she was not, absolutely not, interested in this more than eligible suitor.

It had become disgustingly clear that her father had arranged this dinner solely for her to meet the duke. Only by effort of will did Liz prevent her teeth from grinding. Illness, it seemed, had turned her father into as shameless a matchmaker as any debutante's mother. Liz wouldn't have it! She wouldn't do anything rash to rouse his temper, but neither would she do anything that the duke might conceivably interpret as encouragement!

All three participants were relieved when the waste of a fine cook's talents finally came to an end. As women always left men to their port at a dinner's conclusion, Liz thought she'd be able to escape the men's presence. She was wrong.

"Liz—" Samuel's weak voice was perversely lent strength by its tremble. "Join Grayson and me in the study."

"Why?" Liz sought to reject the unexpected invitation although it was plainly not an invitation but an order.

"I have important news to share with you."

Liz looked from her father to their too devastatingly handsome guest with growing dread. What kind of news so confidential it could only be revealed in the study's privacy would be of any concern to the stranger whose gaze rested heavily upon her? In desperation she mentally searched for some innocuous purpose. Was it related to her father's railroad? Had the duke something to do with those in his own country? A hollow feeling in the pit of her stomach mocked that possibility as an unpleasant joke.

Samuel Hughes, chair pushed by Davis, led the way to the small book-filled chamber which had been his retreat for as long as Liz could remember. A broad mahogany desk straddled one corner of the room, while a plant stand holding the fern Liz's mother had selected stood in its depths. The fern had grown to incredible size, but though its green fronds threatened to fill the space behind her father's usual chair he wouldn't allow anyone to move it from the position his beloved wife had chosen near a decade earlier. As Samuel was maneuvered into place behind his desk, Grayson held a wing chair for Liz before taking a seat on its twin.

"Elizabeth—" Leaning forward to rest his arms on the desktop's satiny surface, Samuel paused to clear a voice apparently strained by the few words he'd spoken at dinner.

Liz tensed and straightened into an uncomfortably rigid posture. Save for introductions, her father *never* called her Elizabeth.

Recognizing the all-too-familiar stubbornness beginning to firm a gentle jawline, Samuel purposely disarmed his daughter with a wan smile of supplication.

"I am rapidly nearing the end of my days." As Liz opened her lips to deny his gloomy prediction, Samuel lifted a trembling hand to wave her demurrals into silence. "The approach of my inevitable end has made me more sensitive to unkept promises given your dear mother on her deathbed."

Without rational thought Liz slowly leaned back, pressing into the chair's thick padding as if it were somehow possible to evade what she feared would follow.

"You know that I gave my oath to see you as well-educated as any debutante."

"And you have, Papa, you have. Indeed, I surpassed my classmates at Miss Brown's School for Young Ladies. You know I was their best pupil in everything from languages to riding."

Again a trembling hand waved away her protestations. "You were indeed. However, that was only the first of the two promises I gave."

Thick amber lashes dropped to rest on sun-bronzed cheeks. Never had they spoken of it, but she knew. She knew.

"I promised your mother that I would see our daughter 'well set up' and, despite your belief and intention to claim that the good care you've given the Double H is a satisfactory fulfillment of that oath, it is not true. No, that promise I have failed to keep, for she sought and won my oath to see you safely and comfortably wed."

Liz's eyes snapped open and she began to so firmly shake her head that it endangered the firm mooring of fashionably upswept red hair.

"Some days past . . ." Samuel relentlessly continued, voice growing suspiciously strong. Liz was not calm enough to notice but the duke's eyes narrowed. ". . . His Grace and I signed formal documents concerning your future."

Turquoise flames flashed as Liz leapt to her feet. "I will *not* wed him! Neither you nor he nor any other can force me to say the words that would make it so!"

Grayson was well bred enough to have sat as quiet witness to the growing discord between father and daughter, but this last was an insult he could not, would not, ignore. There were a great many women of noble blood and far greater beauty in his own country who would joyously welcome the honor this American female rudely spurned.

"So be it." The duke stood and from his impressive height gazed icily down at the unwilling bride. "The contract is null."

Liz returned his freezing glare with one so fiery that by rights it should've burnt the man to cinders.

Then, before another word was spoken or action taken, the brittle tension of their confrontation was shattered by a sharp cry of pain followed by a loud crash. They whirled toward its source.

Clutching his chest in agony, Samuel Hughes lay awkwardly atop fragments of pottery, mangled fern fronds, and the smashed pieces of a wicker wheelchair and toppled plant stand.

* * *

The ceremony was complete and, for the first time since the reverend had begun, Liz lifted her attention from where her stricken father lay on his bed, half smothered by piled blankets. The icy-faced duke, now—horrors!—her husband, looked to be no more pleased by this fait accompli than she.

Gazing down into his bride's brilliant eyes, Gray silently acknowledged how different she was from the woman he'd expected, how complete an antithesis she was to his first wife, Camellia, who had been as pale and delicate as her namesake. The memory cast a shadow of pain over his already cold expression.

Liz saw the darkening of his gaze, and her fine auburn brows met, furrowing a sun-gilded brow. Though she was a tall woman, when standing so close to the coldly controlled duke his shadow enveloped her as he gently pulled her to rest against his powerful chest. Despite the reverend's instructions, she was unprepared when he lowered his head for a kiss. Her senses tilted awry when his mouth met hers with tantalizing pressure. How was it that a man so cold could brush her with fire? Dangerous! Proof the too-handsome duke was dangerous!

Gray was knocked off stride by the taste of this unconventional beauty's untutored but very real passion, while Liz was unnerved by the experience. It was a reaction foreign to her and one she assured herself was extremely unpleasant. She determinedly doused the fire by reminding herself of a chilling concern for her father's health and wretched awareness of just how sweeping a commitment lay in the vows she'd given and the complete mess it made of her plans for the future. Stoically firming lips still burning, Liz reminded herself that for love of her dying father she'd have conceded even more.

"Thank the Lord, that's over." Samuel threw heavy blankets aside, bounced up from the bed, and stripped off his nightshirt to reveal himself fully dressed beneath. "When that wretched snowstorm delayed Liz's train I feared all was lost, but we brought it off in time! Didn't we, Grayson?" His hearty voice was in no way muffled by the handkerchief being exuberantly rubbed over face and throat.

Shocked, Liz blinked at the vision of her "ailing" father suddenly vibrating with good health and actually wiping away his sickly pallor. Powder? White powder! She'd been gulled! Gulled by such artifice as was used for the stage, tricks a woman more concerned with the all-important need for a milky complexion might've recognized from the first.

Gray was equally shocked but might've found the unbelievable scene amusing were he not the butt of its jest.

Planting fists on hips, Liz turned fully toward the one man in all the world she'd have sworn could be trusted. "You've played me for a simpleton!" Blue eyes glittered with fury. *My own father* made me a fool! A fool and something I despise even more—a wife."

"Now Lizzy, lambkin—" Samuel tossed the soiled handkerchief aside and reached out to clasp his daughter's shoulders. "You know I would never do anything to hurt you. Never. I've only found for you a husband such as any of your former schoolmates would swoon to win."

Gray was appalled as the inference of Samuel's initial statement sank in. Although the other man's words would have it seem otherwise, he was an unwitting party to this ill-timed scene. Moreover, it was with growing distaste that he watched the fiery interaction between father and daughter. These Americans had no sense of propriety, no inbred restraint that would prevent an exhibition of private disharmony from playing out before the reverend and, worse still, the two servants present to witness hastily exchanged vows.

From the corner of her eyes Liz saw the duke's frown and recognized its source. She wasn't sorry in the least. She'd be pleased as punch for the whole world to know this marriage was a mockery. Liz twisted free of her father's hold.

"Then you should've introduced my former schoolmates to him!" A fiery glare stilled hands again reaching for her. "You betrayed me! You used my concern, my tenderest emotions, to trick me into this . . . this marriage. You've robbed me of *everything* I love, everything from the Double H to the father I thought loved me enough to respect my wish for an independent life in Wyoming."

Samuel's face went white without the aid of powder. "Lizzy, I do love you. I love you so dearly that I've done all that I've done—*for* you." The unsteadiness of his mournful voice held a supplication of its own. "And I've not stolen the ranch from you. Indeed, by the terms of the marriage settlement the Double H Ranch has become truly yours and yours alone—my wedding gift to you."

"Mine? Of what earthly use can the Double H be to me now that, by the arrangements you've made, I will be banished from my own country . . . and my ranch."

Without the rigid social conventions which no gentleman would flout Gray would've been more than willing to consign his new bride to her uncivilized Wyoming ranch. She obviously preferred its wilds to the status much sought after by others among his equals in aristocratic English circles, a status for which she was clearly ill suited. For the sake of good manners he had restrained himself from earlier interfering in his host and hostess's disagreement, but enough was enough and this was too much.

"Miss Jones—" Gray turned toward a young, goggle-eyed maid standing captivated by the titillating scene. "Would you please see my wife changed for our departure in two hours?"

Liz again nibbled her lip, the vague image of a massive ocean liner looming ominously in her mind. Within hours she and the dangerous, incredibly handsome duke would board the steam-driven beast to be carried across the Atlantic.

Look for *The Keepsake* in Spring 1993
Wherever Paperback Books Are Sold.